Second
Time
Around

JOANN DURGIN

ISBN 978-0-9912252-2-4

All Scripture contained within is from the New American Standard Bible.

Text set in Garamond
Printed and Bound in the USA
COVER DESIGN BY Dino Piccinini

From the Author

My Dearest Readers,

Thank you for welcoming newlyweds Marc and Natalie Thompson into your world. The follow-up to **Awakening**, it features the continuing adventures of Sam Lewis and Lexa Clarke and the TeamWork crew, but **Second Time Around** also stands on its own. What happens when a newlywed bride loses all recollection of her husband? Based on a "real life" story I heard years ago, the dramatic and romantic possibilities intrigued me. Told primarily from Marc's viewpoint, it's an emotional roller coaster as this young couple struggles to find their way back to one another. Marc's deep passion to regain Natalie's love and trust, and his desire to be a better man, will capture your heart and mind. Lessons in grace and forgiveness are learned along the way, and their adventures take the reader from Massachusetts to Montana.

The author's journey is a fascinating process, and the Lord has blessed me once again by opening the doors of His choosing to make this book a reality. To my family—my world, my everything—I love you and appreciate your many sacrifices. To A.P. and Roxanne Fuchs of Torn Veil Books, thank you for believing in me and my stories. To Dino Piccinini, thank you for designing another gorgeous book cover. To Elaine Marie Cooper and Edwina Cowgill, my dear writer friends, thank you for reading the manuscript and giving me invaluable insights to make it stronger. Thank you to my faithful readers for your support and invaluable encouragement (especially Debbie S., Brandi S., Jude U., Beth V., Cindy R., Kristy C., Wendy S. and Barbara S.), and all my friends, church family, coworkers, and faithful supporters and prayer warriors. **Second Time Around** would not be possible without each one of you. To my ACFW family of Christian writers, thank you for teaching me so much and encouraging me to always be willing to learn, stretch and grow as a writer.

One last note: When you reach the point where Marc and Natalie dance together in Montana in **Second Time Around**, I hope you'll listen to the lyrics of Steven Curtis Chapman's sweet and poignant love song, **We Will Dance**. This is truly the theme song for this couple as they discover the fragility and blessings of life and love, and how beautiful a marriage can be with Christ at its center.

Blessings, my friends. Until next time . . .

JoAnn Durgin
Matthew 5:16

Therefore let us draw near with confidence
to the throne of grace,
so that we may receive mercy
and find grace to help in time of need.

Hebrews 4:16

Chapter 1

*I*T WASN'T THE bloodcurdling scream that made Marc's heart pound. Not even the sickening thud. It was the *silence*.

Rushing from the master bedroom on the second floor, he stumbled as he scrambled down the winding servant's staircase. Calling Natalie's name, he dashed into the kitchen.

Nothing.

"Where are you?" His voice echoed in the cold, eerie stillness of the century-old house. Based on the sounds he'd heard, Marc followed his gut instinct. With a rising sense of dread, he darted toward the open basement door. Switching on the light, he tried to see in the dim light. His eyes focused on something lying prone on the cement floor below.

Natalie.

On her stomach—her head turned to the right, arms outstretched—she made no sound, no movement. Marc's labored breath caught in his throat, and an anguished groan escaped from somewhere deep within. Flying down the stairs, he avoided the splintered step that must have caused her fall. The gaping, jagged hole in the wood mocked him. Cursing it under his breath, he sank to his knees on the hard, cold floor beside his bride. He didn't know whether he should touch her, but all he wanted was to pull her into his arms and hold her.

He put two fingers on her wrist. Warm. Beating pulse, but slower than normal. Being careful not to move her neck, he brushed aside strands of silky dark hair as he checked her forehead and then the back of her head. Slight relief radiated through him when he found no bleeding or open head wound. Leaning close, he whispered in her ear. That always tickled and got a rise out of her. "It's me, Marc. Speak to me, sweetheart." His heart pumped harder, and prickles of fear pierced him to his core. He reached for her, but lowered his hand to his side. He had to do something to help.

Managing to run back up the stairs on numb legs, avoiding the splintered step, Marc grabbed the phone from the kitchen wall. His hand shook so much, he almost dropped it. At least all he had to remember was 9-1-1. For a guy who thrived on numbers, he was incapable of anything more. He punched in the numbers, muttering under his breath, shifting from one foot to the other.

God, don't take her from me. It wasn't a request. It was a threat.

~

Ten minutes later, Marc mumbled halfway coherent answers to the EMT's questions as they hooked Natalie to several monitors and loaded her into the ambulance. She was stabilized in a viselike contraption, and the words *head trauma* stuck in his muddled mind. Climbing into the back of the ambulance beside her, he squeezed her hand. Although her fingers were warm, her eyes remained closed, unresponsive.

"Wake up, Natalie. *Please*." Her face, as beautiful as ever, was eerily calm and pale. Almost serene. Even with his limited medical knowledge, he knew every minute could be crucial. He swallowed his anger when the ambulance driver told him there wasn't enough room for him to ride in the back, and told him which hospital. At least an attendant would be beside her, monitoring and checking vitals. A frantic husband would be bothersome and do more harm than good.

With no choice in the matter, Marc rushed back into the house and up the stairs to retrieve his keys. Grabbing discarded workout clothes draped over a chair, he pulled them over his sleeping shorts and dashed back down the stairs. He didn't bother to lock the side door of the kitchen as he flew out of the house. They lived in a safe, upscale suburb with regular patrols. Besides, if anything happened to Natalie, none of their worldly possessions meant a blessed thing.

The siren blared as the ambulance reached the highway. On autopilot, Marc followed the same stretch of interstate and darkened city streets he traveled nearly every morning to his sports advertising agency in the towering Prudential Center. But this time, his destination was one of Boston's finest hospitals, hopefully with world-class physicians on duty near midnight on a Friday night.

Careening into the parking lot like a crazed madman, Marc jerked the silver Lexus to a halt outside the ER doors and jumped out, slamming the door. Even at night, didn't Boston hospitals have valets? Not a one in sight. For once, he could care less what happened to his new luxury car. Even so, tickets and towing weren't exactly foreign—the price he sometimes paid for his impatience. He'd deal with it later.

The ambulance sat nearby, back doors open, but the attendants and Natalie were nowhere to be seen as he rushed toward the sliding glass doors. Why were they so slow to open? "Come on!" Feeling something cold, he glanced at his feet. Great. In his haste, he'd forgotten shoes, but at least he wore socks. Considering he'd been climbing into bed while Natalie retrieved something in the basement, he was thankful he had the presence of mind to pull on the athletic pants and Red Sox T-shirt before jumping in the car. They were newlyweds, after all. Tears stung his eyes, and he blinked hard to keep them at bay.

Rushing through the door, Marc surveyed the quiet ER waiting area. No nurse waited behind the station. Where on earth were they, on a coffee break? "Unbelievable." His curled fist slammed hard on top of the desk and he tamped down a surge of anger. "I need some help here!"

Ignoring the stares of the other scattered occupants, a quick glance at the institutional wall clock reminded him it was nearly midnight. He should be home with Natalie, his arms wrapped around her, watching a movie like they usually did on Friday night. His jaw tightened and his fist rose in the air, ready to strike again.

"Calm yourself down, young man. Pitching a temper tantrum like a three-year-old isn't helping anyone. Especially you."

The clipped tones of a distinctive Bronx accent came from a dour-looking woman who moved at a pace slower than a snail in snow as she made her way toward the desk. Her lips were ruby red, her scrubs covered in a cornucopia of barnyard animals. Marc tapped his foot, chewed the inside of his cheek and counted to at least ten under his breath while she settled her ample frame behind the desk. It rankled to be compared to a three-year-old, but it irritated him even more that she was right.

"Now, let's start at the beginning. I take it you're referring to the young woman they just brought in here. Tell me her name."

"You saw her? Was she moving? Talking?"

Brown eyes peered at him over a pair of wire-rimmed glasses held together by masking tape at the hinges. "Let's take care of the details, sir, and then we'll see what we can find out." The way she said *sir* sounded less than respectful. Even three-year-olds commanded respect.

He avoided meeting the eyes behind the voice that sounded too much like old Junie Prunie Pritchard, his third grade teacher who questioned him on the first day of school about his parents' high profile divorce in front of the entire class. You'd think he might have learned a lesson in tact that day. Instead, he spent the rest of the year backpedaling, hiding behind a false pretense of Beaver Cleaver normal instead of being the only son of a former NBA champion who preferred being on the road to spending time with his offspring.

"Young man," the grim-looking nurse said, bringing Marc back to reality. "You're going to have to settle down and give us some information. It's important. Start by giving me her name."

She looked at him like he had undiagnosed ADD. Probably did. *Focus. Don't let your guard down. Stay strong.* He cleared this throat. "Natalie Dianne Thompson."

"Maiden name?"

"Combs."

"Your name?"

"Marcus Alan Thompson."

"Relationship to the patient?"

Marc grunted as he tried to infuse his voice with a confidence he couldn't quite muster. "I'm her husband." At least pride managed to find its way into his statement. He'd only been able to call himself her husband for eight short weeks. His fists clenched at his sides. He couldn't allow his warring emotions to gain the upper hand. Although necessary, he detested all the paperwork, procedures and the questions which accomplished nothing other than to establish Natalie's identity.

Running an anxious hand through already disheveled hair, Marc swallowed hard and fought for control of what remained of his shaky composure. In all his thirty-two years, he'd never felt this vulnerable. He wasn't used to it, and he didn't like it. *Don't show your fear.* His mouth dry, he licked his lips and tapped his fingers in a nervous march along the top of the desk.

"That's better, but stop the drum line." She put a firm hand over his. "Please." An industrial-looking bandage peeked out from beneath her right sleeve as she poised her hands on the keyboard. Some of the ladies in his agency wore them occasionally. He presumed they were a ploy to engender sympathy until his sister developed carpal tunnel and lectured him on its validity as a medical malady.

"Date and place of birth?"

Think. Same day as Kennedy's assassination, plus twelve years, minus twelve days. "November 10, 1975. Westport, Connecticut." Crazy number patterns worked like a charm to help him remember sports stats and scores. Most of all, it amused Natalie. She liked to try and stump him, but only managed to do it a couple of times. Another reason to love her all the more.

Time to employ self-calming relaxation techniques. Natalie hated it—called it New Age hooey—but it seemed to work for him. Closing his eyes, he deep-breathed. In and out, in and out. In his prior career, the practice soothed him in the bullpen before a big game just as it calmed him at the agency before conducting an important sales presentation. He prayed it might help him now.

The nurse cleared her throat. "I lost you again. Are you gonna help me out here or not?" Her voice registered impatience tempered with a modicum of sensitivity.

Marc's eyes flew open. Those ridiculously red lips upturned ever-so-slightly at the corners.

"That's better. You're much nicer looking with those blue peepers wide open." Her eyes traveled to his head. "That ratty blond hair of yours sure could use a comb, and don't even get me started on the fact you're not wearing any shoes. I realize it's warm for an August night, but this *is* a public building." Shaking her head, the woman clucked like a chicken.

Not sure whether to laugh or scowl, Marc stared. Maybe she was trying to lighten him up. "Yes, Mom. Let's get on with it, shall we?" Leaning on the desk, he fixed her with his most intense glare, which only prompted the stream of infernal questions. If it would help Natalie, he'd recite the Gettysburg Address—standing on his head. He could probably do it, both blessed and cursed with a photographic memory. It was the vision of Natalie prone on the basement floor he couldn't shake.

He turned his head when the nurse waved in front of his face again. *You're losing it. You need to keep it together for Natalie.*

After recording more routine information, the nurse took his insurance card and ran it through a machine. "Take heart. We're almost done." She handed back the card. "Do you know if your wife is allergic to any drugs or medications?" Her tone was once again professional, devoid of emotion.

Marc felt like screaming. Hadn't they wasted enough time? Shuddering, he crossed his arms across his chest and hugged himself since no one else was there to do it.

"Mr. Thompson?"

Marc shook his head. "No . . . none that I'm aware of."

"All right." She made another quick notation in the computer. The deep brown eyes peered at him again, and she appeared more sympathetic. "I don't suppose you know her blood type?"

"A-positive." He remembered from the time they gave blood together, about a year into their relationship. After nearly passing out on the gurney, it turned out to be a fantastic date when he milked it for sympathy and Natalie pampered him the rest of the evening. Even though she knew full well it was a ploy for affection, his wife was a born nurturer.

With a look of pleased surprise and a bob of her graying head, the nurse recorded the information. A couple of minutes later, she pulled herself out of the chair and tucked a clipboard beneath one arm. The heels of her rubber-soled shoes made an annoying squeak on the shiny floor as she marched out of sight.

"Wait a minute!" Marc called. "Don't you want to hear what happened?" Not that she needed to know. Maybe *he* needed to talk about it. But, no. Just the facts.

The nurse pushed through the swinging double doors marked HOSPITAL PERSONNEL ONLY at the end of the hallway and disappeared from view.

"Why don't you have a seat," a gentle voice said.

In the middle of the spotless, antiseptic-smelling hallway, Marc turned to face a blonde nurse with a round, pleasant face. At least this one gave him a genuine smile. She looked about the same age as his mom and wore normal-colored lipstick and plain pink scrubs. But he couldn't throw his arms around this woman, hug her tight and beg her to take away the pain in his heart. Not that he'd do it with his own mom, anyway. Sharing open emotion and affection had never been the thing to do in his family. Natalie's family was the opposite. He'd never seen such an openly loving, accepting group of people. *Parents.* He'd need to make some calls, but should probably wait until he had more information about Natalie's condition.

"I'm sure they'll tell you what's happening as soon as they can." The nurse gestured toward the chairs across from several vending machines. "Go get yourself a cup of coffee and have a seat. I know it's hard to be patient, but rest assured, they know what they're doing in there."

Competency wasn't the issue, but he nonetheless mumbled his thanks and slumped into the nearest chair. He ignored the equally worried stares of the other few occupants of the waiting room. In the back of his mind, he knew they awaited news of a loved one, too, but he didn't care. No, it was more like he couldn't take the *time* to care.

Natalie. Closing his eyes, Marc thought about her dark hair cascading to her shoulders in waves, curling slightly on the ends, framing her face. Luminous, deep blue eyes that could tease and adore, but also spout fire when she was angry or fighting passionately for a worthy cause. Natalie's smile made him taller, more important, more worthy as a man. One look could also stop him in his tracks and start his heart thundering.

An involuntary sigh escaped. Her bright smile charmed strangers, her gentle voice melted harsh words. Her caring hands could make the best blueberry cobbler in the world or corral twenty kindergarten students at a time. She managed to calm him with a simple touch on his arm, excite him with a feather-light brush of her fingertips. Although Natalie wasn't a saint, she was by far the best woman—the best *person*—he'd ever known. Other than the women in his family, no other woman ever accepted him without pretense or some hidden agenda. Then again, he never let anyone else close enough.

He had to win this one. It wasn't a choice. Three years playing minor league baseball had instilled a win-at-all-costs attitude, a tough-minded determination. Starting his own agency in Boston hadn't been easy, either, but he'd managed to make Thompson Sports Advertising a success in an already saturated market. But success and capability in the eyes of the world couldn't compete with medical science. That was a whole different realm in which he had no desire to tangle.

This one was between God and Marc Thompson. He needed God on his team, but he wasn't so sure He was. Blinking hard, he refused to succumb to the tears threatening to fall. *Don't show your weakness.* If his dad taught him nothing else, he drilled it into him that men don't cry. Ever.

"This can't be happening!" He didn't care he'd said the words aloud, anguished as they were and coming from a heart that hurt so much it might burst. Natalie shouldn't be in the emergency room. He shouldn't be wondering what was happening to her behind those closed doors. They belonged at home. Together.

Visions of the old home they'd started to renovate in their small Massachusetts town flooded his mind. It was their dream house where they planned to raise their children, plant flowers and maybe a few vegetables, host dinner parties, get a dog or two, cook holiday meals together, string Christmas lights the length of the wraparound porch and in the towering trees in the front yard . . . . Marc shook his head, closing his eyes in another vain attempt to shut out the horrible vision of Natalie lying on that cold, unyielding basement floor. Could she die? Be paralyzed? The possibilities were bleak, and he shivered, running his hands up and down his arms.

Another hospital staffer, a case worker, came and sat beside him for a few minutes, asking questions about the circumstances of Natalie's fall. Serious but empathetic, she nodded, jotting down his responses, pausing and waiting patiently when his voice caught. It was as if someone else inhabited his body as he answered her questions. Thanking him, the woman told him the doctor would be out to see him as soon as he could.

Not knowing what else to do, Marc hung his head to pray. God brought the two of them together in the first place. Perhaps He had a reason for this accident, although he couldn't fathom anything that could justify it. *I'm not about to lose her now.* It wasn't right to demand favors from the Lord. Since becoming a Christian, he'd listened to enough Bible stories and sermons the last few years to know that much. Still, he couldn't help his thoughts. He'd fought too hard against the odds to win her in the first place.

He snapped his head up, unable to pray. Not now. Not when he was so angry. That's often when people need the Lord most—or so he'd heard—but he couldn't bring himself to utter a rote prayer for healing, comfort or wisdom for the doctors treating Natalie. Like other things in his life, he'd deal with the Almighty. Later.

It's you and me, God. You're not taking her away from me. I'm not going to lose this battle.

Chapter 2

"MR. THOMPSON?" THE British accent sounded cultured, well-educated and belonged to a tall, Lincoln-esque lanky physician in the requisite white lab coat. A stethoscope hung draped around his neck, wire-rimmed glasses sat perched on his patrician nose, and he carried a patient chart. He sported a receding hairline and one of those high foreheads indicating an uncommon intelligence, an inbred seriousness. If this man was Natalie's doctor, she should be in good hands. That knowledge was comforting—to a point. The deep frown furrowing the doctor's brow didn't exactly scream encouragement.

Clearing his throat, Marc rose to his feet, tugging on his trousers with anxious fingers. "Marc Thompson."

The doctor shook his outstretched hand. "Stephen Adams. I'm the on-call neurologist consulting on your wife's case. Mr. Thompson, your wife suffered a closed head injury. She received a hard blow to the head, but it didn't break her skull. You were smart not to move her since the spinal cord could likely have been affected. Thankfully, she suffered no paralysis or debilitating injury, and she regained consciousness on the way to the hospital."

Dr. Adams spoke clearly, slowly, but Marc's addled brain struggled. "We've stabilized her, and for now, she's resting comfortably. Her condition is being monitored, and I'd like your permission to do a brain scan."

Marc tried to absorb it all. At least Natalie had awakened, but a brain scan didn't sound good. "Why?"

"In cases like this, we need to ascertain there's no damage to the brain, no swelling, no internal bleeding. The skull protects the brain, and even though it's not fractured in your wife's case, the brain can hit against the inside of the skull and be bruised as a result." The doctor adjusted his glasses. "We'll need to observe her carefully for a couple of days. If you'll walk back over to the desk with me, I'll have the nurse gather the necessary forms."

Marc's feet moved in slow motion, as though dead weight. At least the blonde nurse stood behind the counter instead of the forbidding, cranky one. "Is it possible Natalie will slip back into unconsciousness?"

"It's possible, but the odds of probability are indeterminable at this point. When you're dealing with head trauma and the intricate complexities inside the human brain, it's . . . complicated." Lowering his glasses, Dr. Adams met his gaze head-on. "We'll take it one step at a time." He handed him several papers. "Is there any chance your wife is pregnant?"

This man wasted no time getting to the heart of the matter, a quality he admired. "No." Marc scrawled his signature on the bottom of several forms. He didn't take the time to read them, assuming they granted his permission for any number of tests, brain scan included.

"Are you absolutely certain?"

"We've only been married a couple of months."

"Then all the more reason." At least the upper crust Brit possessed the good sense not to give him one of those knowing smiles. He'd endured enough well-meaning winks, nods, grins, jabs in the ribs and thumbs-up signs to last a lifetime courtesy of his newlywed status. It was astonishing how grown men could turn into hormonal adolescents when it came to women.

"No." Marc didn't know how much more emphatic he could be as he thrust the papers back into the doctor's hands.

The epitome of calm, Dr. Adams handed them to the nurse. "All the same, I'll need to run a pregnancy test." His voice was firm. "Again, it's precautionary. If your wife is pregnant, it's in the best interest for her and the fetus. Any type of head trauma, especially in pregnancy, needs to be addressed immediately and monitored carefully."

"All right." *The fetus*. It sounded so technical, so impersonal. The thought that his bride of two months could be pregnant never entered his mind . . . until now. He didn't want to think about it. Time to stop acting like a selfish jerk. "Of course. Do whatever you need to do. Just take care of Natalie, Dr. Adams." His voice cracked like it hadn't since he was a teenager in the throes of puberty. "Please." Marc noted the expressive eyes, dark but of indistinguishable color, beneath the glasses. He looked to be around forty, possibly older. His gaze trailed to the long, thin—almost bony—fingers adorned by a simple gold wedding band.

"I'll do my best." The steady voice matched the compassion in those dark eyes.

Marc nodded, but couldn't speak. All he could do was hope the kind doctor's best was good enough. And maybe pray. Later.

~

Time seemed interminable. Every loud tick of the institutional wall clock drove him out of his mind. Marc drained a third cup of the bitter coffee from the vending machine. Pacing the floor, his eyes saw nothing, his mind numb. Crumpling the cup, he tossed it in a corner waste can from several feet away. *Score*. His dad would be proud. He hadn't thought of the man in a long time. Why now? Why tonight?

"There's only so much pacing you can do, son." The words came from a quiet, paper-thin voice as flimsy as the cup he'd just thrown away. Hard to tell if it was male or female. Whirling on his heel, Marc faced a white-haired, bearded man. One hand rested on a cane, his expression a study in compassion. "You must love her very much."

His anger subsided, slowly draining. The man's eyes didn't waver as Marc walked with slow steps to stand in front of him. "Guess it's pretty obvious."

Although he didn't feel like conversation, it was something to keep his mind occupied.

"If all that pacing of yours didn't tell me, it'd be the worried creases on your forehead, the set of your mouth, the way you can't keep your hands still, and all that nasty coffee you're puttin' away." He shook his head with an amused chuckle.

"I can't help it." Marc's shoulders sagged. "I don't know what else to do." That statement was a rarity, but it was never more true.

"Have you tried praying about it, son?"

A frown tugged down the corners of his mouth. "I started to, but it's not like I can expect God to perform a miracle."

"Why not?"

Marc felt the old man's eyes boring into his back as he paced across the room to stand in front of one of the long, vertical windows. His arms found their way across his chest. In the darkness outside, a blurry orange haze surrounded the parking lot lights. It brought to mind all the times he'd sat on an airport runway, awaiting takeoff for business trips that tapered significantly once he married Natalie. All that traveling was essential to establish his business. He'd paved the way, but now it was time to send others.

Considering the old man's question, Marc shrugged. Turning, he walked back to where he sat. "I figure I've already used my supply of favors with God." He ran a nervous hand over his brow. "I'll tell you one thing. I'm not going to lose Natalie. If it's a battle God wants, it's a battle He's going to get."

The man eyed Marc with a curious expression. "If I understand you correctly, you think you only get so many favors in your lifetime. Then once you've used up your quota, that's it?" He fingered the straggly white beard. "First off, you're way too young to think that way. Them's fightin' words, and second, if that was the case, I'd have been dead a long time ago."

"Why's that?" Dropping into an adjacent chair, Marc felt the need to talk yet also wanted to be left alone. But what was the sense in that? All he'd do was worry more. Better to focus on someone else instead of wallowing in his own wretched misery. Natalie would be the first to tell him to get a grip on his emotions and think positively. That thought gave him a small measure of comfort. Marc glanced at the man, really looking at him. The lines on his face were deep, well-earned. The thin outline of a scar ran from his temple to his hairline.

"God gave me a good life." He fingered the beard again with slow movements. "You want to talk about battles? I fought in the Korean War, but lost my best buddy on a battlefield. Died in my arms, but at least he knew he was loved and somebody cared. No wonder they call it 'The Forgotten War.' The rest of the guys took off, but I couldn't just leave him there." The man's voice trailed off for a moment and tears glistened in his eyes at the obvious pain the long-ago memory invoked. "Frank was like a part of me. In the instant I knew he was gone, I felt like he'd taken me along with him."

The man elevated a shaky, gnarled hand in the air. "Knew that man as well as my right hand. Went from kindergarten all the way through high school with him. Served as best man in his wedding, and I'm godfather to his son." He shook his head. "God spared me, but I returned home a bitter, spiteful man. I was full of anger and regret. I also had to face the pain in the eyes of Frank's widow and two kids and wonder what more I could have done. Maybe it should have been me shipped home in that body bag instead of him."

Survivor's guilt. Marc felt a tug of empathy. The memories seemed as fresh now as they did all those years ago. Perhaps they'd never fade. He lowered his hand on a dry, bony forearm. "I'm sorry about your friend. War's a horrible thing."

"Sometimes it's necessary, and I never minded fightin' for my country, son. It's the war inside a man that's worse. That's the war that'll kill you. I lived in an abyss of misery—purely of my own making—here on earth. Until I met and married the best woman in the world. My Ruthie stood by me when I lost two jobs because of seizures, survived three surgeries, suffered two heart attacks and lost our only child to cancer. We had some tough times, but God brought me home safe from the war and gave me a great life for a number of years. I have no complaints."

Closing his eyes, he lowered his head for a few seconds before looking back over at Marc, light-colored eyes bright. "What I'm trying to tell you is that God doesn't keep track—doesn't keep score—of all the good and bad, and the right and wrong like we do. He just is. He knows everything that's gonna happen to us. He's in control even though we're bull-headed and think we're the ones pullin' the reins." A wiry hand patted Marc's thumping knee. "Give her to God, son. It's not a battle. It's not God pitted in one corner and you in the other. If that's the way you feel, you'll never win. You'll lose every time until you're willing to surrender to His will. Only then can you possibly be a winner. Accept His will, whatever that may be. If you can do that, it will give you an almost unbelievable peace. Know this truth: one way or the other, God will take care of your wife."

"How can I just accept what's happened?" Marc said, shaking off the old man's hand. Rising to his feet, he started pacing the floor again. It was the *one way or the other* part of the statement he resented. "I will not allow anything to happen to Natalie!" Of all the fatalistic old coots, he had to run into one in the emergency waiting room. "I can't just give up." With his jaw rigid, the muscles in his cheeks flexed. When the old man cocked his head, his gaze held surprising clarity and an unbelievable calm. Watching him, Marc softened. He had no right to go ballistic on the guy.

"No one's askin' you to give up, son. You're right to want to fight for her, but your battle's not with God. I understand you're angry. God does, too, and I wouldn't be honest if I didn't say I'd probably be mad as blazes, too, in your shoes. How long you been married?"

Marc's eyes misted. He hated it. It showed weakness. "A couple of months." He extended his hand. "Forgive me for going off on you like that." He shook his head. "I'm not myself tonight. Name's Marc Thompson."

"Abe Davis. No forgiveness needed. Sit down and tell me about your wife." He nodded to the seat beside him. "It'll help you to talk it out."

If nothing else, it would help pass the time. Dropping into the chair, Marc blew out a deep sigh. "Natalie's from a good family, born and raised in Connecticut. Went to an all girls' school and got her degree at Wellesley."

A snort escaped. "I don't care how rich her family is, what highfalutin school she went to, or what a fancy career gal she is." The old man met his gaze head-on. "I sure hope you don't either."

"No, no," Marc said, waving his hand. "That's just it." He wiped away a stray tear that managed to escape, noting again his companion's weathered, lined face, the crinkles around the eyes. "Natalie has every right to be a snob, but she's genuine, and has a heart of gold. She teaches kindergarten." He blew out a breath. "She's smarter than I'll ever hope to be, yet she chooses to channel all her energies into young minds. Always finds something unique and special about every single kid in her class. Natalie believes God has a purpose for each one and wants to help them find their special gifts and talents." He wiped away another tear. "Can you imagine that? Her students are five years old, and my wife's trying to set them on a career path."

"Sounds more like your wife's trying to set them on a God-honoring path. Nothing wrong with that."

Marc's shoulders fell. "She's the best person I know." He rubbed a hand over his tired eyes. "We were walking downtown one night and came across a homeless woman. Some thugs had pushed her down on the curb. Her lip was cut, her jaw swollen, and they'd stolen the few things she had. Natalie made sure she was okay, bought her a hot meal and took her to a shelter. If you look up perseverance in the dictionary, you'll find a picture of my wife." A small, wry grin upturned the corners of his mouth. "With my picture next to hers."

It appeared as though Mr. Davis smiled, but it was impossible to see any teeth beneath the mass of beard. "And what do *you* do for a living?" He chuckled. "Something tells me you don't have the patience for teaching."

"I own a sports advertising agency. I used to play minor league ball for the Sox farm team in Pawtucket." Why he threw in that information, he didn't know, and it didn't seem to impress this man. It was a long time ago, and seemed like some other guy's life, not his. He wanted to talk more about Natalie. The old man was right: it *did* help.

"We were dressed for the opera once—me in a penguin suit and Natalie in this incredible evening gown—and she decided to ditch the whole idea. We ended up sharing fries at some burger joint and yakking it up with a bunch of high school kids fresh from a football homecoming dance." He lowered his eyes. "I don't believe for a second she had this sudden craving for fries. And I have no idea why that popped into my head." And out of his mouth

"Think about it a minute, son, and I'm sure you'll figure it out."

Marc raised his head. "My brain's pretty muddled, but if I had to guess, I'd say she did it because she knows how much I hate the opera."

"And what do you give up for her?"

The memory train stopped with an abruptness that startled him. "I . . . well . . ."

"It's not a hard question." He paused. "Is it?"

"Give me a minute." He'd snapped at the old guy again, but couldn't help it. *Watch it, Marc. He's only trying to help.* "I'll tell you one thing. My business has been the most important thing in my life the last few years. Late nights, weekends . . . I was always in my office. But I promised Natalie I'd cut back on my hours, and I have." He looked in the older man's eyes. "Giving up the reins is the hardest thing I've ever done. I didn't call the office on my honeymoon, and I understand my employees laid odds on how long it would take."

"Did you bet on yourself?"

Marc laughed outright at that one. He liked this man's sense of humor. "No. Afraid I'd lose."

Silence for a couple of minutes. "Care to tell me what happened? If it would make you feel better, feel free to unload on me. You listened to me, but it's your choice."

Marc blew out a heavy sigh. Might as well. "We bought an historic home near Wellesley we're renovating. I'd gone upstairs to get ready for bed, and Natalie ran downstairs to get something out of the laundry." Dropping a quick kiss on him with a promise to return in only a minute or two, she struggled out of his embrace to dart down the steps. Natalie was in a hurry to get back to him. So much so she hadn't turned on the light on the basement steps. As if he needed any more guilt.

Marc's breath caught in his throat and he choked. "It's all my fault." His voice sputtered. Everything suddenly seemed so clear. Why hadn't he seen it before? His eyes glazed with unshed tears. "I should have fixed those stairs." Lowering his face to his hands, he slumped down into the chair and his shoulders sagged under the unbearable weight of guilt. "If only I'd done something about them. I knew the wood might be rotting and unsafe. But why did it have to be Natalie? Why couldn't it have been me?" He grabbed his shirt with both fists, bunching it up. He wanted to tear it clean from his body, needed to lash out. "It should have been *me!*" His voice rose, prompting others in the ER to stare.

"It's nobody's fault, son." The man's tone was gentle and oddly comforting. He placed a hand on Marc's arm. It was surprising how warm it was. "No matter what you think you could have done to prevent it, it happened. Accept it, pray, and then get on with the process of living." He nodded his head in the direction of the emergency room. "That young lady in there is gonna need all your love and support. She doesn't need a useless man trapped by the walls of his own guilt. Trust me 'cause I've been there. I know."

"You're a . . ." Marc hesitated, "a very direct person. Are you like an honorary hospital chaplain or something?" With a shaky hand, he wiped away another stray tear. Why couldn't he control them? His skin was crawling from the inside out. Where was that nurse? When were they going to tell him something more, let him finally see Natalie? It seemed like hours, but glancing at the clock, he noticed it wasn't much more than an hour since they'd wheeled her into the ER. It seemed like an eternity.

The hearty laugh was a surprise coming from such a stooped-over, withered frame. "I'm no chaplain, and don't be afraid to show your humanity by shedding a few tears." Reaching into his shirt pocket, he retrieved and handed over a crumpled but clean handkerchief.

"Are you waiting for someone here in the ER?" Marc wanted to change the subject but also wondered why old Mr. Davis was sitting alone. Swallowing his pride and tears, he returned the handkerchief. "Why are you here?" Even to his own ears, his tone sounded insistent, and not particularly nice.

You're losing it. Take it easy on the old guy. He's only trying to help.

"I'm just a tired old man who tries to soothe a troubled conscience when he recognizes one. I can see my work here is done." Leaning heavily on his cane, he rose on unsteady feet.

Placing a quick hand beneath his elbow, Marc helped him regain his balance. "Thanks for listening to all my ranting. I might not sound like I'm grateful, but it *did* help."

Positioning his cane firmly on the floor, the gentleman lowered a reassuring hand on Marc's shoulder. "Remember what I said, son. Give her to God. He'll take care of the both of you. He's not keeping score, so you don't need to, either."

Marc shook his head, watching the man shuffle away with slow, most likely painful, steps. He had to admit, Mr. Davis made sense. But he wasn't going to wave the white flag. He'd never surrender Natalie willingly.

~

A short time later, the buzzer sounded at the empty nurse's station. With a start, Marc rose from his chair, another half cup of coffee in his hand. He'd never consumed so much java within such a short span of time, and he was beginning to feel a caffeine buzz. Not knowing what else to do, he wandered to the window.

He'd approached everything in his life until this point with express intent and purpose: his education, getting drafted to the Red Sox farm team straight out of Yale, building and making his advertising agency a success, and winning Natalie's heart.

Failure wasn't an option.

Leaning his head against the cool glass window, Marc closed his eyes. His wife always teased him that even his dreams must be organized and mapped out in meticulous detail. Even as a kid, he'd been uncommonly focused with an eye toward the future. A few minutes later, he meandered over to the nurse's station. Lost in thought, his fingers absently jingled loose change in his pocket. The blonde nurse looked up with a tired smile as he approached, no doubt resigned to putting up with him. Nothing was worse than when he was agitated, especially pumped high on caffeine.

"Excuse me." He cleared his throat. "The older gentleman I was talking with in the waiting room a few minutes ago. Mr. Davis. I was wondering if you've seen him before?"

The nurse nodded, her expression wistful. "His wife died here in the hospital about two months ago. As I understand it, he doesn't have any family left since his daughter died of cancer. For some reason, he likes coming here. He always sits in the emergency room. For hours sometimes. He'll talk with others, but there are times when he sits by himself in his own little world, staring into space, not saying a word. It's sweet, really, and we don't have the heart to tell him to leave. He never causes any trouble, and I'm sure he's just lonely. He says talking to people brings him comfort." Called away by a patient's summons, the nurse left her station.

"Thanks," Marc said, turning back toward the waiting room. If anything, Mr. Davis was the one who brought others comfort. The nurse said his wife died about two months ago. Meaning the old man's life faded around the same time his life began—when he married Natalie. Sitting in the chair vacated by the elderly man, Marc bowed his head, determined to take his advice and give it all to God. What could it hurt? In his heart, he knew it's what he'd needed to do all along. At all costs, the bottom line was that he'd do whatever it took to get Natalie back. He'd humble himself to the Almighty, and beg if needed.

~

"Hmm?" Marc started and his eyes fluttered open as he realized someone tapped him on the shoulder. Momentarily dazed, he sat up straight as the sight of vending machines forced him back to harsh reality. How could he have fallen asleep? A faint streak of light on the horizon peeked through the windows. Marc cleared his throat. "What time is it?"

"It's half past five, Mr. Thompson." Dr. Adams loomed into full view, and Marc stared at him through groggy eyes. Surely this man was as tall as his dad— at least six-foot-seven. "We have the result of your wife's test."

"And?" Impatience took over. He detested long, dramatic pauses suitable for soap operas but not real life. "The brain scan?"

"No." Dr. Adams shook his head and ran a hand over a long chin covered with a stubble of growth, peppered with gray. "I realize this isn't exactly the best way for you to find out, but I felt you'd want to know straight away."

"Find out what?" Marc said, his voice irritated as he rubbed his tired eyes. "Spare me the medical jargon, Dr. Adams, and spit it out." He looked up. "Straight away." Although he didn't intend it to sound mocking, it did. A stab of guilt ripped through him. One of these days, he'd learn to be more sensitive.

"All right, then." Dr. Adams looked down momentarily before meeting his eyes. "Congratulations, Mr. Thompson. You're going to be a father."

Chapter 3

$\mathcal{M}$ARC STARED AT the doctor and consciously closed his mouth. "Excuse me?" His fingers gripping the sides of the chair turned white. "How . . . what?" Disbelief clouded his mind as he absorbed words he never expected to hear until several years into his marriage.

Dr. Adams sat in the adjacent chair. "From our earlier discussion, it's my impression you and your wife weren't trying to conceive a child."

Marc glanced down at his shiny, gold wedding band. "I guess it doesn't matter much now, does it?" Catching the doctor's look of disapproval, he heaved a heavy sigh. "Of course, children are important to us. Natalie's a kindergarten teacher and adores kids. But, it's not like we made a conscious decision to start our family a few weeks after getting married." Mild sarcasm laced his words. His mind wrestled with jumbled emotions. How could this happen? They hadn't consummated their marriage until their wedding night. A strong Christian, Natalie viewed abstinence until marriage as honoring to the Lord. He found it quaint, albeit old-fashioned, but he loved her without question and honored her desire to wait. It was the right decision.

A Christian only a few years, it was more difficult for him. He loved the fact she belonged to him alone, but it nicked his conscience he couldn't say the same. Now that he thought about it, in his eagerness to be with his wife, he'd gotten carried away in the moment and neglected precautions a few times, both on the honeymoon and after. But that was their private business. No one else needed to know. Not even the good doctor. In any event, if what the doctor said was true, everyone would know soon enough.

"How far along?" It came out a hoarse croak. He grunted and thumped a curled fist against his chest.

"About six weeks." Dr. Adams patted Marc's shoulder and left his hand there.

It was a gesture reminiscent of the white-haired, elderly man. Marc shook his head, dazed. "Forgive me. I think I'm still in shock with all that's happened tonight. This news will take getting used to." His head slumped, his shoulders dropped. Six weeks . . . right after their return from the honeymoon. He couldn't wrap his thoughts around Natalie's condition, much less think of a child. It was too incomprehensible. He looked back up at Dr. Adams. "Is everything . . . okay?"

"For now, everything appears to be normal. However, if your wife . . ."

"My wife has a name," Marc interrupted, his temper rising, his voice curt. "Please call her Natalie."

"Natalie," Dr. Adams said, removing his hand. "I'll continue to monitor her condition. If we need to order further tests, we'll use as many precautions as we can." He stood to leave. "I'll go check on her now. As soon as a bed is readied, we'll be moving her to the fourth floor. In the interim, we'll let you know if there's any change or if any further decisions need to be made."

Marc nodded, hating the thought of any further decisions. It sounded ominous. "Like I said before, just take care of Natalie." Rising beside the doctor, he shook his hand. "Can I see her now? If she's awake, she'll want me with her." *No, it's more the other way around.*

"I don't see why not. I'm sure you'd like privacy. Give me twenty minutes, then feel free to come in."

"Thank you, Dr. Adams." He was rewarded by a weary nod and a wave.

Marc dropped back down in the chair. Staring through glazed eyes at the vending machines, he pondered another cup of the strong coffee. He felt like something stronger, but alcohol wouldn't solve anything. He needed all his faculties about him. Bursting through the double doors and hauling Natalie out of the hospital bed and spiriting her home sounded good.

Hanging his head again, helplessness invaded his entire being. Natalie was exactly where she needed to be, and these people were trying to help her. It was a test of his limited patience, but he needed to stay calm, as hard as it was. This wasn't a business decision, wasn't something he could control or remedy. It was also enough to make him wish Mr. Davis still sat beside him. He might just derive a bit of comfort from that old man.

~

"Mr. Thompson?" It was yet another nurse who'd come on duty with the latest shift change. Time was such a funny thing in a hospital waiting room. He felt like he'd been awaiting word about Natalie for three weeks instead of only a few hours. It had been the longest night of his life, but only ten minutes since Dr. Adams departed to check on Natalie.

When the nurse beckoned, Marc swallowed and replaced the cap on his water bottle, tightening it as he rushed to the counter in seconds, eager for encouraging news. "Please tell me something positive about Natalie."

The nurse's smile was more ingratiating than he liked. "They've moved your wife upstairs to Room 412, and Dr. Adams is with her. I'll show you the way." Following like a puppy nipping at the woman's heels, Marc's heart pounded as she ushered him into the elevator. On the fourth floor a couple of minutes later, he walked beside her, silent, as she led the way behind closed double doors and down yet another endless hallway.

"I have Mrs. Thompson's husband here." Walking into a room with another unoccupied bed, she pushed aside the dividing curtain. Dr. Adams stood on the far side of the bed, one hand resting on the steel rail.

Thanking the nurse and stepping to the other side of the bed, Marc's gaze fell on Natalie—his heart—swallowed by the bed. Everything surrounding her was white, emphasizing the paleness of her face, the deep circles under her closed eyes. He'd hardly ever seen her ill, much less so wan and immobile. She'd hate how her hair was mussed.

Leaning close, Marc smoothed a loose strand of hair away from her cheek and tucked it behind her ear. The diamond earrings he'd given her for their one-month anniversary winked at him. His hand lingered on her cheek, marveling at its smooth softness, like one of his grandmother's porcelain dolls, but without that pretty bloom of pink in her cheeks. He glanced at Dr. Adams. "She's just sleeping, right?"

"Yes, she's resting." The slightest upturn of his lips completely transformed the physician's long, thin face. "But, as I mentioned before, we need to monitor her cognitive function."

Marc liked this man and understood medicine was usually more serious than not. He looked drained, haggard. Not much better than Natalie. *I haven't been the only one going through this all night.* Compassion flooded Marc's strained sensibilities, wondering how members of the medical profession dealt with pain and death as a constant. How did they keep their emotions in check and not be drawn into the lives of their patients? Did their hearts become jaded once they'd seen patients come and go, or did they continue to rejoice in the small victories, grieve over the agonizing losses? He watched in silence as Dr. Adams completed a few more routine tests. Replacing the stethoscope around his neck, he wrote something on the clipboard hanging on the end of the bed.

"Do you think Natalie will wake up soon?" Marc asked.

"She may, or she might drift in and out." Dr. Adams checked a printout from the monitor next to the bed. "We're pleased in that everything we've found is encouraging. You're welcome to wait here for Natalie to wake up, if you'd like." He indicated a chair in the corner.

"So, she's out of danger?" He needed to know there'd be no more unexpected hurdles. The roller coaster of the last few hours was enough to make anyone dizzy and disoriented.

As the doctor patted him again and headed for the door, Marc called to him. "Dr. Adams?" He needed some kind of definitive answer. A pat on the shoulder wasn't good enough.

"Yes, Mr. Thompson?"

"Can I breathe now?" He silently entreated the doctor for something to hang onto to maintain his sanity.

He was rewarded with a nod and another hint of a smile. "Yes, you may breathe. I can assure you, Natalie's life isn't in danger, Mr. Thompson." I'm off my shift now, but I'll check on Natalie later this afternoon."

"Dr. Adams?" As he turned back from the doorway, the good doctor possessed the grace not to show annoyance if he considered his persistent questions bothersome. "When can I take her home?"

"Let's see how much progress she makes in the next few hours. We'll talk later." He sounded even more tired than he looked.

Marc leaned on the steel rails, caressing Natalie's cheek again with a trembling hand. Bowing his head, he finally allowed the tears to fall. If only God could turn back time. If anyone had to be hurt, it should have been him, not his precious wife. He hadn't shed many tears in his life. Never felt like he *could* cry. But his tears now were cleansing, and that could only be a good thing. His emotions spent, he closed his eyes and contemplated crawling into the bed with Natalie, curling himself around her, sheltering and holding her forever.

"Thank you," he said, his voice quiet, raising his head to the ceiling.

Favors or no favors, thank you, God.

Chapter 4

*M*ARC AWOKE WITH a start. Again. His lids were heavy with sleep. Glancing at his Rolex, he was surprised it was shortly before noon. Food smells invaded his nostrils. His stomach rumbled, but he couldn't think about that now. Struggling to sit up straighter, he grimaced at the tightness in his muscles and clamped a hand on the back of his neck, massaging it. Three white-coated doctors, one of them Dr. Adams, gathered near the doorway, deep in quiet discussion.

Stretching his arms above his head, he looked over at Natalie as he yawned. She stirred, eyes still closed. To his knowledge, she hadn't awakened while he'd been sitting by her bedside. Surely one of the machines hooked up to her would alert them if her condition changed. He hated that he'd fallen asleep, but couldn't help it. The exhaustion had been too overwhelming.

The doctors broke apart from their huddle. As Marc pulled himself out of the chair, Dr. Adams nodded at the others. Must be some kind of silent doctor speak. "Let's go out in the hall to talk, Mr. Thompson." He inclined his head toward the hallway.

"No, thanks. I'm not leaving this room. If you have something to tell me, do it here. Who are your friends?" He was too tired and frustrated to care that he sounded brusque. At least he'd been assured Natalie was out-of-the-woods. It was clear these doctors wouldn't be in Natalie's room unless something was happening. A consultation couldn't mean anything good.

"Dr. Perrini is the head of our Neurology Department." Dr. Adams motioned with one hand. "Dr. Hardison is Chief of Staff." Both men, gray-haired and somber, gave perfunctory nods.

"What's the topic of discussion, gentlemen?" Marc snapped, then caught himself. "Look, I'm sorry to be short-tempered, but I'd like to know if Natalie's okay so I can take her home soon."

Dr. Adams walked closer. "That's what we're discussing, Mr. Thompson."

"Call me Marc."

"Marc, let me explain."

"Please do." Marc's eyes widened and he swallowed hard. From the corner of his eye, he saw the other two doctors exit the room. He remembered Dr. Adams telling him he was off his shift, but it appeared he'd never left. While gratifying, he prayed it didn't mean something bad in terms of Natalie's condition.

"Even though we're encouraged by the results of our preliminary tests, we're a bit concerned. It's not necessarily reason to be alarmed." He held up a hand to stem Marc's simmering protest. "When Natalie fell down the steps, her head did not make full contact with the cement floor. Her fall was softened by something else. Often the hands or arms will cushion a fall, absorbing the point of impact. It's an instinctive reaction. She fell at least ten to twelve feet, a fair distance. Chances are, she rolled on the stairs—either head over heels or on her side—and her head probably struck the stairs several times before hitting the floor."

He paused as Marc cringed. "From what you told us, the stairs are made from wood, and that's a good thing. Her brain has suffered some kind of trauma, that much we know. She's suffering a severe concussion, but at this point, there's no way to fully ascertain the extent of the head trauma except to say it was not blunt force. That in itself is encouraging." Dr. Adams lowered his voice. "It could have been much worse, the outcome much more detrimental for Natalie."

Whenever he'd heard the words *blunt force* before, it was usually in terms of a fatality. "Are you discussing the possibility that she might be . . ." Marc gulped, and fought rising nausea. Something twisted inside his gut and threatened to steal his breath. He could barely get out the words. "Might be *brain damaged?*" The mere suggestion horrified him, chilled him to his core. His eyes welled with immediate tears, but somehow he managed to keep them in check. If his intelligent wife had suffered brain damage . . . it was too much to comprehend. He'd rather die.

"It's possible, yes, but I suspect we might be dealing with something else. She's sleeping, not unconscious, and she awoke on the ride to the hospital—all positive signs. The nurses have periodically asked Natalie questions, but they haven't received much response. Our course of action now is to try and understand what's happening inside her brain."

"They came in the room . . . while I was sleeping? Did Natalie know I was here?" Marc's voice rose. *Wouldn't she ask for me?* He hated to think she was awake and he wasn't even told. It was unconscionable.

"We need your help, Marc." The doctor's words brought him back to reality.

"Of course." He swallowed his anger. "Anything you need."

"Try and engage her in conversation. Observe how she responds, if her speech slurs at all. Notice if she seems disoriented, irritable, clumsy or uncoordinated, complains of headaches, loss of hearing or blurred vision. Anything out of the ordinary. Then, if you feel she's ready, ask her a few easy questions. If she can answer those, move on to more challenging questions."

"What kinds of questions?"

"Start with asking her if she knows her name, address, that sort of thing. Then ask something that can only be answered by the two of you."

"And the point of that would be . . . ?"

The doctor's stoic expression relaxed enough to allow a glimpse of his humanity. "We need to determine if her brain was bruised."

Marc frowned. "You keep talking about bruising. What exactly happens when the brain is bruised?" He was tired of all the medical mumbo jumbo and wished the white coats would leave them alone. Unless they could answer his questions with any degree of certainty, what was the point?

Walking across the room, he leaned back against the bedrail, crossing his arms, like he was some kind of bodyguard, protecting Natalie from anyone trying to prod or pry.

"There could be any number of things, but we'll reserve judgment until after you've first had a chance to speak with your wife," Dr. Adams said. "I'll check in with you in a couple of hours."

"Okay. I guess we wait." Pulling a chair over to her bedside, Marc parked himself in it. He'd wait however long it took. Retrieving his phone from his pocket—a state-of-the-art cell phone Natalie teased was his favorite new toy—Marc made a few calls, speaking in low tones. He called his creative director, Trevor, and his assistant, Christy, leaving the message he was taking a few days off. That was such a rarity, it would cause a stir come Monday morning. He didn't elaborate on the reason. They'd speculate, but he wasn't up to any explanations.

Although he hated doing it, he dialed Natalie's parents' number, and spoke with her mother, grateful it wasn't her father. It was one of the hardest calls he'd ever made, and he assured Claudia Combs he'd call again as soon as he had more information. Of course, she wanted to drop everything and come immediately, but agreed to wait until Marc received more direction from the doctor.

"We'll be praying, Marc. Please keep us posted and call if you need anything, if there's anything we can do for either of you. We'll come as soon as you say the word." The greatest thing about his in-laws was he *could* count on them. They wouldn't badger him with questions, wanting to know how this could have happened, wanting to pin the blame on someone or something. They accepted, and got on with life. Not like the person he needed to call next. He steeled himself, dialing his mother's private line, relieved when her answering machine relayed she was on African safari for a few weeks. Good for her, but also good for him. It was better not to deal with her hysterics. With a resigned sigh, he called his sister, only to discover she was apparently keeping his mom company. Maybe this was another case of God stepping in and taking care of things. Funny, it was the same concept old Mr. Davis propounded.

An hour later, Marc was rewarded by Natalie stirring, mumbling under her breath and turning her head. What a beautiful sight. At the first sign of movement, he sat up straighter. "I'm here, Natalie." Taking her hand, he pressed her fingers, being careful to keep his touch gentle. Her eyelids fluttered and she groaned, bringing one hand to her forehead. When she focused on him, he wasn't sure whether to be alarmed or relieved. Something wasn't right. He sensed it as soon as those gorgeous blue eyes met his.

"Natalie?" He tried to keep the rising trepidation out of his voice, but wasn't altogether successful. "Speak to me. Say something. Anything, sweetheart."

"I'm . . . thirsty," she finally said, her voice barely more than a raspy whisper.

Releasing another pent-up sigh, Marc smiled. It felt good, the first genuine smile he'd mustered since this whole trauma began. "That I can handle. Here," he said, pouring a cup of ice water from the pitcher on the bedside table. Placing one supportive hand behind her head, he held the cup to her parched lips. At least his hand didn't shake from all the caffeine flowing through his veins. Perhaps it was diffused by all the water he'd ingested to flush it out of his system.

It scared him to see her like this. But she was alive and talking, and now she was drinking. Taking several slow sips, Natalie licked her lips and laid her head back down on the pillow, her eyes opening and closing several times, blinking hard. As she looked up at him through vacant eyes, Marc's heart thudded in his chest.

"Can I get you anything else?" He smoothed her brow. "I realize I look pretty ragged, but I couldn't leave you. You gave me the scare of my life, you know."

Natalie tilted her head and eyed him with a curious expression. "I'm in a hospital, which must mean you're a nurse?"

Marc laughed. His wife hadn't suffered any damage to her brain if she was aware enough to tease. She sure sounded the same even if the lack of spark in her eyes frightened him. "Well, I'm *your* nurse. Listen, I called your parents and I'm keeping them informed of your progress." He stroked his fingertips along her forearm, something that usually made her smile. Her eyes opened more fully and she withdrew from his touch.

She was probably still disoriented and needed time to readjust. *Don't worry about it.* But something inside triggered another warning bell. The woman had undergone a severe head trauma. It would take time.

"I hardly think that's appropriate, even if you're my nurse. My head hurts and I feel like I've been hit by a truck. Is there something you can give me?" Natalie shifted against the pillows with a deep frown and released a light groan. She looked more alert, and she was speaking coherently, but the continuing lack of recognition scared him.

Dropping his hand from her arm, Marc turned his head. He hadn't been this scared when he was six and his beloved dog, Shep, was struck by a car and died in the street. He'd cried over that lame old dog for days. Or when he'd been drafted to Pawtucket straight out of Yale and thought he'd blown it all in his first couple of games, afraid they'd discover him to be the fraud he was—a minor league athlete trying to measure up to the legend of his champion father. Or the time he found his mother slumped over the kitchen table, her tears soaking the morning paper with the photo of . . . . Marc raked his hand through his hair. It wasn't the time for a trip down memory lane. He focused on Natalie. Her eyes were closed, but he could tell she wasn't asleep.

"What's not appropriate, Natalie?" He squeezed the hand under his. He had to know.

Her eyes flew open. "Holding my hand isn't standard procedure, I'm sure." She withdrew her hand, her frown deepening, and it sent a swift, sharp pain to his gut. Her voice conveyed little warmth or emotion other than irritation. Dread and fear snaked its insidious path into his consciousness, wrapping around his mind and shooting like a bolt of lightning straight to his heart. What was going on? Whatever it was, he'd never experienced such a deep-seated, overwhelming fear.

Trying to cover his shock, Marc turned aside. "I'll be back in a few minutes." Ducking his head, he left the room. While he didn't want to alarm her, a part of him was dying inside. His heart. "Nurse," Marc said, standing in front of the nurse's station, "I need to speak with Dr. Adams. Now." He employed the same commanding tone he used with his employees when he wanted to put the fear of God in them. It usually worked, but then again, the hospital personnel weren't on his payroll.

"Yes, Mr. Thompson?" The unfamiliar nurse gave him a pleasant smile. "Is your wife awake?"

"Yes," he muttered, his voice a low, slow growl. *And looking at me like I'm a total stranger.* Never in his wildest imagination could he imagine his sweet Natalie would look at him through such blank eyes, so unaware and dispassionate. Even when she didn't really know him early on in their relationship, she always had a sparkle in her eyes. Now there was nothing.

"I'm certain Dr. Adams is nearby and will be here momentarily. He asked to be alerted as soon as your wife woke up. I'll page him." She punched in a few numbers on the phone.

"Mr. Thompson . . . Marc." Dr. Adams was as calm as ever when he strode down the hallway a few minutes later. Good thing someone could be calm. If only the physician could be the voice of reason he craved. "Tell me what's happening now with Natalie."

Marc's jaw clenched as he stopped pacing and crossed his arms over his chest. "Well, Dr. Adams, you tell me. My wife apparently believes I'm her overly-familiar nurse."

One brow raised. "Did you ask her any questions?"

"No, I was too dumbstruck. She's speaking clearly and seems coherent. She was thirsty, and took several long sips of water."

The doctor nodded. "Good."

His anger rising, Marc shook his head. "No, *not* good." He marched back into the room and stood beside Natalie's bed. She stared at the slatted window blinds filtering the early afternoon sun.

"Natalie, hello. I'm Dr. Adams." Walking to the opposite side of the bed, one hand on the bedrail, he gave her a nonthreatening smile. Natalie stared at her hands twisting on her lap. It was the only outward sign of nerves. "Do you remember what happened?"

Marc knew her well enough to see the tiny lines forming on the sides of her eyes, the tension around her mouth. His heart lurched when he saw her do a little dance with her fingertips on top of the bedcovers. She did that when she concentrated and wanted to avoid direct eye contact.

Her lips curved in a semblance of a smile. "I'm guessing you're from the UK, maybe near Cambridge?"

Dr. Adam's grin stretched his lips wide, making him appear much younger. "You would be correct. Do you know of it?"

She nodded, but looked confused. "Yes. I . . . I think so."

Her summers spent in England. Great. This was encouraging. Marc shot the doctor a glance and tried not to get too excited. Best to let the professional handle it before he jumped in and made an even bigger fool of himself.

"Do you recall your last name, Natalie?"

"Combs." She shook her head. "What happened to me, Dr. Adams?" Her eyes moved around the room, skimming over Marc, before settling again on the doctor.

"You took a rather nasty spill down the basement stairs in your home last night. You're in the hospital in Boston. We're checking you over and running a few tests." He paused while Natalie digested this information. "We want to make sure you're okay before we send you home."

Marc leaned closer. Standing on the other side of the bed, his skin was crawling, making him want to jump up and down. He could contain himself no longer. "Do you remember where you live?" He had to find out what she knew. It was a slow-burning fire inside, threatening to implode.

She put a hand to her head and closed her eyes. "I live with my college roommates in an old house in Newton."

That statement was encouraging and confusing, all at once. "Where do you work?"

"I'm a kindergarten teacher," she answered after considering the question, her brow furrowed.

Marc forced a deep, controlled breath. "Do you remember the name of your younger sister?"

Natalie's eyes traveled to meet Marc's gaze. "Lisabeth. For a nurse, you ask a lot of questions." She looked over at Dr. Adams. "I asked him if I could get something for the pain. At least now I know what happened to me, and it explains why I feel so horrible. I think every muscle and joint in my body is sore." Her eyes darted briefly to Marc's before looking toward the window. She was no doubt irritated he hadn't followed through on her request like the nurse she thought he was. Averting his gaze, he pressed his lips together.

"Of course," the doctor said. "I'll have something sent in for you straight away."

Marc's chest tightened, and he lost the momentary ability to breathe. His next question sat trapped in his throat. So many things he wanted to ask, but not a one came out for fear of the answer. He shot an incredulous look at Dr. Adams. Indicating for him to follow, he stormed out of the room, feeling all the more ridiculous on the slippery floor in only his stocking feet.

"You rest now," Dr. Adams told Natalie in his calm voice as he headed out of the room. "We'll be back in a few minutes. I'll have some meds and lunch sent in for you."

Get out here now and tell me what's happening with my wife, Marc silently demanded, alternately pacing and sliding back and forth on the shiny, sterile-looking hallway. Stalking over to the nurse's station, he anchored one hand on the counter, waiting.

"Try to calm yourself, Marc," Dr. Adams said, closing the door to Natalie's room and walking toward him.

Marc glared. "How exactly do you suggest I do that? Put yourself in my place. Try being a newlywed with the love of your life in a hospital bed, looking at you through eyes that don't even seem to know you. *Then* we'll talk. Natalie remembers certain things, but it's like she's stuck in some kind of . . . weird time warp. It makes no sense." He met the doctor's eyes, and crossed and uncrossed his arms, not knowing what to do, what to think, what to say. "Look, I know I'm acting like a world-class jerk, but I'm not used to feeling helpless."

"No one likes that, and there are no rules. I'm here to help you. We'll figure this thing out together, but it's going to take some time."

Marc counted to ten under his breath, closing his eyes before opening them. "Please just tell me what you think is happening to her." He waved his hand in the air. "Put aside all the medical jargon and tell me what your gut is telling you." Surely even upper crust British physicians had instincts.

"Go home, take a shower and get something to eat. In the interim, we'll run what tests we can. By the time you get back in a couple of hours, hopefully we'll know more." The doctor's eyes bore into him, leaving no room for argument.

Marc couldn't relent and quietly slink away. Not yet. "Not until you tell me what you *think* is going on with my wife."

The doctor sighed. "It would appear your wife might be suffering from some form of amnesia. Retrograde, in Natalie's case, meaning she recalls certain things from the past, even her childhood, but more recent events are more . . . difficult for her to grasp."

Marc was speechless. "Is retrograde amnesia another term for a bruised brain?" His fists clenched. He loved how doctors were oh-so-politically correct and weighed every word. It was most likely a self-preservation thing, a defense against medical malpractice or other lawsuits. But it didn't help him now in trying to understand what was happening to his injured wife.

"It's not common, but it's possible considering the type of trauma she suffered." His voice low, Dr. Adams began to explain what might be happening in Natalie's brain.

"Cut to the chase, Doctor. Bottom line, amnesia is only temporary, isn't it? She'll regain her memory soon, right?"

"In most cases, it's short-term, yes. However, in other cases, the extent of the brain injury can be more . . . significant."

"Significant?" He didn't like the way the doctor hesitated. *Lord, be with me. I can't handle this. I'm falling apart here.*

"Let's not speculate until we've run more tests." Again with the shoulder pat. "Take my advice and go home and refresh yourself. By the time you return, I'll try to have more answers."

Tests. Always more tests. At least he made it personal instead of using the customary, collective *we*. Marc stared at the doctor, hardly daring to breathe. Amnesia might explain that horrible, blank look in Natalie's eyes, the withdrawal from his touch. He had to see her one more time.

As he walked back into the room, Marc felt Natalie's eyes following him. But for the first time in his life, he hated to look at her. Turning with a great sense of dread, he knew what he'd find. Her cheeks bloomed with a bit more color, but staring at him were the eyes of a stranger. No matter what the doctor told him, all the tests in the world would only confirm what he already knew. It made him physically ill, and Marc's stomach churned as he departed the room without another word.

Natalie was gone.

Chapter 5

MAYBE NOT PHYSICALLY, but the love of his life—the woman who pledged her life and love to him two short months ago—was not in that hospital bed. The realization broke Marc's heart, ripping it down the middle.

Congratulations, God. You won this round. You've got her now.

Through some miracle, his car was still parked outside, right where he'd left it. With a ticket. Snatching the green envelope from the windshield, he crumpled it, shoving it deep in his pocket. If only the nightmare happening inside the hospital could be pushed aside so easily. A young man—a hospital valet judging by his uniform—bounded over to the car. With a frown, Marc lowered the automatic window.

"Sir, I watched over it for you. Fine car like this, I knew its owner had a good reason for leaving it where you did."

"Thanks." Reaching for his wallet, Marc pulled out a crisp twenty and offered it out the window.

"Sorry about the ticket, but at least they didn't tow it."

This kid was annoying, but enterprising. He reminded Marc of himself at seventeen, a hothead kid who parked cars for tips at the country club in Clayton, Missouri, rubbing elbows with the businessmen, and sweet-talking the high society ladies and their pretty daughters. It was one of the few places he ever dropped his dad's name to garner a little extra attention.

Feeling nostalgic, he pulled out another twenty and handed it over. As he drove out of the parking lot, he heard the boy holler his thanks. Glancing in the rearview mirror, Marc caught the smug look on the kid's face as he pocketed the money. "Spend it wisely." Blinking hard, he struggled to sit up straighter in the leather seat and cranked up the talk radio.

A few tears flowed unchecked as he drove home. "I don't care what you say, Dad," he muttered under his breath. Sometimes a guy needed to cry. The events of the past hours more than justified it. Tears for the end of his marriage perhaps. Married only two months, he might already be headed for an annulment or divorce. How was he supposed to feel? What should he do? Never had he felt so completely helpless in the blur his life had become.

He hadn't wanted to leave Natalie, but he needed space, time to think, time to get feeling back in his body instead of the unbearable numbness. Maybe being numb was preferable? Nothing made any sense. The word *surreal* took on new meaning. He slammed his hand against the steering wheel and focused on getting back to the house in one piece. Having an accident wouldn't help anyone, especially his wife.

Tossing his keys on the kitchen table, Marc dragged himself up the stairs. His feet moved by instinct, and he slid to his knees by the side of the bed where he cried out loud in the quiet of the room. His hands touched the beautiful quilt Natalie's grandmother made for their wedding gift. Natalie treasured it so much, and the love represented by the precious gift. Marc ran his fingers over the stitches made by her Grandma Lacey's arthritic fingers. You can't put a price on something like that.

His fingers touched something smooth, silky. With a slight groan, he lifted his head and fingered the lacy pink camisole Natalie had worn right before her fall. Those expressive eyes, those tempting lips, had promised so much. Next thing he knew, she was lying in a heap on the cold, hard floor. Now, his beautiful bride lay in a hospital bed and looked at him like they'd never met.

"God, you can't be this cruel!" Raising one clenched fist in the air, he let it fall back on the quilt. In his heart, he knew it wasn't God's fault, but he needed to place blame or responsibility somewhere. It wasn't Natalie's fault. No, he alone was responsible for not fixing that rotting stair. He let out a curse and burrowed his head in the quilt. When his sobs quieted a few minutes later, he prayed. Even the good Lord must be confused by the see-saw of his emotions. Next, he vowed to get her back. *I will not accept defeat. Natalie belongs to you, Lord, but she also belongs to me for a little while longer.*

"I'm going to get her back." Saying the words out loud gave him small comfort. He repeated it several times over, hoping it wouldn't negate his prayer. Old Mr. Davis wouldn't be pleased with him, and he wasn't proud of it, but he *did* feel poised in one corner of the boxing ring, God in the other. The Almighty knew he hated to lose. In a fog, Marc moved into the bathroom and twisted the shower knob, cranking up the temperature. Shedding his clothes, he left them in a rumpled heap on the floor. As he stepped inside the stall, he closed his eyes and lifted his face, allowing the rush of steamy water to engulf his body.

"God, please hear my prayer," he mumbled as the water from the shower streamed down his face, intermingling with his tears.

~

Slightly reenergized after his shower, Marc pulled on a pair of navy dress pants and one of his best Armani shirts, one normally reserved for his most important client meetings. Or a special date with Natalie. Maybe it was pointless to dress up to go to the hospital, but he wanted to wear the gold monogrammed cuff links she'd given him for his birthday. He couldn't very well wear them with his Henley and jeans. The slightest grin tugged the corners of his mouth upward as he recalled the numbers game Natalie concocted for him to find where she'd hidden the box with the cuff links. She didn't really get the calculations correct on all the clues, but he could care less. She tried, knowing he'd love it. Like Grandma Lacey's quilt, no material gift could measure up to a gift from the heart.

Pausing as he buttoned his shirt, his smile faded. If what the doctor suspected was true, Natalie might not remember much of anything. Wouldn't remember splashing in the rain outside in the garden last week. Neither one had a green thumb, but they'd had fun making a muddy mess and rinsing each other off with the garden hose. Laughed until they were both hoarse. She might not remember working side-by-side to refinish the hardwood floors in the family room, slow dancing in the living room, biking or jogging together several times a week. Or washing dishes and not finishing as they chased each other up to the bedroom? Sitting on the floor of the guest bedroom, arms wrapped around one another as they shared their dreams of one day turning it into a nursery?

That thought sent him back across the room. Marc's head dropped to his hands as he sat down on the bed. *Natalie's pregnant and having our baby.* In all the trauma, he'd forgotten. How could he forget something so important? What kind of man, what kind of husband, was he—not to mention future father? He hadn't thought to tell her mother, but that might have been providential. He wasn't sure whether *Natalie* knew she was pregnant yet. Would he be the one to tell her, or Dr. Adams?

Marc raised his head to the ceiling. "Please let the baby be okay." It was bad enough Natalie had been hurt, but he'd never forgive himself if he'd done irreparable harm to their child because of his negligence. He slapped his forehead several times with the palm of his hand. "How could you do this to your wife and child?" Staring into space, he tried to comprehend it all. Guilt could paralyze him if he let it. But he was stubborn, and had more important things to do. Like get back to his wife. God would have to forgive him, even if he couldn't forgive himself.

A calm surged through him from somewhere unknown, like a blanket thrown around his shoulders, keeping him warm, soothing him. He felt . . . loved. If he didn't know better, he'd think Natalie, or her mom, was sitting beside him. Shivers ran down his spine, but not from fear. Whispers in his heart, in his mind, telling him everything would be okay.

"God, is that you?" Marc darted a quick glance around the quiet bedroom. Maybe he was going crazy, but he didn't think so. He'd never experienced anything like it before. Could this be what the pastor meant by the presence of the Lord? Jumping off the bed with renewed energy, he shoved his feet into his leather dress shoes before heading back into the bathroom to finish his grooming. Passing through the kitchen a few minutes later, Marc opened the refrigerator and grabbed a bottled water. With a quick glance at the food inside, he closed it again. He couldn't begin to think of feeding his stomach. Couldn't even remember the last time he ate. It didn't matter, although he could hear his mother's voice reminding him he needed to eat to keep up his strength. Maybe it wasn't the Lord whispering to him in the bedroom. Maybe it was his *mother's* voice in his head.

Within an hour from the time he'd left the hospital, he was back in the Lexus, headed downtown. Passing the local florist near the house, he stopped in to pick out a dozen pink roses, Natalie's favorite. On a whim, he added a couple of generic helium balloons. A *Get Well Soon* message didn't seem appropriate, so he got a bunch of pretty, multi-colored pastel balloons. They always made her giggle with delight like a little girl, and he'd give anything now to hear Natalie's laughter. Reaching the hospital in record time, Marc made sure to park in a proper visitor's lot before bounding into the lobby. He rushed toward the elevator, clutching the balloons and flowers in one hand. He tapped his foot and took a deep breath as the doors opened.

"Well, hello again, Mr. Thompson."

Moving the balloons higher as he stepped inside, Marc spied the elderly gentleman in the corner of the elevator. "Hi, Mr. Davis." He allowed a smile.

Those light eyes held a bemused sparkle. "Judging by the flowers and balloons, I'd say your wife is doing much better today."

"Yes," Marc said, not wishing to elaborate, "but I'd appreciate your continuing prayers, sir."

"They haven't stopped since we talked last night, son. And they won't stop."

He liked the way he called him "son," especially since it sounded respectful. His dad had been gone for almost ten years but rarely acknowledged him as such when he was alive. After years of being ignored, Marc gave up trying. After his dad abandoned his family, Marc's sole focus became taking care of his mother and younger sister. He'd been forced to grow up and become the man of the family long before he was ready, but he didn't have a choice. Being the man of the family was also about so much more than providing for them financially.

"This is my floor." When the doors opened on the fourth floor, Marc stepped onto the ever-shiny hallway, wedging his foot between the doors before they closed. "Thanks. I should have said it last night. You were just being kind, and I acted like a selfish jerk. I'm sorry."

The folds around the man's eyes crinkled. "You were entitled, young man. I'm glad to see everything is working out."

"I'm not keeping score, but at least God granted me more time with Natalie. Even though it's apparently on His terms, not mine."

In a surprisingly agile move, Mr. Davis clamped a firm hand on the elevator door. Those light eyes bore into him. "Maybe God didn't do it for you, son."

"I beg your pardon?"

"Maybe He did it for *her*."

The elevator doors beeped, and Marc removed his foot. As he caught a last glimpse of the old man's face, he stared at the closed doors. *I'm not going to let that old guy get to me.* Grumbling under his breath, he stormed down the hall with the balloons streaming behind him. Mr. Davis might as well have outright labeled him selfish and egocentric. Maybe he was right. Instead of thinking about all this as something that happened to him, he should approach it from Natalie's perspective. One of the pink roses fell to the floor, but he couldn't be bothered to retrieve it. Let one of the nurses have it. Put it in a vase to brighten her day.

Pasting a smile on his face, Marc rounded the bend past the nurse's station and headed into her room with a brief knock on the open door. When he spied the empty bed, he stopped cold. "Where's Natalie?" He turned and headed back into the hallway. Seeing a nurse a few doors down, he demanded, "Where's my wife?"

She put a finger to her lips and her mouth downturned. He lowered his voice. "Do you know where they've moved Natalie Thompson?" He followed close behind as she walked to the nurse's station and checked her chart. Maybe she was undergoing more tests since that seemed the thing to do in hospitals. Leaning over the counter, Marc tried to catch a glimpse of Natalie's chart, but the nurse pulled the clipboard away from his view with a scolding glance. You'd think he was a wayward child caught with his hand in the cookie jar. Like a three-year-old. That also seemed to be a running theme here in the hospital, insofar as a bothersome, disgruntled husband was concerned.

"Hold on a moment, and let me make a phone call." Punching in numbers on the phone, she turned, her shoulder between them, and spoke in low tones. Maddening. Any more of this, and he might explode.

"Dr. Adams is coming out to see you if you'll have a seat." The nurse gestured toward a couple of chairs further down the hallway. Even though her tone was pleasant, he wasn't earning brownie points for being a favorite of the nursing staff. He couldn't blame them and wasn't overly fond of himself at the moment.

"Please answer one question." Gritting his teeth, he made it sound as congenial as possible. "Is she all right?" He'd hate it if something happened while he'd been away. His guilt was bad enough although Dr. Adams was right to send him home to try and gain some perspective. Apparently, it hadn't worked.

"Please have a seat, Mr. Thompson. The doctor will be with you in a few minutes." Her voice was tinged with faint irritation, which she made only a half-hearted attempt to disguise.

Grimacing, Marc sped down the hallway to the row of chairs. More waiting. He wasn't sure how much more of this he could take. Too nervous to sit, he fidgeted with the bouquet of flowers and the strings tied to the balloons. Where had they taken Natalie? What further tests had they run? More importantly, what had they found?

"Marc." Dr. Adams walked toward him a few minutes later. "Please have a seat so we can talk."

"I can't." Marc's fingers tightened around the balloons and flowers. "What's going on? Tell me. Please." Desperation crept into his voice.

"We performed a few other select tests, keeping your wife's condition uppermost in mind. It does, in fact, appear that Natalie's suffering from retrograde amnesia, but at this point, we have no way of determining whether it's short-term or otherwise."

"And what exactly does otherwise mean?" Marc's eyes bore into the doctor's sympathetic gaze. "Is that the same thing as significant?"

"Permanent, Marc."

Marc's eyes widened, pushing his fear aside. He couldn't allow it to overwhelm him. "What else does she remember? Were you able to ask her some more questions?"

Dr. Adams nodded. "Natalie remembers her age, but not her actual birth date. As you know, she recalls she's a kindergarten teacher, but doesn't remember the name of the school. She has clearer memories from her childhood. She remembers names, significant events . . ."

Marc licked his lips. *Tell me what you don't want me to know.* "And her family? Does she remember her sister? Her parents?"

"For the most part."

"For the most part?" Marc was incredulous, not bothering to hide his shock. "They've always been very close," he said, more to himself than the doctor. "What if they come to see her? Would that help? They're a few hours away, in Connecticut, but they'd come in a heartbeat if it'd help."

"It could, but there are no guarantees. In some respects, it might be better to have them wait, if that's possible. Having too much thrown at Natalie all at once might be much more difficult for her to absorb and essentially impede the process of healing the brain." Dr. Adams shifted his position and pushed his glasses further up on his nose. "It might be a comfort for you to know that in more severe cases of amnesia, the patient often has to relearn the most basic tasks. They revert to childhood tendencies—talking, thinking, behaving like a child. In Natalie's case, it seems strictly to have affected her memory, but she should be able to function fine otherwise."

There was that word again. *Otherwise.* Dr. Adams frowned, his brow creasing, and avoided Marc's eyes. He appeared uncomfortable. The chink in the armor had finally surfaced. He could only guess it was because he knew something he hadn't yet divulged.

"What?" Marc demanded, trying to catch his eye. "First you tell me my wife's pregnant, and now you tell me she can remember some things, others not so much. What is it you're not telling me, Dr. Adams?"

Slowly, the doctor looked back up, meeting his gaze. "Brace yourself."

Marc's heart pounded in his chest, as thunderous as when he'd first discovered Natalie at the bottom of the basement steps. "Okay," he managed to utter in spite of the huge, immovable lump lodged in his dry throat. Then it hit him, and his heart plummeted. His voice deadly calm, low in his throat, Marc dared not look in the doctor's eyes. He couldn't bear it. "Exactly what does Natalie remember about *me*?"

A long moment passed before the dreaded answer finally came. "I'm afraid she doesn't."

Marc collapsed against the back of his chair with a low, guttural groan of despair. "Nothing?" His voice sounded distant and small. As the doctor shook his head, Marc opened his fingers, releasing the cluster of balloons as the flowers fell onto the floor in a pink, scattered heap.

"I'm truly sorry, Marc. I wish I had better news for you. We'll hope for the best." With that, Dr. Adams stood to leave. "Natalie will be brought back to her room shortly, and you can see her then. We'll keep her overnight tonight and discuss our options tomorrow morning."

What good does that do? He wanted to scream. *Nothing.* Even though he'd heard the word a million times, it never sounded as cold, hard and bitter as it did right now. Yet, oddly enough, he'd known. But somehow, suspecting wasn't the same as hearing the words from a medical professional. That blank look from Natalie had said it all.

Nothing.

Chapter 6

NATALIE BOWED HER head, praying for the strength to tell Marc what needed to be said. Saying little prayers throughout the day seemed to help keep her strong. Her mother told her she asked Jesus into her heart when she was six, sitting on her lap at the kitchen table, but her young mind referred to it as the *dinner's prayer* instead of the *sinner's prayer*.

Serious for the most part, Marc had started to relax more around her since her release from the hospital. At first, he'd treated her almost like a child and gone overboard to the point of annoyance. Now he teased her more freely and dropped little kisses on her cheeks, her nose, but avoided her lips. Sitting next to her in church, he tried to comfort her by squeezing her hand. It was difficult to ignore the awkward stares and whispers, even though she knew they were prompted by concern. She opted out of going to Sunday school. Instead of teaching the kindergarten class like before her accident, maybe she should join the five-year-olds. They could probably explain some things to her.

As she closed her Bible a few minutes later, Natalie spied a highlighted passage they'd read that morning. She cherished the times Marc told her how the Lord worked in his life and brought them together. He sat with her in the kitchen every morning, gulping down some disgusting protein concoction he called breakfast while they shared devotions. His work was so important to him, and she knew he was anxious to get to his office, but he was sensitive enough not to check his watch every two minutes. Only every ten.

Her appetite was pretty much gone, her stomach unsettled from the pregnancy and her own conflicting emotions. She knew Marc worried about her, and he tried to tempt her with healthy snacks—fruit, granola, yogurt. Usually, she managed to swallow a few bites of fruit and some dry toast. The morning sickness wasn't too bad, but today it was especially awful. Then again, maybe it was more nerves, twisting inside like a knotted rope.

She couldn't believe she was expecting a child, much less with a man she couldn't remember. Marc told her he made the nurses promise not to tell her she was pregnant, and he assured Dr. Adams he'd tell her as soon as he felt the time was right. Coming into the kitchen the day after her release from the hospital, Marc saw her with a medicine bottle. Anxious, he grabbed it from her, studied the label and peppered her with questions. Leading her by the hand, he sat beside her at the table, explaining how surely God had a master plan in all that had happened. In a gentle voice, he told her how thankful he was the Lord brought them together and how they were expecting a child. It brought tears to her eyes every time she thought of his sensitivity and compassion.

Pulling herself out of the chair, Natalie frowned and headed into the kitchen to start their dinner preparations. She was going to hurt Marc tonight. Wound him deeply. Pulling out the chopper, grater and strainer, she smirked. God had a way of using even the simplest kitchen gadgets as object lessons. In Marc's mind, she might be chopping up his emotions, slicing through his heart and then putting him in the strainer, like a sieve of emotional heartache. She shook her head as she pulled the chicken from the refrigerator. *Help me, Lord. I need to keep it together.*

It was all so difficult, and no doubt he'd be angry. If she couldn't make sense of it herself, how could she explain it so he'd understand? When she called Marc in his office and asked him to come home early, the pleased surprise in his voice pierced her heart. The fact that he so willingly agreed to leave the office spoke volumes of his commitment to her and their marriage. Breezing in the door a few hours later, he kissed her cheek and presented her with yet another bouquet of pink roses—her favorite, he said. His eyes were bright and he acted almost shy around her, something difficult to fathom.

It was the most frustrating thing in the world not to remember dating her husband although they'd dated nearly two years before their engagement. Her husband was an incredibly handsome man—tall, broad-shouldered and athletic with high cheekbones, tiny cleft in his chin, full lips, and a head of thick, blond waves. Hard to believe, but his hair color looked natural, with the kind of sun-kissed highlights women paid big money to achieve. He put some kind of gel in his hair for work, but she loved when it was freshly-washed and soft, begging her fingers to run through it. So far she'd resisted, but it was tempting. Marc's skin was smooth and healthy courtesy of his daily jogs. The only thing marring his gorgeous face was a small, narrow scar just under the hairline on the top left of his forehead, courtesy of a collision on the baseball field.

Pushing a spear of broccoli around her plate, stabbing it with her fork, Natalie contemplated whether to eat it. Her eyes strayed across the table. At least *his* appetite wasn't affected. If Marc didn't love her cooking, he made a good show of pretending to like it. He never once criticized anything she made. He'd gone to London on business a number of times, and it was amusing how he'd adopted the British manner of holding cutlery. In turn, he teased her for cutting her food into minute pieces. He'd always finish his meal first, lean his chin on one hand and watch her eat, a slow grin upturning his lips. Sometimes she'd give him food she couldn't eat, and he'd give her a wink as he ate off her fork The man flirted without even being aware. It was distracting, but it was also unnerving in its intimacy. Marc was only being himself, but she didn't know who *she* was.

"What are you thinking?" He watched her closely, fork poised in one hand, knife in the other.

Natalie dabbed her mouth with her napkin. "For one thing, I'm thinking we sit too far apart at dinner." Great. Now she was getting his hopes up, only to shoot them down. Maybe this dinner was a big mistake. She could only pray he wouldn't hate her within the hour.

His light blue eyes sparkled and the corners of his mouth tipped upward. "Well, that's remedied easily enough." Retrieving his half-eaten plate of food, Marc also grabbed her plate as he swept past, asking her to bring the glasses as he led the way into the kitchen. He nodded toward the table. "You sit. I'll get the rest." Back in the kitchen after retrieving their napkins and silverware, he opened a drawer and pulled out a tapered candle, holder and matches. Lighting the candle, he graced her with a devastating smile. The man was effortlessly sensual. "I vote we eat in here all the time. Much more romantic."

Natalie's heart was sinking fast. She couldn't even respond. She was a coward, not knowing how to broach the subject without making him angry. The only thing she could fault Marc for was his temper, but it was never directed at her. That might change tonight. He'd been impatient at times, but she couldn't blame him. She could tell how frustrated he was with the amnesia, in every way possible. So was she. Marc always made it clear he wasn't mad at her, but this inexplicable psychological condition. He compared it to a thief in the night—unyielding and unsympathetic, robbing her of precious memories of their life together.

Being Friday night, it was movie night. "I'll do the dishes," she said. "You go pick out a movie for us."

Marc grinned. "You sure about that? Last time I picked, you cringed every other scene and covered your eyes at least twice."

She managed a small smile. "Better than you falling asleep during the romantic comedy last week."

"Challenge accepted. I'll find something hopefully cringe-free, but still intellectually stimulating."

Good. That should take him at least ten minutes. She shooed him out of the kitchen so she could plan her strategy while washing their few dishes. For all intents and purposes, they were platonic roommates. Marc made it clear he wanted her, but she didn't *feel* married in her heart. Although she felt a strong physical attraction for him, that's all it was at the moment. She needed more, needed time to fall in love again—with her husband. Since she came back to the house, they slept in different bedrooms, passed each other like awkward roommates, and avoided looking at each other at times. He seemed unsure how to act around her and followed her cues. She didn't feel settled, and no doubt gave him mixed signals. And, sadly, this wonderful home he told her they'd picked out together simply didn't feel like home.

One thing she couldn't deny: Marc got her blood pumping hard and fast with a glance, a touch, a whispered word. Even tired and bedraggled by her hospital bed when she'd first seen him, he'd stirred something deep inside.

Every time she glimpsed the hurt in his eyes, the longing in his expression, she berated herself. This man was her husband. He exhibited many fine qualities, and he loved her. She prayed about it, but wasn't sure what the Lord was telling her to do.

She wasn't blind to the way most other red-blooded, breathing women eyed her husband. It didn't make her jealous, exactly. At least Marc seemed oblivious to it, or didn't care, and he focused his attention on keeping her happy, her needs met. She didn't deserve him, and all the thinking made her head hurt.

Marc called to her after about fifteen minutes. "You coming?"

"Be right there." As she hung the 'Kiss the Cook' apron on the peg on the wall, she frowned. Even the apron's message mocked her. Her feet dragged as she joined Marc in the family room, and she gave him a shaky semblance of a smile.

"Come sit by me." Patting the spot next to him on the sofa, he gave her an expectant grin. He looked so happy, and she hated to think she'd soon take away that optimism. Maybe it wouldn't be so bad. Maybe he'd understand she was doing it for him. For both of them. It wasn't fair to Marc to keep up this pretense.

She expected him to pick up the remote and start the movie, as he'd done before. They sat a couple of inches apart. Last week, he'd put his arm around her a few times, but it proved awkward. So, they sat like friends in a movie theater, both feet on the floor, not touching except for their fingers reaching into the bowl of popcorn at the same time. Maybe it was ridiculous, but it was all she could muster. Something must be wrong with her. She felt Marc's disappointment in her bones, but it was all she could offer.

I hate you, amnesia. You've stolen my life.

~

From Marc's perspective, things had been going well. Each day brought unique challenges, but also a step closer to reuniting with Natalie. He stole a glance. She looked so uncomfortable, her pretty mouth downturned as he pushed the remote and started the movie. Tucking her feet beneath her, she snuggled into the sofa cushions. Of course, she left a good space between them. He wanted nothing more than to kiss away her trepidation and carry her upstairs. Wanted her to let him love her again. But that was *his* way, not the way back to Natalie's heart.

Women needed more than the physical connection. It was one of the credos in advertising—touch the emotions of the female target market, and you'd have a winning campaign. But female emotions were difficult to manage at best. Growing up in a house with two women, he'd learned a few things about the way a woman thinks firsthand. Didn't make it any easier.

That's also when he used to run away from a relationship—when the heart got involved, when a woman wanted more than he was willing to give. Always before, the inevitable closed-in feeling would suffocate him and he'd find a way out. His wife was the opposite—he'd pursued her relentlessly, couldn't get enough of her. With any other woman, he'd have needed a prenuptial agreement. Even though his lawyers and financial advisors insisted—as did Natalie's—it wasn't a consideration.

Now, in an ironic twist, Marc couldn't touch his own wife. She'd withdraw and give him a look like he was doing something she didn't want. She'd always been so passionate, and it was killing him. What a difference amnesia made. He only prayed it wasn't God's payback in some way, punishment for some past sin. He had enough of those. He wasn't proud of his thoughts, but it's the way it was.

The glimmer of hope was the look in Natalie's eyes: that undeniable look of the most basic, human attraction. It was something other than lust or desire. From her, it was more a longing. She'd been through so much, and he couldn't imagine how confused she must feel. Granted, her hormones were probably also out-of-whack with the pregnancy.

He treasured the few times she allowed him to hold her since getting home from the hospital. It chipped away at the protective hedge she'd erected around her emotions. He'd smooth her hair and assure her everything would be okay. He'd tell her how they'd work through it together, and dare to steal a few small kisses on her forehead, her cheek. Sleeping in the guest bedroom was a bad joke, but he'd gotten used to it since it was better than being in a bed with a woman who didn't welcome his touch. "Natalie, what's up? Tell me what's on your mind. Something's bothering you."

Drawing a deep breath, she turned to look at him more directly. "We need to talk."

Marc's heart stopped. When a woman said that, it couldn't mean anything good. "Just tell me straight out."

She looked petrified. Retrieving the remote, she reached for his hand and held on tight as if trying to derive strength from it. "Marc . . . I think I should move out."

His heart immediately dropped to a depth he didn't think possible. Shaking his head, his eyes glazed. "No." His voice was froggy, and he grunted.

"No?"

He released her hand. "Tell me why." He flexed his fingers and his hands fell to his sides. Tiny lines formed around Natalie's mouth and eyes. She wasn't sleeping well and had taken to getting up in the middle of the night to read or get a cup of tea. Sometimes he'd join her if he was awake, and at other times he listened, not sleeping until she came back upstairs. She pushed food around on her plate like tonight, and ate very little. Her clothes hung on her, evidence of the several pounds she'd lost. She should be gaining weight, not the opposite.

"It's not fair to you to stay here and give you hope for something more than I'm capable of giving you right now." She started to reach for his hand, but dropped it to her lap. "Please know this isn't anything final. It's not forever. Just until I get my bearings. We pass each other coming-and-going like polite strangers. We're co-existing under the same roof, but it's so awkward for both of us. I can't bear the disappointment I see in your eyes. You work hard all the time and stay in town late a lot." Her lovely eyes finally met his. "I know it's because you're afraid to come home."

He shook his head slowly. "It's not fear."

"Then what is it?" Exasperation tinged her tone.

He hated to answer that question. "Honestly? It's dread."

She choked, her stare incredulous. "Dread? Of me?"

"Of seeing that look in your eyes that tells me you don't love me, don't want me. It's killing me a little bit every day. I'm trying . . ." He hesitated, swallowing hard. "I'm trying to show you in every possible way that I'm devoted to you and making this marriage work, but it's hard to do when all I see is . . . indifference and . . . apathy."

"You don't understand. It's not either of those things." Her voice broke, and all over again, it made him want to pull her into his arms and hold her. But his hands remained at his sides. It'd be even worse if she pushed him away, especially now.

"Oh, I understand more than you think, Natalie. Believe me." His lips formed a thin line. He couldn't lose his temper with her. It wasn't her fault. Not really. He shook his head. *Of course, it's not.*

"You apparently knew the type of woman I was when you married me. Knew I was a strong Christian."

"I loved that about you, but you can't tell me it wasn't hard for both of us. Especially as we got closer to the wedding date."

She shook her head, the sadness in her eyes piercing through his heart and straight to his soul. "That's just it. I *don't* remember."

He raked a hand through his hair. "Right." He felt like screaming or slamming something, but counted to ten under his breath, waiting until her eyes made a slow path upward to meet his again. "Trust me. Christians or not, it was a struggle, but we waited." Lowering his voice, he captured her hands in his. "You are the most beautiful woman in the world, Natalie, and you were made for me in every conceivable way." *Conceivable.* His shoulders dropped under the weight of it all. "I don't know what else to do. This isn't just about the physical aspect of marriage, you know." With two fingers, he anchored her chin and tilted it toward him. "I miss my best friend."

"She's right here." Her voice sounded incredibly forlorn.

It wasn't the same, and she knew it. They sat and looked at one another for a prolonged moment. "Tell me what to do. I'll do anything. I feel helpless." He felt like begging, and more or less, that's what he was doing.

"I don't know either, and that's the hardest thing of all. But I'll be starting a new school year again soon."

What did that have to do with anything? Her fingers started their little dance on her lap. Grasping both her hands in his, Marc stilled them. He couldn't bear to see it. God help him, it irritated him although that little idiosyncrasy sometimes made him smile under different circumstances.

"Maybe getting back into the routine of school will be anchoring, give me a sense of normalcy. I'll be able to focus on that part of my life, and I'm hoping it'll provide some stability."

True enough. The saving grace was that she'd be starting fresh with a new group of students. It would have been more traumatic if her accident happened during the school year. Her kids would be crushed if she didn't remember their names. It would crush *her*. So, there were some small blessings to be discovered in all this mess.

"Marc, please understand I'm not doing this to hurt you, hurt us. If anything, I'm doing it to *help* us. If I can't remember who I am, or our history together, how can I be the same person you married? I need to find that person."

Shaking his head, he wondered if he was being selfish or if she was being unfair and not giving them a chance. Could it be true in both circumstances? "I fail to see how your moving out of the house to 'find yourself' will help our situation, Natalie. If anything, it'll probably drive the wedge further between us." He withdrew his hands and stood up. "I'll pack my things and move to the club downtown. I'm the one who should leave, not you."

"I talked with Kim and Monica, and they still have the house in Newton. I don't remember it all, but I understand I lived with them after we graduated. While we were dating." She raised her head and met his eyes. "You need to stay here, and I'll move back in with them."

Nothing in his world made sense, but he didn't have the heart to fight. "Fine. Whatever you want." The muscles in his cheeks flexed like they had a life of their own. Turning aside, he couldn't look in those beautiful eyes for fear they'd tell him what he wouldn't want to see. He had to get away. *Now*. Before he said something he'd always regret. He left the room without another word.

"Where are you going?" Coming into the kitchen behind him, Natalie's eyes were wide, making her look as small and vulnerable as a child. "Please don't leave me alone. Not tonight."

Marc snatched his lightweight jacket draped over a chair in the kitchen, thinking of the irony of that statement. He had to do this, had to be strong. "I can't. Don't wait up."

"Why?"

Shoving his arms into his jacket, he closed his eyes for a second, but it couldn't take away the hurt and pain in her voice. "Because it's what you want. Be happy, Natalie. Just don't ask me to help you move out. You're on your own."

Chapter 7

VENTURING HOME WELL after midnight, Marc spied cardboard boxes stacked in the upstairs hallway. Afraid she'd already gone, he walked into the master bedroom. Dropping into the heirloom rocking chair made by his grandfather—the one he hoped to rock their baby in—he watched Natalie sleep. He alternated between praying and dozing. Part of him wished she'd awaken so they could talk, so he could convince her of the foolishness of her plan. But she slept soundly. While a good thing, he suspected the house would be a whole lot emptier later in the morning.

Finally dragging himself to the adjacent guest bedroom in the middle of the night, he fell with exhaustion on the bed, fully-clothed except for his shoes. When he woke up a few hours later, Marc rubbed his eyes and stumbled out in the hall. The door of the master bedroom was wide open, the boxes in the hall gone, as he suspected. Sitting down on the end of the bed, he stared in disbelief at the half-empty closet, hoping it was all a nightmare and Natalie would come around the corner any minute.

Saturday morning was always their favorite time of the week. They'd snuggle and enjoy being lazy together. Either she'd make pancakes or he'd fix microwave eggs and sausage, and feed each other in bed. Eventually they'd go for a run or a bike ride before settling into one of their many fix-it projects around the house. Marc shook his head and ran a hand through his hair, rising from the bed. He had to stop thinking about what he couldn't share with his wife right now or else he'd succumb to a major pity party or go nuts.

His head throbbed. Definitely a morning for some meds. Plodding down the servant's staircase, he stopped halfway, on the curved stairs by the small picture window. A dark-haired, beefy hunk of a man stood in the middle of his kitchen, holding a cardboard box marked—ironically enough—*Natalie's Fall Clothes*. Mr. Muscles stood in *his* house, holding a box full of *his* wife's possessions.

The thought made his stomach lurch, and Marc felt the surge of rising heat. What a way to wake up. Not only did he feel sick, he must be hallucinating. That's the price he paid for ingesting two beers the night before. He hadn't touched alcohol for two years of his own volition, and now he knew why. Drinking never solved any problems, and it was better to stay away altogether. Thank the Lord he'd made it home safe. *Home*. Right. He didn't know which end was up anymore.

He rubbed his eyes again and tried to focus. Maybe it was all a bad dream, and this guy was a figment of his overactive imagination. Nope. Still there. "Who are *you?*"

A dark brow raised, a little too arrogant for his liking. "Roger Clemson."

"I mean, who are you to my *wife*?" He couldn't bother being cordial. Natalie only talked about moving out the night before, and the troops had already invaded. She'd obviously planned this move in advance. It was no last-minute decision.

Natalie bounded in the side door, way too perky and happy. "Morning, Marc." It was like the heart-wrenching conversation the night before never happened. "I made coffee, and your breakfast is in the microwave."

She looked fetching, as usual, on a Saturday morning—in her well-worn Wellesley sweatshirt, jeans and tennis shoes, her hair scooped into a high ponytail. A sudden, sharp pain seized his chest, especially when Roger looked her way. It was no *I like you in a sisterly kind of way* platonic glance. Was this some ex-boyfriend of hers ready to swoop in and take his place? He prayed under his breath he wouldn't have a heart attack with some strange guy standing in his kitchen. A heart attack at thirty-two was bad enough, but the speculation would be rampant with this little scenario.

Roger shifted the box in his arms and avoided his direct glare. Marc cleared his throat and lowered his voice, keeping it just loud enough for Hunk-O-Man to hear. "Tell Roger to leave, Natalie. Now."

Drawing in a sharp breath, she moved to the base of the staircase. "That's not nice." Her voice was low, but controlled. "You told me last night you wouldn't help me move, so what's a girl to do?" Her stare was bold, those rosebud lips pressed together in a defiant line. Oh, yes, she was yanking his strings. Hard.

"I don't care," he growled. "If anyone's going to help you move, it's going to be your husband. Excuse me, Roger," he called, elevating his voice, "*please* be so kind as to get out of my house." After only a moment's hesitation, the man ducked his head without a word and scurried out of the kitchen. Marc gave her a smug, self-satisfied grin, guaranteed to irritate her even more. "Better?"

Natalie crossed her arms and one foot tapped. "I hate to tell you this, *husband*, but there's another guy outside loading my car full of more boxes."

Her boxes couldn't be that heavy, and it wasn't like she was taking pieces of furniture requiring much muscle. All Roger carried was a box of clothes. Bulky, yes, but how heavy could it be? "What happened to your girlfriends? They're not available to help you move out of my life, our house . . . my heart?" He couldn't resist that last one. Twist the knife a little deeper. Again, he wanted to hurt her the way she'd wounded him with all this crazy, moving out business. A long-forgotten curse slipped out under his breath.

"What did you say?" Saint Natalie looked appalled.

Marc snapped his head back to meet her angry gaze head-on. "You heard me. Thanks, sweetheart. You're making this ridiculous moving out scene a whole lot easier." First drinking, and now cursing. Not to mention acting like a world-class jerk around the woman he loved.

"For the record, my roommates have a retreat this morning. They're going to help me unpack this afternoon."

"Well, I'm sure Roger what's-his-name is more than happy to help you move. And in case you didn't hear, I just offered to help, but it seems my offer comes a little too late. Who is he?" He crossed his arms and waited. Surely this guy wasn't waiting in the wings for his wife to cry on that big, broad shoulder. He knew all about vulnerable women since he'd consoled a few in his lifetime. That thought sent him reeling. Guys would line up to take advantage of Natalie. Even if she wasn't vulnerable, she could be naïve. Marc reached for the kitchen counter and gripped it hard. Roger Harvard—Princeton, Clemson, whatever his name was—wanted to be her rebound guy. Over his dead body. Natalie was *his* wife, and that's the way it was going to stay. "Don't even tell me you're already going out with him." If that was the case, she might as well drive the stake in his heart, hammer it home and call it a marriage.

Natalie's eyes grew wide and her frown deepened. "Have you lost your mind? Especially after our conversation last night, I can't believe you'd think I'd go out and latch onto the first man I see. If it makes your ego feel any better, I can't even *remember* any of my previous boyfriends." She had the audacity to flash her diamond and wedding band in his face. "Besides, need I remind you, of all people, I'm a married woman?"

Those rings cost him a pretty penny, but he'd never regret it. Anger aside, he prayed she'd keep them on her finger and make sure all the circling male vultures got the message, loud and clear. "Well," he said, "you could have fooled me." He purposely raised his voice again, in case one of those two guys eager to help his wife lurked within hearing range. "Just make sure Roger and that other guy helping you know you're *still* married."

Natalie made a disgusted sound and stomped toward the side door. "I'll come get the rest of my stuff another time. When you're at your home-away-from-home downtown." She whirled around and put a hand on her slender hip. And there it was, that pouty lower lip. Delectable. The one he loved to nibble and kiss until she finally gave in. If he wasn't so mad, he'd find her irresistible. Not that she'd welcome his advances now. The saddest part was, it only made him ache for her even more. Especially on a Saturday morning.

"Natalie, truce. Come here." Taking a step closer, Marc reached out his hand, beckoning.

She didn't budge. "It shouldn't be too difficult to find a time when you're down at the Prudential Center, slaving away for Thompson Sports Advertising's newest multi-million dollar ad campaign for some exorbitantly overpaid client."

Okay, that was a mood killer. Marc lowered his hand as his jaw simultaneously dropped. How dare she throw his strong work ethic in his face? That was low, especially for her. Did amnesia bring on this round of spiteful behavior? His mind searched for an appropriate reply that wouldn't come out profane. He had nothing. Natalie stalked out the door and slammed it so hard the windows rattled.

He stood rooted to the floor and took a quick survey of the kitchen. Something on the wall above the phone was missing. He racked his mind. Oh yes, a plaque Mrs. Rousseau from church gave them for a shower gift. Their framed wedding invitation. Maybe it was better it was gone. He sure didn't need any more reminders right now. Why *she* wanted it, he couldn't fathom.

Marc dragged himself back up the stairs. The meds and breakfast could wait. It was going to be one of those rare days where he spent a lot of time in bed. Prayer would be good. He pulled out his Bible from the nightstand and sat on the bed. Opening it to a random passage, he started to read, but the words blurred. Before he could concentrate on God's Word, he needed to physically work the anger out of his system. Tugging on a pair of lightweight sweats and a Yale T-shirt, Marc ran for ten miles before he even slowed. He pushed himself to the limit, a cathartic release of all his pent-up energy and frustration. Sweat stung his eyes—or was it salt from the occasional tear he shed?

He'd never had reason to be jealous before where Natalie was concerned, but now he was so jealous he couldn't see straight. He didn't like it, but it was fact. Maybe he should buy a punching bag. Call it Clemson. Splendid idea. Gasping, in need of hydration, he finally headed home.

After his shower, he dried his hair and sat on the bed again, eyeing his Bible. "Lord, I need you. Give me something to cling to, some promise, some hope for a future with Natalie." He had his pick—despair, loneliness, frustration, helplessness, and at the moment, forgiveness . . . they all had their place.

His fingers found the thirteenth chapter of First Corinthians. The so-called famous love chapter. Natalie's TeamWork friends, Winnie and Rebekah, read it at their wedding. He hesitated when he reached the fourth verse. This is where it got really good. *Love is patient, love is kind and is not jealous; love does not brag and is not arrogant.*

Marc hung his head, his heart heavy with unbearable sadness. "I've already broken every one of these rules this morning." Impatient? *Definitely.* Unkind? *Yep. Got that one covered.* Jealous? *Check.* Braggart? *Yeah, you could say that.* Arrogant? *Sure.* A groan escaped and he fell on the bed, flat on his back. It couldn't be much worse, couldn't convict him any more if God Himself stood in the bedroom and lashed out at him. These words were meant for him. Now.

Natalie always said that was one of the greatest things about God's Word. "Trust in Him, and He'll give you what you need, when you need it. Not always what we think we need, but what we need to bring us back to Him, to the truth He wants us to learn."

Struggling to sit up, he leaned against the headboard and propped the Bible on his knees as he continued reading. *Does not act unbecomingly; it does not seek its own, is not provoked, does not take into account a wrong suffered, does not rejoice in unrighteousness, but rejoices with the truth; bears all things, believes all things . . .*

Marc read aloud in the quiet of the bedroom, "Hopes all things, endures all things." He read to the end of the chapter. "But now faith, hope, love, abide these three; but the greatest of these is love." Raising his face to the ceiling, he closed his eyes. "Lord, how I've failed. I love my wife. I know I acted like a jealous idiot. Love can conquer all—the hurt in our hearts, the loneliness, the confusion and the anger. If it's space away from me Natalie needs, help me to be patient and understanding. Whatever she needs to bring her back home."

His shoulders slumped, and he prayed some more. Natalie was right. The Lord had given him exactly what he needed for his bleak, hurting heart. "Lord, hear my prayer. Please." Mentally, physically and emotionally drained, he rolled over and went back to sleep. In the middle of the morning.

Chapter 8

$\mathcal{T}$HE NEXT TWO weeks went by in a blur. He called Natalie every day, sent her a few e-mails and had an overpriced floral arrangement of *Sorry* Flowers delivered. It was worth it. Thank goodness she accepted his apology readily enough for acting like a fool around Roger. Jealousy was hard as anything to shake. It would take time.

He was surprised but thrilled when Natalie asked him to accompany her to a meeting at the school with the principal and teachers. Whether for moral support or whatever, he was thankful. Although they tried to hide it, Marc glimpsed pity in their eyes, and his heart hurt for his wife. Curiosity and questions she could handle, but pity was tough to manage. He could identify. Back in the car after the meeting, as he drove away from the school, Natalie broke down and whimpered like a baby. Ashamed, she tried to stop, but couldn't.

"I can't remember most of them," she said, sniffling and wiping her eyes with the back of her hand. "This is so . . . so . . ." She wrung her hands and burst into hard tears.

Quickly steering the Lexus to the side of the road, Marc cut the engine and drew her into his arms, murmuring that everything would be all right. It felt so good to be able to comfort her, to be *needed* again. Since she'd moved out of the house, he'd felt dispensable—it was a foreign feeling, definitely *not* a good thing.

Meeting a few days later for lunch, on a whim, he brought along their wedding album. Natalie flipped through the pages, listening as he pointed out relatives, co-workers, church friends—some familiar, some not, although there seemed no pattern of recollection. She stared at one particular photo of a pretty, dark-haired bridesmaid named Amy, nodding as he told her Amy and two other bridesmaids were from TeamWork, a missions group she'd worked with several summers. When she asked if willowy, statuesque Rebekah Grant was a model, Natalie seemed surprised when he told her she was an elementary schoolteacher in Louisiana. Drawing the photo album closer, she scrutinized a photo of another lovely blonde with big blue eyes. Pointing to her, she murmured, "Winnie."

Overcome with excitement, Marc swept her in a huge hug.

"You know," she said, lowering the album back to the table, her eyes far away, "I can't explain it except that I have this warm feeling when I look at them, the girls from TeamWork. It's like God's telling me they're important in my life." She shrugged and gave him an adorable grin. "It's true. God's ways *are* mysterious."

He couldn't agree more, but a sharp pang of conscience nipped at him. He hadn't bothered to call any of her TeamWork friends since the accident. Maybe it was time. Neither had they called her, but they probably assumed she was settling into newlywed bliss. He'd need to remedy that, make some calls. It would be hard, but it was important.

Although he offered to take her to dinner at least once every other day, she always had an excuse, usually some school-related or church function. He dragged himself to church the second Sunday morning after the kitchen blow-up, the need to see her overpowering. He figured she'd be there since she hardly ever missed, even since her fall. It might be easier to start fresh, go to a new church where no one knew them. But what would be the point? At least these people loved them, prayed for them. You can't buy love like that, and their church had some zealous prayer warriors. He needed all the help he could get.

He reached for Natalie's hand during the time of prayer, and smiled when she reciprocated. Afterwards, when she invited him to lunch, Marc could barely stomach his food, and was as meek and docile as a lamb. Until Natalie asked what was wrong with him since he was so quiet. They shared a good laugh and enjoyed the rest of their lunch together in relative normalcy, although that concept was debatable.

~

But now Marc was alone again, late on a Thursday night after a long day at work. It was the same routine he'd adopted night after night. He slit the top of the plastic bag open with a kitchen knife and dumped the steaming contents of the bag onto a dinner plate. Grabbing a napkin and a fork, he headed into the living room. Natalie would kill him if she saw his feet on their brand new coffee table, but he left them there as he reached for the remote control.

Consciously pushing thoughts of his wife from his mind, he mumbled a quick prayer. It didn't matter if the food was appetizing. It was something to fill his stomach and his time. He missed her company, her companionship, her food. After she first moved out, she stocked the freezer with casseroles, leaving them when he was at work. But she hadn't made as many casseroles for him lately, and he was afraid to ask why. She'd spoiled him, but he had no desire to learn how to cook when frozen or takeout sufficed just fine.

Punching random channels on the remote control, his finger paused as a scene from a show on an adult channel flashed on the big screen television. Natalie would also kill him if she knew he'd gotten a new cable package. As a vision of a barely-clothed woman appeared, larger than life, Marc's eyes widened as something quickened inside—a primitive, masculine response. "No!" he snarled, switching off the television. "I will not be sucked into a quagmire of sin because I can't make love to my own wife!" Realizing he'd said the words aloud to an empty house, and realizing what he'd actually said, a bitter laugh slipped out.

Looking at the remote control, his hand inched across the sofa. It was wrong, disgusting, and he knew better. Still, he pushed the *On* button and stared as the woman seductively peeled away what little remained of her clothing, accompanied by cheesy music. Under a waterfall. The only good thing to come out of it was the woman couldn't compare to Natalie's natural, wholesome beauty.

"Okay, I'm sorry, God! That's it!" Immediate self-loathing and remorse invaded, prompting him to slam the remote down to the floor with such force the back sprang open, dislodging the batteries. Putting his plate aside, Marc stalked around the corner to the phone on the kitchen wall. With a quick glance, he noted ever-efficient Natalie had saved the number of the cable company on speed dial. "Come on," he muttered under his breath, punching in the number. He didn't want to take his Louisville Slugger to his new, state-of-the-art television, but he'd do it before he was tempted to watch that rot again. Never mind it wasn't the television's fault for his own sinful actions.

As soon as he was patched through to a human being, he growled, "I want to cancel my cable service." Given the condition of his shaky marriage, he couldn't fall prey to temptation if he wanted to stay sane and retain his Christian testimony. It wavered enough these last few weeks, and removing any source of temptation was best. The cable company representative convinced him to keep the package with his sports channels but put a block on the smut networks. He agreed, but vowed to himself—and the Lord—he'd cut them off in a split-second if he was tempted again.

Hanging up the phone, Marc fell to his knees in front of the sofa and raised a prayer, at least his third that hour. "Lord, keep my thoughts pure. Help me not to be so selfish. Show me the way back to my wife, and show her the way back to me. We need each other. But I need Natalie more than I think she needs me, and I know how selfish that sounds. She's the best thing that ever happened to me." The tears flowed freely down his cheeks. "But," he sobbed, "I don't think she wants me." The admission ripped his heart in two.

He gulped and took a deep, steadying breath. "Help keep me strong until I can have a restored relationship with Natalie. I know I'm not supposed to demand, not supposed to call the shots. But I'm begging you, Father. I need your help. Please, God." His body wracking with his sobs, Marc clutched the arm of the sofa. Curling up in the corner, he wept like a baby.

Chapter 9

*H*OW DOES THAT make you feel, Marc?" Like the nurse in the hospital two months ago, the clinical psychologist's expression was devoid of emotion. It was as though he willed a blank look on his face so he wouldn't sway his patient's words, thoughts or opinions. He encouraged him to think for himself instead of trying to evoke a prompted response.

"How do you *think* it makes me feel?" He shook his head and leaned back into the chair, staring at the esteemed doctor across the desk. His fingers twisted his gold wedding band, but he refused to look at it. The newness silently mocked him, a glaring reminder of a promise broken by a rotting piece of wood.

"I don't ask questions, expecting a question in return. I want answers, feelings." Pushing away from the desk, Dr. Fontaine walked around to the front, his dark eyes never leaving his. "The only way to work through this is to confront your emotions. You need to get everything out in the open and deal with this situation one step at a time."

Marc shook his head. "This *situation*? Is that what Natalie is now?"

Leaning back against his desk, arms crossed, Dr. Fontaine stared him down. "Drop the sarcasm. I realize you're going through a horrible time right now, probably the worst you've ever faced, but throwing questions back in my face isn't going to get you anywhere. It most definitely isn't going to help Natalie. If you learn nothing else from this session, please take my advice and stop being so selfish."

He stared, incredulous. "I suppose I'm paying you handsomely for a lecture?"

Dr. Fontaine's laughter surprised him. "That was another question."

"I hardly see how chastising me is going to help anything." Marc shook his head, knowing he sounded precariously close to sulking.

"On the contrary," the psychologist said. "I hate to burst your bubble, but be thankful you still have your wife. She may not remember she's your wife at the moment, and she may never remember, but at least she's alive." He leaned closer. "Natalie could have been rendered an invalid, and you'd be spoon-feeding her and praying she'd talk or walk again someday."

Marc sat up straighter in the chair. He didn't like being scolded, even if it was warranted. "I *am* thankful. Look, I know I've been self-centered, obstinate and entirely obnoxious throughout this whole ordeal, and believe me, you're not the first person to tell me as much." The corners of his mouth upturned. "I'm actually a nice guy when you get to know me. Under normal circumstances."

The doctor's expression softened. "I'm sure that's true. Unfortunately, as you know all too well, these last few months have been anything but normal. Tell me something." He sat in the maroon leather wing chair a foot away.

Crossing his legs, he intertwined his fingers and studied them. "How does your wife's pregnancy enter into this equation?"

Marc bristled at the reference to *equation*, but that was just him being overly sensitive. "I'm not sure I understand. She's pregnant, yes." The last time he'd seen Natalie—longer ago than he cared to admit—it stabbed him in the gut he hadn't been able to muster much enthusiasm for something he always thought would give him incredible joy.

"How do you feel that you're going to be a father with a woman who doesn't remember you as her husband? From what you've shared, a woman who hasn't lived with you as your wife since the time of the accident."

If only he knew. How could he find much joy in having a baby with a woman who couldn't remember what they'd meant to one another a few weeks before? It was enough to make the strongest man bow under the pressure. So, Marc did the only thing he could—he focused on watching over Natalie and keeping his agency afloat while trying to maintain his sanity. He couldn't take the time to worry about a baby. Horrified by his thoughts, Marc lowered his head as tears stung his eyes. "If you must know, it's the final nail in the cross."

"Interesting choice of words."

"What words?" He felt scattered, without purpose or meaning, going through the motions.

"You said 'nail in the cross' as opposed to the more familiar 'nail in the coffin.' I take it you're a man of faith?" Dr. Fontaine sat back in his chair, watching him closely.

"I thought I was." They'd never talked about religion or faith before, mainly because he thought it was a taboo topic for shrinks. "Yes, I'm a Christian." The words sounded defiant, as though daring this man to dispute their veracity. Marc raked a hand through his hair and put a hand on his knee to still its constant thumping, which brought old Mr. Davis to mind. "I'm fairly new at it. I guess you could say I haven't exactly been living up to my end of the bargain. And," he said, his voice dripping with sarcasm, "with all that's happened in the last few months, I feel like I should have been a better Christian."

The doctor was quiet for a moment. "So, you think if you'd somehow been a better Christian, this wouldn't have happened to Natalie? To you?"

That last question sounded a tad accusatory. Or maybe he was being defensive again and reading too much into the questions. "I don't know." Rising from the chair, Marc crossed his arms across his chest and started to pace. "Here's the thing: God tells us He won't give us anything more than we can handle. Lately, I'm wondering if I'm up to the challenge. I feel . . ." His words trailed as he stopped.

"You feel . . . ?" The psychologist had the patience of Job, unlike his patient. He waited as Marc grappled for the right words.

"I feel . . . cheated." That was one way to describe it.

Dr. Fontaine clasped his hands together on his lap. "Tell me more." The expression on his face was eager, and Marc recognized they were getting to the meat now: the kind of soul-wrenching confession that constituted this man's bread and butter. The doctor appeared to be close to salivating.

Marc hesitated, struggling to put his jumbled thoughts into words resembling coherency. "I feel cheated that I have to start all over again with Natalie. She didn't like me very much when I first started asking her out. It wasn't so much me as what I do. I had to break down those barriers she'd erected in her mind against those in the advertising profession. Natalie felt that no one, especially a Christian, could operate a business she believes sells souls for profit."

"What changed her mind about you, besides your scintillating personality?" The voice was droll, but the doctor's eyes held a mischievous glint.

"Watch it. I'm paying you handsomely to insult me," Marc said. They shared a grin. "I employed one of the other qualities in ad men that annoys women like Natalie—persistence. She glimpsed a part of me she somehow grew to love in spite of herself. She discovered the beating heart hidden beneath the sometimes smarmy, ad-man exterior."

Reality crashed into his thoughts, and his grin faded as quickly as it had surfaced. What a roller coaster. Since Natalie's fall, he hated reality. Facing the truth was too bleak and unforgiving. Marc raised his hands, helpless, at a loss to describe his inner torment. "How do you think it makes me feel," he said, his words carefully measured, "to know that I can't freely touch my wife, can't pull her in my arms, can't kiss her and physically show her what's in my heart?" With a scowl, he slumped back down in the chair.

"So, you miss the outward, physical manifestation of your love."

Marc stared. For such an intelligent, learned man, that statement sounded profoundly ignorant, not to mention blatantly obvious. "Yes," he said slowly, "you could say that. I'm a man with a healthy, normal desire for my wife, and need I remind you, I'm supposed to be a newlywed."

"Which makes it even harder."

He paused, fighting the rash response that would not endear him to the learned psychologist. "Dr. Fontaine, forgive me, but am I paying you to state the obvious?"

"Sometimes the best way to help someone is to listen."

He snorted. "Kind of like an overpriced sounding board?" Lowering his eyes, Marc bowed his head and covered his face with his hands. Releasing a loud, muffled groan, he knew the guttural, uninhibited sound conveyed more than words ever could. All he could hear was the ticking clock, every second costing him dearly. But it helped or he wouldn't be there. He raised his head. "I'm sorry. Of course, it's much more than the physical aspects of marriage I miss. Tell me what to do." He needed reassurance that some good would come from Natalie's fall and the amnesia, but perhaps no human being could give him that comfort. Where were those whispered words in his heart when he really needed them?

"Marc, how do you pass the days?"

Ah, sidestep the hard-hitting question with another question. Doctors, especially shrinks, were very deft at that maneuver. "Basically, I bury myself in work." It was the most honest, simple answer he could offer.

"I'm sure your clients are very happy to have you devote extra attention and time to their ad campaigns," Dr. Fontaine said. "From what I know, you're nothing short of a genius. A virtual golden boy."

Marc shot him a quick look, full of irony. An actual compliment? A few months ago, an ego-stroke like that would have made his day. But now, he was indifferent. "Padding my bank account is no consolation prize. I love my job, but I love my wife much more. I'd give it all up in a second if somehow time could be turned back and Natalie's memories could somehow be restored."

"It's good to have goals, but I suggest you keep your day job." The corners of the doctor's mouth, barely visible beneath all his facial hair, tipped upward ever-so-slightly. "You have to go home sometime. What do you do then?"

The smugness was starting to irritate him. Running a hand over his brow, Marc shook his head, trying to concentrate. "I eat out, throw something in the microwave, reheat a casserole. I watch lots of sports on TV, and the best way to fall asleep is to read."

Dr. Fontaine laughed. "You must be reading one of my books." His smile faded. "I understand your wife moved out."

Marc closed his eyes, hating to acknowledge what the psychologist said was true. He hadn't told Dr. Fontaine, even though it was important. It was too humbling. His fingers twisted together as he avoided meeting the psychologist's probing gaze. "It became increasingly awkward for us being in the same house together, especially for her." He took a deep breath. Although not indicative of his failing as a husband, it was a sign to the outside world they were husband and wife in name only. Maybe it was the old selfishness rearing its ugly, prideful head again, but such an admission was ego-bruising. Surely an overpaid shrink knew guys didn't appreciate looking like less of a man, especially to other men. Particularly the son of a famous, globally-respected athlete. "Natalie needs to find the stability in her life. She also thought it might be better for me, in some ways, if she was out of the house."

"And *is* it easier for you?"

Marc met the psychologist's steady gaze. He shook his head, and then shrugged. "The physical temptation has been removed, and that makes it easier. But not really." He blew out a breath. "I miss her companionship. We told each other everything, shared about our work day, watched old movies . . . did everything together." His eyes misted. "My wife is my best friend."

"You and Natalie are in contact, are you not?"

He couldn't help his sarcastic chuckle. *Yeah, right.* "Yes." He cleared his throat. "We trade e-mails a few times a week." Routine *how was your day* kind of stuff. Not *I miss your touch and can't wait to meet you at home tonight.* It was enough to make him groan. Maybe the physical aspects he missed preoccupied his thoughts, but he didn't know how to turn off that part of him. Wasn't it natural to want his wife, especially as a newlywed? Random thoughts and memories invaded his mind at work, and it was often hard to concentrate. "I try to call her once a day, but I don't want to push too much on her too fast." He shot a helpless look across the desk. "It's hard to know what the perimeters are, and I'm not sure how receptive she'll be. As you've said, hopefully she'll give me a clue when she's ready for more."

Marc had begun to wonder if his bride would *ever* reach that point. All over again, his heart hurt, and his head pounded.

"Do you have someone else to do something with—go to a movie, out to eat, see a game?"

"There's a few guys I can call." Marc shuffled his feet on the floor. "But I haven't really felt a need to get together with them lately."

"Why not?"

"I tried, but we all sat around trying not to mention Natalie. It was the albatross in the room, and more than awkward. My buddies mean well, but they can't understand what I'm going through. It's not something I'd wish on my greatest enemy." Not that he had any.

"Have you tried talking with your pastor about Natalie and what's happened?"

"No. I've avoided darkening the doors of the church lately. It would be even harder seeing her there, although the last time I went, we sat together and went to lunch." It was fun, but they'd gone their separate directions afterwards with barely more than a wave, leaving him empty inside. He'd tried another Christian fellowship, but a few of the single women rallied around him to the point where he felt uncomfortable, not wanting to explain his marital status. It wasn't anyone's business. It was amazing how a wedding ring didn't signal a guy was off-limits to some women, and sometimes generated the opposite effect. Even in church.

"What bothers you most about this entire situation?"

He tried not to roll his eyes. Again with the *situation* business. "The fact that my wife has no memory of me and our life together is pretty hard to stomach." An unexpected surge of anger rushed through him. "How can I worship a God who can allow such a thing to happen? How can I thank Him for stealing Natalie away from me?" His heart pounded with an intensity that took him by surprise.

A vision of old Mr. Davis popped into his head again, reminding him against being selfish. It had become increasingly difficult to read his Bible. He knew he shouldn't expect miracles overnight, but he'd been praying and nothing was happening. Wasn't the Lord supposed to be faithful if he was obedient? His impatience probably had a lot to do with it, but still . . . Marc avoided Dr. Fontaine's eyes and looked away in self-disgust. "I suppose that makes me sound like a terrible Christian." It wasn't so much a question as a private thought that slipped out. *Way to go. You're blowing any Christian testimony you might have with this guy.*

"Considering the fact I'm not a Christian, I can't answer that one. I can, however, tell you that you're reacting in an entirely normal way considering the blows you've been dealt." He caught his eye. "They might not be physical blows, but they pack every bit as much of a punch, so to speak. I think we've made some very good headway today. Now, you asked me what to do. I have a couple of suggestions." He glanced at his watch, signaling their hour-long session was almost at an end. "First, you have to face the fact that if Natalie doesn't regain some of her memories soon, you'll have to start all over again. If that's what you want."

Marc swallowed hard. "I beg your pardon?"

"Court your wife a second time. Take her on dates, win her over with your undeniable charm." The doctor's smile was wry. "Show her how you won her in the first place. Don't push her, and give her time to respond. In other words, give Natalie time to fall in love with you all over again." Marc muttered something unintelligible under his breath, and the doctor eyed him curiously. "I didn't hear what you said."

Clearing his throat, he rose to his feet. "Basically, I said, 'second time around.'"

"Yes, I suppose it is." Dr. Fontaine guided him toward the door, one hand on his shoulder. Men apparently liked to do that when they dispensed words of wisdom. "From everything you've told me, Natalie's worth the effort. If any man's up to the challenge, it would be you."

"Thanks. I appreciate the vote of confidence. What's the second suggestion?"

"Talk with someone who shares your faith, someone like a minister or an older friend in the church. Do you have someone like that?"

He didn't. Not really. Sure, he had guys stand up with him in his wedding, but for the most part, they were fraternity brothers from Yale and a couple of former ballplayers. They hardly qualified as spiritual advisors. Then there was Trevor, but he was an employee. Still, as his right hand in the agency, he was so much more than a paid employee. As much as anyone else, Trevor was one of his best friends. *He's also the one who led you to the Lord.*

Marc cracked a small grin. "Are you saying you don't want to work with me anymore?"

"No." Dr. Fontaine didn't smile. "Someone who shares your beliefs might be better able to help you sort through your feelings insofar as they're connected with the spiritual realm."

Walking with slow steps toward the heavy wooden door leading to the outer office, Marc paused, one hand on the doorknob. "Maybe you're right. So, do you think I'm making *any* progress?"

The doctor allowed a small smile. "More than you realize. It's going to be a slow process if Natalie doesn't regain her memory, but we'll hope for the best. You never know what can happen. She could wake up tomorrow, her memory fully intact, or little pieces could come back in the least expected ways and moments. The human brain is an amazing thing, and that's why I love what I do."

Marc nodded. "Thanks. I'll see you next week, and in the meantime, I'll think about what you said." Lost in thought, he made his way on foot in the direction of the house a half mile away from the psychologist's office in the suburban Boston hospital. It was such a lovely day that he'd decided to take a rare walk during the workday. Glancing at his watch, Marc figured he had time to grab a sandwich before heading back downtown and his mid-afternoon appointment. A group of giggling children ran past him, one of the boys brushing his arm as he flew past. He almost yelled to the youngster to watch where he was going but stopped short when he saw her.

Natalie sat alone on a park bench not more than a hundred yards away. His steps faltered, torn with indecision. Memories flooded his mind as he stared. Her hair fell in loose waves to her shoulders, the way he loved it best, and she wore a pretty dress and high-heeled sandals, highlighting her long, slender arms and legs. He wanted to run to her, throw his arms around her, hold her close, and kiss her senseless. *Take it slow and easy, as if you're starting all over again.* Although the suggestion seemed ludicrous, Dr. Fontaine was right. Marc mentally bolstered himself.

Here I go, Lord. Be with me.

Chapter 10

A SHAGGY, WHITE mutt appeared beside Natalie, a leash trailing its way around the edge of the park bench. That was a surprise, and Marc couldn't stop his grin. A soft breeze blew her hair, lifting soft wisps that caressed her cheeks. As he approached, she turned her head in his direction. When her smile surfaced, it made his heart sing—off-key, no doubt. No woman's smile compared to Natalie's.

As he approached, she moved over on the bench, making way for him. Plastering on his best smile with an outward confidence he didn't feel, Marc dropped down next to her, his heart pumping overtime. So much was at stake. Why was she here in the middle of the day? Shouldn't she be at the school? He told her about his bi-weekly appointments with Dr. Fontaine just as she told him about her various appointments with her own doctors.

"Hi." Dark blue eyes met his.

"Hi, yourself. Who's your friend?" He scratched the mutt's ears and made a friend for life. The dog cocked its head to one side, watching him with big, limpid brown eyes. What a lovable mug. "Hey, little guy." A small, rough tongue licked the side of his hand, and he chuckled.

"This," Natalie announced, "is Elwood."

"Elwood?" Marc grinned. "Interesting name."

"It's from *The Blues Brothers*."

His eyes widened. Turning to face her on the bench, he laid gentle hands on both her shoulders, unable to tamp down his rising excitement. "We watched the movie together once and, now that I think about it, we talked about liking the fun names . . . for the dogs we might adopt someday. This could mean something, Natalie. Maybe a little piece of your memory is coming back." Hey, he'd fight these battles as he went along. A little or a lot, he'd take what he could get.

~

Natalie hated to take away the enthusiasm in Marc's voice, the hope in his eyes. Again. Seemed that's all she'd been doing lately. Her heart skipped a beat as his gorgeous blue eyes met hers. "Or it could be that Kim and I watched the movie the apartment a few nights ago." As expected, her husband's countenance clouded, disappointment etched into his handsome features. He looked like a little boy whose favorite toy had been dangled in front of him only to be yanked beyond his grasp. He probably felt that way about a lot of things.

58

And it was all her fault. She wasn't a cruel person, but the look on his face made her feel like one.

Bending over, Marc scratched behind both Elwood's ears. "Well, I suppose it's good you've found yourself a companion." He shot her a wry grin, easing her discomfort somewhat.

"You mean a companion of male persuasion that's not human?" She laughed as he feigned shocked surprise.

"Amnesia or not, you know me pretty well." He laughed quietly. "Since you started it, I don't mind saying I hope he's warming your bed at night." He grunted and averted his gaze. "When did you get him? I assume he belongs to you." His eyes dropped to her wrist with the leash wrapped around it.

"I picked him out at the shelter a couple of days ago." She smiled. "His little ears shot up in the air, and he tilted his head and gave me one of those please-take-me-home-with-you looks. I couldn't resist." She looked over at him. "Actually, I thought he might be a good companion for *you*."

"Me?" Marc hesitated, running his hand along the mutt's back, wishing she'd find *him* irresistible—not a dog—no matter how cute. "I'm hardly ever home. Business is really good and things are hectic at the agency . . ." His voice trailed, and he blew out a sigh, his gaze falling on Elwood. "He sure does have big eyes."

"You work too hard, Marc."

His grin disappeared. "Care to guess why I do that?" He looked remorseful the second the words escaped. "Sorry."

She steeled herself. It had to be said. "If you want to file for an annulment, or a divorce, I'll understand. You have a life to live, and I don't want to keep you from it."

"That's not what I want and you know it," he shot back. "I know you don't either. Christians don't give up, and I can't believe you even suggested it." Now he sounded angry.

"What I want is to be fair to you, and I know how hard this is." She twisted her hands together on her lap before starting that little dance thing with her fingers. A single tear slipped down her cheek. "I know you feel it was unfair of me to move out of the house, but I want you to know something."

He turned to face her, hopeful optimism etched into his expression. Propping his elbow on the back of the bench, his eyes dropped to her lips.

"I miss you." That brought his gaze upward to meet her eyes. She loved his smile, liked the way he looked at her now. "I miss the way you make me tea and leave it in the microwave, knowing I'll probably be up in the night and find it there. I miss our morning devotions." She smiled a little. "I even miss seeing you gulp down those horrible breakfast shakes. You have a way of . . . really getting into my thoughts even when it's a *very* inconvenient time. I'm afraid my students, and probably most of the school staff, think I've gone mental."

"Could it be that missing me is the reason you're sitting here today, on this bench, on a school day, not to mention in the *middle* of the day?"

"It might have a little something to do with it." When Marc leaned toward her, she felt an undeniable tug in her chest and consciously fought to stop twisting her hands together. Her eyes widened as she realized she wouldn't mind if he kissed her on the lips. He'd already worked his way around her face. A tear rolled down her cheek, followed by another. She sniffled and looked away. "See, I told you I was mental." One minute she was fine and the next she'd cry. Why couldn't she control her emotions? Opening her purse, she fumbled for a tissue.

"Let me, Natalie," he whispered, scooting closer on the bench, caressing her cheeks with both thumbs. "You may not remember, but whenever you cried—which wasn't often since you met me, for the record—I'd kiss away your tears." To prove his point, he pressed his lips against the wet trail on first one cheek and then the other. It was incredibly sweet how the forthright businessman could turn surprisingly gentle.

Closing her eyes, she enjoyed his tender touch. "You're a very . . . romantic man, aren't you?"

"I'm going to do my best to help you remember." Marc's arm circled around her on the park bench, but then he removed it almost as fast. "Sorry." He sounded disgruntled.

"It's all right. You've already kissed away my tears. Now," she said, lifting his arm, "let's put that arm back where it belongs." His eyes softened, and she sensed his relief. "How was your therapy session today?"

Marc stared at some of the children playing around them, but she could tell his mind was elsewhere. "Dr. Fontaine seems to think I'm making some headway."

"That's good news, isn't it?"

He stretched out his long legs and shifted his position, but left his arm around her shoulder. "He also told me to stop being so selfish." He shrugged. "So, how are *your* sessions going? I'm sure your doctor didn't tell *you* to stop being selfish."

She sighed as she tucked a stray section of hair behind one ear. "They're going as well as can be expected, I guess, but they obviously haven't brought me any closer to recovering my memories." She hated telling him that, but he should be used to it by now.

Marc frowned. "Are they repressed memories or are they totally gone? I mean, does the doctor think your memory's completely lost, or is it in there somewhere, waiting to be tapped into if it's somehow triggered?" Slumping back against the bench, he lowered his head into his hands. He sat that way for a long moment before looking back up at her. "I'm not making sense to myself, so I can't expect you to understand."

Taking his hand in hers, Natalie squeezed. It was the reassuring, comforting gesture of a caring friend, but she understood it wasn't what Marc hoped for, what he needed. She couldn't give him that. Not yet, but hopefully someday.

The Adam's apple in his throat moved up and down. "What if you don't remember? What then?" She could tell how much it took out of him to ask. From what she knew, he rarely expressed doubts about anything.

Touching the side of his chin, she needed to look at him. Such a handsome face with its masculine, angular lines and planes. An involuntary sigh of longing escaped, and she caught the way his eyes lit. His gaze melted into hers before settling on her lips again. She was thankful he seemed to find her pretty, but it also drove her crazy out of her mind. With him looking at her like that, it took a few seconds to find her voice.

"I don't know how, Marc, but I'll come back. With more love for you than before. If you can just hang in there long enough." It sounded like she was trying to convince herself. "Maybe it's not fair to you to ask you to wait even longer, but . . ." *Please, Lord, let him wait for me. Help us find our way back to each other.*

Marc planted a soft kiss on her lips, the first since her accident. Her heart responded, and so did all the rest of her. Why should she be surprised? This man *knew* her. And, somewhere deep inside, she knew him in the intimate way only a wife could.

He pulled away after a moment and released a deep sigh. "That's all I need to hear. I'll wait, however long it takes." His eyes caressed her lips, lingering there. With a gentle finger, he trailed an achingly slow path along the edge of her face, tracing her cheekbone before skimming his thumb across her lower lip. She was powerless, under his potent spell. It was the most sensual thing she could imagine, especially when he graced her with that devastating smile guaranteed to turn her to mush. "I love you, Natalie." When he brushed her cheek with a whisper of a kiss, a deep yearning stirred. "We'll work through this together."

She opened her mouth, but couldn't speak. If she told Marc she loved him in the heat of this moment, it would only be hormones talking. Even so, would that be so wrong? He *was* her husband. Moral convictions and upbringing in the church aside, maybe she should tug him by the hand, lead him back home and march straight up those stairs to the bedroom. He would love it, but she wasn't ready. Above all, she treasured honesty in their relationship. Deep down, so did he. The sad, honest truth stared her in the face. She didn't *feel* married. Trembling with emotion, she closed her eyes, dazed by his nearness. Moving her head to his shoulder, she put her hand near his heart, seeking the reassurance of his strong, steady heartbeat. His arm tightened around her shoulder and he kissed the top of her head.

Marc needed a wife, a soulmate, a helpmate. A lover.

She snuggled into him, burying her head and enjoying the quiet moment. She loved his warmth, his desire to protect her. They sat that way for a long time until he looked at his watch. The selfish part of her wanted him to stay much longer. As they said good-bye, his eyes searched hers, seeking answers and a promise for tomorrow. Caressing the side of his hand with her thumb, she raised it to her lips and planted a gentle kiss.

His eyes widened as she took his hand and placed it over her heart. Pressing his palm flat against the thin cotton of her dress, her hand over his, she relished the look of love etched into her husband's face. With her other hand, she smoothed his bangs away from his forehead.

Although she couldn't find words, surely Marc knew.

She offered him Elwood's leash, but he shook his head. "Maybe in a couple of weeks. Not now." He turned after one last kiss on the cheek. "Be careful going back to the school. There's construction all over the place. I'll call you tonight."

After helping Elwood scamper into the passenger seat, Natalie watched as Marc strolled down the street. At least she'd given him renewed hope, as evidenced by his confident strides, the lift of those broad shoulders. A few hundred yards away, he turned and blew her a kiss, sending her heart into overdrive. Climbing into the leather seat of her Audi, her smile sobered. She couldn't hide from the hard truth much longer. A man like Marc Thompson might have the best of intentions, but if things didn't change, he wouldn't be around forever.

It simply wasn't possible.

Chapter 11

"Hey, Marc." Trevor Monaghan stuck his head inside the office door. "You're looking pretty ragged, my friend."

"Well, hello to you, too." Marc gave him a half-grin and laid his pen on the desk. "Flattery will get you nowhere. Judging by your goofy look, I'd say you've been spending time with the lovely Miss Kilbourne." All their flirting around each other the last few months was enough to drive him crazy. Even though he frowned on office romances, this one seemed inevitable. Last week, he'd advised Trevor to declare his intentions and get on with it, especially since everyone else in the office could see they belonged together. "About time you two connected. No doubt it's a match made in God's infinite wisdom."

Trevor smiled. "Thanks, considering the sentiment comes from one of the most successful advertising gurus in the country." He plopped his lanky frame down in the chair opposite Marc's desk, the wide grin spreading across his face.

While flattering, Trevor overstated the case. Marc sat back in his chair, crossing his arms behind his head. "I wouldn't go that far. Don't need that kind of pressure." He met Trevor's gaze. Talk about Irish eyes. "I couldn't do it without you, that's for sure. So, enough sap." He grinned. "Tell me. When's the wedding?"

Trevor laughed. "Don't rush us. But things are going great. No thanks to you, I might add."

"How so?"

"You were supposed to arrange a little office get-together, as I recall, in order to facilitate our blossoming friendship. Oh, how quickly they forget," he joked when he gave him a blank look.

Marc shook his head. "Sorry, Trev. I haven't exactly focused on social events the last few weeks. Refresh my mind." He made a mental note to plan something special for Christmas for his staff. They were too invaluable for the lifeblood of his agency, and he couldn't neglect them or they'd start grumbling. And those kinds of rumbles could lead to bigger trouble.

"I'm just teasing you. No need to worry. I'm doing just fine on my own without the crutch of an office event to win over Christy's affections. How are things with you?" He sobered at Marc's deep scowl. "That good, huh?"

Marc rubbed his tired eyes. "Tell me what good it does to have gained all these material things," he said, gesturing around his modern office with its expensive framed art and sculptures, "when I can't have the one part of my life that means the most."

"You worked awfully hard to get where you are," Trevor said, his voice quiet, but without the slightest hint of chastisement. "You don't turn off your life's blood because you got married. I mean, come on. This is me, Marc.

Natalie's great, but she can't fill every void in your life." He gave him a quick look. "Neither would you want or expect her to."

Marc met his gaze head-on. "You're right in one respect," he admitted. "Partying in the Red Sox clubhouse, tickets to every Celtics game and going to the Patriot's kick-off parties is a nice perk, but Natalie *does* fill the gaps in my life. I'm floundering without her."

"Like a drowning man in the bay?"

He snorted. "More like the annoying guy who's thrown off the lifeboat and can't swim. I'm calling out, but nobody's answering." He paused a moment. "Maybe they don't want to. I'm stretching my arms toward the lifeline, but I can't seem to reach it, no matter what I do."

Trevor nodded. "Sounds to me like you could definitely benefit from a talk with Pastor Ron. He might be able to give you a better perspective. I'm really sorry you're being put through all this."

He made it sound like he was being punished. Maybe he was. But by whom—God Almighty? "You know, both you and Dr. Fontaine have told me I should speak to our pastor." Since Trevor attended the same church, Marc knew Pastor Ron well. Since he trusted his creative director on a daily basis with crucial business decisions, it seemed he should do the same in his personal life. "Considering I trust your collective judgment, maybe that should be my next move."

"You mean I'm giving you the exact same advice as that high-priced shrink?" Another of Trevor's trademark grins surfaced.

Marc nodded and smiled. How he appreciated this man. "None other."

"Then, in exchange for my fee, you and Natalie can treat Christy and me to an outrageously overpriced dinner once everything . . ." His voice trailed and his gaze dropped. "You know what I mean. Sorry."

"I do, and thanks. Stop apologizing. It helps more than you know to talk about it."

~

Before the Sunday evening service, Pastor Ron Shelton sat next to Marc in his study. "Natalie's met with me a few times. Give her time. The Lord can work a beautiful miracle in this situation, and we're going to pray toward that end." The lines around the senior pastor's eyes crinkled. There was that word again. *Situation.* This time, it didn't bother him. Feeling the need to unburden himself, Marc confessed his recent temptation and subsequent humbling before the Lord.

"I'm sure you're stronger than you give yourself credit for," Pastor Ron advised. "Keep your eyes on Him, and God will never tempt you beyond what you can bear. The success of your agency shows how resourceful and resilient you are."

"Meaning He must have some serious tempting in store to test me," Marc said. The sarcasm was ill-advised, especially around a man of God. "I'll never be able to be content or fully rest in the Lord again until Natalie and I are back together. I'm trying my best, but that's the bottom line."

"I know you are, but as best you can, try to grow and learn from it."

"To be honest, what the Lord wants me to learn from this experience is something I might not ever understand."

"I'm sure it will all be revealed in due time. In some ways, I have no doubt your relationship with your wife will be stronger for having gone through this trial. Trust in the Lord, and don't blame Him. Remember, God doesn't go by our timetable. It's all in His control."

The words pierced Marc's heart as he recalled his rash outburst in Dr. Fontaine's office. *Do I blame you, Lord, for what happened? For taking Natalie away from me?* "I don't want to blame God, but it's all very confusing." He shook his head and rubbed the back of his neck. "I need to pray, if you don't mind."

"We'll do that, and I'd like to share some scripture with you. But first," Pastor Ron said, standing to walk around the desk, "I want to give you something." Flipping through a small book on his desk, he wrote a name and phone number on the back of one of his business cards.

Returning to his chair, Pastor Ron handed the card to him. "Sam Lewis is Domestic Missions Director of TeamWork Missions based in Houston. Natalie's volunteered with their organization in a few summer work camps, at least a couple in San Antonio. She's very passionate about the work TeamWork does, and I've heard her speak to the ladies and the youth group here at the church about the impact the missions made on her life. It's my hope Mr. Lewis and his wife might be able to give you some insight to help." He met Marc's eyes. "Call it the Lord's leading, but it's at least worth a phone call."

Marc nodded. "Thanks. I know the name Lewis since Natalie's talked about them in the past. Some of the TeamWork ladies were in our wedding, but Sam and his wife weren't able to make it." He scratched his head. "Unfortunately, Natalie doesn't remember much about her experiences with them." But she *did* remember Winnie's name. That was a promising start.

As they prayed together a few minutes later, Marc wanted to believe the Almighty heard his prayer. The battle lines were slowly fading, but it remained difficult to worship when he couldn't fathom God's purpose in allowing this horrible thing to happen to his wife. She didn't deserve it. But neither did all the abused children and wives in the world. Or all the victims of floods, earthquakes, other natural disasters or acts of horrific terrorism. Bad things sometimes happen, even to the best people in the world. Didn't make it any easier to stomach.

"Thanks, Pastor Ron," Marc said, shaking his hand on the way out of his study. "I appreciate your time, and I'll call Mr. Lewis tomorrow." Why not? He had nothing to lose and maybe something to gain. Pausing outside the sanctuary, he spied Natalie surrounded by a few ladies. She nodded and listened, and it was good to see them engaging her in conversation. When another pregnant woman approached, Natalie slid over on the pew. She smiled and returned the woman's hug, and turned to say something to a couple of young children with her.

His wife needed the encouragement and support from her friends, and he was thankful for them. It wasn't the time to interrupt. Heading for the side door of the church, Marc avoided the greeters positioned by the front doors. Maybe he should slide in a back pew and stay for the service, but he couldn't do it. Not when his heart attitude wasn't right.

God forgive me, I just can't.

Chapter 12

*M*ARC DRUMMED HIS fingers on the desktop, focusing on the clock on his desk. He'd been preoccupied all morning, and it wasn't like he was accomplishing much work. He had to plan his strategy for how to approach the conversation with Sam Lewis. How could he summarize the story of what happened to Natalie in sixty seconds or less? He wasn't a very good ad man if he couldn't figure that one out. You'd never know he made countless cold calls each month and often socialized with the insanely rich and famous. Yet he was nervous to call Sam Lewis because *this* time, it was personal.

"Thanks for calling TeamWork Missions. May I help you?" The young, feminine drawl brought a smile to his lips. The native Texan accent held such an inherent welcome. "Hello?"

Marc snapped to attention. This was an actual living, breathing woman on the other end of the line. Such a refreshing change from the usual recorded greeting. "Sam Lewis, please."

"Sam's out for lunch with his wife right now, sir, but if you'd like to leave your name and number, I'm sure he'll call you back this afternoon."

"Thanks. I'll call back later." Replacing the phone, Marc sat lost in thought, ignoring the nagging in his mind. He could at least have left a message. An hour later, taking a break from watching the latest ad campaign on the screen in his office, he tried again. The same friendly voice patched him straight through to another extension with no hesitation whatsoever, as if she'd been waiting for his call.

"This is Sam."

"Mr. Lewis?"

"Guilty." Tinged with humor, the deep drawl was pleasant, welcoming.

"This is Marc Thompson, Thompson Sports Advertising, calling from Boston." Great. He'd used his professional voice out of habit. Sam would think he was trying to sell him some kind of marketing promotion and rush to get him off the phone.

"Ah, Beantown. Love the Sox. Second in the AL East this year wasn't bad. Tell me, what can I do for you, Mr. Thompson?"

Marc warmed to him immediately. He spoke his second language—sports. He'd expected a stuffy, older-sounding gentleman, but this man was neither. "Call me Marc, please."

"And I'm Sam. How can I help?"

This guy was great. "I'm calling about my wife, Natalie." When he heard no immediate response—no confirmation or name recognition—he hastened to add, "I believe you know her as Natalie Combs."

"Of course. How is Natalie?"

Oh, how to answer that one? All his carefully rehearsed spiels no longer seemed important.

"Marc? Is everything all right?" Compassion resonated in the warmth on the other end of the line.

"Yes . . . I mean, no. Her foot pushed through a rotting piece of wood on the basement stairs in our home, and she fell and hit her head on the basement floor. Now, she's suffering from amnesia, and the doctors aren't sure how long it will last." Wow. His life had become a soap opera.

"I'm so sorry." Sam's voice was quiet. "I know you two married only a few months ago. Lexa, especially, hated that we couldn't be there, but we were already committed to a TeamWork trip overseas that week. Is the amnesia . . . severe?"

Might as well spell it out for the man. "It's retrograde amnesia, meaning she has a lot of childhood memories up through college. The sad fact of the matter is, the last few years are barely a blip on her radar. To be blunt, she doesn't remember anything about me. At least not since the accident. We're having to start all over again, pretty much from square one." He hesitated and cleared his throat. "The blessing is that she seems okay otherwise, and other than the memory loss, she's fine. Amnesia's a very strange, unpredictable beast."

Sam was silent for a long moment before he finally spoke again. "Does she remember anything about TeamWork or our volunteers?"

Marc blew out a deep sigh. "Something about Amy looked familiar, and she remembered Winnie's name when she saw their photographs in our wedding album. She said she felt God was somehow telling her how important TeamWork is in her life. Before her accident, Natalie mentioned you and Lexa quite often, and she talked about how much she loved working the missions with all of you."

"Natalie's one of our most faithful volunteers," Sam said. "My heart goes out to you, brother."

The heartfelt emotion in his voice touched Marc somewhere deep inside. He'd only talked with this man a couple of minutes, but felt he'd known him much longer. Now he could understand why Natalie always spoke so lovingly of Sam and Lexa and the others. The TeamWork director used none of the pat phrases—didn't tell him he'd pray for Natalie, pray for him, that it's "all in God's plan" or "it'll be okay"—and then sign off. From what he knew of Sam, praying was second nature. An idea came to mind, and Marc made an impetuous decision, something he rarely did. "Sam, if it's okay with you, I'd like to come meet with you in Houston so we can talk about this more in-depth. I understand from our pastor you've been a good friend to my wife, and she helped you with a couple of mission camps in San Antonio. He's actually the one who gave me your number and suggested I call."

"I'm glad you did. Natalie's also worked a number of TeamWork projects in the Northeast. That's where she met Amy Jacobsen and recruited her. If you feel there's something Lexa and I can do to help her, we'll be more than happy to try. We can talk more privately at the house. It goes without saying you're more than welcome to stay with us. Will Natalie be coming?"

"No, I'll fly solo on this one," Marc said. "I don't want to impose, but how does tomorrow sound?"

He sensed Sam's smile. "I can tell you're not a man to let any grass grow under his feet. We'll look forward to meeting you. Once you make your flight reservations, give me a quick call or shoot me an e-mail with your itinerary. I'll meet you at the airport."

"Will do." Marc scribbled Sam's contact information. "If Lexa has any hesitation whatsoever, I'll be more than happy to stay in a hotel. Thanks, Sam. I really appreciate this."

He chuckled. "Trust me, Lexa will insist you stay here, and we'll look forward to visiting with you. I'll be praying for a safe trip, brother."

Hanging up, Marc sat for a few moments, staring at the phone. That was the second time Sam called him brother. From most men, it would annoy the tar out of him. But this guy was different. He sounded more genuine than most, and he'd been around enough insincerity to discern the difference. Spinning in his chair, he turned his attention to the computer. Normally, Christy took care of all his travel arrangements, but this one he'd handle on his own. Typing in the specifications, he was thankful he had the financial resources to buy a ticket without the benefit of two weeks' notice. Even so, he cringed as he processed the credit card payment. If it helped Natalie, he'd buy a ticket to another planet.

Preparing to leave the office a few hours later, Marc's spirits were much higher as he shot off a quick e-mail to Sam with his flight schedule. Contacting Sam and Lexa was a positive step in trying to reconnect with Natalie and helping her find her life again, and he had a good feeling about it. While he couldn't impose the impossible burden on Sam and Lexa of being the primary key to Natalie recovering her repressed memories, he held high hopes. They had to count for something.

~

"Marc? Sam Lewis. Welcome to Houston."

He pumped the other man's hand, surprised when Sam pulled him into a quick, warm hug before releasing him. Although lean, he sported the impressive muscles of a professional athlete. The Texan had to be at least six-foot-four since he bested his own height by an inch or two. "How'd you know it was me?"

Intense, light blue eyes met his. "It's stamped on your forehead." Smile lines surrounded his mouth, and dark, wavy hair streaked with a few silver strands at the temples peeked out beneath a black cowboy hat. He looked to be about his age, maybe a few years older. Sam laughed when he shot him an amused glance. "Wedding photos. Winnie sent them to us. Did you check a bag?"

Marc nodded at his computer case and the small overnight bag he carried. "This is it. I've traveled a lot and learned the benefits of not checking baggage. Besides, I doubt your wife wants an overnight guest for more than a night or two."

Sam reached for his bag. "You're welcome to stay as long as you need, and that's a promise. We want to help. Whatever it takes."

He tried to keep the shock from his tone. "Are you this nice to every stranger?"

The smile lines deepened considerably. "Welcome to Texas, my friend. This way." As they approached the automatic revolving doors, Marc caught the openly admiring glances directed at Sam from more than a few women as they passed through the terminal. The man was a walking chick magnet, and could be a rugged model in a Ralph Lauren ad campaign. He sure looked the part of the outdoorsy, quintessential cowboy with the Stetson, western-style sports jacket, white cotton shirt and jeans. Marc's eyes trailed down to Sam's well-worn, leather cowboy boots. As much as anything, he exuded self-confidence untouched by arrogance or pride. At least he didn't swagger.

Sam's strides were long, purposeful, and Marc hurried to keep pace. As soon as they passed through the doors, a blast of warm air assaulted him. "I'd forgotten how miserably humid it can get here in Houston, even at this time of year." Unable to keep the disgust from his voice, Marc shrugged out of his suit jacket and draped it over one arm, loosened his tie and opened his collar.

"It can be humid almost any time of the year, but somehow you get used to it," Sam said. "Helps that I'm native born. You don't sound like an inbred Yankee."

"I'm originally from a suburb of St. Louis. I went to Yale and fell in love with New England, Boston in particular." No sense in going into all the reasons now. He preferred hearing more about Sam and Lexa. "Where did you meet Lexa?" They drove along the highway in Sam's late model white Volvo station wagon. It seemed good humor came as naturally as breathing with this man when he chuckled again.

"I met my wife when she signed on for the summer work camp in San Antonio in 1997, her first TeamWork mission. We were both from Houston and financial planners. Neither one of us saw the other one coming. It was rather like . . ."

"Love at first sight?"

Sam darted a quick glance in his direction. "More like spontaneous combustion."

They shared a laugh.

"How long have you been married?"

"Two years this past August. By the time that work camp ended, I'd committed to an overseas mission with TeamWork for a year. I had to get the wanderlust out of my system. I'm glad Lexa was feisty enough, brave enough—and loved me enough—to wait."

"An entire year away from each other?" Marc shook his head. "That must have been rough." The irony of that statement didn't escape him. At least Natalie lived in the same state, but sometimes it might as well be another planet.

"It was a tough summer at the work camp. There was a lot happening, between Lexa and me in finding our way to one another . . . and in other ways. We had some situations with some of the other volunteers. As a result, I made the life-changing decision that I needed to make the move out of financial planning and work in full-time ministry."

"Where were you stationed during your overseas mission?"

"I was in several countries during the course of the year, but the deepest part of Africa the last few months. You hear things about missionaries, but most people stateside don't have a clue. I thank the Lord every day He brought me back home after some of the atrocities I saw. Things Lexa doesn't know to this day." He darted a quick glance his way. "Things I'm not about to tell her."

Marc nodded, humbled. "Was it hard to reconnect with her after a year?"

The humor surfaced again. "As soon as humanly possible—on the very day I returned—I proposed. Right in front of the Alamo, believe it or not. Before I left, I promised her we wouldn't wait long. Normally, there's a three-day waiting period, but my grandfather lived in San Antonio for a few years. Helps to have a judge as a close friend of the family." Sam smiled. "And then I arranged for a pastor friend of mine to marry us."

"The same night?" Marc could hear the incredulity in his own question.

"The very same. Like you, I'm not a man to let grass grow under his feet, either. We were married with lots of yellow roses and hormones in overdrive. She doesn't have any family left, and my family pretty much told me not to come home unless Lexa was my wife. They watched over her while I was overseas, and fell in love with her, too. Not a hard thing to do." He shook his head with another smile. "Lexa's prayer was that I'd show up and not leave her standing there in front of the Alamo, but she jumped aboard the marriage train soon enough, especially once I gave her my grandmother's engagement ring and promised her the prized family peach pie recipe."

"Sometimes I wish I'd whisked Natalie off somewhere like that and eloped. Keep it simple. Saves a lot of time and headaches, not to mention money."

"Best decision I ever made to marry Lexa. She's the perfect foil for me, and helps keep my head on straight. She rounds out the rough spots in this old cowboy, challenges me every single day."

"Any kids yet?"

"No." The smiled faded only a bit. "Lexa's more than ready. She's terrific with kids and seems to think I'll make a good father." As he turned onto a tree-lined, quiet residential street, Sam waved to a young mother pushing a stroller and a man mowing his lawn.

Marc tried to ignore the arrow to his heart at the mention of the word *father* and Sam's unwitting reminder, although he'd brought it on himself by asking. That was another piece of the puzzle with Natalie he'd probably need to tell them. As Sam turned into a driveway, Marc was surprised by the beautiful, two-story red brick home with white shutters and lovely landscaping. The perfect suburban home to raise a family. Somehow, he'd expected a sprawling, ranch-style home in the middle of this lovely neighborhood.

A very pretty, petite woman stepped out the front door and onto the walkway. A long, blonde braid hung over one shoulder, and she wore a simple blue dress that flirted around her knees in the light breeze. But it was her welcoming smile that warmed his heart. Glancing at Sam, Marc was floored by his obvious look of love.

She extended her hand as they climbed out of the car and headed in her direction. "Hi, Marc. I'm Lexa Lewis. It's so nice to finally meet you." Like her husband's, the drawl had to be native Texan. It was surprisingly deep for such a tiny woman, but charming.

"Thank you. The pleasure's all mine." Her cheeks bloomed a pretty pink when Marc gave her a quick, spontaneous kiss. When he pulled away, Lexa's aquamarine eyes momentarily mesmerized him. This couple's future offspring would be genetically blessed.

"You're a bit late," Lexa said, planting a kiss on her husband's cheek as he leaned close. "No doubt you were regaling Marc with stories of how you relentlessly wooed me."

"I'll always woo you, Lexa. And if I stop, you'll set me straight." Sam touched her cheek with the back of his hand, his fingers lingering for a couple of seconds.

Marc hid his grin. These two were too cute for words. Who says "woo" anymore? It was quite possible time stood still. It might be a long wait to eat if they kept getting lost in the other like this. Maybe he should save them all some time and offer to treat them to dinner at one of Houston's finest restaurants.

"Please, come in." Lexa broke the spell as she headed inside the house and gestured for him to follow. Overhead fans circulated a cool breeze, and Marc eyed the high ceilings and spacious, open floor plan. This was a home he could live in, a warm and welcoming reflection of its owners.

"We're going to start dinner," Sam said. "Come into the kitchen and keep us company unless you'd rather go to your room and rest."

"I'd enjoy the company. You can tell me more about TeamWork." He caught Lexa's smile.

"I think our guest already knows the magic word, Sam."

Leaving his things in the living room, Marc followed them toward the back of the house. An overflowing vase of fresh flowers stood on the entranceway table, family portraits adorned the wall by the wide staircase, and books were everywhere—crammed onto bookcases and scattered on tables. A photo of Sam in an Air Force uniform caught his eye as his host held a swinging door, standing aside and waiting. Sunlight reflected off the hardwood floors and streamed through a large picture window in the breakfast nook as Marc walked into the kitchen. More ceiling fans—a staple in the home—whirred softly above them.

"I see you were in the Air Force."

"That's Will, Sam's younger brother," Lexa said. "The first time I met Will, I almost kissed him, thinking it was my husband." She laughed when she spied Sam's raised brows. "He's a candidate for the NASA astronaut training program."

"We used to call my brother 'Star Sailor' when we were kids," Sam added. "Going into space is all he ever talked about. Still does." Removing his jacket, Sam draped it over a nearby chair. "He's got a one-track mind, my brother. If there's any justice, he'll be accepted into the program."

"Impressive. I have a lot of respect for our astronauts." Marc released a sigh as he settled in a chair in the cozy breakfast nook, noting the spacious backyard with its lovely landscaping. Perfect romping grounds for all those future, genetically-blessed Lewis children. But there wasn't a horse, stable, tumbleweed, cow or armadillo in sight. Somehow, he expected at least one of them.

As they pulled steaks and vegetables out of the refrigerator and worked together, Sam asked questions about his agency. Lexa told him about her work as a part-time financial planner for Alamo World Financial, and how—as Sam mentioned in the car—her husband had also been an independent financial planner when they'd first met.

"Sam liked financial planning for the people factor," Lexa said, handing him a glass of iced tea, "helping them see that solid financial planning was a lot like securing their eternity. Something to look forward to and not be afraid of." She darted a sweet smile in her husband's direction as he arranged steaks on a platter and prepared to carry them to the grill on the back patio. "But he pegged me for a numbers girl right from the start."

"A numbers girl?" Marc liked the sound of that. With his weird fascination with numbers, he could get onboard with that idea.

"I love numbers, but I also hid behind them. They're safe and dependable. You see, numbers don't disappoint the way people can."

Marc wasn't sure how to respond, but he understood exactly what she meant. "I've always had this weird thing I do that helps me remember number patterns, but relating well with people is also a large part of what I do in my business. I depend on both in the advertising game."

"Natalie's so proud of you, and she respects what you do, Marc. She told me how you built your agency from the ground up with pure grit and determination, and that you're brilliant at what you do."

He raked a quick hand through his hair, but couldn't meet Lexa's eyes. Couldn't bear to see the pity. "She might have been proud of me at one time, but I'm afraid she doesn't remember now."

"Natalie told me a long time ago, when you were dating." Lexa gave him a slightly sheepish glance. "But Lisabeth told me last night. Right after she talked with Natalie yesterday afternoon. Your wife admires you. Very much."

He looked up so fast his neck popped. "What do you mean?" He massaged the back of his neck and tried not to stare. Surely there weren't many women named Lisabeth. Did Natalie know he'd flown to Houston? He purposely didn't tell her about this trip. He tamped down the quick rise of emotion.

Those aquamarine eyes were kind. "As far as I know, Natalie doesn't know you're here, and your heart's in the right place in coming to us."

Sam's beautiful wife must be a mind reader.

"I called Lisabeth and told her we hadn't heard from Natalie in a while, and wondered how she's adjusting to married life. It wasn't my place to tell her you were coming for a visit. She told me about Natalie's accident, and she encouraged me to call Winnie, Rebekah, Amy and the other girls in our TeamWork crew. None of us knew about it. We're all concerned, of course, and we want to help. The other girls agreed to wait and not call Natalie, or do anything else, at least until after your visit so we'd know more."

At least Lexa's tone wasn't chastising. Shaking his head, Marc lowered his gaze. "Forgive me. I should have called, but I couldn't bring myself to do it." Standing, he moved over to the opposite side of the counter from where they worked side-by-side.

Lexa stopped wrapping plump ears of corn in foil and gave him a gentle smile. "We all love Natalie—*and* you—and we want to surround you, and your marriage, in prayer. Remember, there's a lot of power in numbers." Ah, so she had a point with the numbers talk. Wise woman.

Marc wondered how they could love him except as an extension of Natalie, but he understood they did, and that filled him with unexpected contentment. They'd help them get through this continuing nightmare. His eyes were full when he glanced at Lexa and then Sam. "Every day I wake up with the same prayer—that somehow Natalie will regain her memory. That it's all a bad dream." He blew out a sigh and looked away. "But every night, when I crawl back into bed, nothing's changed. And I wonder if it ever will."

"I've learned there's nothing too impossible for the Lord," Sam said, his voice quiet. "He'll work this out between you and Natalie. Good will eventually come from it, but we need to be patient. I know it's easier said than done."

"Love is the most powerful emotion we have," Lexa said, glancing at her husband. "Every time we find it, it's a gift. We have to believe the love you and

Natalie share will overcome all the odds. We just need to find the key to unlocking her memories."

Sam nodded. "We need to pray."

Marc raised his head. "Right now?"

Those smile lines deepened. "Why not? No time like the present."

Why did he have the feeling this couple would become very dear to him in the future? Maybe because they already were. He admired how they said *we* instead of *you*. He didn't mind at all. He welcomed their prayers, their help, their love. Marc's eyes traveled to their intertwined hands, and he nodded. He didn't hesitate as he placed his hand over Sam and Lexa's. They both grabbed onto his hand and held on tight. It was like he'd done with his Pawtucket teammates before every ballgame, but this time, it was different. Sam and Lexa would hold on as long as he needed.

TeamWork took on a whole new meaning.

Chapter 13

A FEW HOURS later, sitting in the living room after a delicious grilled steak dinner, Marc patted his stomach. He couldn't wait to loosen his belt. "If you two eat like this all the time, how you don't weigh a ton is beyond me."

"Oh, we manage to work it off." Sam laughed and winked at Lexa.

Blushing furiously, she gave his arm a playful swat. "We work out in the gym together."

"Well, in any case, I'm not entirely certain I shouldn't be getting myself a hotel room tonight." He caught their surprised expressions.

"My sincere apologies, Marc," Sam broke in without hesitation. "I hope we didn't make you uncomfortable."

He shook his head. "No, of course not. It's just . . . hard." He was pretty transparent with his feelings, but hoped his envy wasn't obvious.

"Forgive us. I'm sorry," Lexa said. "I hate to think we're being insensitive. How hard this must be for you. I can't even imagine."

He shot her a grateful glance before lowering his eyes. These two were the best example of a Christian marriage he'd ever met. During the course of their dinner, he'd witnessed the countless gentle touches on the hand, the loving glances. Marc swallowed his sigh. As they ate, Sam and Lexa had thoughtfully avoided discussing his situation with Natalie, and he was grateful. It would have been difficult to eat if he kept getting all choked up.

"In our painfully misguided attempt to make you feel welcome," Sam said, bringing him back to reality, "all we did was make you realize what you're missing with Natalie. We want to help. Name it, and we're there. If you're up to it, start by telling us how you two met and what's happening with Natalie now."

That's all it took to open the floodgates. Marc gulped and began his story, telling them how he first met Natalie through a client at a Patriots football game at Gillette Stadium. She was dragged there by a cousin with an extra ticket given to them by his own ad agency, hoping to sway her into a passion for the game. Didn't work. Although he didn't get to spend much time with her that day, he was pleasantly surprised when one of her matchmaking cousins pushed Natalie's phone number into his hand.

"I tried for weeks to get a date with the gorgeous brunette I'd met briefly at the game. I plied her with the usual—flowers, candy, offers of dates and fine dining." He shot them a sheepish grin, pausing to gather his thoughts. It was amazing how easy it was to talk with Sam and Lexa. "I would have given her the world. Still would if I thought it would help get her memory back. Funny thing how money can't buy something that precious."

"How did you finally convince Natalie to go out with you?" A smile played about the corners of Lexa's mouth.

Marc laughed. "She found me out."

"How do you mean?" Lexa shifted on the sofa and tucked her bare feet beneath her.

"I volunteer at a home for troubled teens once a month. I'd all but given up hope trying to get Natalie to go out with me. Then I ran into her by accident at the home one Saturday morning."

The faint lines around Sam's eyes crinkled. "I love those so-called accidents by God's design. Lexa and I can attest those can be the best kind. So, what do you do at the home?"

"Help with reading programs, sports activities, basically whatever they need. That particular day, another volunteer told me Natalie watched as I worked with one of the teenage guys, teaching him to read. Great kid, but he has dyslexia and it was keeping him from playing on the basketball team. My sister has dyslexia and had the benefit of one of those expensive reading programs, so I was able to give him a few helpful hints."

"So, did you ask Natalie out that same day?" Lexa smiled when she caught Sam shaking his head. "Women need details. I've never heard this part of their story."

"We went out for lunch, yes, but Natalie didn't like the fact that I was in advertising." Marc rubbed his forehead. "Like a lot of people, unfortunately, she was skeptical that someone in my profession could be sincere. It was pretty hard to accept, to be honest." He blew out another sigh. "We obviously worked it out, but it wasn't easy."

"We all have baggage," Sam said. "I'm sure Natalie saw exactly what I see in you."

"Which is?" Marc looked up sharply.

"A man who gives his all to whatever he's doing. A man who wants to serve God. A man who simply wants to love his wife. Wholly and completely."

Unwelcome tears threatened, stinging the back of Marc's eyes. They'd think he was a complete sap if he kept tearing up all the time. Accepting the tissue Lexa handed him, he took a deep breath. Might as well get it all out now. "There's more." His words were so quiet both Lexa and Sam strained forward on the sofa. "Natalie's pregnant. It happened right after we returned home from our honeymoon."

Lexa's sharp intake of breath was audible as she brought a quick hand to her mouth. "Oh, my."

Marc nodded. "My sentiments exactly."

"Of course, that's great, but given the amnesia . . .." Lexa's voice trailed.

"Well," Sam said, "that throws an entirely different light on everything, doesn't it?" That intense gaze fixed on him. "I take it the pregnancy wasn't planned?"

"Sam!" Lexa shot him a surprisingly strong glare.

"It's okay. We certainly didn't plan on starting a family so soon. It's no secret Natalie loves children. I love them, too, but we're newlyweds, and didn't always think about taking precautions." Pressing his lips together, Marc gave them a knowing look. Sam and Lexa watched, silent, waiting, as though they sensed there was more to tell. He could trust them, and they wanted to help, so they needed to know. Everything. "We're not even living under the same roof right now. About two weeks after the accident, Natalie moved back into the house she shared with her former college roommates. Funny thing," he said, "she remembered certain things about them, but not her own husband. It became difficult for her, being nothing more than platonic roommates. It's not what I wanted, but I had to let her go and do what was best for her."

Lexa spoke first. "If Natalie can't remember marrying you, I'm sure she's struggling with the idea of being a wife. Her faith has always been so strong." Her brow furrowed, and she bit her lower lip.

Marc sighed. "The truth? I'm a fighter. I've rarely failed at anything I've set out to do, and the thought of losing Natalie forever scares me to death."

Sam's caring, intelligent eyes seemed to bore straight through to his soul. Elbows on his knees, he leaned close. "As long as this is about reconnecting with Natalie and not a statement to the world about how Marc Thompson never fails."

"I've thought long and hard about that. I've always been competitive, but I assure you, I don't want to go through life without Natalie. Not only is she the best thing to ever happen to me, but I know the Lord brought us together against the odds. I intend to honor my marriage vows until the day I die." Aw, man. The tears. Inhaling a deep breath, he plowed on even though his voice cracked. "I need help, and that's why I'm here." It was one of the hardest, yet most honest, admissions he'd ever made. Being an equally strong man, Sam must surely understand his inner conflict. He refused to give up his wife without a major effort to restore the relationship.

After Lexa pushed another tissue into his hand, Marc wiped his eyes but managed a grateful smile. "Natalie's my best friend. There's so much to love."

"Tell us." Lexa's voice was gentle.

It might bring on the tears, but it helped to talk with Mr. Davis the night of Natalie's fall, so it might help him now. "I love how she splashes in the rain like a carefree kid and doesn't care that she's getting drenched. She gets all sentimental and mushy when she hears the National Anthem at a ballgame. Natalie finds the violin hauntingly beautiful, and says it speaks to her soul, but what's really beautiful is the kindness she shows strangers, the way she listens with equal patience to a five-year-old or an eighty-year-old. I saw her give the coat off her back to a woman with three kids downtown one day. The kids all had coats, but the mother was shivering so much her lips were turning blue." He wiped his eyes again. "Natalie has a real heart for the underdog, and gives so much more than her time and money. When she sees a need, she fills it. That's

78

my wife." Although he felt like a romantic sap, it was all true. Sam and Lexa deserved the bare-bones truth.

"So, then, time is of the essence, now more than ever." Sam slapped his hand on his knee, determination written in every nuance of his face. "Natalie must recover her memory, the sooner the better, and we all need to work together to help her—whatever it takes. Prayer is the first key." He tossed him one of those don't-even-tell-me-you're-not-praying looks, rising to his feet and starting to pace. With the set of his jaw, the firmness of his lips, the tilt of his head, Sam looked not unlike a general commandeering his troops.

Sitting up straighter, Marc lifted his chin. "As often as I can." He felt like a kid in Sunday school, participating in a Bible drill. But, oddly enough, he didn't mind. This was about Natalie. Nothing else mattered.

"You've discussed her condition with her doctors? Exhausted everything you can find to jog her memory?" Sam continued to pace.

"I've tried everything I can think of to fill in the blanks for Natalie, but in a lot of ways, it's like someone else lived that part of her life." Marc touched his chest. "She needs to know it in her mind as well as feel it in her heart, but other than the Lord—and the blessing of time—I don't quite know how that's going to happen."

"I have an idea." Sam's hands found his hips, and his forehead furrowed. The loud ticking of the grandfather clock's pendulum was the only sound in the room for at least a minute. With raised brows, Sam glanced over at Lexa. She nodded slowly, her eyes never leaving his.

"We have another work camp coming up, a short one," Sam said, sitting back down beside Lexa. "Normally, the work camps last a couple of months, but this one's only a couple of weeks. It's not an official TeamWork-sanctioned mission, but one designed to help a friend to the organization. If you can get away, perhaps you can convince Natalie to come, and being together with the TeamWork volunteers again might somehow jumpstart her memories."

"I think the goal is to recover any part of her memory." Lexa's drawl wrapped him in its warmth. "It might translate into remembering people or events from past missions, and Natalie might uncover other things hidden deep in her subconscious."

A completely male, protective instinct arose. "What would Natalie be expected to do? I wouldn't want her to be subjected to heavy lifting or working, given her pregnancy. I have to protect her at all costs."

Sam smiled, his expression sympathetic. "We'd keep that thought uppermost in our minds. Marc, we can't pretend to know what either you or Natalie are going through, or know exactly how to help. Getting away might be a definite advantage. Of course, you'll need to get the okay from her doctors to take her outside the realm of her normal environment."

"I'll check with her doctors and psychologist, but I can't imagine they'd have any objections."

Sam nodded. "If this is something you want to do, then we're there for you."

"Mission Natalie?"

"More like Mission *Marc* and Natalie." The corners of Sam's mouth upturned.

"I don't know." Could he in good conscience leave his agency for a couple of weeks? That would take some maneuvering. "I'll have to think about it. Where is this camp? I understand you're often assigned to a camp in San Antonio." He was afraid his hesitancy betrayed the fact he wasn't exactly thrilled at the prospect. Nothing against the city itself, the Alamo, the Spurs, or anything else. Then again, he needed to be willing to go wherever the Lord led. That's why he was sitting in Sam and Lexa's living room, after all. Geography wasn't the real issue. Whether or not the inner control freak inside would allow him to leave his agency for that long was the problem.

"Why don't we have some dessert," Sam said. "You can think about it overnight, and we'll talk more in the morning. For now, you stay put, and we'll get the coffee started." He gestured to the bookcase. "Take a look around. You might find something interesting." The gentle giant ushered his tiny wife through the swinging door into the kitchen. Although she kept her voice low and controlled, as did Sam, Lexa had definite questions for her husband as Marc overheard her peppering Sam with questions. He must have surprised her with his suggestion.

Stir crazy, Marc glanced at the wide variety of books on the shelves lining one wall of the spacious room and moved across the room for a closer inspection. He loved books, but hadn't taken time to read much except for the occasional sports autobiography every few months.

Bible commentaries, Christian novels and non-fiction as well as sports books dominated the Lewis collection. He broke into a wide grin as he spied a Red Sox picture book and an autobiography written by Larry Bird. So, the man from Houston really was a Boston sports fan? Wasn't that a kick. He assumed Sam only said those things to be congenial and break the ice during their phone conversation. Most sports fans from this area of the country—especially native Texans—were loyal to more regional franchises. Based on the University of Texas memorabilia scattered about the room, he figured the Longhorns also held a special place in Sam's heart. Very fitting.

He stopped cold, staring at the spine of a book. *The Life and Times of Jumpin' Phil.* Couldn't be. Marc pulled the hardcover autobiography down from its place. Daring to look at the cover, his breathing slowed. His father's features, from the dark blond hair, blue eyes, and determined expression so much like his own, stared back at him. Why had he never seen this book? Never even known about it? He knew why—summed up in one name—*Mom.*

For a few seconds, Marc flipped through the book, noting a few early photos of their family, before his parents' acrimonious divorce. Going back to the front, he noted the publication date. Five years after the divorce when his dad retired from the NBA. Did Sam know Jumpin' Phil Thompson was his father? If he didn't, it wasn't the time to tell him. This trip to Houston was about Natalie, nothing more. Snapping the book closed, he shoved it back in its place. It would be harder to shove the memory of this book back where it belonged. Just a little light bedtime reading. Yeah, right.

Sam and Lexa continued their banter as he heard cupboards opening and closing. Something in the oven smelled pretty great, too. He cleared his throat loud enough for them to hear before rapping on the swinging door. "Is it safe to come in?"

"Come on in and have a seat." He heard the smile in Sam's deep voice.

"I thought I'd join the party." As he seated himself at a counter stool, Sam sat across from him as Lexa poured coffee into oversized ceramic mugs and placed sugar, artificial sweetener and a pitcher of cream on the counter. When she opened the oven and pulled out a huge, simmering pie, Marc grinned. "So, that's what smells so great. Let me guess. Grandma Lewis' special recipe?" He caught Lexa's look of pleased surprise from the corner of his eye.

Sam grinned. "Sure is. Best homemade pie in the state of Texas, bar none."

He hadn't thought he could eat another thing, but he could make room for Lexa's pie. Might need to work out a little harder once he returned to his club in Boston, but the indulgence would be totally worth it. Wow. He was starting to sound like a woman on a diet.

Sam watched as he sampled the pie and pronounced it delicious. Heaven help him if it wasn't, but thankfully, it was. "You should think about going into the pie-making business, Lexa." He took another bite, amused by the look on Sam's face. It was gratifying to see how they took such satisfaction in the accomplishments of their mate. As they sipped their coffee and ate the pie, they chatted about random things and laughed easily together.

Bidding them good night an hour later, Marc puzzled over the location of the upcoming work camp. They hadn't mentioned it again, but Sam said they'd talk more about it in the morning. Maybe after Sam and Lexa ironed out more details between the two of them. They obviously loved Natalie, and such an unselfish love was humbling.

After checking his messages from Trevor and Christy and answering a few client e-mails, he climbed into the big, four-poster antique bed made by Sam's dad. It was a beautiful piece of sturdy craftsmanship. Marc told his host about the rocker his grandfather made that sat in their Boston home. Should he take up a hobby? It might give him something to keep his hands and mind occupied so he didn't dwell on things, and help him focus elsewhere. He shook his head. It was a good idea, but he'd never find the time.

"So, where exactly is this work camp?" he whispered in the quiet darkness of the bedroom. He crossed his arms behind his head and closed his eyes. *Lord, maybe being with her TeamWork friends is exactly what Natalie needs. Help me know if it's the right thing to do.*

Chapter 14

*M*ARC MADE THE trip from Boston's Logan Airport to the suburbs countless times, enough so he didn't need to concentrate other than to watch out for the other guy and unexpected detours. Pulling into the driveway, he cut the engine and sat lost in thought, hands still on the steering wheel, his eyes unseeing. Coming home to an empty house filled him with sadness, and an emptiness. The physical ache for Natalie stirred inside him again. Closing his eyes, he bowed his head while lifting a silent prayer for guidance . . . and patience. *Lots of patience, Lord.* A soft knock on the car window caused him to jump, and he whacked his forehead on the steering wheel. "Ouch."

"I'm sorry, Marc. I didn't mean to startle you." The concern in Natalie's voice filled his heart as he slowly opened the car door. She placed a gentle hand on his forehead once he climbed out of the car and stood facing her.

He resisted the urge to lean over and kiss her. Instead, he shrugged, massaging his brow, giving her a wry grin. The hint of mischief in her eye sent his pulse soaring. "You can knock me senseless if it makes you smile at me like that." He hadn't glimpsed this playful side of her since her tumble down the steps. She looked incredible in a pink sweater and jeans, her hair pulled up in a pretty twist on top of her head. Pre-amnesia, he'd have kissed her senseless right there on the driveway, released her hair and carried her inside and up the stairs. *Focus.* "To what do I owe the honor of your presence, my love? Sorry," he said, holding up one hand. "Force of habit."

"I don't mind a bit. Come on, let's go inside. I made us a good dinner."

"You did?" he stammered. "Why?" The question slipped out. "I mean, this is a terrific surprise. I appreciate it." *Appreciate?* He appreciated the kid who delivered the newspaper every morning and the guy who delivered his sandwiches to the office when he didn't have a client lunch. Sure, they expected a generous tip, but from his wife, it was so much more than mere appreciation. His pulse thrummed and surged throughout his body. He loved that Natalie said *us*, meaning she intended to stay. At least through dinner. He couldn't expect miracles, but this was encouraging.

She laughed. "Why make dinner for you? Because you just got back from a trip and deserve a good dinner. I called your office and Christy told me you were getting back today from a trip. There's only so many nights you can eat takeout or frozen."

Grabbing his overnight bag and computer case, Marc reached for her hand. Did he dare believe she'd missed him? He'd only been gone overnight. He wondered if his ever-efficient assistant also told Natalie he'd been in Houston. "If I'd known you'd be here, I wouldn't have come home empty-handed. I'd have brought you flowers, at the very least." From the corner of his eye, he glimpsed her Audi a little further down the street. In his preoccupied state, he hadn't noticed it. As they walked through the front door, hands intertwined, he dared to slip his other hand around her waist.

"I don't need flowers or anything else. Spending time together is all we need," she said.

The warmth in her smile, the genuine affection in her voice, melted his heart in so many ways. The aroma of a homecooked meal wafted throughout the house. "Smells great. What can I do to help?" Marc followed her through the front foyer and into the kitchen.

"Relax, go change or whatever you need to do, and I'll let you know when dinner's ready. It shouldn't be much longer than twenty minutes or so."

Removing his suit jacket, Marc draped it across a chair, determined not to leave her, thankful she was here with him in their house. He watched her move about the kitchen, busy with the dinner preparations, half-listening as she told him about her classroom and new students. It seemed so *normal*. For even a few minutes, he glimpsed what they'd shared before and what he hoped they'd become again: a married couple. Lovers. *Parents*. She asked him to help carry the dishes to the dining room table, and smiled when he insisted on lighting candles. When he bowed to ask the blessing, he was pleased when her hand reached for his again and held on tight.

They enjoyed casual dinner conversation as they ate the delicious roast chicken. Natalie told him amusing stories from the classroom and he told her about some ideas he'd been tossing around for the agency. It was the most comfortable, easy meal they'd shared in months. Marc didn't have the heart to tell her he hated scalloped potatoes and asparagus made him gag. She'd never made them for him before, but tonight they tasted delicious as he swallowed one slow bite after another. Lots of water helped force it down, drowning the bitter aftertaste of the asparagus. The best part of the meal was the blueberry cobbler. As he spooned the last bite into his mouth, he released a contented sigh. "This is my favorite dessert. How did you know?"

"I pulled out the cookbook that looked the most well-worn. The page for the cobbler had notes scribbled all over it and a few dried stains that looked suspiciously like blueberries."

"Well, it's delicious, as always. Thanks. Here, let me help you with the dishes," he said as he cleared their plates from the table. With a grateful smile, she handed him a dishtowel.

With the last pan dried a few minutes later, Natalie folded the dishtowel and laid it on the kitchen counter. With a small smile playing about her lips, she leaned close, her breath tickling his ear as she whispered, "I'm going upstairs. Why don't you join me in ten minutes." It wasn't a question. It sounded . . . enticing. Her lips gently nuzzled his cheek.

Blood coursed through his veins and Marc wiped a bead of sweat from his brow. What in the world happened in the twenty-four hours since he'd been in

Houston? His throat dry, he watched as she slowly ascended the servant's staircase. She looked as slender as the day he first met her, with no visible, outward sign yet of the new life growing inside her. Pausing on the stairs, she turned and gave him another warm, playful smile. A hope for their shared future glimmered in his mind. For the first time since she'd moved out, Natalie was taking a step back in his direction. From all indications, a very *big* step. Maybe Sam and Lexa's prayers had a direct pipeline to God's ear.

Marc paced like an anxious groom eager to join his bride before darting into the bathroom off the kitchen. Grabbing the spare toothbrush and mouthwash he kept beneath the sink, his eyes strayed to the small clock mounted on the wall. The next ten minutes would seem an eternity. Finished gargling a couple of minutes later, he leaned against the sink and closed his eyes.

Lord, I don't know what's going on in the mind of my beautiful wife right now, but . . . thank you.

Returning to the living room, he resumed his pacing and checked his watch. The very second the ten minutes passed, he climbed the stairs, forcing slow steps when all he wanted to do was run like an overeager kid. Natalie waited for him in the doorway of the master bedroom, wearing a light blue silk robe, loosely tied at the waist. Her hair curled at her shoulders, and she twisted her hands together in front of her before dropping them to her sides.

Climbing to the top landing, his eyes never leaving hers, Marc crossed the hallway. He caught a whiff of the tantalizing perfume that drove him wild. Talk about an aphrodisiac. The scientist who invented that scent deserved millions. The first time Natalie wore it—on their honeymoon—they didn't leave their Italian villa for two incredible days. The dim light reflected the luminosity of her eyes as they focused on him. She looked alluring, but vulnerable.

Natalie had planned this evening—the dinner, the playfulness, the provocative invitation to come upstairs. Surely she wouldn't tease, wouldn't tempt him and not intend to follow through with her seduction. Did she remember anything about their honeymoon—the tenderness, the intimacy, the unbridled passion? His pulse soared to a new height.

Taking him by the hand, she led him into the bedroom. Candles glowed inside, and he heard the mellow, smooth sounds of a jazz quartet. She'd certainly set the mood—not that it would take much. He almost couldn't breathe as she untied the robe and lowered it. As it puddled on the floor at her feet, Marc kept his eyes trained on her face. He could tell she wore a sheer negligee she'd taken on their honeymoon, but if his eyes lingered south of her lovely, long neck, there'd be no turning away. This was the dream he'd had for weeks—months, really—and he hardly dared believe it was reality. If it was a dream, he hoped never to awaken. "Is this what you want, Natalie?"

She nodded and lowered her eyes, and it brought to mind her shyness the first night of their honeymoon. *This is like her wedding night again.* The thought staggered him, and was incredibly sentimental and frustrating all at once. Given permission, his eyes traveled the length of her in a slow, leisurely path. She was incredible. Beautiful. *His.*

Make her remember.

His hands encircled Natalie's waist as he drew her to him. She made no protest and willingly leaned into him, curving her body into his. Oh yes, this woman was made for him. Marc's hands rested on the delicious curve of her hips as he lowered his head. Their lips met, tentative at first and then with increasing desire. He needed to take it slow, but it was difficult to hold back as he cupped her face between his hands and poured all the emotion, all his need and longing, into kissing his wife. "Natalie, you feel so good. I've missed you so much," he whispered, kissing her neck in the way she loved before moving back to her mouth. "I love you." His voice was thick, husky with desire. His pulse throbbed everywhere.

She smiled and, sifting gentle fingers through his hair, drew him closer. Her body language spoke volumes. She wanted this, wanted *him.* Natalie's warm lips were as supple and welcoming as always. Although she kissed him back with true passion, there was still a nagging tug in the back of Marc's mind. *Something's not right.* For one thing, she didn't tell him she loved *him.* Call him a latent romantic, but sometimes a guy needed to hear it, especially from his wife.

Pushing aside the thoughts, he concentrated on showing Natalie how much he loved her, how desperately he wanted and needed her in every possible way. He kissed her deeply and caressed her face, his fingers tracing a slow path down to the small of her neck. A moan of desire escaped from his throat as he whispered her name, glorying in their intimacy and the promise of the night.

Natalie's hands shook as they traveled an upward path toward his shoulders before dropping to his shirt, unbuttoning one slow button at a time before parting it with gentle fingers. Oh, how he'd waited for this moment. Enjoying the closeness, the touching, Marc tried to ignore the faint line tightening her brows as he unfastened the cuff links and pulled the shirt away from his shoulders. His gut clenched hard as her lips quivered. Those rosebud lips weren't trembling from desire.

Something's not right here. She's only doing this for you. It's a gesture borne from her desire to be a good wife and perform her wifely duties. Nothing more.

He stifled a groan, and his heart sank quicker than a felled tree crashing to the ground. Placing his hands over hers, Marc stilled them against his chest. Natalie's eyes questioned, but she said nothing. Swallowing the huge lump in his throat, he lowered his head. Drawing her hands away, he blew out a sigh from the deepest recesses of his heart. It took everything within him to do it.

Lord, you know I can't do it. I hope you appreciate this sacrifice. I want her more than anything, and I'm her husband, but you know I can't take advantage of this situation.

"Not like this, Natalie. Not like this." His anguished words were barely more than a whisper. He averted his gaze or he'd stare longingly at her loveliness beneath the negligee. His fingers shook as he buttoned the middle of his shirt and slumped down onto the bed. Releasing another soft, low moan, Marc lowered his head to his hands, his elbows resting on his thighs. "You don't remember making love with me, do you?" Even though he hated it, the question begged to be asked. He knew the answer in his heart. Of course, she didn't.

She doesn't even remember being married to you.

Those shaking fingers, those big eyes, those trembling lips, said it all.

"Marc, I'm failing you as a wife." Sitting beside him, Natalie shed silent tears. "I want to make you happy. You have expectations as my husband, and I'm willing . . ."

Putting a finger over her lips, he kissed her damp cheek and took hold of her hand, squeezing it. "I know you are, sweetheart, and that means the world. You're not failing me. But until it's something that's fully in your heart, I can wait. I don't want it to be an experiment, a test. I want you to make love to *me*, your husband and soul mate, not just some great looking man who begs you to love him."

She didn't crack a grin at his lame attempt at humor. Oh, the sweet irony.

"God's teaching me patience, I can tell you that much." Tipping her chin, he waited until she looked him directly in the eye, "I'm not going anywhere." Brushing her lips with his, he curled a strand of dark hair around one finger.

"I'm not sure I deserve you, Marc. I *do* love you. You must know that. I just need more time."

It helped to hear her say she loved him. "I know. But I want you to know it up here," he said, lightly touching her forehead, "as much as you feel it in here." He placed a careful, gentle hand on the soft flesh above her heart. "It needs to be something we're both ready for together, not something you feel you have to do in order to keep me happy."

The relief he saw in her eyes nearly broke his heart. But it was more than her eyes—it was in her shoulders, her body posture, everything. He'd never felt such deep-seated hurt in his life, but it wasn't her fault. He needed someone to blame, but again, the finger of blame pointed to him alone for not fixing that blasted, rotting stair.

"How could I ever forget you?"

Marc shook his head. "I don't have an answer for that one. What I *can* tell you is that I'm going to do everything in my power to help you regain your memories. If not the old memories, then we'll make new ones together." He faced her on the bed and, taking her hand, softly kissed her palm. "No matter what happens, you'll grow to love me even more than you did the first time." He kissed her cheek again, pleased when she leaned into it. "That's a promise. And I always keep my promises."

"Dr. Fontaine's wrong, you know." Natalie's head dropped to his shoulder. That perfume was driving him crazy, and her hair smelled like sunshine mixed with flowers. He couldn't have her, and it was killing him.

He snapped out of his reverie. "In what way?"

"You're not selfish. If you were, we'd be making love right now."

Shaking his head, Marc chuckled under his breath. "Please don't remind me. I'm not only selfless, I'm incredibly stupid to boot." He retrieved her robe from the floor. "I also need to cover you up before I can think clearly much less speak coherently."

She smiled a little as he pulled the robe around her and draped it across her shoulders. He had to focus on what he had to tell her without being faced straight-on by the fact she was clothed so revealingly and was so absolutely tempting. The Lord had to give him a lot of credit for self-restraint.

"I have a plan. Something that might help," he said. Those eyes were bright and trusting as Natalie wiped away a tear and met his gaze. He never wanted to let this woman down, never wanted to betray her trust, that blind faith. "My trip to Houston yesterday wasn't for the agency. I went to see friends of yours."

She shook her head. "Friends of mine? In Houston, Texas?" Her blank look told him all he needed to know.

"Sam and Lexa Lewis. Sam's a director for TeamWork Missions. His wife, Lexa, helps him with summer work camps, and you've helped out with at least two of their summer work programs in San Antonio in the last few years, and you've worked some other New England missions, too. Three of the girls from TeamWork were in our wedding as your bridesmaids. Remember, I showed you the photos and told you about them—Winnie, Amy and Rebekah. You pointed to Winnie and said her name."

Natalie's eyes widened and she nodded, but didn't speak.

"Sam and Lexa have another work camp starting in two weeks, and they've invited us to come along. I think we should go, sweetheart. Maybe it'll help you recover some memories by being around people who love you, and being involved with a ministry you're so passionate about."

Her eyes softened when he called her sweetheart, another small victory. "Where is this camp?"

"Well, it's not San Antonio. Apparently, TeamWork sets up a camp wherever there's a need, although it's primarily a foreign missions organization. On the downside, the planned work camp is much colder than San Antonio. On the plus side, it's not as dirty and dusty as Texas."

"Where, exactly?"

He met her eyes. "Montana. Big Sky Country."

"At this time of the year?" She frowned and rubbed her brow.

"I know. But, hey, we live in Boston, so how bad can it be? It's only for a couple of weeks."

"It'll be November. We'll freeze to death."

"But think of all the romantic opportunities to cuddle up together. Warm fires, hot chocolate, snowball fights . . ." He raised a suggestive brow.

"Were you always this much of a flirt?"

Putting his arm around her, Marc kissed her cheek, his lips lingering. "No, I was even *more* of a flirt. But only with you."

"Let's talk more about it tomorrow. I'm not even sure if I can take time off work yet."

"Don't worry about that. I'll call Principal Leighton. They're all committed to helping you recover your memories. I can be pretty persuasive, you know." He nudged Natalie's shoulder, feeling like a teenager.

"There's one thing I know." Her voice sounded small, uncertain.

"What's that?" When her robe slipped off her shoulder, he stole a quick kiss on her collarbone before repositioning it. They'd made great strides tonight.

"You must really love me to go to Montana. The fact that you're willing to leave the agency for a couple of weeks says a lot in itself." A hint of a smile curved those luscious lips. "And something tells me you're not exactly fond of the idea of roughing it out on the range."

Marc threw his head back with his laughter. "See? The plan's already working, and you're starting to get your memory back."

Chapter 15

$\mathscr{I}$T WAS TWO full weeks before they departed for their Montana adventure. Time to lay the groundwork and build a strong foundation for winning back his wife's heart. Sam sent Marc e-mails, answering his questions and explaining their upcoming mission helping a former TeamWork director who owned a ranch outside Helena.

The ranch owner and a number of his regular ranch hands were called elsewhere for a couple of weeks, resulting in a need for extra hands to help with the cooking, teaching the children of the remaining ranch hands, and the general care and feeding of the horses and cattle until their return. That's where TeamWork came in. Natalie could help the children with their schoolwork, and he'd help Sam and the other men with chores around the ranch.

His telephone conversations with Natalie were becoming more regular, and were often in the same teasing vein as before her accident even though there was plenty of routine talk about the weather, state of the economy, and the otherwise mundane everyday stuff. Deciding he wanted to try sharing joint custody—his own ridiculous, misguided term—of Elwood, Marc drove over to the apartment house one evening to pick up the mutt. What he didn't expect was all the paraphernalia that came along with him. Who knew such a small creature needed more than a soft bed, a bag of dog food and a bone or two? Maybe it was God's way of preparing him to be a father since babies apparently needed more than a bottle and diapers. He had so much to learn. At least Elwood didn't seem to mind going home with him.

Natalie also gave him reports from her visits to the obstetrician and told him she'd registered them for childbirth classes. She e-mailed him a schedule so he could make sure the dates were on his calendar and clear his calendar. So far, everything looked good with the baby, and the pregnancy seemed to be progressing normally. That was a relief.

At her next doctor visit—only a few days before they were scheduled to leave for the work camp—she'd have her first sonogram where they could see their baby and hear the heartbeat.

"Will you come with me, Marc?"

"Of course, I'll be there. Wouldn't miss it."

For a lingering moment, he forgot her memory was gone. The idea of being a father was quickly growing on him. The last time he'd seen her, he couldn't miss the sparkle in her eye when she talked about the baby. She was starting to make plans, but that also unsettled him since they lived apart. At least she included him. Still, he needed to increase his efforts.

"Come to dinner with me tonight," he said. "I just signed a new superstar client. We need to celebrate." As if he needed a reason. "Name the place."

"Sure. How about Peppino's?"

"Sounds great. We haven't been there since . . ." He stopped cold. His heart throbbed as blood rushed to his head. "Natalie, do you remember Peppino's?"

"What do you mean?"

Excitement enthused his voice. "Peppino's is not your average, run-of-the-mill place. It's a hole-in-the-wall, family-owned pizza joint off Boylston Street. We discovered it by accident last year after a game at Fenway. It was raining, and we ducked inside to stay dry. It's one of the best-kept secrets in Boston. We go at least once a month, and it's one of our favorite places in the city. The owner and some of the staff even came to our wedding." Dr. Adams told him the sense of smell was potent and could sometimes trigger memories. Maybe the smells of garlic and other Italian spices would help.

"Wait a minute . . ."

"Do you remember something else?" This was a breakthrough moment. He could feel it in his bones.

"Did they put anchovies on our pizza by mistake once?" The rising excitement in Natalie's voice matched his.

"Yes!" Marc pushed away from his desk and sprang to his feet. He ran his hand through his hair and grinned like a kid. Not that it was a pleasant memory, by any means. "You had a bad allergic reaction. I rushed you over to the ER at Mass General. Maybe you remember because the reaction was so bad."

"Let's definitely go tonight. Peppino's, not the ER." She hadn't sounded so happy since before her fall. "Maybe I'll remember something else."

"Definitely no more hospitals until the baby comes. I'll pick you up at seven. Wear something fabulous." Hopefully, she could sense his smile. Natalie usually dressed up to go to Peppino's, if it wasn't after a Sox game, and he'd wear his suit. It was just one of the fun, silly things they liked to do. The thought sent his pulse into overdrive.

"I'll look forward to it. See you tonight, Marc."

How he loved the sound of that infectious giggle, sexy and throaty. It was great to hear. His heart pounded like it was their first date all over again, and in a lot of ways, it was. What a weird thought. He couldn't concentrate the rest of the afternoon. Before leaving the office, Marc took time to shave in his private bath. Feeling optimistic, he splashed on the cologne Natalie gave him for his birthday. His smile lasted all the way from the Prudential Center to Newton. As he pulled the car to the curb in front of the old, two-story restored home, Natalie stepped outside the front door, talking with one of her roommates. She turned and gave him a lovely smile. He waved, feeling silly all over again at the odd situation they found themselves in.

She wore a blue dress he'd never seen before that clung to her in all the right places, at least from what he could see beneath her lightweight coat. He whistled under his breath. How he loved every inch of this woman. While his wife dressed modestly and didn't flaunt her curves, she couldn't hide them if she tried. She was the essence of femininity, and he'd caught the frequent stares from other men.

Natalie was the prize he'd earned, but the gift from God he wasn't sure he deserved.

Focusing on her as she still talked with Kim, relief flooded through him that she didn't look as gaunt. The woman was grace personified, fluidity in motion. She'd been a dancer and, like a lot of little girls, dreamed of joining a ballet company one day. But that was before adolescence hit. The years of dance training were evidenced in the way she held her shoulders, the tilt of the head, the proper posture. Finished with her conversation a minute later, Natalie walked down the stairs, headed toward the car. It took him a few seconds before Marc realized he was staring like a teenager in heat. *Get a grip.* Climbing out of the car, he moved around to open the passenger door. Offering his hand, he assisted her as she settled herself in the seat. "You look gorgeous."

She glanced up at him with that shyness so reminiscent of their first date. "Thanks. Only the best for Peppino's." Marc's heart skipped a beat. Did she somehow remember how they always dressed their best for the obscure pizza joint? Her eyes narrowed, drinking in the sight of him with barely-disguised admiration. That was enough to get his pulse racing again, but in a very good way. "You're looking very handsome yourself, stranger."

Stranger. No matter how innocent the word, it stabbed his heart. Still, the look in her eyes made him glad he'd chosen the light blue striped shirt—one of her personal favorites—when he'd grabbed it that morning with no idea where this day might lead.

"I like your cologne, too."

"You should since you gave it to me for my birthday." Closing her door, he refrained from saying what was in his mind, something she'd probably find incredibly forward. But the look in her eyes was promising. *All I ask is a good night kiss, Lord. That's all. Really.*

Sliding behind the wheel, he planted both hands on it. They were dating again. Although surreal, it was . . . almost like role playing. But amnesia was no game. As he drove them downtown, Marc kept up a steady stream of conversation by relaying amusing stories from his childhood and a few things from the last few years when they were dating . . . the first time around. Natalie asked questions, but none seemed to jumpstart any memories. Still, they had fun and laughed easily together. As they talked, he stole glances at his wife—the curve of her ankle, the gorgeous long legs, hands folded demurely in her lap. He was thankful she wasn't twisting her fingers, doing that nervous little dance thing. While rather endearing, it also drove him nuts.

Her mother and sister visited the week before, and Natalie told him they'd filled in some blanks for her about her childhood. While he missed seeing them, he understood their primary focus was helping her regain her memories. Lisabeth called him several times during their visit. "Keep the faith," she said, telling him how the family continually prayed for them. It was a comfort, especially since her father made his initial misgivings about his daughter dating an ex-baseball player painfully clear. *A second-string player*, he'd called him. No matter that his agency was thriving, it was his perceived failure on the baseball field that most men remembered.

He suspected her dad meant more in terms of life rather than athletics. He'd finally come around to accept him, and they got on reasonably well, but it was impossible to forget. It didn't help that Natalie's dad was a summa cum laude graduate of the no-man-is-good-enough-for-my-little-girl school of fatherhood.

Maybe Gregory Combs compared him to his famous father. A lot of men did. The comparisons were inevitable, and he lost to his dad every time.

What son could ever compare to a two-time NBA champion? It was better to leave others with their ideals intact. It was bad enough his own opinion of his dad had been shattered when he'd left the family and divorced his mom when he was nine. A thing like that caused the only boy in a family to grow up real fast. It would have been easier had the man come around every now and then. Periodically, he looked up his dad's photo in a sports anthology to remember what he looked like since his mother banished all mementos of him in the house. He'd learned the hard way that bitterness could be all-consuming, often as damaging to the innocents on the sidelines.

"You've got that look on your face. I've seen it a few times lately," Natalie said, breaking him out his thoughts a short time later as they sat in Peppino's. She put down her fork. "You look sad. If you feel like talking about it, I'm all ears."

Marc sighed. He didn't wish to relive painful memories. Certainly not tonight. He'd never shared the most personal part of it with her because it wrenched him to his core. On their honeymoon, he'd almost opened up, but then stopped himself. Now, his wife had too many other things on her mind. *Oh, Lord, what an ironic thought.* There seemed to be a lot of those lately.

But she'd made the observation and deserved his answer. He told her how his dad always provided for them, financing his education at Yale not covered by his athletic scholarship, and his sister's undergrad years at NYU and master's at Columbia. Yet, given a choice, he would have preferred his father's presence over the amenities his money could buy, the Ivy League education and the trust fund. He'd never remarried, and never had more children, as far as he knew. When Phil Thompson died ten years ago from an inoperable brain tumor, it was tragic to hear the once towering, strong athlete had been reduced to skin and bones, the life sucked out of him in mere months. As the end drew near, his dad retreated further, refusing treatment, not wanting to see anyone. Not even his children.

It was his final, deepest rejection.

When he finished his story, Natalie reached across the table, covering his hand with hers. "I'm so sorry." Withdrawing her hand, she averted her gaze. Something was on her mind. If he waited long enough, she'd tell him.

Taking another bite, noticing her habit of cutting even pizza with a knife and fork, he raised a brow. "Tell me what you're thinking."

She dabbed at her mouth with her napkin and met his gaze. "From everything you've told me, you loved your dad, but it's like you felt this overpowering need to prove yourself worthy."

Marc sipped his ice water. The woman was uncanny in reading him. Amnesia hadn't altered that ability. "True enough." If he was honest, he'd admit he wanted to best the man because he'd broken his mother's heart. "But I failed miserably in trying to achieve what Dad accomplished in the world of professional sports." It was his greatest achievement-to-date in failure.

"You failed at nothing." A trace of anger laced her words. "From what I know, you were a very good player, but it wasn't in God's plan to send you to the majors. Look at what you've accomplished." The anger faded, replaced by unmistakable pride. "You took charge of your life. You purposely walked away from professional sports and used that analytical, logical brain God gave you to full advantage. As a result, the Lord's blessed you beyond what you could hope for. It's a tough business, but you're a rousing success. Not many men—including your dad—would have been able to do something like that."

Natalie's words reached him somewhere deep inside. "And, ironically enough, I'm now in the business of getting endorsements and exorbitant sums of money for superstar athletes. Go figure." His laugh was bitter. It didn't change the fact he loved what he did for a living. Still, she'd paid him a huge compliment. Marc squeezed her hand and smiled his thanks. His perceptive wife understood more than she'd actually said—he'd always been in competition with his famous dad.

"Even if he never said the words—and even though you started the agency after he died—I hope you know how proud your dad would have been."

How he appreciated her words. His eyes filled, and he lowered his gaze before clearing his throat. When she squeezed his hand again, he almost lost it. She rambled on about something inconsequential, giving him precious time to recover his sensibilities. In that moment, Marc loved her more than he thought possible. What an incredible woman. Natalie might not remember many surface things, but she had innate compassion and understood him.

He was careful not to overload her with too much information all at once since Dr. Fontaine warned it might be too much to handle. *Slow and easy.* He knew the wait staff and the owner of Peppino's wondered what was going on between them, but with their customary smiles, they took expert care of their dinner needs and stayed in the background. His tip conveyed his appreciation.

"How about a walk or a duck boat ride?" He reached for her hand, thrilled when she took it.

"A walk sounds great." After their serious, heartfelt dinner conversation, Marc kept it light. When Natalie shivered, he removed his suit jacket and draped it around her. She snuggled into it and thanked him with one of her trademark smiles. She always appreciated his chivalrous, gentlemanly gestures. As they strolled Boston Common hand-in-hand, she asked more about the dates they'd shared in the past, and he was more than happy to oblige.

It was a beautiful, star-filled night. Spying the new Red Sox relief pitcher across the way talking with a group of guys, he stopped himself from bounding over to introduce himself. It wasn't the time. If he was meant to sign the promising athlete, it would happen. *In God's time, not yours.* Pulling up in front of the house a couple of hours later, he leaned his head back against the seat. Neither he nor Natalie made a move. "I honestly don't know what to do now."

"Neither do I." Her sigh was audible. "I suppose we say good night."

"No." He shook his head.

"No?" She sounded confused and hopeful all at once.

The last time he said *No* like that, she moved out of the house the next morning. Better say something quick. "I'm walking you to the door. What kind of husba . . . date would I be if I didn't escort a beautiful lady to her door?"

"Not just yet." She put her hand on his arm. "Thanks for tonight, Marc. I had a great time." Her touch sent electric currents coursing through him.

"It was fun reliving those memories, telling you about them, laughing with you, being with you," he said, turning to face her. "I wouldn't want to be anywhere else, with anyone else, doing anything else tonight." The expression on her face made him want to take her home so bad he ached all over again.

"You're pretty hard to resist when you say things like that," she said.

And you're hard to resist when you look at me like that. He cleared his throat and straightened in the seat. "Then why resist?" Even though he joked, he meant it. Perhaps that was unfair, and he hated the tinge of irritation in his tone.

She eyed him, biting her lower lip, not saying anything for a moment—a lengthy, pregnant pause. "There's a part of me that wants to move back into the house with you and resume our relationship—in every way." The way she looked at him, there was no mistaking her meaning. "But, like you said, I have to know it as well as feel it." Natalie hesitated and lowered her voice. "You're right. This is about so much more than the physical aspects." She looked at him with wide eyes, and appeared surprised to see his smile. "Did I say something amusing?" She sounded slightly wounded.

"No, not at all." Although he rather regretted his whole noble *know it, feel it,* speech. Taking both her hands, Marc caressed her with his eyes. "I was only talking about a good night kiss, and nothing more, as hard as that might be to believe." Her cheeks bloomed with color and a grin tugged at the corners of that luscious mouth. How he wanted to taste those lips again.

"Well then, that's no problem." He wasn't laughing as Natalie took hold of his suit coat lapels and tugged him close to plant a thorough, lingering kiss on his waiting, receptive lips. Her kiss was as hungry as his own, her passion one of the many things he adored. She'd surprised him in amazing ways, and he missed their intimacy more than ever Memories flooded his mind, threatening to overwhelm him.

"That was . . . well, that was an unexpected fire starter." Marc reluctantly broke free from her embrace, massaging his neck and looking at her askance. That kiss was great, but it would be difficult to forget when he crawled into bed tonight—alone.

"Sorry," she said, but she didn't look or sound the least bit apologetic. "This is such new territory, isn't it? I don't mean to tease you. I hope you know that."

"We'll just have to keep fumbling our way, Natalie, but I think we're definitely on the right track. Let me walk you to the door." Placing her hand in his as he helped her from the car, she gave him a tentative smile he couldn't decipher. Affection? *Definitely.* But maybe a little bit of fear of the unknown. *She is pregnant, after all. With your child.* His eyes moved down to her stomach. "Are you having any morning sickness? I understand it can be pretty bad sometimes."

She nodded. "Just a little queasy some mornings. Overall, it hasn't been too bad. Crackers help. And lots of dry toast."

"Do you need me to stock anything for you? Soda crackers? Melba toast? Ice cream? Pickles?" *Me?*

She laughed. "I haven't had any peculiar cravings yet, but I'll let you know."

I want you to have cravings for your husband. "I want to know what you're feeling." He captured her gaze and they stared at one another for several long seconds. "I imagine it's hard for you in some respects, isn't it?"

Natalie's glance told him she was surprised by his sensitivity. "In some ways, yes. I know the Lord has a plan, and He'll help me—help us—through the amnesia and the pregnancy." She blew out a prolonged sigh. "It's hard to explain, but I know I have the love of the Lord in my heart." She gave him a look that tugged at his gut. "I can *feel* it. Some things, I guess you don't forget."

Marc nodded. "I think the things of the Lord are sometimes unexplainable. They just *are.* We just have to trust He always knows what He's doing and wants the best for us." He wanted to somehow lessen the tension so she'd kiss him again. His one-track mind had taken over. They stood together on the front porch, facing one another. It was awkward, yet sweet in an odd way. It brought to mind his first date. He'd stood on Alicia Plummer's front porch—just as he stood with Natalie now—shuffling his feet, an awkward fifteen-year-old shoving his hands deep in his pockets, wondering whether to try and kiss the girl good night. While thankful those days were long gone, and he'd gained a certain amount of finesse with women, he felt equally uncertain now—about his future with his own wife. "Your roommates must find our situation interesting."

"You could say that. For the record, they think I'm crazy."

"In what way?"

She tilted her head, her lips curving into a coy grin. "Like I said, you're a smart man. Surely you can guess without me having to spell it out."

"Spill it. You can't make a statement like that and not tell all." He had an idea what she meant, but—call him egotistical—he wanted to hear it from her. That kiss in the car was a prologue. If he didn't feel her lips on his again soon, he'd burst with frustration. He took a step closer.

She laughed again. He loved the sound, so genuine and totally lacking in pretense. "Let's just say your charms are obvious. Even though they like the extra rent money, my roommates can't understand why I'm living here and not with you at the house."

"Is that your polite way of telling me I'm hot?"

"It's at least their perception," she said, grinning. "They'd kill me for admitting as much to you."

"What do *you* think?" He took one step closer. "Your opinion is the only one I want."

"Well, if you don't know after that whopper of a kiss I just planted on you in the car . . ."

Marc bundled her in his arms. Leaning close, he glimpsed the need in her eyes. This kiss was slow and tender. She tasted familiar, sensual. Her silky hair brushed against his fingers as he anchored one hand behind her neck, drawing her closer. Her skin was warm, her lips soft. He smiled against her lips when she took the initiative to deepen the kiss. It would be hard to stop, but he lost himself in the pure enjoyment of holding her in his arms, the feel of her, locked in a passionate embrace. How he'd missed her. The rest of the world could simply fade away.

"Marc," Natalie breathed, finally pulling out of the kiss. Her breathing was staggered, and he detected the obvious longing in her voice.

He forced calming breaths. "Hang on. I'm still trying to catch my breath." He smiled as she put a gentle hand on his chest, near his heart. Surely she could feel how fast it was pumping. Desire coursed through him, making his head spin. It was on the tip of his tongue to ask her to come home with him, back to their bed. Even if only to sleep, he needed her beside him.

His hold on her tightened as he dared to move his hands further south on her hips. If he thought she wouldn't be offended, he'd move his hands to her belly, see if there was the slightest swelling beneath that fabulous blue dress. Curve his hand over any baby bump that might be forming. The thought thrilled him. It was *his* child, after all, so didn't he have every right? But, even though she was his wife, he couldn't touch her that intimately. Not yet. He shouldn't push her.

Natalie pulled away, interrupting wishful thoughts. She avoided his eye contact and looked away awkwardly. "Thanks for a lovely evening." With a final kiss on his cheek, she hurried inside the house and closed the door.

All he could do was stand on the doorstep and stare, praying he hadn't offended her. Maybe she didn't trust herself and needed to make an abrupt getaway for both their sakes? They'd made great headway, but it was time for another self-coaching moment. And a cold shower. Tonight he'd made significant progress in winning back her affections, if not her heart. It had been fun, spending time with her like it was their first date. But it was so much more. His wife's insights and depth of compassion had shown through, loud and clear. He smiled as he climbed back into the Lexus, replaying the evening in his mind. The shy glances, the whispered comments, the laughter, the great food—with nary an anchovy in sight. Not to mention those killer kisses couldn't lie. The strong physical attraction between them was more powerful than ever.

As he climbed under the sheets a couple of hours later, Marc grinned at the sight of Elwood on his back, legs in the air, watching from the floor. Laughing, he tapped the bed, and the mutt wasted no time jumping up beside him. Nudging aside his arm, the dog laid his head on his chest and gave him the head tilt maneuver accompanied by the *please rub my stomach* look. Elwood had mastered it. This dog was good for his sanity, his soul. If only his canine friend could talk, he'd spill some pretty juicy stuff. Elwood snuggled closer and half sprawled across his chest as he scratched behind the dog's ears. The warm, steady rhythm of another heart beating next to his felt great. "You're not exactly what I was hoping for, but you'll do, buddy." The Lord had given him exactly what he'd asked: a memorable good night kiss from his gorgeous wife.

If he hadn't already been in love with her, he would have been after the date they'd just shared. Marc buried his head in his pillow and released a low moan. After one great date, he couldn't expect Natalie to fall into his arms and allow him to carry her home and up the stairs to Wonderland. He was beginning to think it might be more like Neverland.

"I miss you, Natalie," he murmured, turning on one elbow, face-to-face with Elwood. "I hope you miss me, too." The dog shifted and stretched before sliding down to the pillow beside him. Natalie's pillow—just the way she'd left it. He hadn't been able to wash it because it smelled like Natalie. Still did, even after all these months. Elwood didn't seem to mind. Maybe in his doggie mind, it reminded him of his mistress, and gave him some kind of comfort, too.

Oh, man. He was going mental and needed some sleep. At least for now, he could rest, content in the small victories.

Chapter 16

$\mathscr{A}$ FEW DAYS later, Marc sat in Dr. Fontaine's office. He hesitated, gathering his thoughts. "I feel as though we're at an impasse of sorts. Kind of like a plateau. We've reached a certain point in reclaiming our relationship, but now we're stalled." Sure, they'd shared some great kisses on their date, but he wasn't sure when he'd see her again, much less kiss her. Maybe the reminder of what he'd been missing made him more impatient. If too much time passed, would he lose the ground he'd recently gained? He wouldn't trade their date at Peppino's, and for more reasons than the physical reconnection.

"You're not sure what to do next, how to get past the plateau."

"That's right." He loved how this guy had a propensity for stating the obvious.

"You should consider taking a break from Natalie, from the two of you." Marc opened his mouth to protest, and Dr. Fontaine raised his hand. "Hear me out. It's understandable you've given yourself a timeline because of the baby, but this is a situation where you can't force affection, can't force memories." He regained his eye contact. "You can't force Natalie to fall in love with you again, at least not overnight."

He eyed the doctor before lowering his head, staring blindly at the hardwood floors partially covered with a high-quality Persian rug. "So, what do I do?"

"You're scheduled to go to Montana together soon, correct?"

Marc nodded. What in the world did he mean by a break? How could that possibly help?

"What I suggest is not scheduling so much time with Natalie before you leave."

"Why? What purpose would that serve?" How could he do that? Why would he even want to? It had to be one of the psychologist's less-inspired suggestions.

"You need time to grieve."

"Grieve? No one's died." All the fancy degrees from institutions of higher learning didn't mean this man was right.

Dr. Fontaine sat back in his chair and steepled his fingers. "I'm talking about time to grieve for your marriage, Marc. For what you've lost."

Sadness overcame him. Turning his head, he didn't want the doctor to see his pain. "Since Natalie's fall, I've had a long time to grieve."

"I don't think you have. You've been in shock, going through the motions. Your head's still trying to wrap itself around what happened to her, and to you, in dealing with the daily ramifications of the amnesia and how it's impacted your relationship. What I'm talking about is stepping back and taking a good, hard look at where you've been, where you're at now, and where you want to see this relationship ultimately go." He sat up straighter. "And then figure out how to get there."

"Where I want it to go? Natalie's the best thing that ever happened to me. I'm not giving her—giving *us*—up without a major battle. We've made some good headway in reconnecting as a couple in the last few weeks, and I want to build on that foundation, not stall it—or tear it down completely.

"I'm not saying it's a battle. That's *your* perception. I'm merely suggesting this as a way to strengthen your relationship."

Marc shook his head. "Forgive me, but I'm not following. How can staying away from Natalie strengthen our relationship?"

"By consciously giving her space, perhaps it will have the opposite effect by reminding her how much she misses you. From everything you've told me, you're reconnecting on a daily basis and seeing her as much as possible. I'm not saying not to call her, e-mail or share any communication whatsoever. I'm merely suggesting that you don't take her to dinner, go to a movie or any other kind of special date until you leave for Montana. If you need to contact her, stick to the basics like planning your trip. Nothing more." Dr. Fontaine trained his eyes on him, holding them steady. "I realize how hard it'll be, but it's only for a short time. Don't worry about a timeline, Marc. Step back and be patient."

"Is this advice based on the old theory that absence makes the heart grow fonder?"

The doctor allowed a smile to crack through his austerity. "It's been known to work for centuries, but that's not why I suggest it. Simply put, you need time, just as Natalie does. I want you to give yourself the luxury of that time. You're going to be together for two solid weeks in Montana, and no one knows what that experience will bring. Perhaps a little break before you leave will prove beneficial."

Marc digested the thought. "Maybe you're right. Only the Lord knows what'll happen in Montana." Sensing his reference to the Lord might make the psychologist uncomfortable, he shrugged. "I'm not going to apologize for my faith."

"No one's asking you to apologize." The words were spoken with equal conviction. "I understand some things about Christianity. Even though I don't share your faith in a risen Savior, I can appreciate its meaning in your life. If anything, it makes you a stronger man, and a better husband to Natalie."

"I only pray that's true."

~

Not seeing Natalie proved difficult although Marc recognized Dr. Fontaine made a valid point. He hoped to spend a lot of time with her in Montana—in-between all the chores Sam threw his way. The hard labor might prove therapeutic and be a welcome physical release to relieve the stress of the last few months. As it was, the guys at his fitness club stared at him in wonder as he bench-pressed, cycled and pushed himself to the limit. They speculated he was training for a marathon. Let them think what they wanted: in a way, he *was* in the race of his life. No question about it: he'd win this one.

So many times, he picked up the phone or started an e-mail to his wife, only to pause and stop. If he communicated with her, he'd end up asking her to do something, desperate for her company. Instead, he poured his energies into his other passion—running his ad agency.

Trevor knocked and poked his head around the corner of his office well past the dinner hour one evening. "It's late, even for you, boss. Anything going on I should know about?"

Marc beckoned him in. "I didn't know you were still here. You should be out with Christy, wooing her with your undeniable Irish charm."

The younger man laughed. "Who says woo anymore?"

Exactly. He chuckled under his breath, scribbling notes on the storyboard in front of him. "I'm trying to make sure everything's in order before I leave. Besides," he said, putting down his pencil and looking at his friend through tired eyes, "considering the person I'm leaving in charge of my agency is inordinately distracted by romance, I've got to do everything I can to secure my business."

"Very amusing." Trevor dropped into the chair opposite his desk. "Go home. This," he said, waving his arm around the spacious corner office, "will all still be here in the morning. And the next. And again next month. It'll be in good hands while you're gone."

"I know." Marc leaned back in his chair, and crossed his arms behind his head.

"I'm surprised you haven't been out with Natalie as much this week. I thought things were going better between you two. Everything okay?" His eyes narrowed. "If that's too personal, say the word."

"It's fine." It'd probably do him good to talk about it. "In one of my sessions with Dr. Fontaine, he suggested I give our relationship some space before leaving for Montana. He said I hadn't taken the time to grieve, for lack of a better term."

Trevor looked puzzled. "Grieve? What do you mean?"

Marc tapped his pencil in an absent staccato on his desk. "The good doctor thinks I haven't taken the time to absorb what happened." The pencil stopped. "When Natalie fell down those stairs, she took a part of me with her, too, you know." He hesitated. "My heart."

"I can't even begin to imagine how hard it's been for you."

He glimpsed the compassion in Trevor's eyes. "Dr. Fontaine said I should concentrate on forging new memories since we're basically starting over. But he advised waiting until we get to Montana." He blew out a deep sigh. "The bottom line is that I miss Natalie."

"I hope you don't have to help her get over the whole 'I hate advertising thing again.'" Trevor whistled under his breath and shook his head. "The first time was hard enough. I know she came to accept what you do, but you don't want to have to go through that all over again. Not that you wouldn't. Your devotion to your wife is admirable, and I have to say, a beautiful thing to witness."

"You mean for someone like me? Type A, nose-to-the-grindstone workaholic? I don't understand it myself, but thankfully, it hasn't come up as an issue. Score one for amnesia." Marc tossed Trevor a wry grin. He thought of Natalie's words to Lexa about how proud she was of him. He was glad Lexa told him, and that Natalie herself told him at Peppino's. "Present circumstances aside, you know I've grown closer in my walk with the Lord the last couple of years," Marc said. "It's changed the way I run the agency in some respects." He'd always equated Christianity with being soft, but he couldn't run a successful advertising agency by being a pushover. Perhaps not surprisingly, the agency thrived even more once he gave his heart to the Lord.

"You lost me again. You run a tight ship. You always have, but you're a good guy at heart. Everyone knows that, and your stellar reputation in this cut-throat industry affirms it." Trevor's brows drew together.

Picking up the baseball paperweight on his desk, Marc balanced it on his hand. "Case in point—Reggie Remoulet. You must have wondered why I passed on the opportunity to sign him for that Reebok account."

"Other than losing your mind, yeah, I wondered. But I've worked with you long enough to know you had a good reason. You're not a man to do anything without substantiation. You're too intuitive."

Marc sat up straighter. "I'm telling you this in complete confidence, Trev." He met his eyes and held them steady. "I discovered some . . . unsavory information about Mr. Remoulet. He beats his wife. On a semi-regular basis, apparently."

His friend's eyes widened and he released a low whistle, slumping back in the chair. "Wow. No kidding."

Walking over to the window, he leaned against it. Marc barely glanced at the street many floors below. It made Natalie nervous when she saw him positioned like this. That thought sent him straight back to his desk. "The man should be behind bars instead of on a playing field. I prefer to think that even before I had Christ in my heart, I never would have signed Reggie on the dotted line, knowing he'd just put his wife in the hospital with a black eye and broken ribs." His eyes settled on his dad's framed Celtics jersey hanging on the wall. "Reggie's got kids, too."

He returned his focus to Trevor as he sat down again. "Let another agency deal with him. You and I both know there are enough blood-thirsty sharks in the pool without scruples or morals who'd be more than willing. Here's the thing. If I'd glimpsed the slightest sign of remorse or possibility of redemption, I might have signed Reggie, but I didn't see it, so I couldn't find it in my heart to justify an ad campaign based on lies. What exactly would I be peddling?" Marc shook his head. "That's not the way I run my agency."

"Again, I think you're selling yourself short. You're an honest man and always have been, Marc. All your hard work and effort shows in the success of this agency. Without integrity, you'd have nothing to show for it. And, at the risk of swelling your head, your employees think pretty highly of you, too."

"Thanks. Couldn't do it without you."

Trevor's broad grin was a great thing to see. His pulled up his shoulders. "So, wait until you hear what I'm planning for Christy for Thanksgiving."

Marc allowed a smile. "Tell me. I'm all ears."

~

Arriving home after ten that night, Marc poured himself a bowl of cereal. *Nutritious dinner, old man.* He sank down into the soft, plush cushions of the sofa and looked over at Elwood sitting at attention, panting for food or affection. Or both. "Okay. Come with me, buddy." Going back into the kitchen and retrieving the dog's dish, he prepared another bowl of cereal, being careful not to add much milk. Shep used to love milk, but the vet always said not to give it to a dog often. "Knock yourself out, but don't get used to it. It's a special treat." Tail wagging, Elwood dug into the bowl and enjoyed lapping up the milk.

Returning to the living room, Marc sat in the quiet darkness. The blinking red light from the answering machine caught his eye. His first thought was to dismiss it. It only blinked once. Probably someone trying to get him to buy or donate something. The thought it might be Natalie brought him to his feet, and he quickly crossed the room. Pushing the button, he smiled when his wife's voice filled the room.

His eyes fell on the soft Irish blanket draped neatly over the sofa. He remembered that blanket from the night after their return from their honeymoon. Still on Italian time, they'd gone to dinner downtown and window shopped, but neither of them could sleep when they'd returned home. If he figured correctly—and based on Natalie's projected due date—the odds were high that was the night she'd gotten pregnant. Elwood padded back into the living room and took up residence by the sofa. Realizing he hadn't listened to Natalie's message, Marc pushed the button to replay it.

"Marc, hi. It's me, Natalie." A rush of emotion flooded through him as he heard her voice—so sexy, completely female, and all grown up. Elwood sat up at attention, letting out a boisterous bark, his tail wagging. Closing his eyes, Marc focused on her words. "I wanted to remind you of the ultrasound late Thursday morning. Call me tomorrow and we can talk about it." She hesitated.

"I've missed talking with you this week. I hope everything's okay, and I'll talk to you tomorrow."

She didn't say, *I love you*, and she didn't say, *I can't wait to see you again*.

"But, she did say she missed talking with me." Marc scooped Elwood into his arms and carried him upstairs. The mutt was a captive audience as he brushed and flossed. He couldn't stop smiling as he walked into the bedroom, the loyal little dog at his heels. "And that, my canine friend," he said, peeling off his shoes and socks, "is what I call progress." Removing his shirt and stepping out of his pants, he let them fall on the floor in a crumpled heap before crawling into bed with Elwood snuggled beside him. Falling asleep with the smile still on his face, he made a mental note to call Natalie tomorrow morning as soon as possible.

Chapter 17

$\mathscr{M}$ARC RESISTED CALLING Natalie at the crack of dawn. Armed with the best night of sleep he'd had in a long time, he waited only long enough to reach his office. Throwing his coat on the sofa, he swung around the desk and into his chair in seconds. Cradling the phone, he turned on his computer and glanced at his calendar as he punched the speed dial for the school. He smiled when he heard the customary cheerful greeting. "Good morning, Martha!" He adored the grandmotherly receptionist from Alabama who called everyone "sweet cakes" and "honey pie" and smelled like peppermints and gardenias. Every school needed a Martha.

"Why, Marc, is that you, sugar?" The enthusiasm in Martha's voice was infectious. "About time you called. You'd better be coming around to see me. I told Natalie just last week that I needed a big old hug from her handsome husband."

A grin curved his lips. "I'll try to remedy that soon enough. I miss you, too." He jotted a note on his calendar to stop by the school soon and take Martha a box of her favorite chocolates. She deserved Godiva, but preferred the cheaper, drugstore variety.

"I miss Natalie when she's not here. Is she feelin' any better?"

Marc stopped, his pen poised above his calendar. "What do you mean? Is she sick?"

The receptionist laughed. "Nothin' that won't go away in a few months, dear."

Morning sickness. He'd hoped that might be over by now. "I'll check on her. Thanks, Martha." Replacing the phone, he sat lost in thought. No matter what Dr. Fontaine advised, he wanted to see Natalie. Roommates were one thing, but they couldn't give her the comfort the expectant father could. Besides, it wasn't like her mother and sister were next door or even the next town over. Otherwise, he'd consider having them drive up from Connecticut.

No, this is definitely a job for a dutiful, loving husband.

Pulling on his coat, he told Christy he'd return at some point. "Don't wait up!" If he was honest with himself, he wanted to be the kind of husband and father his dad never was.

"Everything okay, Marc?" The compassion in Christy's voice was touching. She'd been his assistant from the beginning days of the agency. Like Trevor, he couldn't do it without her. It was unusual for him to take off this early if he didn't have a scheduled meeting. He'd been doing a lot of things differently as of late.

He tossed her a smile. "Everything's fine. If you need anything while I'm gone, call Trevor." Noticing the flush in her cheeks at the mention of Trevor's name, he waved as he pushed open the glass doors and headed toward the elevators. He started to whistle, something he rarely did.

Stopping at the drugstore on the way to Natalie's apartment, Marc pestered the pharmacist about possible remedies for morning sickness. The man finally shook his head in exasperation. "Sir, go home to your wife. Hold her hand, smooth her brow, and tell her how much you love her. This will all take care of itself in a few months. Trust me." His smile more than intimated he wasn't the first husband in the history of the planet to go through pregnancy. He selected a fun-looking mystery novel and a couple of magazines he'd seen Natalie read before and a big box of chocolates for Martha. The day was unseasonably chilly, so hopefully they wouldn't melt in the car.

Next stop was the florist where he chose beautiful, long-stemmed pink roses with baby's breath. *Baby* being the key word. Hopefully, she'd appreciate the sentiment. Marc pondered calling her on the way to the house in Newton, then thought better of it. Best not to give her the opportunity to tell him not to come. He hoped she'd feel well enough to answer the door since most, if not all, of the other girls should be at work. Leaving everything at the front door wasn't an option. He needed to see his wife, probably more than she wanted to see him.

Reaching the house, he retrieved his purchases and flowers and hopped out of the car, taking the outside steps two at a time. His heart pumped as it always did in anticipation of seeing Natalie. He hoped his presence might give her some small measure of comfort. Instead of pushing the doorbell, Marc knocked on the heavy, wooden front door. Kim peered at him from behind the sheer lace curtains covering the living room window.

With a warm smile, she ushered him inside. "Hi, Marc." Seeing the flowers, her smile grew wider. "Looks like someone's here to brighten Natalie's day."

"That would be correct. At least I hope she'll be happy to see me. I called the school and Martha told me she's under the weather." That was one way of putting it. He nodded toward the stairs. "Is she in her room?"

"Yes. Second door on the right."

"Thanks," he called, already halfway up the stairs. He'd never been allowed up to her room when they were dating. Funny how these things work out. With a gentle knock on Natalie's bedroom door, Marc paused, listening. Not hearing anything, he knocked louder. Hearing a small groan, he pushed the door open. The bed was empty as Marc walked into the middle of the spacious bedroom. Putting the roses on the bedside table, he pulled the magazines and the book from the bag and placed them beside her pillow.

"Natalie?" He shrugged out of his overcoat and tossed it on a chair.

"In here." Following the voice to the small adjacent bathroom, his eyes opened wider. Natalie sat on the floor, rocking back and forth, head face-down on her bent knees.

Dropping down beside her, he gathered her in his arms. She looked up with a combination of shocked surprise and relief, but leaned into him. He followed the pharmacist's advice and smoothed her brow and kissed her damp forehead. He'd save the "I love you" part of the man's suggestion until she wasn't in imminent danger of being sick. Pushing dark hair away from her face, he leaned his head against hers, and couldn't help but notice she wore a nightgown that dipped strategically in the front. *Focus.* "Is it bad?"

In response, she gagged and clamped one hand over her mouth. On her knees in a heartbeat, she retched none-too-delicately, clutching the sides of the toilet so hard her knuckles turned white and shook from the effort. Not knowing what else to do, Marc held back her hair as she alternated between retching, dry heaves and gasps.

"I guess that's my answer." He pulled her into his arms again when it seemed she had nothing else left to give, ignoring her frown at his lame attempt at humor. Grabbing the damp washcloth from the edge of the sink, he pressed it against her forehead, murmuring sweet endearments. Her body trembled, and his heart swelled like it might burst. *Poor baby.* Seeing her suffer triggered deep, protective instincts. Natalie rarely complained of anything more than a headache, so it must be pretty bad. He gently wiped her mouth with the washcloth and leaned her back against him, tightening his hold until she stopped shivering.

Part of him wanted to tell her how sorry he was he'd done this to her. Another part of him was ecstatic. He prayed it wasn't perverse to feel that way. When they held their baby in a few short months, it would be worth it all. One other thing Marc knew: no matter what an esteemed Boston psychologist told him, he had a personal timeline.

Comforting Natalie until she was better, he gave her privacy in the bathroom for a few minutes. He ran down the stairs to the kitchen and filled a glass with ice water. As he waited in the bedroom, he vowed that by the time they brought their child home from the hospital, their relationship would be fully restored. A baby deserved no less than two loving parents who not only loved one another enough to bring her into the world, but wanted to raise her in the love and joy of the Lord. Together. Under the same roof.

In his heart, Marc suspected Natalie carried their daughter—a sweet little girl he prayed would inherit her dark hair, gentle manner and incredible smile, and hopefully his intense blue eyes but none of his irascible traits. Call him crazy, but he'd started referring to his child as "she" in his daily prayers.

Natalie looked at him through tired eyes as he helped her settle against the pillows. Her eyes drank in the roses, her smile weary. "They're gorgeous. Thank you. There's a vase under the bathroom sink, if you can fill it with water." She spied the glass of water on the table. "Thanks for hydrating me, too."

Coming back into the bedroom, he paused, watching her. Her eyes were closed. Even with her hair matted to her head in places, her eyes red-rimmed, pale and withdrawn, she was the most beautiful woman he'd ever seen. He'd do anything to drain away her sickness, take it on himself. Placing the vase on the bedside table, he gathered the roses and arranged them the best he could, trying to be quiet so as not to wake her.

"Oh, no." Natalie groaned as her eyes fluttered open.

"What's wrong? Need to go back in the bathroom?"

"Look at your shirt."

His eyes traveled down his shirt and found the telltale stain. "Well, I suppose I could leave it there and claim it as a badge of honor." Catching a whiff, he wrinkled his nose and shot her a wry grin. "But then again . . ." Good thing he kept extra shirts in his office.

"That's just gross." Natalie waved her hand, and the thought probably wanted to make her gag. "We'd better try to wash out that stain before it sets." She struggled to sit up.

"You rest. I'll take care of it." Not thinking, he started to unbutton his shirt. It seemed the most natural thing in the world, but when Natalie's eyes widened as he unfastened his cuff links and proceeded to pull the shirt from his shoulders, his fingers paused. He hadn't put on an undershirt.

"Sorry," he mumbled, crossing the room to the bathroom. Once there, he closed the door and removed the shirt. Leaning against the sink, head bowed, Marc blew out a deep sigh. Holding the stained section of the shirt under the running water, he rinsed it before lightly wringing it out and smoothing it flat against the sink. "Natalie," he called, opening the bathroom door, "where's your hair dryer?"

"What?" she called from the bed.

Opening the door a bit wider, he stuck his head out the door. "Where's your hair dryer?"

"What?" Her voice sounded louder, stronger, and that hint of mischief intrigued him.

"Where's your hair dryer?" Marc repeated, stepping around the door, minus the shirt. Seeing Natalie's bemused expression, he laughed out loud. "You sneak." His chest was one of the things she loved most about him, so who was he to waste the opportunity? It was worth it, seeing the undeniable look of longing in her eyes. Amnesia or not, some things never change. Maybe he should beat on his chest like Tarzan and call her Jane. Elwood could be Cheeta, and the baby she carried Boy. Except it was a girl. He just *knew* it.

She giggled, and it thrilled him. "What in the world are you thinking?"

He gave her a sheepish grin. "Just being stupid."

She shook her head slowly. "I disagree. Right now, you're the sweetest man in the world." Her eyes looked brighter, the color had returned to her cheeks. "Thanks again for the flowers, the book, the magazines . . . everything. It was incredibly wonderful of you to bring them all to me this morning. Still," she added, her tone wistful, "you'd best go put your shirt back on before you drive me crazy, you sexy man."

If he didn't take her advice, he'd be on that bed beside her. Considering she was feeling nauseous, that wasn't the brightest idea. "I'll be right back." A few minutes later, his shirt buttoned all the way up to his neck like a Pilgrim, he repositioned his tie and fastened the cuff links. She turned her head and gave him a small smile.

"You're wearing the cuff links."

His eyes widened, and he walked closer to the bed. "Do you remember them?"

"You wore them on our date to Peppino's." His disappointment must have been obvious when she hastened to explain. "I don't know for sure, but I think I gave them to you." She hesitated. "Didn't I?"

"Natalie," he said, his eyes moist, "you gave them to me for my birthday this year. You even made up clues for me to try and find them."

"Clues? Like a game?"

He sighed. "Yes, a numbers game. I'll tell you another time. You need to rest now. The significant thing is that you're starting to get memories back, sweetheart." Wanting to hold her, but feeling it was best to abstain, he sat down beside her on the bed. "I wanted to bring you some kind of medicine, but the pharmacist couldn't recommend anything safe for morning sickness. Seems a waiting period of several months is the only prescription."

"Marc, don't you know?" Her voice was quiet, a smile tipped the corners of her mouth.

"Know what?"

"The best medicine . . . is *you*."

He shook his head. "It's not fair, you know. Telling me something like that and then sending me on my way. It will be next-to-impossible trying to work this afternoon with those words in my head."

"Call me later today. Maybe I'll feel better." When Natalie squeezed his hand, the old familiar gleam was in her eyes. "We could grab some supper."

His day kept getting brighter. Dr. Fontaine could take his advice and shove it right out the window. He wasn't going to bypass any prime opportunities. Tilting his head, he surveyed her. "If I didn't know better, I'd say you've missed your husband this week."

"And I'd say, you know me pretty well." She gestured toward the bathroom. "We've never . . . done that before, have we? You know, the sickness part?"

He winked. "No, that was a first, but our wedding vows included it, so you're covered. Goes with my job of being a good, dutiful husband." Dropping a light kiss on her cheek, he whispered, "I love you, Natalie." Grabbing his coat with a quick wave, he swept out of the bedroom and down the steps. As he drove back to the office, he marveled over how sometimes the smallest victories turn out to be the sweetest.

~

When Marc spoke with Natalie later in the day, her morning sickness had extended into the evening.

"I'm really sorry, but I still feel lousy. I wouldn't be good company for you tonight, trust me. Can we go to lunch together after my doctor's appointment on Thursday? It's only a couple of days away."

"Sure. Sounds great." He should have known he wasn't fooling anyone, much less his perceptive wife as he swallowed his disappointment. "Besides, I've got Elwood to keep me warm." Small consolation, even if the mutt was adorable and affectionate. "Have you been sick all day?"

"A little this afternoon, but it wasn't as bad as this morning. Now I know why it's called *morning* sickness."

"Make sure you get plenty of fluids. I don't want you getting dehydrated. No more trips to the hospital."

"Monica and Kim are taking good care of me. I'll be fine."

"Do you need anything?"

"Thanks, but I think I just need to rest."

"Sure you don't need me to come and read you a bedtime story? I could act it out—without my shirt on." He'd do a striptease if it made her feel better. Whatever Natalie wanted from him was hers for the asking.

She laughed, sounding more like herself. "I'll take a rain check on that offer."

His brows raised. More encouragement. "I'll call you tomorrow, and we can make plans. Since you mentioned lunch, I assume you're taking the whole day off?"

"That's right."

"Then we'll make a day of it, or at least the afternoon. It's not every day a couple hears their baby's heartbeat and sees their child for the very first time." *Our daughter.* He wondered if and when he should share his prediction with her. Perhaps he should keep that one to himself for the time being. She was silent for a long moment. "Natalie? You there?"

"I'm here."

"You're awfully quiet. Care to share your thoughts?" He hated phone conversations when he couldn't see her face to gauge her reaction.

"Every day, I understand a little more why I fell in love with you. Thanks for coming over and taking care of me today. It meant so much."

She couldn't see, but he hoped his wife could sense the huge, unstoppable grin that spread from ear-to-ear. Oh yes, it meant so much.

Chapter 18

*M*ARC IMAGINED THE clear, jelly-like substance the ultrasound technician squirted on Natalie's stomach must feel really cold. An instrument that resembled a stethoscope with a large, round metal button on one end was positioned on her abdomen. Pushing down with gentle pressure, the technician moved it quickly from one side of her stomach to the other before centering it slightly beneath her navel. All the while, the technician kept her eyes trained on the small monitor. In a seemingly unconscious move, Natalie reached for his hand, intertwining her fingers with his. Her tremulous smile tugged at him.

Without her asking, he'd waited outside, giving her privacy while she changed into the gown. He wondered if she'd be modest and self-conscious and not want him in the room with her during the actual procedure. But she'd invited him, and judging by the way she squeezed his hand, she not only wanted him there, she *needed* him.

"There's your baby, Mr. and Mrs. Thompson." The technician pointed to the screen with a smile. "Here's the head." They both strained forward in their eagerness for the first glimpse of their child.

Stealing a quick glance, Marc's breath caught as he glimpsed the awe in Natalie's eyes. She looked like a child herself, eyes bright, completely enthralled. He watched the moving image on the screen, heard the swishing of the heartbeat. What a beautiful sound. They'd actually created another human being. It was surreal. Without a doubt, their baby was the best thing he ever had a part in creating. He squeezed Natalie's hand a little tighter. If he had any say in the matter, this would be the first of many children, but it probably wasn't the time to voice that opinion. They didn't even live in the same house.

"Marc?"

He snapped to attention. "Sorry. What did you say?"

"The baby's heartbeat is strong." The relief in Natalie's voice was apparent.

"And everything looks good?" He had to know for his own peace of mind.

"Perfectly normal," the technician said without hesitation. If anything was wrong, he'd pick up on the cues. He thought about asking the technician if she could tell the baby's gender, but decided against it. Let Natalie ask if she wanted.

After a short visit with the doctor, they left the women's health center, hand-in-hand. She couldn't stop smiling as she glanced at the ultrasound photos one last time before tucking them in her purse. Marc wanted to stare at them all day himself since they were more enthralling than any of his ad campaigns. Nothing in the world was prettier than his wife's smile, and he hadn't seen her this happy in way too long. He felt on top-of-the-world himself.

"I'll bet that squishy stuff felt weird." He helped her into the car, tucking the bottom of her coat inside the door, noting her grateful smile.

"It was really cold." She laughed. "Did you hear my stomach growl when we were talking with the doctor? That was pretty embarrassing. But I don't want to talk about that. Why don't you tell me where you're taking your hungry wife for lunch?"

"I have something very special planned for us, but it's not Peppino's this time." The car purred to life, but Marc couldn't leave the parking lot. Not yet. Not when everything in him wanted to kiss her. "I'm so proud of you, Natalie." His eyes fell to her stomach. He couldn't help it, given what he'd just seen in the office.

"Thanks. You had a little something to do with it, too, you know." Her cheeks colored and she diverted her attention to the window.

"That was the most incredible thing I've ever seen in my life. Our dau—our child," he said.

Natalie drew in a sharp breath. "What did you say?" She turned in the seat to face him. "Marc, do you believe we're having a girl?"

He smiled a little, relieved she didn't seem upset. "Yes. I can't tell you why, exactly, and I could be wrong. I just have this gut instinct, a feeling in my bones, intuition, foresight—whatever you want to call it—that you're carrying our daughter. I hope that doesn't bother you."

She shook her head. "No, of course not. I have the same feeling."

When she looked at him like that, her beautiful eyes so trusting, he couldn't stay away. Leaning toward her, he lowered his head as she moved closer, her lips parted in sweet invitation. She sighed and settled into the curve of his arms as he brought his lips down on hers. He kept it light rather than full of passion, but felt heady and dazed with the feel, the taste, of Natalie. "Thank you," he whispered, reluctant to release her.

"Are you thanking me for the kiss . . . or otherwise?" Nestling back into her seat, she fastened the seat belt, her eyes not leaving his.

"Both. Thank you for carrying our child and taking such good care of . . . her."

Turning her head, still leaning back against the headrest, Natalie smiled. "And thank you for giving her to us."

He cleared his throat. "Okay, we're like one small step away from a Hallmark ad here. Time to take my beautiful mother-to-be to lunch." As he drove, Marc couldn't stop smiling as she reached for his hand.

And yes, Lord, the slightly larger victories are even sweeter.

~

Settled a short time later in Amore, one of Boston's finest downtown restaurants, Marc's heart skipped a beat as he spied a woman he'd hoped never to see again in this lifetime. Ashley Williams. She looked the same as the last time he saw her, a year before meeting Natalie, but she'd been spitting-nails mad at him then. His trail of ex-girlfriends wasn't exactly a happy one.

Ashley's long blonde hair was swept on top of her head, and she wore a tight, low-cut dress that showcased her ample assets. Bright red—her favorite color, appropriately enough—with fingernails painted to match. Her feet were encased in some kind of high-heeled, scandalous death trap of a shoe more suited for night-time escapades than daytime lunches.

Averting his gaze and praying she didn't notice him, Marc buried his head in the menu. *Of course, nothing can be easy, Lord.* Darting a quick glance in her direction, he found those cat-like eyes settled squarely on him. Disgust clenched his gut the way she eyed him like prey. Flavor of the month. She wanted him for lunch, and then intended to chew him up and spit him out. She was a barracuda, embodying in human flesh every song ever written about a man-eating female. A few years ago, he'd have gladly welcomed an afternoon delight with Ashley, but that behavior was long gone.

Thank you, Lord, for saving me from myself.

Seeing Ashley cross the crowded room, headed in his direction, he rose to his feet, nearly overturning his water glass. *No, no, no.* This couldn't be good. He righted the glass and smoothed the bunched tablecloth with a shaky hand. Ashley shouldn't bother him. She was in his long-dead past, and couldn't hurt his relationship with his wife.

Oh yes, she can.

Natalie looked up at him, a question written in her expression. The honesty in those deep blue eyes rendered him a spineless fool. Usually he was suave, self-possessed. Now he was a mess, a coward. "I'll be right back." He shot her a nervous smile and tried to slow his breathing. With a nod, she continued studying her menu.

Marc's heart pounded and his pulse throbbed in his ears as he tilted his head toward the outer foyer. Ashley's satisfied grin was much too smug. *She's just your ex. Nothing to worry about.* Still, nothing would be worse than Ashley approaching the table where he sat with Natalie. These two women had nothing in common.

Except you.

"Ashley." He greeted her with a perfunctory kiss on one cheek. He shouldn't have done it, but social graces were long ingrained in him. He'd greet any female acquaintance in the same manner. Honey-colored eyes bore into his. At one point, he believed he was in love with those eyes, along with all the rest of Ashley Williams, but now he felt nothing. Except remorse.

She narrowed her gaze and a seductive smile flirted about those pouty lips. They looked even fuller, courtesy of a skillful doctor. A small laugh escaped, which she took as encouragement. It really didn't take much for this woman.

"Marc, darling, how are you?" Her affected socialite accent sounded like a feline's purr. "You're looking well. *Very* handsome." That sultry voice dripped with innuendo. Yes, it never took long for this woman to make her point. It sickened him how he could ever have been attracted to this woman enough to take her into his bed. It hadn't been a one-time thing, either. On a purely physical level, the woman was more than attractive, but she had not an ounce of the inherent sweetness, sincerity or innocence of his wife. His taste had improved dramatically since ditching Ashley. Score another one for the Lord.

Shame swept through him, over him, and invaded every pore of his being. His only excuse was she'd come along at a time in his life when he was on top of the world—a professional athlete, full of himself. She'd fed into his ego and every male fantasy. *How could I have been so stupid?* Marc's heart sank to a new low, all the way down to his expensive leather shoes. Ashley Williams was so far removed from the godly, incredible woman sitting in the dining room, waiting for him. He couldn't take the chance Natalie would ever see this woman or know the past he shared with her. What was done, was done. Over. Finished.

Ashley ran a possessive finger up his arm, making a slow trail with her painted index finger from his wrist all the way to his shoulder, watching him with an expertly-arched brow. She stepped back, devouring him, drinking in every inch, moving upward from the tip of his shoes, up past the dark, double-breasted business suit and deep red tie before finally resting on his lips. "Why don't you come around and see me sometime? It's been a long time. I've missed you." Leaning close, she whispered, "Same address. I'm sure you remember."

When she licked her lips and winked, Marc bit his lip not to laugh. "I'm married, Ashley." His voice was firm as he pried her fingers from his arm. "I'm not interested. It's nice to see you, but if you'll excuse me . . ."

Before he could react, she pulled his head down to her lips. "You know I've never been able to resist you," she whispered. "Come home with me, Marc. Let's share dessert." Subtlety was never her strong suit.

With a disgusted grunt, Marc nudged her away from him. He tried not to be rough, and he'd never manhandled a woman in his life, but Ashley pushed him to the limit. Enough was enough. He had to get out of there.

But he wasn't fast enough.

Chapter 19

*H*E'D NEVER FORGET the look on Natalie's face, the barely-veiled contempt in her eyes, as she rounded the corner and spied her husband in a private tête-à-tête with another woman. *Oh, Lord, please help me.*

"I'm ready to leave, Marc." The words matched the icy stare she gave Ashley. When Natalie turned her eyes on him, fire boiling beneath the surface, he wanted to melt into the floor.

"Hello, darling." Ashley surveyed his wife beneath those ridiculous eyelashes. "I'm Ashley, an old *friend* of Marc's." Her words dripped meaning. She wasn't the least bit embarrassed she'd been caught kissing another woman's husband in public. Knowing her as well as he unfortunately once did, she'd consider it a personal triumph and take some kind of perverse satisfaction from it.

"And it's going to stay that way, *old* friend." Natalie matched Ashley's stare before turning on her heel and striding back through the restaurant toward the entrance. Her shoulders were straight, her head held high. Oh, but the woman was dignified and full of class. Unlike the Scarlet Woman standing beside him, her hand on his arm, as clingy as ever. It was altogether fitting her name started with the letter *A*.

"What a precious wife you have," Ashley cooed.

"Oh, shut up." Shaking off her hand, Marc stormed through the restaurant after his wife. He'd never been more proud of her. *Way to go, Natalie!* In spite of the rising panic in his chest, he was thrilled she sounded like she'd be willing to fight for him . . . if it ever came down to that. Which, of course, it never would. He was torn between giving into the loopy grin hidden beneath the surface or wanting to shield himself from her impending wrath. It was coming all right.

Behind him, he heard Ashley's laugh. She'd think him weak, but he could care less. All that mattered was his wife. He had to make this right. Of all the stupid clichés, Natalie had to witness a woman from his past kissing him in one of Boston's finest restaurants. A kiss he neither encouraged nor wanted, and now she thought the absolute worst of him.

How could things have gone from the top of the mountain to the fiery pit so fast?

Signaling their waiter, Marc handed him a ridiculously generous tip for a couple glasses of water. This day was going nothing at all like he planned. Trailing behind Natalie, he spied her heading into the ladies room. Handing the coatroom ticket to the attendant, he gathered her lightweight coat and kept vigil. He couldn't take the chance she'd slip out the back entrance and hail a taxi. When she emerged a few minutes later, she barely glanced his way and shrugged off his attempts to help her into the coat. Apparently, he'd done enough for one afternoon. They waited in awkward silence for the valet to bring the Lexus. Glancing at her watch, Natalie turned and headed in the opposite direction.

"Natalie! Where are you going?"

She fixed her gaze on the sidewalk. "I'll call a taxi to take me back to the apartment."

"You're staying put. I'm taking you home." His tone left no room for protest. She pouted, but said nothing. Probably storing up her zingers for when they were alone in the car. His wife could dish it out pretty good, and he loved it when he wasn't the focus of her wrath. But when he was . . . look out.

"You couldn't wait for me, is that it?" Natalie seethed once he'd ensconced her in the passenger seat.

At least she didn't make him wait long. *Here it comes.* "Natalie, there's nothing going on between me and Ashley, and you know it." Were they in some stupid movie? He wished he could snap his fingers and banish this new nightmare. One of his biggest mistakes, his personal Pandora's box, had come back full-force to haunt him—haunt *them*. He needed to make sure to bury it so far down it would never surface again.

"Even if there's nothing going on now, you apparently have a past with that . . . that woman. Tell me something: Did I know about Ashley before we were married?"

"I told you about her, yes," he said, hoping she'd leave it at that. He couldn't lie to her—he never had, and he never would. Not that he'd been completely honest and told her the extent of his past relationships. Thankfully, confident and secure, she never asked questions. What did it matter? Dwelling on the past was counter-productive. He rationalized that not telling her was protecting her. It wasn't lying. Not really. Just following the age-old "don't ask, don't tell" rule. If anything, it was more the sin of omission. *Admit it. You'd lose her if she knew, and you couldn't face the loss, the failure.* Ashley Williams was a long distant memory. She meant nothing now except to remind him of his past stupidity.

Stealing a glance, Marc sensed Natalie's internal struggle as she slumped down further in the seat and crossed her arms. She stared out the window to avoid his scrutiny. At least she didn't spout further accusations or go off on a rant. That wasn't her style. In his mind, the stony silence was worse. It continued until they were almost back in Newton, and it was no ten-minute drive.

"You still haven't eaten," he said, turning onto the street of the apartment house.

"I'm not hungry."

"You have to eat something. For the baby, if not for yourself."

"Well, thanks for the reminder, you adulterer."

In some twisted way, Marc found it funny. But he wasn't a total idiot. Laughter would not be good right now. *Is it adultery, Father, if I committed sin with a woman before I was saved? Before I was married? Before I'd even met my wife?* No time was right for confessions like this, but he wasn't ready. Problem was, would he ever be ready?

"I'm not an adulterer." *Please, Lord. Let her drop it.* "Don't let that ridiculous scene spoil the joy we felt earlier today. I'm with you, and I've only been with you since the moment we met. You know that—or at least you did at one time."

"Apparently there's still some things I need to learn about you." Her words were so quiet, he almost didn't hear them. But he did, and wished he hadn't.

As soon as he pulled the car in front of the house, Natalie climbed out before he'd come to a full stop. She slammed the door. He winced. His car was important to him, and she knew it. That slam told him *she* knew how important it was.

"Natalie!" He tried to quell his extreme frustration, but his tone betrayed him. Climbing out of the car, he scrambled to catch up to her. "Don't run away from me. Let's talk this out."

Headed toward the front door, she halted and turned, partially facing him. Again, she avoided his eyes. "I'm fine. I just need to be alone right now." The look on her face made it painfully obvious she wasn't fine.

"Calling me an adulterer is a serious accusation. If nothing else, I deserve an explanation of why you're so mad."

"Okay." She stepped closer. "Remember how mad you were the morning I moved out? You couldn't stomach the fact that Roger and Kyle—my roommates' boyfriends, for the record—were helping me move out of the house. You were so jealous you couldn't see straight. I want you to think about how mad you'd be if you'd come down those steps and found me in Roger's arms, *kissing* him." She waited a moment, watching him. "And don't think I couldn't tell you were out drinking the night before. I could smell it on your breath. It was embarrassing."

"Not that it excuses the drinking, but you'd just told me the night before you didn't want to live with me in *our* house anymore." He lowered his voice, not wanting their fight to become a public spectacle. "How did you honestly expect me to react? In essence, you told me you didn't want *me*."

She threw her hands in the air. "I never said it was forever! I don't know how to talk with you. This is the thing: that morning, you made me feel like I was somehow betraying you. But, after what I witnessed at the restaurant today, I'm wondering if the exact opposite is true."

Marc shook his head, dazed with disbelief. Where was this anger coming from? "I can't believe you'd think such a thing. Haven't I proven my devotion to you, done everything I could to prove my love for you since your accident?" He ran a hand through his hair and swallowed his anger. "Whether you like it or not, I'm your husband, and I'm not going to let you think I'm a cheater. It's not true, and in your heart, you have to know that." His voice broke. "Don't let this negate all the positive steps we've taken in the past few weeks, Natalie. No matter what you think of me now, promise you won't make any more impetuous decisions." His eyes met hers. "We need to pray about this mess and ask the Lord to help us."

She hesitated, and her eyes filled. "Listen," she said, "since we're committed to this Montana project for TeamWork, I'm not going to back out now. I'll meet you at the airport on Saturday, as planned, but don't expect too much." Without another word, she hurried inside.

With a heavy heart, Marc got back in the car. As he started to pull away, he caught something from the corner of his eye. His foot on the brake, he lowered the passenger window as he spied Natalie coming back toward the car. The woman actually stomped. One hand traveled to her hip and she leaned in close, planting her other hand on the edge of the door.

"By the way, Marc," she said through clenched teeth, finally meeting his eyes with a glare, "you've got a red lip print on your cheek. You might want to clean it off before you go back to your office, especially since it didn't come from your *wife*."

Driving to a nearby fast food chicken franchise—muttering to himself all the way—Marc marched inside and ordered Natalie's favorite meal, complete with the extras, condiments and the juice she preferred. Handing the manager an exorbitant tip for one of his employees to hand deliver the meal to Natalie—something not in their normal job description—he left knowing *he* was the chicken.

Storming back into the office, his mood completely boomeranged from earlier in the day. After telling them he'd be out the rest of the day, they were surprised to see him blow back into his office and slam the door. Ignoring Christy's hurt expression after he lashed out at her when she brought him a spreadsheet and asked a valid question, he was irritable and short with everyone who dared cross his path. He couldn't be bothered, preferring to wallow in his misery, a definite flunky of the Dale Carnegie school of winning friends and influencing people. Not to mention totally obliterating any semblance of a Christian testimony he might have had. Holing up in his office, Marc did little more than sulk, his eyes blurring as he stared at the spreadsheet in front of him.

Trevor rapped hard and barged inside his office without an invitation less than an hour later, slamming the door. Why was everyone slamming doors today? As if he didn't know. Usually the consummate professional, he was acting like a Class A jerk.

"You need something, Trev?" His voice abrupt, he barely looked up, pretending to work.

"Look at me." Trevor planted both fists on his desk and waited. Normally, he was very even-keeled and rarely showed anger.

"You've got my attention." He'd hurt Christy, and Trevor didn't take kindly to it. Well, good for him, standing up for his woman. A stab of guilt ripped through him. He needed to stop being a chauvinist and concentrate instead on being a friend.

"Stop it." Those green eyes blazed into him as Trevor raked his fingers through all that thick red hair. "I don't know what happened today, but I'd say it's a fair bet it has something to do with you and Natalie. The fact of the matter is, you can't go around yelling at everyone and taking it out on them. I hope you're proud of yourself. You've got Christy and half the women in this office in the ladies room having a good cry."

Marc's eyes widened. He shook his head. "I'm sorry." Not only was he pitiful, he was mean to take out his anger on his loyal, valued employees. What a louse.

"You should be, and you owe them an apology. Time to grovel, my friend. No matter what's going on—and even though you're the guy who signs their paychecks—they don't deserve your anger." With that, Trevor spun on his heel and departed, leaving the door open.

Marc lowered his head to his hands, and prayed for forgiveness. With a renewed sense of purpose, he strode out of his office a few minutes later, intent on making amends, starting with Christy. Surrounded by a majority of his thirty employees in a nearby restaurant an hour later, he managed to eat a sandwich. Trevor caught his eye and smiled. It soothed his conscience somewhat, but not much. He'd have to lay low and watch it. He was the boss, not some adolescent kid who couldn't control his emotions or his personal life.

The group enjoyed the unexpected afternoon off from work with good food and lively conversation. Marc sat back in his chair, nodding his head every now and then to give the impression he listened, but his mind wasn't in it. The one person from whom he most sought forgiveness would be going to Montana with him in only two days.

Doubts about the upcoming trip swirled in his muddled mind. He hoped he didn't have to endure Natalie's wrath for the entire two weeks at the work camp. It was intended to bring them closer together, not the opposite. Marc blew out a heavy sigh. His work was definitely cut out for him.

Lord, give me strength, he prayed for about the hundredth time that day.

Chapter 20

*I*T TOOK NATALIE almost ten minutes to notice Elwood in the car as he drove them to the airport early Saturday morning. She'd intended to meet him there, but he'd convinced her it made no sense to go separately. Judging by her body language as she settled herself in the passenger seat, it promised to be a long day. As it was, it was going to take more than nine hours and three flights to get from Boston to Helena. If they could manage to get through that, they should be well on the road to reconciliation.

Hearing a whimper, Natalie twisted around in her seat, her eyes wide. "Why is Elwood in the car? Are you dropping him off somewhere?"

"Elwood's coming with us."

"He *what*?" It was nearly a screech. His attempt to please her by bringing the dog might have been misguided, but he thought it would make her happy. Not to mention he'd miss the little guy.

"Have a heart. He begged me to come along." Marc graced her with his best impression of the dog's limpid, pleading eyes.

She shook her head, the slightest hint of a grin tugging at her lips. When she directed her attention out the window, his quick glance encompassed her jeans tucked into boots, topped with a white cotton blouse and dark gray sweater plus a warm, navy blue down jacket. Her dark hair was pulled back in a high ponytail, and curly wisps escaped down the nape of her neck. She always thought her neck was too long, but he found it beautiful. All the better to nibble and kiss. Might as well push that thought aside since there was a current nibble-and-kiss embargo.

As they rode in silence, he sensed Natalie doing an assessment of her own. She loved it when he dressed down and wore jeans, a sweater and didn't put gel in his hair. It struck him that his clothes were nearly identical to hers, except his sweater was a lighter gray. His laugh escaped.

"Something funny?" Her tone dripped sarcasm, and she raised a skeptical brow.

"Look at us. We look like we just stepped out of an Eddie Bauer or J. Crew catalog." Glancing over at him, she let out a short laugh. Good. Break the ice a bit. The flight to Montana was going to be even longer if he couldn't crack through that frozen wall. "How are you feeling today? Any more morning sickness?"

"It got a little worse the last few days, probably just nerves about this trip." She turned her head, her cheeks flushing with color. Probably mad at herself for saying so much to him all at one time.

119

"You should have called me. I could have at least provided a little beefcake to cheer you up." *She can objectify me all she wants, Lord.* Natalie shook her head and looked out the window, but not before he caught her grin.

~

Marc checked their bags at the curb and handled the arrangements for Elwood, then they passed through the Logan Airport security checkpoint. "We have about an hour before we board. Do you want something to eat?" He nodded in the direction of the fast food franchises as they headed toward their departure gate.

"Not really. Go ahead if you want something." She sat down and pulled out a magazine.

He tried to catch her eye, but she either ignored him or didn't notice. "Have you eaten anything today?"

"Leave me alone." She returned to her magazine, but appeared a little shaky. Not to mention the magazine was upside down. When she saw his head tilt and grin of amusement, she slapped the magazine down on her lap and blew out a prolonged sigh. "No, I haven't eaten anything."

"Then you need something. I have a vested interest in this pregnancy, too, you know." Even if she wasn't taking proper care of herself, she needed to nourish their baby.

A little snort escaped. "You love to remind me that it's *your* baby, don't you?" She waved her hand in the air. "You're like some kind of Neanderthal, staking his claim on his woman."

He didn't like her tone, much less the sentiment. Closing his mouth, he glanced around the airport and swallowed his frustration. He sat down beside her, counting under his breath. "Is this anger the result of seeing Ashley the other day?" Even though she shook her head, when she looked up briefly, he glimpsed the glimmer of pain in her eyes. Regret squeezed him. He'd hoped she'd had time to cool off, but it'd only been a couple of days.

Nothing with Natalie comes easy.

Except for a couple of brief phone conversations to discuss their travel arrangements, Marc hadn't made any other contact with her since that ill-fated lunch at Amore. Especially after their last parting, he knew she needed time and space away from him. That realization cut him down hard, but he wasn't going to force unwanted affection on anyone, especially his own wife. Could it be Dr. Fontaine's advice wasn't so far off-base, after all? "I'll be back in a few minutes." He sounded more curt than he intended.

Walking to a nearby deli counter, he ordered a couple of breakfast sandwiches. As he waited, his eyes traveled back to Natalie. He wanted to watch his wife, hold her with his eyes when his arms could not. Her head bowed as she read the magazine, and she tucked a wayward strand of hair behind one ear.

The corners of her mouth lifted as a small girl waddled beside her chair, falling down on a heavily-padded bottom, giggling in delight. Putting down her magazine, she played with the child as she chatted with the frazzled mother seated in the opposite row of chairs.

She's going to make such an incredible mother. With every glance, every movement, every lilt in her charming laugh, Natalie was grace personified. His mother-in-law told him how nurturing she'd been from the time she was a toddler the same age as the one playing beside her now. She pulled the little girl onto her lap with the obvious encouragement of the child's mother. It was perhaps inevitable she'd become a teacher. Bouncing the laughing child on her knee, both Natalie and the toddler looked happy, the mother relieved for the short break.

"Sir?" The voice of the deli manager broke into his musing.

"Thank you." Taking the bag of warm, wrapped sandwiches, he grabbed the bottles of juice with his other hand. As the toddler played beside her mother once more, Marc took his seat and offered a sandwich to Natalie. When she didn't take it, he placed it on the chair between them with a napkin, along with the juice, her favorite—some combination of berries, kiwi and mango.

"Thanks," she mumbled, not meeting his eyes.

Pure and simple, she was mad at her husband, and he needed to give her time to calm down. Usually she was irritated over little things but got over it quickly. This one was much bigger, and he'd have to wear her down, but the Lord knew he embraced a challenge. He hoped getting away from Boston might help. He said a hurried prayer and took the first bite of his sandwich, busying himself by looking around at everyone else. Airports were great for that. He stole a glance at her from the corner of his eye, somewhat appeased she was eating. With cheeks a little pale and her face drawn, she didn't exactly look like the healthy, expectant mother he wanted to see.

A few minutes later, she crumpled the empty wrapper and walked across the waiting area. Marc followed her with his eyes as she headed down the terminal. So did the guy sitting in another waiting area across the way until a woman came over and sat down beside him. Out of boredom, he picked up the magazine, needing something to keep his mind occupied. His eyes widened as the title jumped off the page: *How to Recapture Your Husband's Love— After He Cheats.*

Marc dropped the magazine with lightning speed. It was as though the pages burned him, searing through his flesh. Is this what Natalie had been reading? Could she actually suspect him of infidelity? That stunned the spit out of him. *Is she so insecure of my love that she'd believe such a ludicrous thing?* The only good thing was the article was about *recapturing* love. Small consolation.

In some ways, that tumble down the steps was their personal fall from grace. It was unusual for Natalie to stumble, much less fall with such dramatic consequences. Never mind that it was caused by a rotting stair and through no fault of her own. Her fall brought his indiscretions to light, making it *his* fall from grace in the eyes of his wife. Surely she never believed him to be perfect. Even though they never talked about it, surely she must suspect he had some history with other women by virtue of his background and not becoming a Christian until his late twenties, but neither had they come face-to-face with a former lover before.

Maybe on some level it was a good thing they were starting over, but instead of starting on even ground, the advantage was definitely in her corner. Before he could ever hope to win her back, he'd need to first reestablish her respect and trust. That, he feared, might prove the hardest thing of all. When Natalie returned to her seat a few minutes later, he'd managed to recover from the shock of that offensive article and replaced the magazine on her chair.

An impatient frown wrinkled her brow as she opened her purse and dug around inside. "Do you have any loose change or a couple of dollars? I want to get some gum or mints at the concessionaire and hate to break a twenty."

"I think there's some change in the pocket of my jacket. Look there." He nodded toward his jacket draped on top of hers. Stretching out his legs, Marc returned his attention to his cell phone as he listened to a voice mail message from Trevor.

"I hope you're not going to keep that thing chained to your ear the entire time we're in Montana." Though her voice was low and controlled, Natalie sounded accusatory.

"No," he said between clenched jaws, "but I have an agency to run." He didn't mean to snap, but his defensiveness rose when she criticized his work ethic.

Her frown deepened. "I'm sure Trevor is more than capable of handling things for a couple of weeks." Meaning she believed he overemphasized his sense of self-importance.

"Need I remind you, it's *my* agency?"

"Trust me, I know. You remind me often enough." She didn't sound particularly proud of him now.

He swallowed his anger. "You might also remember that it's the success of the agency that pays the mortgage on our house. You don't even realize . . ." He stopped, not wanting to create another scene, this time in a very public place.

Those blue eyes blazed. "Tell me what you were going to say."

He fixed her with his steady gaze, softening at the sight of her. "I work hard for you. For us. For our baby and our shared future together. You work hard, too, and trust me, I appreciate everything you do." He made a rash decision he hoped he wouldn't regret. "I promise you this—once we step foot on that plane, the cell phone goes away, and you won't see it again until we get back to Boston."

She'd pulled loose coins from his jacket pocket, but she also discovered something else. Her face blanched as she stared at the slip of paper in her fingers. *Oh, no.* For a former ballplayer, his reflexes sure were slow these days. As Natalie's eyes slowly traveled upward to meet his, Marc knew. Knew she'd read that short, but blunt, note. As conveyed in the incredible sadness crossing her face, she accurately surmised both the meaning and the sender.

He hadn't worn that jacket in a few years. Obviously hadn't thought to look in the pockets. Closing his eyes, he steeled himself. He never expected his wife to find a suggestive note from Ashley Williams in her innocent search for spare change.

Oh, yes, he remembered that note well, and his cheeks colored with the memory as he berated himself for not destroying it. He'd forgotten about it, pushed it out of his mind. A scowl tipped down the corners of his mouth. He dared not look over at Natalie. Shoving the note in his hand, she darted away to get her gum or whatever, no doubt wanting to get as far away from him as possible.

Slumping into the rigid confines of the chair, he crushed the paper in his hand and aimed for the nearest trashcan. *Score.* Yeah, right. Resting his head on the back of the chair, he wished the ground would open up and swallow him whole. It'd probably be safer than sitting next to a woman who found him dirtier than pond scum. He stared through blind eyes at the water sprinklers on the ceiling. Nothing he could say would appease her.

He thought she'd give him the silent treatment, but now it would be a downright freeze-out. Not only was Natalie subdued, she was seething, spitting mad. She wouldn't be talking to him the entire way to Helena. She'd study that article about cheating from Massachusetts to Montana. His hand clutched the arm of the seat that much harder.

It was going to be a *very* long trip.

Chapter 21

NINE-PLUS HOURS LATER, after jetting from Boston to Milwaukee, to Denver, to Helena—with short layovers in-between but thankfully no delays—they finally landed in Big Sky Country. Might as well have been agitated, spun around like mad until he was dizzy and hung out to dry. Natalie uttered all of sixty-four words to him since boarding the flight in Boston. He counted.

As soon as the plane landed and taxied to the gate, she unfastened her seatbelt and jumped up from her seat. Stretching his legs, he stifled a groan. Without a doubt, it was indeed the longest day of flying in his life, including his trips to Hong Kong and Australia. At least she hadn't tried to swap seats. Reaching for her hand, Marc attempted to draw her back into her seat. "The plane's early. We've got time. Let the others go first." The windows were so fogged from the frigid temperatures he couldn't see a thing on the ground.

Natalie stared ahead for a long moment before dropping back down beside him. His fingers reached into his pocket, touching his cell phone. *You promised. Don't make things worse.* He darted a glance. Although he couldn't read her expression, she didn't appear angry. *Thank you, Lord, for small favors.* If anything, she looked rather frightened.

"Are you nervous?" One look at her trembling lower lip told him that was a dumb question.

She blew out a long sigh. "Yes."

This would be the time for a hug, but she might not be receptive. He placed his hand on her arm. "Talk to me." He was sincere, but it might also score some points on the old sensitivity meter.

"I'm supposed to know these people, be good friends with these people, and I don't know if I'll feel anything. That's a scary feeling." She twisted her hands before crossing her arms.

"I suppose it's like going back to the school—having to relearn names, personalities—basically starting from scratch." Squeezing her arm, he gave her a smile of reassurance.

Her expression registered surprise. "Thanks for trying to understand." She turned her head, blocking any further conversation. One compliment at a time must be her quota.

"I think it's okay to get up now." It felt good to stand and stretch.

As soon as the words were out, Natalie hopped out of her seat again. Reaching above to the overhead compartment, she startled as he stepped into the aisle and unlatched the lock. "I'll get it. You just had the one carry-on, right?" She nodded as he retrieved both their bags. Standing so close, he felt her warmth, and the familiar longing stirred inside. For a moment, he allowed his gaze to brush over her eyes, her nose, her mouth. Her eyes met his, but lowered first.

He cleared his throat, breaking the spell. "Let's go meet Sam and Lexa." Daring to put his hand on the small of her back, he cringed when he felt her back stiffen, even through her fifty layers of clothing. Following the steady stream of passengers into the main terminal, a smile upturned his lips.

Sam Lewis stood out in the small crowd, especially with that black Stetson. Lexa stood beside her man, as lovely as ever. Marc leaned close as they walked. "The tall guy in the black hat is Sam, and the tiny blonde beside him is Lexa." When Natalie hesitated, her steps faltering, he propelled her forward. At least this time she didn't cringe.

"He's very handsome, and she looks like she could fit right in the palm of his hand." He heard the amusement in her voice as he waved to them.

"Natalie!" Lexa walked toward them, warm and welcoming. His wife gave them a shy smile. Not missing a beat, Lexa opened her arms and pulled her into a hug, similar to how Sam hugged him when he first arrived in Houston. "I know you might not remember us, but if not," Lexa said, a twinkle in her eye as she winked at him, "you'll get to know us all soon enough."

"To know us is to love us." The warmth in Sam's tone was equal to his hug as he enveloped Natalie in a quick embrace before shaking hands with him. "Nice to see you again. Glad you could make it. Let's go get your luggage."

It was hard to ignore the admiring stare Natalie gave Sam. The man had an aura about him, a presence hard to define but impossible to ignore. Kind of like some of his star clients. Only they knew people looked at them in awe, and expected it. Sam was either oblivious or didn't give a whit.

"They're all here, Natalie's closest friends from TeamWork," Sam said. "Except for one young man who's working through some personal issues." A hint of sadness tinged that deep voice and a shadow crossed Sam's face as they waited by the baggage carousel, but it was gone a moment later, replaced by his customary smile.

"How did you manage that?" Marc asked. The man was a miracle worker.

"It was the Lord's doing. Can't take the credit," Sam said.

Humble, too. Telling Sam he needed to reclaim Elwood, Marc departed. When he returned a few minutes later, Elwood barked and jumped around inside his carrier.

"Who's this little guy?" Lexa asked, peering inside. "Hey there, little fella. He's so cute." Tilting his furry head, Elwood piped down and graced Mrs. Lewis with his best impression of a downtrodden mutt.

"Traitor," Marc muttered under his breath. "This would be Elwood Thompson."

Sam laughed. "My wife attracts all the guys. Let me guess, *Blues Brothers?*"

"Exactly. Natalie named him. Seems to fit. Let me take him outside for a few minutes so he can get out his aggression for being subjected to that long trip. I thought it might help Natalie to bring him. I hope that decision wasn't a mistake."

"Based on Lexa's reaction, I don't think it is. The women will love having him around."

Marc nodded. "Be back in a few minutes."

Thankfully, Elwood relaxed once he exercised on his leash. Shivering in the cold, he tugged his jacket tighter around his neck, crossed his arms over his midsection and prayed under his breath. *This had better be worth the trip, Lord.*

Their bags were sitting at Sam's boot-covered feet as he walked back into the baggage claim area. "Is Natalie okay, Marc?"

Glancing over to where she was engaged in conversation with Lexa, Marc sighed. "Physically, she's fine." Sam wasn't talking about the amnesia, but he wasn't willing to get into anything deeper. He couldn't open the floodgates now, or there might be no stopping him. It wasn't the time or the place.

"Forgive me for being direct, but I sense some pretty bad tension between the two of you." That piercing gaze shot straight through him. This man was most likely a student of human nature, which would also explain why Lexa called him "Mr. Freud" a few times during his Houston visit.

"How can you tell?" Defensiveness was never flattering, but he couldn't help it. Sensing his stare, Natalie looked his way without so much as a glimmer of affection.

"Sorry if I offended," Sam said. "Lexa tells me I'm too direct sometimes and need to back off. I don't want to send you running in the opposite direction, especially since you've just arrived. Welcome to Montana, by the way."

"Thanks. It takes a lot to offend me. I know you want to help, and I can use your insight. Besides, you didn't tell me anything I didn't already know."

"We'll work through this thing together. I hope you'll allow me the honor of being your friend. Whatever you need, that's why I'm here."

"I appreciate it, Sam. More than you know." He didn't trust himself to look at him.

Natalie looked much more at ease as she and Lexa rejoined them.

Sam led the way out of the terminal and into the parking area. "Have you eaten lately?"

"Breakfast sandwiches this morning. Not much since. Seems the airlines aren't big into food service these days."

"That was hours ago," Lexa said. "You must be starving. Sam, let's take them to that fun little steak place we found the other night."

"Sounds like a plan." Sam stopped beside a white SUV, and opened the back door on the driver's side. "Natalie?" He made sure she was settled before doing the same for Lexa while Marc loaded their bags in the back.

Instead of seating Lexa in the back with Natalie, as expected, he put her in the passenger seat. Stepping to one side of the SUV, Marc could tell Natalie wasn't pleased, judging by her continuing frown. Marc blew out a sigh as Sam came around to the back of the SUV. "Thanks a lot." It was muttered under his breath, not intended to be heard. When Sam laughed, Marc cocked a brow and gave him a wry look. "I hope you realize you're making me look bad here."

"Don't worry. When I'm done with you, you're going to smell like a rose," Sam said, closing the back of the SUV as Marc picked up Elwood's carrier to put in the back between the two of them. As if they needed any more barriers, but it was the only place it would fit.

Sam regaled them with the history of some of Helena's landmarks as they exited the airport and headed out on the highway. Marc only heard every other word, but at least they were fun, interesting facts.

Lexa beamed. "Can you tell my husband's a history buff?"

Natalie used to look at him like that. Not that she'd remember. Settling back into the backseat of the car, disgruntled, Marc leaned one elbow on the armrest and stared out the window at the snow-covered ground. Even though he was used to snow in Boston, it made him feel cold all over thanks to the freeze-out going on in the back seat. A few miles down the road, he caught Sam watching him in the rearview mirror. Their eyes met and held. Unsure whether to be grateful or irritated, Marc shifted and turned his head. He had a pretty good feeling Sam knew what was going through his mind. The man had him pegged already.

A short time later, the foursome sat in a cozy booth at a steakhouse outside the city. Lexa told them it was a twenty-minute drive to their final destination of Milestone Ranch. Marc hadn't told Natalie the name of the ranch, and she looked vaguely amused.

"Natalie, tell us about your work at the kindergarten," Lexa said as their salads were delivered. After Sam asked the blessing, Natalie answered their questions. Watching them draw her into the conversation, Marc was grateful for this couple's sensitivity, especially since she'd clammed up after being forced to sit beside her husband.

"Can you tell me a little bit about the past TeamWork missions in San Antonio?" Natalie asked as the server delivered the main course. Both Sam and Lexa entertained them with amusing stories of how Lexa defied his orders not to work at the worksite on Sundays, resulting in a stand-off with a pesky armadillo. They learned about the kidnapping attempt and adventure they shared toward the end of their time together at the memorable TeamWork camp three years before. He'd never heard that story before, and Natalie showed no signs of recollection.

"I'll say one thing," Marc said, shaking his head, "life is never dull with Lewis and Clarke."

Natalie's eyes widened. "Clarke is your maiden name?" She grinned when Lexa nodded. "Lewis and Clarke. Seems very fitting."

Sam intertwined his fingers with his wife's. "We were destined to be together the moment she called me Sam Clarke by mistake—right after she'd fallen off the top of one of the houses we were building and I caught her."

"In more ways than one. I still can't believe I did that." Lexa shook her head with a sheepish grin.

"Calling me the wrong last name or falling off the house?"

"Both." She leaned her head against Sam's broad shoulder. "My only excuse is that I was knocked off-kilter by your overwhelming presence."

Sam smiled and grunted. "So, Marc. Your turn. Tell us more about what's happening with your agency these days. What impressive new clients have you signed?" While they ate, Marc told them about a few of his major ad campaigns, past and present.

"I'm sure you're a wonderful boss," Lexa said after he told them of his plans for an upcoming Christmas ski outing he'd planned in Maine for his entire staff.

"Those people are my lifeblood," Marc said. "Without them, I wouldn't be able to survive, professionally speaking. They're creative, supportive and loyal, and I couldn't ask for more. They give above and beyond, and definitely more than I deserve. They're a great team, and I thank God every single day for them."

"You must be very proud of him, Natalie," Lexa said, darting a quick glance his way.

"I am. Marc works hard and definitely deserves his success." Natalie avoided looking at him, but it was a nice compliment and shot a thrill of adrenaline straight through his system. It also gave him hope. Freezing cold temperatures or not, Montana was already starting to grow on him.

Chapter 22

*S*AM SAT ACROSS from Marc in the kitchen of the main house later that evening, sharing coffee. Exhausted from the trip, Natalie had retired to the women's cabin an hour earlier. The other ladies had been kind and welcoming, doing their best to make her feel comfortable. For that, he was grateful, although he found it difficult to hide his irritation she hadn't bothered to tell him good night. The slight angered him, but he knew he was being selfish. It had been a long trip, and she was pregnant, after all.

They talked sports for a few minutes before Sam hit him with the question he knew he wanted to ask all along. "Is there something in particular that's happened between the two of you to cause this frostiness?"

Marc sighed. He wasn't eager to reveal everything on their first night at the ranch, even though he trusted Sam. "Suffice it to say something . . . more like someone . . . from my past resurfaced the other day. Now we're both fighting a ghost."

Sam stirred his coffee before taking a sip. "Ghosts are dangerous, but they can be banished instead of sticking around to haunt."

"What are you, some kind of modern-day prophet?" Marc kept his tone light, teasing.

Sam snorted. "Hardly. Don't put that label on me or I'll sorely disappoint you. Are you tempted by this ghost?"

It was uncanny how this man could read his mind even though he spoke metaphorically. Sam was no fool. The TeamWork leader was with him every step of the way. "The only ghost I'm tempted by is the ghost who looks me in the eye with absolutely no idea who I am, what we had, what we were and where we need to be again."

Sam waved his hand. "Enough with this ghost talk. Does this woman from your past have a name?"

"Ashley."

Sam lowered his coffee mug. "Is Ashley a threat to your marriage, Marc?"

His head snapped up. "No. It was over about a year before I met Natalie."

"I'm listening, if you feel like talking about it. Your choice." Sam sat back in his chair, hands behind his head.

"It happened a few days ago. On one of the worst days possible."

"That's usually the way it works."

True enough. "We'd been to our first ultrasound, saw the baby and heard her heartbeat. It was incredible. We were on top of the world."

"So, you're having a girl." A grin creased Sam's lips. "Congratulations."

"We don't know for sure. It's just a strong . . . intuition or whatever . . . but Natalie and I both feel the same way. Of course, we'll be thrilled with a boy, too. After her accident, I'm just thankful she didn't lose the baby, and everything seems to be progressing normally."

Sam nodded. "Good to hear it. I didn't mean to interrupt. Please go on."

Marc fiddled with the handle of his mug, avoiding Sam's gaze. "It all came crashing down around us in one of Boston's finest restaurants. I'd taken Natalie there to celebrate. But what should have been a happy occasion . . . well, it turned into something entirely different."

"So, I take it you had a close *personal* relationship with Ashley?"

"Yes." Marc met Sam's eyes. Might as well spill it since this man already suspected the nature of his past liaison. "In every sense of the word." He paused, grateful Sam showed no condemnation. It would be hard to really open up if this godly man seemed judgmental. "Seeing Ashley only made me wish I could relive certain periods of my life. Maybe I wouldn't be so stupid, wouldn't make the same mistakes."

Sam shifted his position and sipped his coffee. "What periods of your life?"

"When I played minor league ball for three years, for one."

"You did? Where?" Sam sat up straighter and looked intrigued.

"Pawtucket."

Those blue eyes widened. "You played on the farm team for the Sox?"

Marc nodded, smiling. "Yep."

Sam whistled under his breath. "I'm impressed. Ever get called up to the majors?"

"Nope."

"Still, that must have been an awesome experience. Something for a lifetime, really. Every kid's dream." Sam grinned a little. "If it weren't so blasted cold here, I'd form a softball team and sign you up as captain."

Marc allowed a small smile. "I have some great memories, yes, and it was an incredible experience in a lot of ways, but it was the memories on the field and in the clubhouse that were sweet. Off the field, I wasn't such a nice guy. I met Ashley my sophomore year on the team. Suffice it to say she liked ballplayers. Liked them a *lot*. I was a player, and I'm not just talking about on the baseball diamond."

"How long have you known the Lord?"

"My closest associate at the agency, Trevor, got saved a few years ago. He led me to Christ about a year before I started dating Natalie."

"So, about the same time you stopped seeing Ashley."

Marc took a sip of his coffee. "Right. A couple of weeks after, as a matter of fact."

"And was it *your* decision to break it off with her?"

Not understanding how that mattered, he nodded. "Choosing to quit baseball was the first step toward finding my new career and starting the agency. That's when I said good-bye to the relationship. I needed a new start, a different life. Finding the Lord was the most important step in connecting with Natalie. But marrying her is the best thing I've ever done." He faltered, a lump lodging itself in his throat. "Natalie's everything I hoped for in a wife." Marc shook his head, the smile fading. "Enter amnesia." He fixed his gaze on Sam. "And now she's expecting our child, and to tell you the truth, I'm scared to death."

"Of what, exactly?"

Marc sat back in his chair and blew out a long sigh. "Of losing her forever. But like we talked about in Houston, this is about more than fear of failure. She makes me better, softens my rough edges, like you said about Lexa. She gives me great ideas and unique insights for some of my ad campaigns, even though Natalie inherently despises the idea of advertising. His shoulders slumped and he ran a hand across his brow. "Things were finally going great in reconnecting with her, but running into Ashley stirred up trouble."

"Define 'running into.'"

Marc sighed. "I should have forgotten about manners for once and walked away, and it's to my detriment that I didn't." He looked up, meeting Sam's eyes. "Ashley kissed me, Sam, but I assure you it was one-sided. I need you to believe me on that point."

"Why wouldn't I?" Sam held his gaze steady.

He nodded. "Thanks. I appreciate that. To complicate matters, Natalie found a note from Ashley in the pocket of my jacket while we waited at the airport. A very to-the-point note that left no doubt about the nature of my relationship with her. I hadn't worn that jacket in a few years and forgot all about that stupid note." Marc shook his head. "I can't figure out why God would bring us close together again, and then allow something like this to happen. I'd like to hear your theory on that one."

Sam leaned closer. "Fair enough. The Lord has a way of taking care of us even though we don't ask. In your case, He knew the truth needed to come out. It was no accident or coincidence that you ran into Ashley, Marc. If you weren't going to tell Natalie of your own volition, He made sure it happened. She probably needs a little space, as much as anything, to adjust."

"Yeah, well, Montana's the place for that." He couldn't keep the sarcasm out of his tone. "But it's not why I brought her here." Sam was probably right although he hadn't looked at it that way. Still, it was only the first night at the ranch. Enough confessions for one night. The rest could wait. "Thanks for not judging me."

"It's not my place. You're my brother in Christ. Sometimes it's hard to forget the past, but you have to remember your slate was wiped clean. Before you go back to your cabin, let's pray together—for you, for Natalie, for the Lord's guidance in bringing the two of you back to one another. Like I said, we've got ourselves a mission of a different type here in Montana."

Bowing his head, Marc's eyes stung with unexpected tears. Sam would stand right beside him on this daunting venture to reconnect with his wife. That kind of unconditional love was humbling. As he hurried to the men's cabin a few minutes later, he wondered what lessons the Lord might have in store for him at Milestone Ranch.

Chapter 23

$\mathscr{M}$ARC'S SPIRITS WERE a bit higher as he awoke the first full morning at the ranch until he heard Sam's rousing voice welcoming everyone to their two-week mission. Sounding altogether too cheery and annoying, the TeamWork leader smiled and gave him a friendly pat on the back as they took their seats at the breakfast table. He hadn't slept well, and although he'd never admit it, he missed Elwood. He'd made sure Natalie had the dog to keep her warm. Score one for being magnanimous even though nobility didn't keep him warm at night, especially in Montana. In the winter. He ran a tired hand over his eyes, stifling a yawn.

Sam smiled and called out to the others as they made their way into the room. Seeing that most of his volunteers and a few of the ranch hands had arrived, he removed his Stetson to ask the blessing on the food and their day ahead. Like the TeamWork crew, the regular ranch hands lowered their hats and bowed their heads. Taking the plate Lexa offered, Sam helped himself to a few strips of bacon and a healthy portion of everything else. The man could pack away the food, but he obviously worked it off somewhere. Marc watched as he dished up a heaping spoonful of peaches. Catching his grin, Sam laughed. "The peach *is* God's greatest fruit, you know."

"So you say." He listened but didn't participate in the all-too-cheery bantering at the table as they ate. More than a few times, Marc's gaze strayed Natalie's way. She was quiet, but at least she was eating as she listened to the other ladies. He trained his eyes on her, willing her to look his way, but she avoided looking at him. No small surprise there.

"Give her time. You can try talking with her tomorrow," Sam said. Even though he knew the man was right, it was difficult. Confronting Natalie now would be premature. After a day or two at the ranch, her defenses might soften a bit and give him an advantage.

Finished with his breakfast a few minutes later, Marc wiped his mouth and put his napkin and silverware on top of the empty plate. "So, what wonderful work do you have planned for us today, boss?"

"Marc, buddy," Sam said, "just be thankful I didn't wake you up at four to milk the cows." Both Sam and Lexa laughed at how fast he snapped up his head. "No, my friend, you get that task tomorrow morning." Sam laughed even harder at his scowl.

What in the world have I gotten myself into here?

~

"Everyone connected with TeamWork is so wonderful, Natalie said as she worked alongside Lexa as they cleaned up in the dining hall. Everyone else had scattered to their various posts. Knowing she wanted a little time alone with Lexa, Winnie whispered on her way out the door she'd start the kids on a project until she could join them.

The other girls had been so considerate in respecting her space and not plying her with questions. "I'm sure it's hard for them, not knowing what to say because they don't know if I'll remember things . . . or even remember *them*."

Lexa handed her a clean cloth to wipe one of the long tables. "We all love you, and want to help you and Marc in whatever way we can. We can tell you our memories from the past TeamWork camps, if that helps. Or, like I told you at the airport, we can start fresh and create new memories." She smiled. "When the Lord first led me to sign up for TeamWork, I felt lost, too. Even though it's not the same thing, I still wasn't sure who I was or what I wanted in life. But the Lord knew, and He led me exactly where I needed to be."

Natalie bit her lip, her eyes filling as she stopped wiping the table. Lexa was so nice, and she felt drawn to her.

Noticing her tears, Lexa was at her side in a second, one hand on her arm, the other lightly touching her back. "Talk to me if it helps."

"Trust me, I've had a few meltdowns over all this. I start feeling sorry for myself, but then I realize how blessed I am. I've met people who had to start over again as though they're babies, relearning how to walk, talk, feed themselves . . . everything." She sniffled and wiped her eyes with the back of her hand. "It's just so hard." Collapsing into one of the wooden chairs at the table, Natalie found it difficult to focus through her tears. "I'm married to a gorgeous man whom I truly want to love, but I don't remember him and what we shared together before I fell down those basement steps." She started to rise. "I shouldn't be telling you this."

Lexa pushed her back down with a gentle, but firm, hand. "Yes, you should. I think you *need* to tell me, at least while you're here in Montana. You're obviously burdened. Have you had someone back in Boston to share all this with?"

"My mom and sister came to help. They're great, but no one really knows what it's like. My psychologist gives me suggestions, but he's not a close, personal friend. I have friends at the school where I teach, but I don't really remember them. My roommates listen, but even though they pray for me, they can't understand, either." She shot a helpless look as Lexa dropped into the chair beside her. "Like you said, the Lord knows what we need for our heart, and maybe that's why He led us here to Montana with you, Sam and the Teamwork crew." She laughed a little and dabbed at her eyes with the tissue Lexa pulled from her pocket and handed over. "Maybe I should ask the doctor if there's a support group for people like me. *Amnesiacs 'R' Us*, or something like that." She lifted her shoulders in a shrug. "I guess it's pointless to talk about a life we can't even remember."

Lexa hugged her tight. "Let us be your support group. Winnie, Rebekah, Amy and Cassie, and all the TeamWork men. Natalie, you *will* work through this."

She mustered a wan smile. "I hope you're right."

Lexa smiled. "Of course, I am. Ask Sam. He says it all the time." Those blue-green eyes looked so wise, but she couldn't be any older than thirty. She possessed a rare serenity and calm, no doubt derived from her strong faith. "That smile looks much more like the Natalie I know. She's coming back, you know."

Natalie leaned closer as Lexa supported her chin with one hand and dabbed beneath her eyes with another tissue. "You think she's really in here somewhere?"

"I know she is."

She sniffled, wishing she felt as confident as Lexa sounded, wanting to cling to those words. "Besides, it's not like we can expect God to work miracles in two weeks."

Lexa's smile was mysterious. "Then again, why not?"

~

At the end of the first full day working the ranch, Marc ached everywhere, all the way down to his bones. He could say one thing with certainty—working himself to exhaustion was one way to keep his thoughts trained on something other than his situation with Natalie. He wasn't sure whether she was more mad or sad. Maybe it was a combination of both. After avoiding him at breakfast, by the time he arrived for lunch, she'd already departed with the other women, except for Lexa and Cassie.

The TeamWork leader did his part to keep him busy. As he worked, Marc got to know the other men—Kevin Moore, Dean Costas and Eliot Marchand. They worked together with the foreman, Clifford Mason, and the ranch hands, getting to know them and following their direction to repair broken fences, feed and herd the cattle and sheep, and exercise the horses. It was good, solid work and therapeutic for the soul.

He hadn't done so much physical labor since training for the Sox. Could it be the Lord prepared him for life on the ranch with his recent spurt of exercise at his Boston fitness center? While he definitely wasn't as fit, he could more than handle his weight around the ranch. It also increased his appetite. He embarrassed himself by how much he ate at dinner until Eliot told him how many pieces of chicken *he'd* consumed.

Natalie was tired, and didn't show up for dinner. He asked Lexa to fill a plate and intended to take it to her himself until Winnie told him she'd do it. He didn't like it, but reluctantly agreed. Maybe it was best he didn't talk with Natalie when he wasn't in top form, anyway. Barely keeping his eyes open during Sam's thankfully brief devotional in the dining hall, he trudged back to the cabin with the other guys.

"I don't know about you, but I've never been so tired." Marc stifled another yawn as he and Kevin collapsed on adjacent bunks in the men's cabin. He craved sleep, especially since he was expected to rise at the unearthly hour of four the next morning—as Sam reminded him no less than three times during the course of the day. God Himself probably still rested at that hour. From what the other guys told him, Sam's tenacity was legendary. That and his devotion to his wife.

"Are you married, Kevin?" Marc crawled under the covers and pulled the heavy woolen blanket over his chest. He hadn't noticed a wedding ring, but hadn't really looked.

"No. I'm hoping, though." Kevin gave him a rather sly grin.

Propping himself on one elbow, Marc surveyed the other man who looked to be a few years younger. "Maybe I should be asking if you have a girlfriend."

"No. I'm hoping, though," Kevin repeated, laughing, pulling his thermal sleeping shirt over his head and crawling under the covers.

"Anyone I know?" Somehow, Marc suspected something was going on—or about to be going on—between Kevin and the lovely Rebekah Grant.

Kevin turned his head to look at him. "You noticed?"

Marc laughed aloud. "How could I *not* notice? Your tongue was practically hanging out."

Kevin winced and scratched his head. "Was I that obvious? I'm going to have to watch myself."

Maybe he shouldn't have phrased it that way. "Tell me about it, if you want." Reclining, Marc crossed his arms behind his head and released a sigh, settling on the pillow. "I'm a good listener." Kevin was private, quiet. Total opposite from his own temperament. He'd seen how much Sam depended on him and trusted his judgment. This guy seemed about as solid, straight-arrow, true-to-the-Lord as you could get.

"I'm sure you've noticed how gorgeous Rebekah is, but doesn't even know it," Kevin said.

All true. The woman could be a fashion model, based on looks alone, but in a prettier, softer way. Marc nodded.

"I've watched her for a few years now, at the various work camps, and gotten to know her. There's something between us, but I'm too shy for my own good."

"Only way to get to know her is if you stick your neck out and give it a shot. Beautiful women are often lonely on Saturday nights." Marc shot him a tired grin. "Don't you live near her? You're both from Louisiana, right?"

Kevin nodded. "I live a half-hour away from where she and Josh grew up. Rebekah still lives there and teaches third grade."

"I take it Josh is Beck's brother?"

"Oh, sorry. I didn't realize you might not have heard about Josh. He's actually Rebekah's twin."

Marc didn't bother to cover his surprise. A male version of Rebekah Grant? That he'd like to see. "Does Josh usually work the TeamWork camps, too?"

"When he can." Kevin hung his head a minute, and Marc propped himself on one elbow again. Something wasn't right.

"What gives? Is something wrong?" Marc said.

"Sorry. I can tell Sam's still grieving over what happened with Josh." Kevin's eyes met his. "Sam threw him out of the TeamWork camp—Lexa's first work camp, and we haven't seen him since. Lightning strikes started a fire in a couple of the houses we were building that summer. Josh stayed behind with Sam to make sure the fires were out and when they got back to the camp, Josh said something that got him all fired up, and Sam flew at him and pounded him. Then Josh started fighting back. I broke up the fight, and the next thing we knew, Josh was gone."

Marc's eyes widened. It was hard enough to believe Kevin Moore told him that much. But Sam in a fist-fight with another man? Especially with one of his TeamWork guys? It didn't seem possible. "Do you know what started the fight?"

Kevin blew out a breath. "You might as well know, especially since you're part of the TeamWork family."

At least he hadn't said *now that you married into the TeamWork family*. These people were great, and it was gratifying to see how they'd welcomed and embraced both he and Natalie since coming to Montana. He snapped to attention as Kevin's voice broking through his musing.

"Josh is a good guy—a great guy—but he had some . . . moral issues. From what Rebekah tells me, he's doing fine and has done a lot of relief work in the aftermath of Hurricanes Mitch and Floyd. He graduated from law school ahead of schedule, and he's a rising associate at a top firm in Baton Rouge." He shook his head. "I think there's a part of Josh that's too embarrassed to come back to TeamWork. I'm praying he will someday. I know that's Sam's prayer, too."

Kevin didn't sound judgmental. Josh must be the man Sam referred to when he spoke of the volunteer not currently with them because he was working through his own issues. He'd glimpsed the deep sadness in Sam's eyes, and couldn't imagine what it must have taken to throw Josh out of his TeamWork camp.

"So, Josh turned a bad situation into one for good."

Kevin nodded. "He's a winner. He'll overcome it and be all the stronger. I feel sure Josh will come around eventually. I know the whole situation still weighs heavily on Sam's mind, especially since he and Rebekah have always been very close."

Marc stretched back out on the bed. "I don't know Sam well, but I can just imagine." Another yawn escaped. "I think that's enough of a bedtime story for one night." His voice was raspy with exhaustion. "Just answer one question."

"Sure." Kevin looked over at him.

"I've noticed how everyone else calls her Beck, but you call the lovely Miss Grant by her given name. Is there a reason for that?"

A wistful look crossed Kevin's face. The guy really had it bad. "Beck's too masculine a name for such a beautiful woman. She'll always be Rebekah to me."

"Makes perfect sense," Marc said, turning over and pulling the blanket to his chin again. "Good night. Sweet dreams, buddy."

"You too."

Thankfully, he didn't have any trouble falling asleep . . . until he was awakened by Sam looming over him and tapping him at precisely four o'clock in the morning. Rolling over, Marc willed him to go away, leave him alone. Even more annoying, Sam pulled a chair close to his bunk and whistled "Great Is Thy Faithfulness" under his breath, low enough not to wake the other men, but loud enough to get under his skin. He came to Montana to win back his wife, not participate in torture disguised by another name.

Chapter 24

$\mathcal{D}$OWN ON HIS haunches, Sam observed Reagan closely. Marc clamped one hand over his mouth, swallowing his third yawn in less than a minute. Would he ever catch up on his sleep? "Sam, tell me something. Why is this cow named Reagan?"

"I imagine because the owner of this ranch, Simon Tucker, is a staunch Republican. Cows usually have names like Maybelle or Clover. Now, Reagan— you don't forget that name."

"True enough. What was her mother's name? Nixon? Eisenhower? Truman . . . wait, he was a Democrat." Marc chuckled. "Care to tell me why we're standing here staring at her? I thought the whole reason you so rudely awakened me at this unearthly hour was to milk her."

"Not Reagan. I think she's going to be giving birth in the near future."

Marc's eyes grew wide. "Are you serious? As in *this* morning?"

"I don't joke about childbirth. Or calf birth, in this case." Sam rose to his feet, hands on his hips, but he looked stoic. "We'd better leave Reagan and go about our business. We'll milk the others and check on her periodically. Let's give her time to let nature take its course."

"Shouldn't we call in a vet? Surely they have lots of those here in Montana."

"I'll radio Lexa and have one on standby, but from what Simon told me, things pretty much naturally take their course."

"Simon says, huh?" Sam ignored his attempt at humor, and Marc waited while he called his wife, following as he led the way to another stall.

"Cliff went into Helena for the morning, and the other ranch hands are scattered, but I think we'll be fine. I'm sure Reagan is probably more calm than we are," Sam said.

Marc let out a short laugh as he read the name on the stall in front of him. "Ike. Of course."

Sam pulled over two short, wooden stools and buckets. It was rather comical to see such a tall man seat himself on that stool so low to the ground and position his legs.

"I thought there were machines to do the milking."

"Some dairy farms and ranches have machines, yes, but here at the Milestone Ranch, we do it the old-fashioned way. By hand." Sam grinned when Marc raised a skeptical brow. "They've put us in charge of the four cows here in this area." He waved his hand to encompass the nearby stalls. "Except for Reagan, they'll get milked twice a day for maximum production. We'll switch off milking duties with the other guys. That way, everybody's happy."

"Right. I'm sure you'll be more than happy to remind me when I'm on the schedule." Marc removed his gloves and settled himself on the stool and gaped at what looked like a very full udder. Putting one hand on Ike, he smoothed his hand over her, gradually moving down. When he touched the udder, he was surprised by its heaviness. "I think Ike's more than ready." Scooting closer, Marc pushed up the sleeves of his jacket as best he could and blew on his hands. "I like a challenge. Tell me what to do."

"First, you'll need to massage the udder to get her ready and relax her muscles." Laughing, Sam shot him a wry grin. "Don't even say anything, buddy."

Marc howled. The man already knew him well. "Wouldn't think of it."

Sam demonstrated how to properly clamp the teat between his thumb and the rest of his hand, squeezing with firm, gentle pressure in order to coax a steady flow of milk from the massive beast.

Once he got the rhythm, Marc alternated hands and kept at it. "If only Natalie, not to mention my employees, could see me now." He'd either be a hero or a laughing stock. In less than a minute, he was rewarded by the sound of milk squirting against the metal bucket. Who'd have thought getting up in the middle of the night could be so gratifying?

"If this doesn't bond the two of us, I don't know what will." The corners of Sam's mouth dipped a little. "Watch it. You're pulling down. That'll stretch her out."

"Oh, sorry." Marc concentrated on his task-at-hand, as it were.

"Isn't this the life?" Sam shot him a sly grin a few minutes later. "Beats sitting in an office, wouldn't you say?"

"Sure. For two weeks, anyway." After thirty minutes, Sam switched stalls to milk another cow—no doubt with a Republican presidential name—and told him he'd go check on Reagan.

"What's next, boss?" Marc asked a short time later, rolling his shoulders to ease out a few remaining morning kinks caused by hunching over an udder with intense concentration. Eyeing the buckets at his feet, he was pleased with the results of his efforts.

"Time to gather the eggs in the henhouse," Sam said.

Marc frowned. "I can hardly wait." Sam shot him an amused look as they left their buckets of milk for the other men to retrieve and take wherever they needed to go next. Leading the way out of the barn, Sam stepped around to the back. Following close behind, Marc stopped short. Clucking like the stuff of nightmares made him dizzy and the overpowering stench filled his lungs. Goodness, it was enough to fell a grown man. He wasn't sure whether to gag, hold his nose or laugh. Maybe he should multi-task and do all three. He shuddered, both from the cold and the smell. Maybe he'd freeze to death and wouldn't have to worry.

He watched as Sam demonstrated, trying not to breathe in, coughing a few times as his friend retrieved eggs and placed them with extreme care in the wire basket. As he tried his hand at it, one of the pesky mothers was feisty and wouldn't let him close. "Move it, will you? Come on, sweetheart," Marc said. "I've got enough trouble with human females. Don't give me a hard time." He jumped when he heard a loud call behind him, and tossed a quick glance over his shoulder. A rooster stared him down with its beady eyes and spread its wings.

"Take it easy," he said, withdrawing his hand, backing away, ignoring Sam's chuckle. The man might find it entertaining, but he'd like to keep his hand.

"Don't mind Charlie," Sam said. "He's the proud cock of the flock defending his harem, but he's harmless. That's his way of showing off, and how he courts the hens."

"Even so," Marc muttered, wiping his hand on his jeans, "I think I'll skip this coop. It's all yours." Moving down the row, he listened as Sam explained the pecking order.

"It's nature's way of determining which bird eats or drinks first. A chicken goes before any bird it can peck, and follows any bird that can peck *it*."

"Interesting theory. Guess that's where the expression 'hen-pecked' came from." Something about getting up in the middle of the night must make him punchy. "Tell me something, Sam."

"What's that?" Sam already had an impressive stack of eggs in his basket.

"How on God's green earth do you know how to do almost everything? If I didn't know better, I'd say you're on the next space shuttle."

Sam stopped, giving him a startled look.

"You're *not*, are you?"

"No, but Will's in the NASA training program now. There's already speculation he might be chosen as a shuttle commander." Sam's pride in his younger brother's accomplishments was obvious, but his eyes held a sadness when he talked about him. Something was there, but it wasn't his place to push.

Marc smiled. "Glad to hear Will made it. You knew he would. That's great. So, tell me, exactly how many other Lewis dynamos *are* there in the world?"

Sam laughed. "Six of us total, three female, three male. Trust me, there's a whole slew of stuff I can't do, and have absolutely no concept how to do. A lot of it is pure instinct, the rest the good Lord's leading."

As they worked, Marc threw Sam a sidelong glance. "So, ever help a cow in childbirth before?"

"No, this will be a first. Like I said, it's supposed to come naturally. I'm hoping everything will go smoothly, and we can stand nearby and watch the miracle happen without having to intervene."

"I hope you're right. Now, if we've got most of the eggs, I suggest we get out of here. I can't take much more of the henhouse, and Charlie's looking at me kind of funny."

Sam threw his head back with the force of his laughter. "This way," he said, telling him to leave the eggs for one of the ranch hands to collect. As Sam disappeared back into the barn, Marc lingered behind, marveling at the sheer

140

massiveness of the structure. Solid and sturdy. He shivered from the cold, and rubbed his hands together, blowing on them for warmth.

"I think it's time! Get in here, Marc," Sam called. "I might need you."

The panic in Sam's voice couldn't be good. He rushed to his side, wondering how he could help. Bent over Reagan, Sam wiped the back of his hand on his brow. "I think she's in some kind of trouble." He chewed his lower lip, one hand on the large animal, moving in slow circles. "She's straining." Marc followed where Sam pointed to a large opening in. the creature. "If something doesn't happen soon, we're going to have to help her."

Calling in the vet might be good, but Sam apparently wanted to handle this on his own. "What do you want me to do?" Marc asked.

Sam leapt to his feet and grabbed a chain looped over the wooden post in the corner of Reagan's stall. "I'm afraid the calf might be breach. We may need the chain to give her a little help. That's what Cliff recommended if we ran into trouble."

Marc raised a brow, not willing to ask how a chain would facilitate matters. The set of Sam's mouth was grim. They both stood, not speaking, watching Reagan—feet planted apart, arms crossed. He wasn't sure how to pray in circumstances like this, but pray he did. Standing beside him, his head bowed, Sam did the same.

When a rush of water flowed out of Reagan a few minutes later, Sam breathed a huge sigh of relief. "Thank the Lord. That was dicey. It shouldn't be long now, although I understand the birth can happen anytime between two minutes up to two hours." He glanced over at him. "Now we wait, but you might want to remove your jacket. It could get a little messy."

With reluctance, Marc slipped out of his jacket as Sam did the same. Reagan gasped and jerked from side to side. Fear struck his heart, remembering Shep dying in the street all those years ago. Maybe that's why he unconsciously hadn't wanted another animal . . . until Elwood. "Can you tell what's happening? Is she okay?"

"It's normal. Those are her contractions." Sam placed a steady, comforting hand on the large creature, murmuring soothing endearments as he patted her in an attempt to keep her calm. His ministrations had the desired effect when Reagan quieted and laid her head back against the pillow of hay, stretched out in the stall. "From what I can tell, it looks like she's almost there. I don't want to try palpating a cow, but I think we're getting close."

Marc leaned closer, fascinated. "I don't know a blessed thing about palpating, and don't *want* to know, but I think I see something." They waited a couple more minutes, shoulder-to-shoulder, marveling at the natural progression of events as they caught glimpses of the little one about to emerge. The cow moved from side to side again, rocking in a back-and-forth motion. It wasn't long before even stronger contractions rocked the massive beast. In a few more minutes, the nose of the calf peeked at him before disappearing.

Reagan's noises echoed in the barn, and Marc prayed she wasn't either in some kind of danger or extreme pain. "Shouldn't we do something to help her?" He fell to his knees beside Sam.

"No. Just watch one of God's miracles. You'll be seeing your own miracle in a few months. This is just a prelude. It shouldn't be long now."

Reagan continued the rocking motion and within another few minutes, the calf's nose emerged again and the entire lower portion of its face was visible. "Wow. Just look at that," Marc said. Another big push, and the calf's entire head emerged. He stood entranced, barely able to move a muscle. Glancing at Sam, he could tell he was equally fascinated.

Within minutes, the calf slid out in a wet rush of fluid onto the bed of hay. Sam jumped back, pulling Marc with him. It was amazing how Reagan struggled to her feet right away and began licking her calf. She cleaned her offspring multiple times before nudging the youngster. The wobbly calf struggled to stand on its spindly legs, and it wasn't long before it stood on its own.

Marc shot a grin at Sam. "So, what do you think we should name this little one?"

Sam chuckled. "Any suggestions?"

"Lincoln seems fitting." He tilted his head, studying the calf. "Can you tell if it's a boy or a girl?"

"Judging by Ike, I don't think it matters. Lincoln's a fine choice."

"I can't believe how quickly Lincoln was able to stand up. That's incredible." Brushing his hand over his shirt, Marc stared at the sticky goo and grimaced. The front of them bore the evidence of what they'd witnessed, but it was totally worth it. Smart thinking to remove their jackets. Engrossed in what was happening, he hadn't even noticed. "Now, I think we'd better go change."

Hearing soft cheers and claps, they both turned in surprise. Most of the other TeamWork volunteers stood behind the stall. Sam saluted his troops as both retrieved their discarded outerwear. "Think I'll head over to the main house to get a hug from Lexa and a strong cup of coffee. Care to join me?"

"Sure. A hug from Lexa sounds real good." They both laughed. "I'll meet you there in ten minutes." As they headed out of the barn, a hand touched his arm.

Natalie.

"That was amazing," she said.

"I didn't do anything." He shook his head.

"Yes, you did." Her eyes met his

"Reagan did it all on her own. We were there in case she needed something. Which, thankfully, she didn't."

"That's all she needed. I'm sure your presence was comforting to her." Natalie's eyes looked more yielding, and a gentle smile curved her lips.

"Sam and I are going for some coffee in the main house. Care to join us?"

"Better not. I'll talk to you later," she said in a quiet voice, hurrying away. Whether Natalie was more touched by the sight of the calf's birth or the fact that he and Sam were there for Reagan, he couldn't be sure. Pulling on his gloves and tugging his hat down over his ears, Marc smiled. In spite of the temperatures, it seemed his wife's heart might be starting to thaw.

Chapter 25

$\mathcal{S}$AM LEANED AGAINST the counter, talking with Lexa in low tones when Marc entered the kitchen. Seeing him, Sam grabbed two mugs and headed for the coffee. Lexa waved him away. "I'll get it. You and Marc sit and talk."

"That's why you're the boss." Sam smiled and dropped a light kiss on her cheek.

Looking away, Marc pushed aside his sudden pang of jealousy and focused on the clock above the sink.

Lexa carried their mugs over to the table and poured their coffee. "There's sugar on the table and I'll get the cream. Do you want something to eat, Marc? You must be hungry. I heard you two had quite the adventure this morning. They're already calling it the 'Miracle in the Barn.'"

"I'm fine, but I appreciate the offer." Unbelievable as it seemed, he wasn't hungry.

Sam dropped a spoonful of the sugar into his mug and stirred slowly. After putting the pitcher of cream on the table, Lexa quietly departed. Letting out a loud yawn, Sam stretched his arms high. "Only a day here, and you're already becoming a TeamWork legend. Good work. I'm glad you were there this morning."

Marc shook his head. "Like I told Natalie, I did nothing."

"Sometimes your presence is all that's needed."

His eyes widened. "That's exactly what she said, too."

Those smile lines deepened. "Then it must be so. It's also a good thing that she initiated the conversation."

"An encouraging way to start the day, yes. I invited her to join us for coffee, but she hurried out of the barn like a bat out of . . ." Marc stopped himself.

Sam yawned again, bypassing the comment. "It's hard to believe it's only a little after seven. Whether milking cows or rebuilding homes, when I'm at a TeamWork camp, it feels like I've already put in a full day by noon. I'm sure you'll know what I mean soon enough."

"I understand it *now*, but in a lot of ways, it's also very satisfying." The look on Sam's face confirmed his sentiment. Whether sharing about the Lord or leading a work camp, Sam thrived on what he was doing. As much as anyone he'd ever met, he was completely at ease with himself and the world.

"That's why the TeamWork camps are so challenging," Sam said. "For one thing, you never know what can happen, but every one of them is a learning experience, in a number of ways."

"I envy you, Sam." Maybe it was more admiration than envy.

Sam's eyes narrowed as he sipped his coffee. "You've got everything you've ever wanted, too, Marc. You just have to be patient a little longer." He shook his head. "I can't imagine what it's been like for you."

Marc savored the hot, flavorful brew as it slid down his throat. "To say it's frustrating is an understatement. It's like finally getting something you've always wanted, and then it's ripped out of your life without warning."

Sam shook his head. "If anyone told me right after Lexa and I married that I had to start all over again with her, I'm the first to admit I wouldn't handle it well. I'm generally not a very patient man." Sam's eyes met his. "I think that's something else we might have in common."

"I'll be honest with you, Sam."

"Please do."

Marc took a quick breath. "Because of her background and religious upbringing, she won't . . . enter into a physical relationship again. And she won't until she loves me again. *Fully* loves me, whether or not she remembers loving me the first time around. I understand, but it also cuts me to the core." His shoulders slumped. "The night I got back from Houston, she waited for me at the house. She'd prepared a special dinner and then invited me upstairs." He looked away, gathering his thoughts. "She was . . . willing, but I couldn't let her."

Sam nodded. "Neither would you want Natalie coming to you without that love in her heart. It wouldn't be the same." That deep voice resonated with compassion. "I know it's about much more than the physical longing you feel for her. Now that she's pregnant, I'm sure you feel the added pressure to reconnect."

"Exactly. As much as anything else, I want her back with me in the house." Sam would understand his deepest yearnings. "It's the house we picked out together. I don't want a child of ours going off with Natalie to some apartment. She needs to be back home, and I need to be there for both of them." Marc shrugged and shot a helpless glance across the table.

"Like I told you, I'm a pretty direct man, so I'm going to spell it out for you," Sam said. "From my perspective, anyway. Take it or leave it."

"Sure. I admire direct. Works for me. It's what advertising's all about, after all."

Sam fixed him with that piercing, blue-eyed gaze. "You need to get everything out on the table with Natalie. Based on what I've seen and heard, I can only assume you didn't tell her everything about your relationship with Ashley—or anyone else—before you married. And, that's obviously now a problem. Confess everything, be completely honest with her. That's the best way to start and move forward from here. You won't be totally free to reconnect otherwise. But tell Natalie while we're in the beginning stages of the work camp. I know it'll be hard, and please know I'm here for you in any way I can. Just as Lexa's here for Natalie."

Marc stared at the table. *Tell this man. He cares and wants to help.* "I think you know why I haven't told her." He cast his gaze downward, ashamed to look Sam in the eye, this man who was quickly becoming his mentor. He was unworthy of Natalie, aware he didn't deserve her love. Just as he never measured up to his dad, he could never measure up to her ideal of a husband.

"Marc," Sam said, leaning forward in his chair, his tone more gentle. "Natalie fell in love with the man you *are*, not the man you were. The Natalie I know is a very forgiving, loving woman. Surely she knew—at least could have guessed—that a man in your position would have had opportunities and temptations."

"Call it what it was. Like I said, I was a player. I'm not proud of it, but I was everything Natalie hated, everything she was raised to avoid. I used women for my own selfish pleasure."

"You're being too hard on yourself."

"Am I? You don't know that."

Sam sat back in his chair and blew out a breath. "Like I said, given your background, she couldn't expect you to be a saint." He settled that penetrating gaze on him again. He'd make a good cop. "If I hadn't invited the Lord into my heart when I was knee-high to a grasshopper, I don't know that I might not have given into temptation. It's everywhere. I understand."

Those last two words meant the world. As much as another man could, Sam understood his inner conflict. "Sex outside of marriage is unforgiveable in Natalie's eyes. That's why I never told her in the first place. I couldn't bear the thought of her being hurt, and the thought that she'd push me away forever."

"How do you know she won't forgive you unless you ask?"

Marc shook his head slowly, his heart sinking. "She won't forgive me, Sam."

"Well, then, it sounds like you don't trust your wife very much."

He swallowed the quick rise of anger. "How can you say that?"

"Because I've worked TeamWork missions with her. Those are experiences that reveal true character, show where the heart lies." Sam's gaze narrowed again, pinning him to the chair. He couldn't move if he wanted. "I've seen Natalie sing and rock a child to sleep while her mother lay dying of HIV in the next room."

Marc's breath caught in his throat. He never knew that, although his wife was a great humanitarian who put her faith in action.

"Natalie's raised some of the most heartfelt prayers I've ever heard, beseeching the Lord on behalf of someone she's never met. She's been a great friend and confidante for Lexa, and all the other women of TeamWork." Sam's eyes softened. "I admire how she wants to help shape young minds. She loves them unconditionally, and children respond to that love. She can reach them on a level most adults don't, either because they don't want to, or because they can't. I've seen glimpses of the nurturing mother she'll be when she takes a small child by the hand and leads them in a prayer, asking Jesus into their heart." He leaned closer. "I've seen what a great mother she is *now*."

Marc swallowed hard. "Natalie will be an incredible mother. I've always known that. She'll want to share about the Lord with our children, but sometimes I wonder exactly how the amnesia affected her faith. She says she can feel the love of the Lord, and even though she remembers certain verses of scripture, others are gone."

"I like to think the Holy Spirit takes over in cases like Natalie's. There's a basic trust she placed in the Lord in coming to Him, and He's carrying her through."

"Sounds like that 'Footprints' poem. He'll carry her, but I want to be there, too, holding her hand along the journey, or at least waiting for her on the other side." Marc's eyes misted. "I only pray she'll want me there."

Sam leaned back in his chair, his arms crossed. "You *need* to be there for Natalie *and* your baby, every single step of the way. Whether she knows it or not, she wants you beside her. Believe in that, brother." His gaze lingered. "Now, then, you know what you need to do."

"It'll hurt her. I don't want to cause her any more heartache." He hated the indecision in his voice, the hesitancy. It wasn't like him, but this was unlike any business decision. It affected his heart, not just his brain.

"Trust me, it'll cause both of you more pain in the long run if you *don't* tell her. For whatever reason, the Lord's giving you a fresh start. Grab the opportunity, be honest with her, and move on. Otherwise, you run the risk of running into another . . . ghost . . . somewhere down the road. I don't think you want to live with that fear hanging over your head."

Sam was right. "I'll talk with her, but be prepared for another long talk afterwards. I'm sure I'll need it."

Rising to his feet and coming around to stand beside his chair, Sam lowered his large hand to his shoulder. "That's why I'm here." The fingers squeezed. "Thanks for your honesty. I want you to think about something. It's not sex outside of marriage in the traditional sense. You hadn't met Natalie, weren't married, and weren't a Christian. *Big* distinction. Remember, the blood of Christ paid for your sins. Trust me, Natalie knows that, too."

His heart swelled with affection. Sam's counsel was so wise, and it was difficult to believe they were about the same age. His shoulders dropped a bit. He felt so inadequate and had so much to learn. "Thanks, Sam." Marc rose slowly from the chair, his heart beating fast. "Is Natalie in the schoolroom now, do you know?"

"I believe so. I'll be praying."

With a small salute and a nervous smile, Marc prepared to walk across the ranch to the schoolroom. In spite of the temperatures, it might be a long walk.

Chapter 26

$\mathscr{S}$TEPPING INSIDE THE schoolroom, Marc closed the door against the howling wind and rubbed his hands together. The smell of wood burning and pine permeated the room, and the warmth from the fireplace was comforting. Amy and Winnie worked in a corner with a small group of kids as he scanned the small makeshift schoolroom, but Natalie wasn't in view. A door led off from the main room. Maybe she was back there? He prayed she wouldn't be upset that he'd interrupted a teaching session. Even though it was only a temporary assignment, Natalie would approach it as seriously as her teaching position back home.

A little girl who looked to be about nine or ten with long red braids and freckles looked up from her work. Closest to the door, she sat at a table by herself, her pencil poised above her paper. Big brown eyes followed Marc as he traversed creaky wooden floorboards. When he turned and smiled, she quickly moved her head down, embarrassed to be caught gawking.

"Looks like you have an effect on little women, too." Winnie's native Texas drawl was charming from the sweet, pretty blonde nicknamed the "Mother Hen" of the group. "I'm sure you'd like to speak with Natalie."

"If she's free. Sorry to just barge in here, but it's important." He pulled off his gloves with considerable effort since they were almost frozen to his hands. Pulling off his hat, he ran his fingers through his tousled hair, smoothing it down.

Winnie's smile was understanding. "I know it is, or you wouldn't be here. I can't imagine how tough this must be for both of you." She nodded her head toward the door at the back. "Natalie and Beck took a couple of the younger boys in the other room. They were acting up, but I haven't heard a peep out of them in close to an hour. Your wife has a very calming presence."

"That she does." Marc hoped that held true in a few minutes when he spoke with her. When he winked at the little girl, she blushed ten shades of red.

"If you can wait, I'll have her come out as soon as possible. It shouldn't be long." Winnie glanced at her watch. "We have a break in a few minutes. Do you want a cup of coffee?"

"No, thanks. Just had a cup with Sam. Got enough fuel in me for now." Amy gave him a bright smile, and he waved. Lowering himself onto one of the small chairs, he teetered on the edge. Catching himself, he heard Pippi Longstocking's giggles as he righted his adult-sized frame on the kid-sized seat. "Almost missed the chair," Marc said with a sheepish grin. Glancing around, he counted six children, all belonging to the ranch hands. It looked like they were equally divided between boys and girls, but most looked to be older than kindergarten age, the age Natalie preferred to teach.

It was silent in the room except for the sounds of scribbling on papers and the popping embers in the fireplace. The girl's brow furrowed, and she appeared to struggle with a math problem. Tilting his head, Marc tried to get a good look at her paper. She looked at him and released a sigh. "You any good at multiplication and division?"

Well, that's a question loaded with irony. We're having a baby and multiplying, and yet Natalie and I are very divided.

"I'm excellent at it, young lady." He looked around and whispered, "Am I allowed to help? I don't want you to be accused of cheating."

"I think it's okay." She gave him a cute grin as he moved his chair closer. He didn't have much experience with children, but felt drawn to help her.

"I'm Marc. What's your name?"

"Ashley."

He swallowed the sudden lump in his throat. "Very nice to meet you." Of course, she couldn't be a Mary or Lisa or any other name under the sun. He couldn't even say the name aloud. *Good one, Lord. You don't need to beat me over the head.* Crouching beside her, he scanned the page and pointed to one of the math problems. "Let's start with this one." Mustering his most patient voice, he helped her work through it. Wanting her to reason it out on her own, he waited until she reached the correct answer.

Her brown eyes widened, and she started on the next one with renewed interest. It was true—knowledge was empowering. Ashley worked through it, saying each step out loud, looking at him for reassurance and encouragement. The grin of satisfaction on her face said it all. No wonder Natalie loved working with children.

"I think you've got it. Try the next problem." As Ashley began working through it, Marc heard a noise behind them and turned. Deep blue eyes met his. He rose to his feet, almost losing his balance again. "Sorry. I didn't know you were here." Ashley ducked her head with another shy smile and continued her work.

"I think you might have missed your calling." Natalie's voice was warm, her eyes equally so, warming parts of him he thought were dormant since arriving in Montana.

"I need to ask you something." With a smile for Ashley, he took Natalie's arm and steered her over to the closest corner. He felt many of the eyes in the small room on them. Catching Rebekah's attention, Marc nodded, grateful when she took the lead in engaging the other children in conversation. "I want to take you to dinner tonight. Just the two of us, away from the ranch."

She pondered the idea for a long moment. "Is something wrong? Everything okay with the agency?"

The question surprised him. "I wouldn't know. I haven't talked with Trevor since we've been here." It hadn't been as hard to keep his word as he'd thought, but better for Natalie to focus on the sacrificial aspect. "Trust me, we need to do this." He implored her with his eyes.

"Well, that's enough to get my heart pumping. You're scaring me a little bit." Reaching for his hand, Natalie squeezed it for reassurance. A good sign. Even more so since it seemed a natural reaction, instinctual.

"I'm sorry. I didn't mean to scare you. I need . . . *we* need . . . to talk."

A frown creased Natalie's brow as she released his hand. "I have to get back to the kids now, but I'll meet you by the main house at six tonight."

~

As they worked out the horses later that afternoon, Marc and Dean discussed the joys and pitfalls of starting a business and advertising revenues. A native of a small town outside San Antonio, Dean owned a small but thriving chain of leather goods stores throughout Texas. During the course of the conversation, he made an offhand comment about having to rearrange his schedule in order to attend the work camp.

Marc looked up sharply. "Aren't these camps usually planned well in advance?"

Dean's brown eyes grew wide and he blanched. "Ye-e-e-s," he said, drawing out the word. "Normally they are." Without saying more, he climbed onto one of the horses, saluted and galloped in the opposite direction.

What's that all about? Marc left the comment alone until a short while later when he strolled over to where Dean and Eliot stood together, talking in low tones. "So, this camp wasn't planned months in advance?"

"No," they said in unison, looking decidedly uncomfortable.

"Tell me something, gentlemen." A suspicion formed in Marc's mind. "Exactly how *long* have you known about this particular TeamWork mission?"

They looked at one another, making it painfully clear neither one wanted to answer.

Marc moved closer, arms crossed over his chest. "It's not really a hard question."

Kevin approached, whistling. "Hey, guys. What's going on?"

"I was asking Dean and Eliot how long they've known about this work camp. Care to answer the question for them? They seem struck by a sudden case of shyness . . . or else forgetfulness."

"Uh, well," Kevin said, the color draining from his face. Although not a man of many words, Kevin was generally much more articulate. When he glanced at the other two men, they shrugged and shot him helpless looks. Something was definitely afoot.

"Well, then, I'll get the answer from our fearless leader. I don't think Sam has either a shy or forgetful bone in his body. I think we've worked out the horses long enough, don't you?" Silent nods. "Let's round them up and take them back to the stables."

As usual, Marc spotted Sam immediately. Unless the man's head was bowed—in prayer or otherwise—he was never hard to find. As soon as possible, the other men hightailed it out of the stables. "Sam, a word, please?"

"Over here." Sam motioned to him from the nearby stall. "Did you find Natalie?"

"Yes. We're going to dinner tonight. I need to borrow a car, by the way."

"Done." He paused, studying him. "What's on your mind? Spill it."

"Something's just come to my attention. Quite frankly, I'm not sure whether to deck you or hug you."

Sam turned, his brows raised, a question in those narrowed eyes. "Care to explain that statement?" Hands finding his hips, he looked every bit the rugged cowboy.

"I understand this Montana mission wasn't planned in advance. It's something you cooked up, just a few weeks ago, as a matter of fact." The latter statement was a guess, but Sam confirmed its accuracy by the expression crossing his face.

"True enough." Sam started to walk away.

"Wait." Marc placed a hand on his arm. "Why would you do something like that?"

The TeamWork leader turned. "It's time to get a few things straight. Why *shouldn't* I do whatever I can within my power to help Natalie? Why *wouldn't* I do something to help you as a fellow brother in Christ?" Those intense eyes bore into him as Sam took a step closer. "Marc, you need to accept the fact that sometimes people help one another. Because that," he said, moving even closer, staring him down, "is what Christians do. Stick around. This is TeamWork in so many ways. Trust me, you ain't seen nothin' yet."

Nice speech. "I obviously have a lot to learn when it comes to unselfish Christian love and the TeamWork family. They go hand-in-hand. I understand that now." He looked at him with renewed admiration. "Tell me something. When I was with you in Houston, you didn't answer my question about where this work camp would be because *you* didn't know at the time. Right?"

Sam raised a brow. "Do you really need me to answer that question?"

Humbled, Marc swallowed hard. "How did you accomplish it in such a short time? Overnight? Arrange this camp, bring these people . . . ?"

Sam blew out a breath, looking into the distance before settling his gaze on him again. "I made a few select calls when you were in Houston that first night. I'd heard the Tuckers lost some of their workers for the season. They've been so instrumental to TeamWork through the years, and they put out an appeal. When you called and told us your story, and then came to Houston, I figured this was the Lord's answer. I made a few more calls to round up the troops," he said, waving his arm around the stables, "and here we are." Sam cracked a grin.

"Don't think a Texas boy, born and raised, would purposely choose to come here in the freezing cold of his own volition. My TeamWork volunteers all love Natalie, and they didn't hesitate to drop everything at a moment's notice once they knew the circumstances behind the request."

The man was really getting fired up now. Marc took an instinctive step backward.

"Look," Sam said, hands on his hips again, feet spread apart, "I'm sorry if that offends you in some way, but get used to it. If it's macho pride, or a bruised ego working against you, let it go. Just accept the fact that we're all here for you. I told you we want to help, and this is where the Lord brought us." Dropping his hands to his sides, he leaned in so close they were almost nose-to-nose. "Accept it, brother."

Marc nodded, stunned speechless before finding his voice. "I accept it with undying gratitude, Sam. You and your TeamWork crew have given us an unbelievably unselfish gift."

Sam nodded, and the beginnings of a grin slanted his lips. "Good. About time. Now, I need some help, if you're willing."

"Thought you'd never ask." As the two men walked over to another stall, Marc shot his friend a grateful glance. "I'm glad we're here. From your lips to God's ear."

Sam handed him a full bucket of oats. "Oh, I'm sure God's listening. Just make sure you stop long enough, and listen hard enough, to hear what He's whispering. That's the key."

That was enough to shut him up, and they worked in silence as they tended to the horses in separate areas of the stables. Humility didn't begin to cover how grateful he should be to Sam, Lexa and these wonderful people. Marc lowered his head and murmured a quiet prayer, keeping one eye on the horse in the stall.

~

"Sam, how do you and Lexa do it?" Marc asked a short time later.

"Do what, exactly?" Sam rotated his shoulders before hanging his steel bucket on a nearby peg, falling into step beside him as they headed out of the stables together.

With all the cold, their muscles would tense up if they didn't keep moving, so he followed Sam's example, rotating and stretching to get out the kinks. "How do you keep your marriage so . . . fresh?"

Sam laughed. "That's a loaded question. It takes work, but after all, we're still sort of newlyweds ourselves." He pulled the collar of his jacket tighter about his neck and pushed the Stetson further down on his head, covering his ears as the bitter wind blasted them full in the face. "Come with me."

Marc chuckled under his breath. Subzero temperatures aside, heaven forbid a man from Texas would wear anything on his head other than a Stetson.

Hastening his pace beside Sam, he darted a quick glance at the darkening gray sky as they made their way to the small office adjacent to the main house. Crossing the grounds, they nodded and waved to a few of the ranch hands.

Opening the door, Sam held it open and quickly ushered him inside. "Have a seat." Rubbing his hands together, he flipped the switch on the space heater near the desk.

"Yes, Captain." Marc dropped into the chair opposite the desk, relieved for the warmth inside the small, sparsely-furnished office. Shivering, he ran his hands up and down his arms.

Reaching into the middle drawer, Sam pulled out a set of keys and handed them across the desk. "Take the Pathfinder tonight. It has a full tank of gas."

"Thanks. I owe you one." Marc pocketed the keys.

"You owe me nothing. Now, you asked a question. Don't let us fool you, Marc. We have our moments. Lexa can dish it out as good as she gets, but that woman is smart. She's passionate about the Lord, she's fierce in her determination to do His work, and she's relentless in expressing her passion for me. There's nothing more I could ever ask from a wife and a solid, Christian partner."

The look on his face was intriguing. "To be honest, before the Lord brought Lexa into my TeamWork camp, I always thought I wanted a woman like *your* wife, one who'd been a Christian for a long time. But the Lord knew better. Her mother died when she was eight, and long story short, she was left on the doorstep of her faith, raised by a gruff father who wanted nothing to do with the things of the Lord."

"Well, thanks for not pursuing *my* wife, although I can't imagine why you didn't."

Sam returned his grin. "I've always been partial to blondes. Opposites attract, as proven by you and Natalie. Of course, God's providence has everything to do with it. When the Lord brought Lexa to my TeamWork camp, I learned how to look at faith through her eyes, and she taught me more than she knows. She was young in her faith, but so willing to grow and serve Him. It was one of the most beautiful things I've ever witnessed."

Marc leaned back in the chair. "Natalie's taught me a lot, too, but I'm not sure how much I'm teaching her. That's why I need to hear your pearls of wisdom." He motioned with one hand. "Carry on, oh wise one."

Sam shot him a look. "The Lord knows Natalie needs you, just as I need Lexa. Now," he said, scooting his chair closer to the desk, "I have a few personal marriage rules. I've never shared them with anyone else, and I think you could benefit from them now." He shrugged. "They're pretty much common sense, but it doesn't hurt to be reminded."

"You've got my attention."

Sam's deep smile lines surfaced and the faint lines around his eyes crinkled. "Listen carefully, and maybe you'll learn something."

Chapter 27

"OKAY, HERE GOES," Sam said. "As trite as it sounds, never let the sun go down without resolving any differences between the two of you. It was impossible to master that one with Lexa before marriage, but after, when we were sleeping in the same bed, it was much easier. If there are cross words, work it out. Pray about it, talk it out, fight it out, but do whatever you have to do to resolve it before you go to bed. Makes things infinitely easier, believe me." Sam paused and lowered his voice. "I know that's difficult with the way things are between you and Natalie right now, but do the best you can. You're doing it later tonight by going to dinner with her. Don't expect miracles, but keep praying."

"Right. Please go on," Marc said, sitting up straighter, eager to hear the rest.

"Rule number two. Always be honest with your partner, as long as it's not something that will hurt or wound her. If you feel it's something she needs to know, tell her. Don't hold back. Pray about it, and go with your gut. I'm not talking about commenting on what she's wearing. I'm talking about letting her into your heart, your soul, sharing your emotions and what you're feeling."

Marc nodded. "And number three?"

Sam grinned and straightened in the chair. "Always think of her needs first—emotional, physical or whatever. Pay close attention. Really listen if she opens up and wants to talk. Help her out around the house. Offer to help or do the grocery shopping, watch the kids down the line when you have a whole brood of them." Sam grinned as he shot him a look. "This is also where the 'in sickness and in health' part of the marriage vows come into play. Pregnancy is tough under normal circumstances, but do whatever you can to ease her discomfort." He waited a moment before continuing when Marc made no comment. "Obviously, if she's ill, do what you can to ease her pain or discomfort. Bring her food and cook it yourself. Bring her medicine, run to the store, rub her feet. You accomplish this one by putting your love into action, by demonstrating the love you have for her in physical, tangible ways."

"This is great stuff, Sam. Common sense or not, you should write it down. You'd probably make a bestseller out of it. Guys need to hear it, and women would buy the book and make sure their men read it." He grinned at the surprised look on Sam's face. "Any more rules?"

Sam's wide smile indicated he was just getting started. "I also have scripture verses that accompany each of these rules. I'll write them down and give them to you later. Okay, rule number four. Tell your partner on a daily basis how much she means to you, how much you love her. It takes more than merely showing her. Women need the verbalization of our love more than men do. Say the words, 'I love you' every single day, and mean it." He paused. "Bored yet?"

"Not a bit. Carry on."

"Next rule. Be the head of your own household, but respect your wife as your equal in all things. Actually, this one should be at the top of the list since it comes first in my own mind." Sam leaned forward, making sure he had his complete attention. "A woman can't respect a man who doesn't take charge of his own household. A *Christian* woman expects the man to be the leader of the home, both physically and spiritually. We have the God-given right and responsibility to take care of our wives and families and put them before ourselves. There's no question as to God's commands in that regard, Marc. We are to honor and respect our wives as our equals while still being strong and decisive in all things, as much as humanly possible. And, part of this rule is to pray both independently as well as together, on a daily basis."

Sam sat back in his chair, crossing his arms behind his head. "Rule six. Guard your heart, your eyes, your mind and your soul, brother. This one is tough for most men. We have to keep our focus on what's right and pure in God's eyes and turn away from all temptation, no matter the source. Temptation is everywhere. The lines between right and wrong get blurred, and sin takes root and festers. Rationalizations are made to excuse unacceptable behavior. When push comes to shove, so many make the wrong choice, even Christian men. We have to always be on guard and alert."

 Marc nodded. How well he knew the truth of that one firsthand. "There's one more rule?"

"Yes, and this one is every bit as important as all the rest. You need a place where the two of you can slip away to be alone. A secret rendezvous place, a place with no distractions, and no one else to take your attention away from your partner. For however long you need, a few hours or a few days. Focus on your wife. Listen to her, talk with her, share your thoughts, your hopes, your heart. Basically, follow all of the above rules. And then, you love her." Sam stopped, making sure he had his eye contact. "Pick your own, private definition of what that means, but take the time to *love* her."

The man made a lot of sense. "Do you and Lexa have a place here in Montana?"

A smile played about Sam's lips. "Yes, as a matter of fact." Following where he pointed, Marc spied a small, brass skeleton key hanging on a hook behind the desk. "Ever since Lexa and I married, I've scouted a location for *our place* as diligently as I've scouted the TeamWork work camps. I always rent or borrow a little cabin, or find a tent, hut, cave, tepee, sleeping bag—whatever's available." He paused, catching Marc's wide grin. "A place where I can take my wife away from everything and everyone else." A wistful expression crossed Sam's face. "Before we married, there was this pitiful tree on the west side of the camp in San Antonio. Lexa and I would meet out there late at night and share quiet time. Again, it's all about opening your heart and being totally honest with your partner."

"So, if you and Lexa disappear together, I shouldn't ask questions. I have to hand it to you, you're a very wise man. I do believe you're also the most romantic soul I've ever met."

Sam's laugh was deep and hearty. "I'm pretty much a romantic fool, but don't let it get around. I have a reputation as TeamWork leader to uphold. It'll be our secret. But, between you and me, I'll accept it as the highest form of compliment."

"Thank you. I'm really glad you, Lexa and the other TeamWork volunteers are here. Like I said, it's a true gift." He extended his hand as they both rose to their feet. Grasping Marc's hand, Sam pulled him across the desk in a big bear hug.

"Anytime, brother." Sam released him, and Marc grunted. Nothing like tearing up in front of another guy, but he wasn't surprised when he saw tears in Sam's eyes as he turned to go.

"Marc?"

Something in Sam's tone turned him back around. "Yes?"

Sam nodded his head toward the wall. "If you ever want to borrow that key, it's yours for the asking."

Heading out the door, renewed hope filled his heart. First, he had to get through dinner with Natalie.

Chapter 28

By BOSTON STANDARDS, the restaurant left something to be desired, but it boasted decent food and a nice atmosphere. Gazing across the table at Natalie, Marc made small talk, mostly about the ranch and their work. Neither one of them ate much of their dinner and pushed the food around their plates before giving up altogether. The uneasy stirring in the pit of his stomach grew increasingly persistent the longer they sat. He couldn't wait to escape so they could talk privately.

"Now that we're done with that awkward dinner, care to tell me what's on your mind?" Natalie shivered and ran her hands up and down her arms as they sat in the car outside the restaurant a short time later. Marc blasted the heat, chastising himself for his lack of foresight in warming the car like he usually did back home in Massachusetts. The frigid temperatures must have frozen his brain cells.

"I'm sorry." Shifting position, he still couldn't bring himself to look Natalie in the eye, knowing what he had to tell her might crush her. He couldn't bear to see the look in her eyes, but he knew Sam was right. If he didn't tell her, never again would he be able to fully love her the way she deserved, and the way he needed to be loved by her without pretense or anything standing between them. That second rule of Sam's about total honesty was a hard in a situation like this.

Marc struggled for the right words. He prayed his wife could find it in her heart to forgive him. Hoped she'd understand his motivation was to protect her, not keep anything from her that would eventually hurt her. Hurt *them*. Of course, most would call it cowardice.

Natalie breathed in deeply, exhaling slowly. "Marc, just tell me whatever it is so I can deal with it."

"Okay, I . . ." He faltered for an extended moment.

"You . . . what?"

He shook his head, staring at his hands as an overwhelming sadness coursed through him. Drawing in a quick breath, he closed his eyes for a split-second. *Just spit it out and get it over with.* "Natalie, I had relationships with three other women before I met you."

She blinked, but didn't look shocked. "Well, that's not surprising. I may be mad as blazes at you, but you're a very handsome man." She stared down at her hands twisting in her lap. "That's part of what makes this all so difficult for me. Having said all that, I'd be more surprised if you didn't have girlfriends before you married me."

His eyes softened as he watched her. So intelligent and sophisticated, Natalie was also an innocent. Raised in a strong Christian home, she was naïve to the ways of the world. But that was a good thing, and he adored that quality in her. *Tell her. Get up the nerve and say the words.* Marc opened his mouth, finding it extremely difficult to tell his wife the sad truth. He couldn't remember anything ever being this hard except that long ago morning when he found his mom at the kitchen table, slumped over the newspaper. He pushed the thought aside.

"I'm talking about more than girlfriends." *Oh, Lord, this is so hard.* "Physical relationships." He didn't want to look yet couldn't keep his eyes away, needing to see her reaction. She strained forward, her expression impossible to read. Praying she wouldn't ask him to repeat it, not sure he could. She didn't cry, didn't scream, didn't do anything but stare into space. Maybe it would be better if she *did* let it out. Natalie trained her focus out the front window of the SUV, her jaw tight, her chin defiant.

His heart told him what it was. Pure and simple, his wife was devastated. If she let down her guard, she'd crumple. Perhaps more than anything, it was her disappointment in him that broke his heart. He'd failed her. Not that she put him on a pedestal, but she'd admired him, and look what he'd done to shatter that trust, that faith, that admiration. Deeply ashamed, Marc couldn't face the hurt and pain in those beautiful eyes. "I can tell you once, and then we never have to speak of it again."

The laugh she let out wasn't one of mirth. It was brimming with sarcasm, barely-contained anger, and it cut him like a carving knife. "Why? So I can know who else will be carrying a part of my husband with them forever?" As she finally moved her gaze to him, meeting his eyes, she burst into tears. Hard, body-rocking, heartrending sobs. When he tried to pull her into his arms, Natalie turned aside, pushing away his hands, crying even harder. It was the most awful sound he'd ever heard other than that bloodcurdling scream the night of her fall, which now seemed so long ago. Her shoulders heaved, wracked with her anguish.

His hands poised mid-air. What could he say or do to comfort her? Rejection was a horrible, miserable feeling, especially from his wife. The seed of doubt planted itself in his mind, insidiously threading its way through his subconscious. "Please, Natalie. I need to tell you." His voice broke, ragged, and he tried to touch her, but she pulled away from him.

"Don't you touch me, Marcus Alan Thompson! This isn't a confessional. Or is it?" She glared at him, and brushed falling tears away with the back of her hand. "Tell me one thing. Did you actually love any of those women?"

"I thought I loved one of them, but what I felt for her is nothing compared to what we have, Natalie. Nothing. You must believe me." It wasn't love. It was nothing more than lust, but admitting that would only drive the stake deeper into her heart. The other two relationships lasted barely more than a few months, six at most. Most women were too clingy, unlike Natalie who made him work for everything he'd achieved in terms of their relationship. But he liked that. She was different from every other woman he'd known in all the *best* ways. The Lord changed his heart when he became a Christian, and as much as anything else, that decision made a huge impact on his relationship with her.

"Please don't tell me the one you thought you loved was Ashley what's-her-name. A milk bottle has less plastic than that woman, Marc. For the record, that note I found was from her, right? Tell me, Marc, did the *A* in that note stand for 'Ashley' or 'Adulterer'?"

He hung his head. "Yes, if you must know, the note was from Ashley. It was from a time when I was young and incredibly stupid. She threw herself at me, and, at that point in my life, I couldn't resist." As soon as the words were out, he realized it was the wrong thing to say.

"Oh, so it was all her fault, was it? Last time I checked, it takes two." She hesitated. "Did I know all this before we were married?"

That was the dreaded question, the one he prayed she wouldn't ask. The one that could make—or break—them forever. *Please, Lord. Let her forgive me so we can get past this.*

"I repeat, did I know this before we were married?" Her words were slow, purposeful, and her voice rose with barely-contained anger. Mixed with unbearable hurt.

"No." His pulse throbbed, pounding in his ears, pulling him down even further into the abyss of self-loathing and desperation.

"You *lied* to me?" Unmistakable betrayal laced her words as Natalie dropped her eyes.

In that moment, he hated himself all over again for doing this to her. "In my misguided thinking, I thought I was protecting you. I love you so much, Natalie, and I wanted you as my wife more than I needed my next breath. I know the Lord brought the two of us together for a reason, but I couldn't risk losing you. There seemed no reason to tell you because those relationships were in my past, over long before we met. More than anything else, I couldn't bear the thought of not claiming you as my wife." His voice broke again as his shoulders slumped. "I couldn't bear the failure."

"So we've been living a lie, and you'd rather stick it out with a woman who is—for all intents and purposes, your wife in name only right now—because Marc Thompson can't face failure." Shaking her head, Natalie turned away in disgust. "When are you going to get over yourself? You are *not* your father, and neither should you want to be."

Marc clenched and unclenched his fists a couple of times and counted to three under his breath before answering. At least she'd tacked *right now* onto the wife-in-name-only part. Small consolation. As if he needed any reminders. But he refused to drag his father, or his feelings about his dad, into this discussion. For a woman suffering amnesia, her mind possessed an amazing clarity all its own.

"We haven't been living a lie." The stirrings of anger boiled beneath the surface. He wasn't sure how she'd react, but neither did he expect to feel this way. Mad. "I freely admit that I was a coward. Trust me, we were gloriously happy for the two years we dated, during our engagement, and then for two beautiful months after we got married. I was faithful to you from the moment we met, and *you* are the woman I want beside me for the rest of my life."

Natalie snapped her head up, and the force of her stare bore straight through to his gut. "And when you made love to me, were you really making love to me, or to Ashley or someone else?"

"Stop it, Natalie! Don't even go there." His voice was a low growl, his back teeth grinding as he fought to keep his temper in check. "I wasn't raised in a Christian home with parents who shared a strong marriage like yours, with the same values, standards and morals. I know that doesn't excuse my behavior, but it's the way it was. And, as long as I'm getting it all out in the open, I passed up a *lot* of opportunities." He knew it was wrong to throw that in her face, but couldn't help himself. "Do you have any idea what it's like to be in the public eye as a professional baseball player?"

She snorted. "No, but I can just imagine." Sarcasm oozed from her.

"You have to give me some credit for restraint, and believe me, it didn't stop the day we married." He cringed. That last one was out-of-line, a low blow. Even the night he stormed out of the house when she told him her plans for moving out, a curvaceous blonde set her sights on him. His fault for going to a hotel bar, but it was enough to send him running in the other direction. A few years ago, he would have made a completely different decision. The wrong one.

Lord, a little help here, please.

Natalie snorted. "Well, you *are* quite the catch, after all. With a head that big, I don't see how you manage to fit it through the door. Why now, Marc? Did you wake up this morning with this sudden, overwhelming urge to confess your sinful past?"

He counted to ten under his breath. "I don't know what you want to hear. Surely you suspected I wasn't a saint since I wasn't a Christian until a year before we met. But since we're basically starting over, I wanted you to know, I *needed* you to know. And now you're punishing me. Maybe I was wrong, and this was all a big mistake, especially if you can't find it in your heart to forgive me."

Not knowing what more he could say, he turned the key in the ignition and, after pausing to make sure she was buckled in, headed out onto the highway. With each silent, passing mile back to the ranch, his heart broke a little more, piece by agonizing piece. Walking her to the door of the women's cabin, he stood and watched as she started inside. "Don't push me away forever, Natalie. I'd give anything not to cause you pain."

She paused, her hand on the door, turning to the side.

"I've only loved you—and thought of you—since the day we first met. Remember that and *cling* to that. Forgive me. I love you more than life itself." Although he knew she'd heard him, Natalie bit her lip and escaped inside the women's cabin.

Turning, Marc stomped through the snow in the direction of the main house. Knocking once, he opened the door, knowing it was normally unlocked. Sam sat at the desk in the family room. Seeing him, he removed his glasses. "I'll make the coffee." Following him to the kitchen, Marc sighed. It promised to be a long night.

Chapter 29

$\mathcal{M}$ARC COULDN'T KEEP his eyes from straying in Natalie's direction during dinner two nights later. Keeping away from her this long was torture, but she was avoiding him like he carried some infectious disease. *I came to Montana to win her back, not push her further away.*

He knew Sam watched closely, but he didn't dare look him in the eye. Even though he could understand Natalie's feelings—especially considering her background and strong faith—he'd done his part by confessing everything and asking for forgiveness.

If they were going to get on with the process of restoring their relationship, she'd have to forgive him. Her blatant disregard was already wearing thin. He had only so much patience, and growing irritation was settling in fast. The ball was in her court, but it didn't look like she was willing to volley. Kevin moved over, making room at the table for Sam.

"Rule number one," Sam said under his breath, putting his glass of water on the table and dropping down beside him.

Marc's fork poised above his plate as he released a heavy sigh. He wasn't really hungry and didn't taste the food. "Remind me. You confused me when you moved one of the rules to the top of the list." He stopped, catching the look on Sam's face. "I'm guessing it's the one about never letting the sun go down on your anger."

"I believe I used the term 'resolving differences,' but same idea, yes. Do everything within your power to start on the path to resolution. It's time."

Stealing a glance at Natalie, Marc found her eyes on him. She turned away first. "I'm afraid it's a little late for that one, Sam. Natalie's been angry with me for a while, you know. And, truth be told," he said, blowing out a deep sigh, "I'm not exactly feeling like Mr. Congeniality."

"Do what you can each day." Sam waited until he looked over at him, holding his gaze steady. "Forget about a timeline and focus on working through this thing together." That deep voice lowered as he leaned closer. "If that means hashing it out—shouting, stomping, yelling, throwing things or whatever else you need to do—so be it. But be honest with each other and get to the bottom of your anger. Then you can work on getting past it."

"I'm not sure I'm up to it. Everything's still fresh and raw."

The man didn't flinch. "Sometimes that's the *best* time." A large hand clamped on his shoulder as Sam drained his glass and left the table. Marc watched as he moved among his TeamWork crew and the other ranch hands, smiling and talking. Every now and then, Sam caught his eye, and he also caught Lexa stealing glances his way, her eyes sympathetic. Natalie left the table, and he heard the ladies talking in the other room.

Pushing his plate aside, Marc bowed his head, overcome with the sudden urge to pray. A short time later, he looked up to find Kevin, Eliot and Dean gathered around him, their heads also bowed. The others had all departed, giving them privacy. He needed to leave before he got all misty again. Standing, he nodded to each of the other men in turn as they raised their heads. "Thanks, guys." What an understatement.

At least now he knew what he needed to do. He needed to confront Natalie. Let her see his anger. Maybe even give her a choice, but make *her* fight to keep this marriage together.

~

Waiting until after the evening devotions, Marc approached Natalie as she talked quietly with Amy and Winnie. Perhaps the women intended to keep her with them long enough for him to find her. *What am I, in high school? Go and talk to your wife already.* "Natalie?" The women stopped mid-conversation.

"Do you need something, Marc?" Her eyes met his for a fleeting second before she looked away and crossed her arms.

The physical ache for her pounded in his heart, throbbed in his veins. More than anything on earth in that moment, he wanted to hold her. Out of the corner of his eye, he caught Amy's wince. *I need you.* "We need to talk." He looked down at his feet for a moment before looking into her eyes, tilting his head to one side, gracing her with his best Elwood impression. She probably wanted to slap him silly, anyway, so he had nothing to lose.

"All right," she said with a resigned sigh, uncrossing her arms. The ladies walked away without another word, but not before Amy and Winnie both winked. When Amy gave him the thumbs-up sign behind Natalie's back, Marc turned his head so as not to laugh out loud and sucked in his cheeks.

At least she allowed him to assist her into her jacket, mumbling her thanks. He might be a louse, but he was a gentleman. Walking beside her in silence except for the crunching of snow under their boots, Marc shoved his hands deep inside his jacket pockets as he led the way toward one of the large, towering evergreen trees a short distance away from the buildings.

Montana really was beautiful, but he'd been so bothered by their situation, he hadn't had taken the opportunity to fully appreciate their gorgeous surroundings. He breathed in the crisp air, catching Natalie's hint of a smile. Surely she felt it, too, and appreciated the beauty of God's creation so evident here. His already churning stomach warned him their discussion might get heated. Still, their personal issues shouldn't be fodder for everyone else's conversation. That was probably a moot point, anyway. Nonetheless, he made certain they stood just far enough away from anyone else who might be within earshot.

Arms crossed again—probably for warmth as much as anything—Natalie's eyes avoided his. "What do you want to talk about?"

"Do you really have to ask that question?" He was already on the defensive, and needed to cool the sarcasm. Not a good sign.

"Oh, we're playing a game now, I see." She sounded equally testy.

"The only one playing games here is *you*, Natalie." His voice came out a low growl. When he glimpsed the fleeting look of hurt cross her face, it nipped at his conscience.

"Go ahead. Get it out. Tell me what's on your mind tonight. More confessions?"

That was all the encouragement he needed. "Fine. You know what your problem is?" Marc tried to temper his rising anger, but Lord help him, it was difficult. He despised raising his voice to his wife, of all people, but she'd angered him. He'd reached the point where he had to let loose and spill his emotions, once and for all. It might prove detrimental to their relationship, but it might also be soothing and somehow cathartic. The die was cast.

Natalie stared, her mouth a firm line. "Why don't you tell me, and then we'll both know."

"You can't accept the fact that you married an imperfect man."

"What does *that* mean?" The sight of her softened his resolve. She looked so vulnerable with her feet planted apart, as if prepared to do battle, those beautiful eyes blazing.

The tiniest grin tugged at the corners of his mouth, but giving into it would be a huge mistake. "You can't accept the fact that the man you married had a past before you." The momentum was going again now. "God forbid I dared to love someone other than you before we were married."

"No," she said, her voice rising. She took a small step forward. "The reason I'm mad is because you didn't *tell* me about those relationships *before* we were married, Marc. Because you didn't trust yourself, and more importantly, you didn't trust *me* to be mature enough to handle it. By covering up your past, you lied to me, you lied to us, and you made our marriage a sham in the process."

"Oh . . . you . . . woman!" Marc yelled, not bothering to keep his voice low. Forget about calm. It was long gone. "Our marriage was . . . is *not* a sham, and you know it!" He took a step closer, and they stood toe-to-toe, their boots touching. "Even if you can't remember how great we are together because of this horrible thing called amnesia, surely you can tell by the way I've treated you the last few months." He leaned closer. "I. Love. You." Inhaling a deep breath, he prayed for calm and lowered his voice. "Natalie, don't you know you're the only woman I've ever really wanted? The only woman I cared for enough to ask to marry me? Did you ever once stop to think that maybe, because I was a sinner, I gave into temptation? Maybe my past sins made me a better man, a better husband to you . . . "

She snorted. "Oh, that's rich, Marc. You can't honestly expect me to excuse your past behavior by telling me it somehow prepared you for me."

Not knowing what else to do, what else to say, he nudged his foot between her boots and leaned as close as humanly possible without toppling her over. They were almost nose-to-nose, but to her credit, she didn't flinch and stood her ground. "Maybe it did, Natalie. I never had any complaints from you." Ignoring the warning look in her eyes, he plundered on. "You are my *wife*. You, Natalie Dianne Combs Thompson, are the *only* woman I want by my side, facing life together, working together to solve problems and sharing everything. The only woman I want in my bed for the rest of my life. The only one I want to kiss, the only one I want to touch, the only one I want to bear our children. Those are the most important things here. So, deal with it and get *over* it."

By the fierceness of his tone, he forced her to look at him. Her eyes canvassed his face, and her soft breath fell on his cheek as she blinked hard. It was enough to distract him, but he had to keep going. "The man standing before you is the same man you fell in love with and married. He has the love of the Lord in His heart, but he didn't for a long time." Great. Now he was talking in third person, but he had her undivided attention. "From what I know, Jesus was a forgiving Man. And we're supposed to forgive others when they sin, especially when they don't understand what Christ did for them on the cross." He reached for her hands, surprised when she didn't struggle out of his grasp. Her eyes met his, another victory. "I've seen how kind you are to total strangers, how generous, how loving." His hold on her hands tightened. "I'm asking you to extend to your husband the same courtesy you'd extend to a complete stranger. Do you think you can do that?"

"I . . . I . . ." she said, lowering her gaze from his. A tear slipped out and made a path down her cheek as she withdrew her hands from his and took a small step backward.

It was do or die. Time for the ultimatum. It worked in business, and he prayed it'd work now. The stakes were totally different, but this was so much more important than any business deal. Maybe it was harsh, but he had to know. "I'm going to give you a choice, Natalie. Either take one step closer to save our marriage, or take one step back and walk away. But if you walk away," he said, "don't look back. I'll fight you for our daughter. If I can't have you, I want our daughter with me. Always." He hadn't planned on saying it, but there it was.

Natalie's mouth opened and she stared at him, aghast. "I can't believe you just said that! This isn't one of your high-powered business deals, Marc. This is our *life*. Are you willing to just give up everything—give up *us*?"

He shook his head, his heart heavy. "No, of course, I don't want that, but you're making it abundantly clear with your words and your behavior—not to mention your total disregard of my feelings—that you can't forgive my indiscretions in the past. And, believe you me, I don't want to live in that kind of self-made purgatory the rest of my natural life. I love you too much—and I have too much self-respect—to stick around watching you hate me for the rest of your life. I sure as anything don't want to subject our daughter to that kind of hate. I grew up with it, and I can tell you, it's *not* pretty. If you want me gone out of your life, so be it. Just tell me, but tell me now. I can pack my things and be out of Montana—and out of your life—tonight."

Shifting his position, Marc pressed his lips against her cheek. Maybe that was unfair, but he had to know how she'd react. "Just tell me now." A falling tear landed on his mouth, and he left it there.

"I can't," Natalie said, her voice broken, the tears falling in rapid succession. "I'm tired of the tears, tired of the anger. I don't want to lose you." Her voice was barely more than a whisper. With her finger, she touched his bottom lip, absorbing the moisture from her own tear before cupping his chin with one hand. "I'm not walking away from this marriage . . . and I pray you don't, either." She gulped, looking up at him with shining eyes. Avoiding his eyes, she moved back a little. "I hate what you said in the car the other night, but I know it took a lot of courage to tell me. I couldn't sleep, and kept thinking about all the sweet, wonderful things you've done for me since my accident." Her eyes moved up slowly to meet his. "Marc, there's a big part of this equation you don't understand."

He stepped closer. "Tell me. Help me understand, Natalie, so we can get past this." He forced his arms to his sides even though he wanted to pull her to him and never let go.

She bit her lower lip, probably in an effort to stem its trembling. Meeting his eyes again, she released a shuddering sigh. "At first, after I saw you with Ashley and then read that note, I thought you'd resumed a relationship with one of your past . . . girlfriends." She held up her hand when he started to protest. "I realized soon enough that wasn't the case." She turned away from his view, her shoulders shaking.

"Natalie? What is it? You can tell me anything."

"I thought," she said, choking on her words and sputtering, "I thought I'd failed you. I disappointed you, and you didn't want me, even though you said you did. This horrible amnesia has stolen away the *real* me, and I'm only a shell of the woman you fell in love with and married." Her eyes met his for a brief second before she looked away again. "I'm so confused, and I don't know if I'll ever remember who I am, who you are, and who we are together. And that breaks my heart. I hate amnesia, but I know I love you. You're my *husband*."

He swallowed hard. "Answer one question." She didn't say anything, waiting, watching. "Does our marriage have a chance?"

Her eyes widened, and she nodded. "I don't think we'd be here in Montana otherwise. The Lord's made it pretty clear He's in it for the long haul, so I think we need to be willing to do the same. Don't you?" She shrugged and gave him the slightest hint of a smile that gave him incredible hope. "I just need more time to absorb everything."

She might say she needed more time, but time wasn't going to solve anything. Natalie needed her husband now. He couldn't spend another moment without her. Marc pulled her to him and crushed his mouth down on hers. His wife could be the most infuriating woman in the world, but also the softest and most vulnerable. In his heart, he knew she wanted the marriage. It was a soothing balm to his hurting, weary heart. Although he'd never doubted his love for her, he, too, was tired of the tears, the anger.

Marc kissed her long and hard. She briefly pushed against him with weak arms, but he held her fast, bundling her closer, his arms wrapped completely around her. If anything, she leaned further into his kiss, responding by pressing her lips equally hard against his. Her hands moved around his neck, her body yielding to him, fully involved in the kiss.

It was almost as though she battled him with her lips, an outpouring of mixed emotion and anger. This kind of weapon he'd willingly suffer. When she fell asleep that night, he wanted her to remember the feel of his lips on hers, the warmth of their bodies pressed so closely together. As she awakened in the morning, he wanted her to put a finger on her lips, remembering the passion of their kiss.

Marc increased his efforts, slowly deepening the kiss, a low moan escaping when she responded in kind. Whether or not Natalie understood it, she was fighting back for her husband, and for their marriage. Fighting *hard*.

Chapter 30

$\mathcal{N}$ATALIE AWOKE WITH a start. Sitting up too fast, she felt dizzy and brought a hand to her forehead. Forcing herself to take a few deep breaths, she steadied herself before swinging her feet over the edge of the bed. A rumbling stirred deep in her stomach, maybe hunger, maybe something more.

A smile played about her lips as her hand smoothed down over her flannel-covered stomach. She'd noticed a definite curve there when she was in the shower the day before. Sometimes she still couldn't believe she had a new life growing inside her, but she prayed constantly for her baby. With everything so messed up with Marc, knowing she'd have a baby to love in a few short months gave her renewed hope. She only prayed the consequences of her fall hadn't somehow harmed her child.

Her bare toes brushed over something soft. Peering over the edge of the bed, she spied gorgeous pink bedroom slippers. She pushed her toes into them. Ah, cozy, and they fit perfectly, but they must belong to Winnie or Beck since their beds were the closest. Taking them off with a wistful sigh, Natalie fumbled under the bed for her old slippers, slipping them on and pushing herself off the bed. Hearing the blustery wind howl outside, deep shivers ran through her.

Walking across the room, she squinted against the sunlight streaming through the window as it reflected off the snow. Feeling silly, she drew a heart on the frosty window. Her finger paused. She'd done this before. Without thinking, she drew N *loves* M inside the heart. Stepping back, startled, her eyes widened. A strange sensation blanketed her, and she wrapped her arms across her middle. Just like the arms that wrapped around her once before, putting a hand over hers as together their fingers traced the outline of a heart on a window. In Massachusetts. He'd pulled her close, whispered words of love.

It was a memory.

Tears welled in her eyes, and a small cry escaped. "Are they coming back, Lord?" Or was she remembering Marc holding her the night before, kissing her with so much passion? Moving her fingers to her lips, she traced their outline as she stared out the window. She'd been surprised by the strength of her desire as she'd kissed Marc, but it was more than passion. It felt *right*. Maybe the force of that kiss had dislodged something in her addled brain. Was that crazy? Maybe. But the Lord was mighty, and He could accomplish miracles in unconventional ways.

She shook her head. Passion in the heat of the moment couldn't excuse the fact she wasn't sure she could trust her husband. He didn't seem to understand what tore her up inside wasn't his past dalliances with other women—and she knew that's all they were. Of course, it saddened her, but she could tell it made him sad, too. Anyone could see how contrite and repentant he was.

What ate at her was his need to hide the truth of his past before they married. That was the hardest part to accept. He claimed it was to protect her from possible hurt, but she wasn't so sure. How did she know there weren't other, deeper secrets he was hiding? He seemed to have laid it all at her feet. Then again, she wasn't sure of a lot of things right now, including her own mental stability and obvious inadequacies. Was it possible the hormonal changes of pregnancy made her irrational?

Something stirred inside again, and she put a quick hand over her abdomen. *Where is everyone? Why is it so quiet?* All the other beds were neatly made, everything in its place. Darting a glance at the clock on the dresser, she gasped. *Nine-thirty!*

Scrambling back to her bed, she grabbed the clothes she'd laid out the night before and her cosmetics bag to head to the small bathroom. She shot a longing glance at the bedroom slippers at the same time she felt a blast of cold air. The door creaked open and Winnie and Amy blew inside the cabin, shivering and rubbing their hands together.

"God bless Texas!" Winnie grinned and yanked her gloves off her hands, removing her hood and shaking out her blonde ponytail. "Montana's great and all, but give me heat and humidity any day over this torture."

"How are you this morning, Sunshine?" Amy crossed the room and put an arm around her. "Feeling okay?"

"I'll give you sunshine." Natalie suppressed a girlish giggle. Being around these two brought out her silly side. "Why didn't you wake me up this morning?"

Amy glanced at Winnie and shrugged. "We thought you could use the rest."

"You *are* sleeping for two, you know." Winnie's smile was infectious, and her big blue eyes never looked brighter.

"That expression doesn't wash with me in terms of eating, so it doesn't apply to sleeping either, Winnie, but I appreciate the sentiment. Actually," she said with a sheepish grin, "it felt wonderful to sleep in." Nodding toward the window, she shivered again, praying all the while she didn't get sick. "It looks even colder today. Do I need an extra layer?"

"Probably a good idea," Amy said. "Listen, we need to scoot back over to the schoolroom, but we're planning a little road trip into Helena after lunch to get some fabric. Mother Hen over here is feeling domestic," she said, shrugging a shoulder in Winnie's direction, "and she's decided to teach us how to make curtains. Imagine that." She smiled when Natalie giggled again.

"Lexa's driving," Winnie said, crossing her eyes at Amy. "Please say you'll come. It'll be fun."

"When you put it like that, sure. I'll come over to the schoolroom soon."

Amy waved her hand. "We'll handle the kids this morning, and Cassie's taking over this afternoon when we go into town. For now, you just enjoy a long, leisurely shower."

Winnie grinned. "Lexa specifically requested that you come over to the dining hall. She wants to fix you a hot breakfast. Expectant Mother's Special, or something like that. My advice is to eat up all this attention while you can. Literally."

"All this and getting to sleep in, too. Thanks. Oh, someone left their slippers under my bed by mistake. If they don't come get them soon, I might have to claim them."

"Yes, you might just have to do that," Winnie murmured behind her. Turning to head into the bathroom, Natalie caught the conspiratorial look passing between Winnie and Amy.

~

After her shower, Natalie hurried over to the dining hall where she found Lexa sifting flour at one of the long tables. She blew a long strand of blonde hair away from her face. Flour was smudged on both cheeks, the sleeves of her sweater pushed up to her elbows.

Cassie stood at another table, rolling out crust. "Morning, Natalie. You look pretty today." It was hard to decide which was sweeter—the smile or that incredible Alabama drawl. Her compliment was welcome since she didn't feel particularly pretty.

"Hi, Cassie. Thanks." Winnie told her Cassie was the newest of the TeamWork ladies, and she hadn't worked with her at the other previous work camps. Removing her jacket, Natalie quirked a brow. "So, Lexa Homemaker, what are you baking today?" She shared a grin with Cassie. The work table was covered with measuring cups, bowls, and other baking supplies and ingredients. One thing she'd learned—when Lexa put her mind to something, she did it wholeheartedly, skimping on nothing.

"Well, you see," Lexa said, wiping the back of her hand over her brow, smearing a line of flour in the process, "Sam loves pie—basically any kind of pie. As long as it has a flaky crust with something stuffed inside, he eats it like it's going out of style. Of course, peach is his favorite, but it's not exactly the height of peach season. Thankfully, I found some great blueberries at the local market. Frozen fresh, so they'll do. When God gives you blueberries, you make pie. So, I'm making my cowboy a pie worthy of his big old Texas appetite."

"Well, that's a very touching sentiment, and I know how much Sam will appreciate your efforts, like he does everything else. I'm a little late for breakfast since there was a conspiracy to let me sleep in this morning. Don't let me interrupt your pie making. I'm just going to grab something quick before going over to the schoolroom." Pushing away from the doorway with a grin, Natalie headed into the kitchen.

Lexa wiped off her hands and pulled her by the arm, steering her back to the long table. "Here. You sit down and talk with Cassie while I get something extra special for you this morning."

"Thanks, but I'll be glad to get it . . ." Her words were silenced as Lexa instructed her to stay put in no uncertain terms before disappearing through the swinging doors.

After no more than five minutes of getting to know Cassie, she was rewarded as Lexa returned, weighed down with a heaping platter of pancakes, enough for several people. "A little bird told me this is your favorite type of pancake." Going back into the kitchen, Lexa emerged with a pitcher of warm, fragrant maple syrup and a tall glass of milk.

"Was this bird a peacock, by any chance?" Catching Lexa rolling her eyes, Natalie smiled. "I should be thankful Marc knows my preferences since I sure don't. You're treating me like a queen. Thanks, Lexa. These smell great." She darted a curious glance at her plate. "Forgive me, but . . ."

"Streusel pancakes," Cassie said. The look on her pretty face was interesting, too. She shrugged. "Peacock told me to whisper it in Homemaker's ear."

Maybe it was an IHOP Specialty or something. Feeling that rumble in her belly again, Natalie said a quick prayer and took a hearty bite of the pancakes. They practically melted in her mouth. "Oh, Lexa." It came out an almost indecent moan. "This is soooo good. If your pies are anywhere near as scrumptious, you should start your own business." She took another bite.

"That's an intriguing thought." Lexa accepted her invitation to sit at the table for a few minutes, and they chatted about the ranch and the curtains they planned to make. "I'm glad to see your appetite is healthy again," Lexa said a few minutes later. She shrugged when she caught Natalie's quick glance. "Marc told me you weren't eating much the first few months of your pregnancy."

Natalie's breath caught. She cleared her throat and prayed she wouldn't burst into tears. She'd shed enough tears lately to last her a good long while. How much had Marc told Sam and Lexa? From the corner of her eyes, she noticed Cassie leaving and slipping out into the kitchen.

Lexa reached across the table for her hand. "I'm sorry. Did I say something to upset you?"

"No, no." Wiping her mouth with her napkin, she put it beside her empty plate. "Am I being a fool?"

A frown creased Lexa's brow. "Why would you think that?"

"I have amnesia, but I'm not blind. Marc shows me he loves me in everything he does, everything he says, and even in what he doesn't say. He's considerate of my feelings, he's kind to others . . . at least for the most part." She managed a small grin.

"All true."

"I feel the need to unburden myself about something." She hadn't planned on bringing it up, but in Lexa, she'd found a kindred spirit. It seemed fitting, especially since Sam and Marc had already formed such a strong bond.

"I'm all ears, but hold that thought." Jumping to her feet, Lexa darted back into the kitchen. Relief was etched into her expression when she reappeared a couple of minutes later.

"Sorry, Natalie, but Cassie left, and I can't let Sam's pies burn." She patted her hand in a move reminiscent of Winnie as she reclaimed her seat at the table. "Please, continue."

Natalie blew out a sigh. "Let's face it, if Marc wasn't such a gorgeous man, I probably wouldn't have given him a second look. I must be incredibly shallow."

Lexa didn't bother to hide her grin. "That might have attracted you to him initially, but I know you well enough to know you would have seen through any façade. You're genuine and unassuming, and you wouldn't marry a pretentious man."

"I guess part of what I'm trying to say is that I'll probably always be fighting off other women. Even on our honeymoon, other women hit on him. Right in front of me!" It was true. Although she couldn't recall the details, she remembered an Italian woman making eyes at Marc at dinner one night, and another one on the beach wearing next-to-nothing.

A bemused grin twisted the corners of Lexa's mouth.

A bristle of irritation nipped at her. "I didn't find it so amusing."

"Of course not, sweetie." Lexa squeezed her hand and leaned across the table. "But, don't you see? You *remembered*. I don't think Marc would have told you something like that. But, even so, he belongs to you. Let them look all they want, but they can't have him."

She met Lexa's eyes head-on. "What I'm struggling with is that Marc *did* belong to a few other women before me."

"Oh." Lexa withdrew her hand and looked down for a moment.

"I didn't know that when I married him, apparently."

Lexa looked up sharply. "And how do you know this *now*?"

"He told me."

Silence filled the room for a long moment. "Well, that's a good thing when you think about it."

"Care to explain exactly how it can be a *good* thing? My husband wasn't the man I thought he was when we married. He kept secrets from me. Marc had physical relationships with three other women before he met and married me." She heard the defensiveness rising in her own voice. Still, she couldn't help but wonder how Lexa would feel if she discovered something like this about Sam *after* they married. But she couldn't voice that thought aloud. From what she knew, Sam and Marc had totally different backgrounds.

Lexa shifted in her chair, but she didn't look uncomfortable. She rested her chin on one hand, elbow propped on the table. "I think the key words are 'before he met me.'" She raised a hand when she saw her open her mouth to protest. "Chances are that also means before he became a Christian. Think about it and hear me out. Marc knows you were raised in the church, and taught Christian values and moral values, but he wasn't. That makes a *huge* difference in the way a person makes decisions once they're an adult and unleashed into the so-called real world. Not to excuse his behavior, but the man played minor league baseball. And yes, he's very handsome. We've all heard stories about professional athletes. At the risk of sounding crass, it's almost expected they have as many female conquests as they do trophies. Then Marc became a successful businessman, building his own advertising agency. Powerful men are irresistible to a lot of women."

Leaning closer, Lexa placed her hand on top of hers. "Not that it makes you feel any better, and not that it condones his behavior in any way, but there could have been so *many*."

She shook her head. "I can't bear the thought of it."

"Men don't always have the emotional connection women do. I don't know the circumstances of Marc's relationships with these other women, and I don't need to know. Neither do you. They're in the past. My advice, if you want it, is to let it go or it will tear you up inside. Even if Marc was in some kind of ongoing relationship with any of these women, it wasn't ordained by the Lord the way his relationship with you is right. Cling to that hope. The Lord brought you two together, Natalie. From what I understand, Marc fought hard to win your love over some pretty big odds. He's a fighter, and truth be told, he deserves your respect and forgiveness."

Natalie stared into space, not speaking. It seemed everyone was ganging up on Marc's side, against *her*. She knew that wasn't Lexa's intent, but she couldn't help the sting of hurt.

Lexa spoke again before she could respond. "In some ways, Marc and I have some things in common. I was a nominal Christian when I first came to the TeamWork camp in San Antonio and met Sam. Sam figured me out right away, and I knew it was only a matter of time until the rest of you caught on." Lexa paused. "Granted, I didn't have previous physical relationships with other men, but neither was I what Sam thought he wanted in a woman."

The waterworks started. "I wish I could remember you and Sam and everyone else in TeamWork, but I can't." Natalie's shoulders heaved as she put her head down on her crossed arms. A small wail escaped, and it didn't even sound like it came out of her. Grabbing hold of Lexa's warm hand, she poured out her heart. The stored pain came flooding out of her, tears streaming down her cheeks. "It hurts that I can't remember my first date with Marc, our first kiss, anything. He told me about all those things, but it's like it was someone else's story, not mine. Not . . . ours." She hiccupped a few times and blew her nose, finding it hard to stem the flow of tears.

Lexa moved around the table to sit beside her, and handed her a tissue. She prayed quietly, and made small circles on her back with a gentle hand once the sobs quieted. Wiping her cheeks with the back of her hand, Natalie managed the beginnings of a smile before another small sob escaped. "I don't know why I had to go through this, but I trust in the Lord enough to know He has a reason." When Lexa's arm moved around her, drawing her close, she leaned her head on the other woman's shoulder. "I hate that I don't remember much from before, Lexa, but I know that I couldn't love you any more than I do right now."

Lexa hugged her and planted a light kiss on her cheek. "And you're one of the kindest women I know." Smoothing her hair away from her face, she gave her a loving smile. "And you *are* starting to remember. The Lord's giving you snippets of memories here and there, and that's a precious gift. I guess the key to all this is that you can't change Marc's past, but you need to somehow accept and resolve it. If you love him enough, you'll forgive him and move on from this point. There's an awful lot of sin and heartache in the world. Not to say that Marc's past isn't a heartache to you. I'm sure he hated to tell you, but he did it." Lexa's eyes softened. "I want you to think about something."

"What's that?" Sniffling, she dabbed at her eyes. Lexa made a lot of sense, and she'd already given her a lot to think about.

"A lot of men would never be able to humble themselves to their wives and admit their failings. Marc was afraid to do it before he married you, but for whatever reason, the Lord's giving you a fresh start now. By telling you, it shows how much he's grown in the Lord. Marc took a big leap of faith because he loves you. Now," Lexa said, patting her hand, "it's *your* turn to return the favor." Pushing away from the table, she gave her a knowing smile. "If you'll excuse me, I have some pies to bake. If you need me, you know where to find me." Lexa departed the room, humming under her breath.

Bundling into her jacket, lost in thought, Natalie unzipped the pocket and reached inside in a search for her gloves. Nothing. That was odd since she'd had them on when she arrived. She looked down, puzzled. This jacket had way too many pockets. Reaching inside another pocket, her fingers touched something deep inside. Paper. It must have been there since the year before.

She pulled it out, chewing on her lower lip as she unfolded it. Recognizing her husband's precise but strong cursive, she released a sigh, mentally bolstering her attitude. Their track record with notes hadn't been the best in recent days.

Natalie—warning: this might be corny, so be prepared. I'm an ad man, but I'm the guy who runs the business, and I never claimed to be a copywriter, but here goes. How do I love thee? Let me count the ways. I love the way your nose scrunches up and you say "Brown Cow" when you try to stop a sneeze. I love the ridiculous way you cut pizza with a knife and fork and tease me because I use my knife and fork like a Brit. I love the way you do that little dance thing with your fingers on your lap when you're nervous.

I love the way your eyes light up with wonder like a child when you see a star on the top of a Christmas tree, the way you can't swim in a straight path, the way you cried when you couldn't make Baked Alaska, but you tried anyway because you know I love it. No one can make blueberry cobbler the way you do, so it's my forever favorite.

You are such an incredible woman, and I can't wait to make you my wife. I'm never more proud than when you're on my arm at some social function. Never more happy than when you give me that look that tells me you love and accept me for who I am. I still can't believe you chose me, Marc Thompson, a man with so many faults. But, with your help, I'll be a better man. Thanks for your faith in me, and your love.

You're beautiful, you're compassionate and sensitive, and you're going to make an awesome mother someday. And the greatest thing of all? You belong to the Lord, and by God's infinite grace, you belong to me. Natalie, you make me happier than I ever thought possible.

All my love and devotion,

Marc

Natalie's hands shook almost uncontrollably. Dropping the note, it fluttered to the floor as she stumbled back to the table. "Lexa!"

Chapter 31

NATALIE FELT BAD one of Lexa's pies burned a little around the edges, but Lexa assured her Sam wouldn't mind. "Totally worth it. I'll just scoop out the middle, put vanilla ice cream on top, and he'll never notice the difference," she said with a reassuring smile.

Sufficiently recovered a short time later, Natalie visited the schoolroom for the last half-hour of the morning before lunch. Feeling restless, she didn't want to go back to the cabin, and staying busy with the children would be good. Closing the door behind her, she stamped the snow off her boots and pulled the wool cap from her head, shaking out her hair and smoothing it down.

Nathan looked up as she stepped inside the schoolroom. "Miss Natalie's here!" His announcement sent a flurry of bodies scurrying, and Winnie and Amy helped pick up supplies scattered on the table where they'd been working.

When she stepped closer to see what they were working on, Winnie took her by the arm, steering her to the desk at the front of the room. "How was your breakfast?" Winnie nodded at Amy.

"Absolutely scrumptious." Pulling back, Natalie looked Winnie full in the face. "What's going on? You don't have a subtle bone in your body, Miss Doyle."

"That's what you think." Winnie nodded at Amy again. "Ready?" When Amy nodded, Winnie forced her down into the chair behind the desk. "Sit, please. The kids have a little presentation."

"A presentation? For me?"

"Yes. Sit back, watch and listen."

For the next twenty minutes, Natalie watched, enthralled, as the kids reenacted the story of David and Goliath. They really put their all into it and were quite talented. Of course, no reenactment of a biblical tale was complete without shenanigans from the sidelines. Jake pulled Ashley's braid, and she retaliated by punching him in the arm. Poor Denny kept stepping on everyone's toes, but other than getting a few frowns and swats, he emerged unscathed.

When they finished, Natalie jumped to her feet and clapped with enthusiasm. *Whoa.* Maybe she shouldn't have done that so quickly. She stretched out a hand, fumbling for the desk. In a heartbeat, Winnie and Amy rushed to her side, steadying her.

"I'm fine," Natalie assured them. "With those pancakes in me, I shouldn't be lightheaded."

Amy smiled. "Maybe it's a sugar rush from all the syrup. It's pure and potent stuff."

Natalie grinned and winked at the kids to reassure them she was all right. Bless their hearts, they looked concerned as they stood behind their teachers.

"That's probably it." Recovering her equilibrium, she moved over in a group hug. "You all were so great! I can't tell you how much your play meant to me."

The kids buzzed with excitement, chattering like magpies. Amy signaled to them, and they retrieved brightly-colored papers from the table and brought them to Natalie. One by one, the children presented her with cards of caring, love and thanks for being their teacher. Ashley threw her arms around her and whispered, "Your husband's smart. And really cute." Her cheeks flushed as she ran off to join the other girls.

Natalie tossed a curious look Winnie and Amy's way as the children were dismissed. "I don't know what prompted this, but thank you."

The quick glance shared between the two was intriguing. Winnie shrugged. "The kids told us they wanted to do a play and we thought you could use some . . ."

"Encouragement," Amy said. "Even though they've only met you in the last few days, these kids all love you, Natalie. You're going to make a terrific mother. The best." Leaving the schoolroom after dismissing the laughing children, the trio wrapped their arms around each other as they headed in the direction of the dining hall.

Later that afternoon, as they shopped for fabric for kitchen curtains for the main house and other miscellaneous items, Lexa and the other ladies surprised her with a bottle of body lotion she adored. "I didn't see this lotion for sale here . . . in the general mercantile . . . in the middle of nowhere." It was pretty pricey, and she normally bought it at Macy's. It was unfathomable they'd find it here in rural Montana, of all places.

"You'd be surprised what you can find if you look hard enough." Lexa gave Natalie a look she wasn't sure how to interpret.

Something about this scenario didn't add up. Several things today didn't make sense. It exhausted her thinking about it. She turned the bottle over in her hands, lost in thought as they piled into one of the SUVs to return to the ranch. "Everyone's being very secretive today," she said.

"Just accept it and enjoy the benefits," Winnie said with her trademark giggle.

"Thanks for the lotion. I love it, and I appreciate your thoughtfulness." Natalie leaned back against the seat and closed her eyes. Picking up on her cue, the others kept their voices down so she could rest during the trip back to the ranch.

~

"Why is everyone doing all these nice things for me today?" Natalie glanced at the other ladies in the cabin a short time later. "This is all Marc's doing, isn't it? He's having everyone do all these sweet, thoughtful, entirely wonderful things for me." It was so confusing.

Winnie put one hand on her hip, darting a helpless look in Amy's direction. The door of the cabin opened and Lexa breezed in. She did a little dance as she shivered and then leaned her full-body weight—all one hundred pounds of her—against the door to close it, blocking out the bitter, cold wind.

"And that's what I call timing." Winnie darted a glance toward the ceiling. "Thanks, Lord. I owe you one."

What in the world does that mean?

Amy spoke up. "Lexa, Natalie's wondering what's up today, with all the nice things happening."

Lexa tugged her woolen cap off her head and pulled out her long braid as she moved into the center of the room to stand beside Winnie. Her cheeks were bright pink, and she smiled. "You really don't know, Natalie? You can't guess?" Her eyes sparkled with merriment, or perhaps mischief.

"I have no idea. Be Extra Nice to the Confused Woman Day, I guess."

Hooking their arms together, Lexa and the other ladies took steps toward where she stood beside her bed. In a semi-circle, they hemmed her in. At least they looked friendly enough.

A nervous laugh escaped. "What is this, an intervention?"

"Maybe, in a minute," Amy said.

Lexa nodded at them and hummed a note, and they started in, "Happy birthday to you, happy birthday to you, happy birthday, dear Natalie . . ."

"It's my *birthday* today?" Natalie slumped down onto her bed, befuddled. How could she forget? Even with all the surprises, it hadn't even crossed her mind.

Amy frowned. "I know you don't want my opinion, but although you're another year older, you're definitely none the wiser."

"And what's *that* supposed to mean?" She couldn't be mad at Amy. Not really.

Winnie shot a warning glance in Amy's direction, raising one hand. "Amy . . ."

"You're obviously punishing that sweet man for only wanting to be a better husband to you. Yes, Marc told us it was your birthday." Hands on both hips, Amy's eyes blazed into hers. "Some of us already knew that, of course, but it was really sweet how he wanted to make sure we did. For starters, he told Cassie how much you loved streusel pancakes, and none of us had ever heard of them before."

"They were delicious." Natalie brought her hand to her forehead.

"Thanks." Lexa nodded, pleased.

Amy's sigh was audible, her impatience to continue obvious. "Marc and Sam disappeared for over three *hours* the other day to drive into Helena to buy those pretty pink bedroom slippers—yes, they belong to you—and that fancy schmancy lotion you love so much. Marc said the doctor told him one way to trigger memories is through the sense of smell, and he thought the lotion might help."

Amy crossed her arms and stared her down. "You and I both know most men wouldn't go to those lengths. Marc loves and desperately wants to please you, Natalie, and he's doing it in ways he knows will be special and meaningful for *you*."

Natalie lowered her eyes first, but Amy was only getting started. If she was trying to make her feel guilty, it was working.

"Of course, Marc also knows how much you love children and handmade things, so that explains the schoolhouse play and the cards. You may not know this, but we had to tackle one of the female ranch hands when we first arrived here. She set her sights on your husband, and thought she'd reel him in before we set her straight on the fact that his wife was right here in the camp and, if anything happened, she'd have to answer to the rest of us." Amy let out a short laugh. "You don't mess with Sam, and especially his TeamWork crew, or you'll have to answer to Papa Bear."

"That's Amy's new nickname for Sam," Winnie said.

They all looked over at Lexa. She nodded. "Seems fitting. I like it."

Not sure what to say, Natalie remained silent. Amy wasn't done yet. "And then, when we went into town for supplies and Sam and Marc walked in the general mercantile, you should have seen how fast the head of every single woman within throwing distance swiveled and zeroed in on the both of them. Sorry, Lexa," she said, throwing an apologetic glance her way. "They're both tall, strong, manly men, and they get female attention. But the point is, they don't care and seem downright oblivious because they only have eyes for their wives. It's a beautiful thing, I tell you. I only hope I'll be so blessed one day."

Lexa surprised them by laughing. Other women coveted their husbands, and the woman laughed. "They can drool all they want. They're making fools of themselves because they're not getting anywhere. I trust Sam. I know how to keep him happy, and I intend on doing it all the rest of my days." When she glimpsed their collective look of surprise, Lexa laughed even harder.

"Well, okay then," Winnie said.

Watching them, Natalie was grateful to be part of such a great group. They put the meaning of TeamWork into action at every possible opportunity.

Amy sat down on the bed beside her, pulling her close with one arm draped around her shoulders. "Here's the thing. You marry someone like Marc, he's going to get female attention. Get used to it. My humble advice, take it or leave it, is to get over yourself and forgive that man or he might eventually start looking elsewhere. I don't think that's what you want, is it?"

"This is just too much too absorb right now," Natalie said, leaning into Amy's hug. "By telling me to *get over* myself, do you honestly believe I'm being selfish? And does everyone in this room know my personal business with

Marc?" An uncomfortable silence greeted her question. Looking from Winnie to Amy, she dared not look at Lexa. How could they know?

Winnie sighed. "We don't know any details, and we don't mean to impose or intrude in your personal lives. It's obvious something's going on between the two of you other than the amnesia, but we can only guess what it is. Judging by your reaction, I think we've got it nailed down pretty accurately. The point is, Marc's courting you all over again, making new memories, but he's hoping you'll recover those hidden memories. He's trying so hard, Natalie. Marc's a lovely, thoughtful man, and we all love him. Even more so because he loves *you* so much."

It was hard to miss all the other nods in the cabin. Natalie blew out a breath. Seemed she was outnumbered—again. But how could she be mad when these women were so sweet and caring? It was clear how much they wanted to help. "Marc calls it 'second time around.'"

Winnie beamed. "Exactly."

Quiet until now, it was Cassie's turn to speak. "We can all see how much you mean to him. The only other time I've ever seen a man look at a woman like that is, well . . ." They all glanced over at Lexa. Bless her heart, she started laughing again. Soon, they all laughed, and Natalie couldn't help but join in. It was infectious, and the release felt good.

"You know," Natalie said, "I don't think I could find better friends. Thanks for helping me get through this." Something stirred inside, something hard to define, but it was definitely there. "Wait a minute." She held up one hand.

"What is it?" Still sitting beside her, Amy's arm around her tightened.

Cassie moved close, falling to her knees beside the bed, her blue eyes wide. "Do you remember something else?"

It was another breakthrough, and it got her heart pumping. "Winnie, you helped me fix something on my bridal gown right before the wedding, didn't you?"

Winnie's smile was bright. "You had a tiny tear in your veil. You fussed about it, but we arranged it so no one could tell." She sighed. "You were the most beautiful bride I've ever seen, and Marc was your gorgeous groom. Made for each other might sound silly, but that's exactly what everyone said about the two of you. You were the fairy tale come true."

Natalie grinned. Winnie was so sweet, and she appreciated her sentiment. She needed to tell Winnie privately that she remembered her name when Marc showed her their wedding photos.

"I'm not sure I want to know what you remember about me." Amy nudged her shoulder and laughed.

She chewed the inside of her lip, her brows drawn. "Well, I don't remember anything specific."

"Go ahead. Out with it," Amy said with a skeptical expression. Forthright, bright and funny, Amy had once been much more hesitant at confrontations, at least according to Lexa and Beck. An editorial assistant at a large New York publishing house, she'd come into her own, not afraid to speak her mind. That's what was also rather intimidating.

"I'm guessing you helped coordinate everything at our wedding."

"Which is oh-so-polite Natalie speak for telling me how bossy I was. And you would be right."

As the other girls departed to begin preparations for dinner, Amy hugged her tighter. "I don't mean to be harsh with you. Even if you don't remember, I hope you can tell how much we all love you and Marc, and want the best for you."

Natalie nodded. "I know. It means the world. In spite of the fact that I'm freezing here in Montana," she added with a small grin, "I'm glad we're here. You all are so great, and I can't thank you enough for all you're doing for us." Once the other girls departed, it was Winnie's turn to sit down beside her on the bed. Lost in thought, Natalie wondered if maybe she'd start remembering more things now.

"I might be grasping at straws," Winnie said, "and I'm certainly no biblical scholar like Sam or Kevin, but I think it's interesting that your veil tore before your wedding."

Natalie sighed. "Tell me. My brain is muddled." She offered a tired smile, but had to admit she was intrigued.

"In the Holy of Holies, the veil represented the separation of man—because of sin—from the holiness of God. Only the high priest was allowed to pass through the veil once a year, on the Day of Atonement. But when Jesus died, the veil was torn in half. In other words, Christ's death on the cross made *us* right before God."

Natalie drew her knees to her chest, wondering where Winnie was going with all this.

"Bear with me," Winnie said, her voice quiet. "You might think I'm crazy, but hear me out."

When she smiled, Natalie felt so drawn to this woman's sensitivity and compassion. No wonder she was called the Mother Hen and everyone loved her dearly.

"Marc's sins died when he became a Christian. Maybe you should think of your torn veil as Christ's atonement for Marc's past. That tear, especially on your wedding day, symbolized a new beginning for both of you, and freedom from the past." Winnie shrugged and gave her a sheepish grin. "So, do you think I'm a total nut case?"

"Not at all," Natalie assured her, giving her a quick hug. "If anything, you're very wise and intuitive. I understand what you're saying, and it makes perfect sense. Thanks for sharing that with me."

Winnie patted her hand. "We're all here for you. Anytime you need us, just say the word. Remember, too, the Lord knows what you're going through now, just as he did on your wedding day, and every day. He's right beside you, every step of the way. He doesn't want you to go through this alone, and neither do we. Remember that, sweetie."

"Winnie, there's something I want to tell you." A fleeting look of alarm crossed over her features, but it faded quickly as Winnie listened to the story of how she'd remembered her name. "Marc thought it was a breakthrough. When I looked at the photos of you, Beck and Amy at the wedding, it's like I knew."

"Knew *what*, exactly?" Winnie's voice was so gentle, so soothing.

"I knew the Lord sent you all to help. To love Marc and me enough to help us get through this trauma together. Thank you from the bottom of my heart."

Watching Winnie leave after a quick hug, Natalie wondered how she ever got along before she met Sam and Lexa Lewis and their TeamWork crew. They were gifts in and of themselves in so many marvelous ways. This unexpected birthday was turning out to be very special.

Chapter 32

$\mathcal{S}$ECURING THE HORSE to a nearby tree, Marc walked, hands in his pockets, shaking from the cold. Whether he shook because of the freezing temperatures or his own volatile emotions, he couldn't be sure. He'd made decent headway in regaining Natalie's trust and love, but even though she told him she didn't want to give up on their marriage, another part of him knew her blind faith in him was shattered.

It's called trust, Marc.

Maybe the ghosts of his past would never truly fade, but always lurk around somewhere, ready to surface and haunt again, triggered by unknown circumstances. Spying a fallen log, he sat down, elbows propped on his knees, his head falling to his hands. He willed the tears to come, but they were stubborn. "Natalie, I love you. Happy birthday." Marc's voice echoed in the stillness, mocking him. Everything mocked him these days, from his shiny gold wedding band to the Montana wilderness.

"God, help me, please." He needed the heavenly Father to help save their marriage, and he should have called on Him first. *I won't lose her.* Sure, he'd prayed, but like everything else in his life, he didn't want to willingly relinquish control. It all boiled down to a battle of wills. He'd been calling the shots far too long and hadn't fully surrendered to God's will. Approaching the throne of grace, laying it all at the feet of the Savior should have been his starting point, not where he'd ended up as a last resort.

Dear God, he prayed, *help us get past this. I don't know what else to do, where else to turn. I thank you for Sam and his wise counsel and Lexa's wise counsel to Natalie. I don't know what we'd do without them. But you've blessed us with a baby together, Lord, and I know it's Your will that we stay together. I love her with everything in me, and I want us together as a family.*

The pain had been buried inside him far too long, but he'd been too stubborn. Holding onto it this long was a mistake, and he needed the release. No one else was around. No one but God. Giving into his anguish, the loud, long, slow moan trapped in his throat flowed out of him. It was almost unearthly, and along with it came the tears. They fell freely, freezing as soon as they hit the hard, cold ground.

Shivering, arms crossed in front of him, Marc rocked back and forth, watching his breath escape. His body wracked with loud sobs. Like they so often did, his dad's words came back to haunt him. *Men don't cry. It shows weakness.* He'd excelled at school, earned a scholarship to Yale, but it was never good enough to gain the attention or affection of his famous dad. "No more, Dad," he said through clenched teeth, his fingers curling into fists inside his gloves. "I will not allow you to dictate my life!"

His dad died alone. No matter what they'd been through together—how he'd wronged them—he was still family. If only the mighty Phil Thompson had reached out, Marc would have been at his side in a heartbeat. So would his mom and sister, but he'd suffered in silence because of a distorted perception of what it meant to be masculine and strong. And, in doing so, denied his children—and the only woman he ever truly loved—the opportunity to say good-bye.

Sitting in the wilderness, his heart aching, Marc shed more tears for the sadness of it all. "You were wrong, Dad," he said, wiping away more tears, rocking back and forth on the log. He was stiff from the cold, but he didn't care. Once his sobs quieted, a sense of calm passed through him, the same as after Natalie's fall. Maybe this *was* the peace that passes all understanding? He loved his dad in his own way, but he was gone. If he'd learned anything from how his dad lived his life, he had to make *his* life count—by doing things his own way, not patterning his life after a man who didn't know how to live. Marc stopped rocking, and listened to that still, small voice.

Abraham.

Marc glanced around, but other than the horse, he was alone. Okay, so maybe he *was* going crazy, or else the Lord planted the name in his mind. It wasn't just any name. It wasn't Robert, or Harry, or even Sam. Abraham in the Bible was known for his great faith. *What are you trying to tell me, Lord?*

He sat for a few minutes, thinking. Then it hit him with sudden, full clarity. Abraham was asked to do the unthinkable when God told him to offer his son, Isaac, as a sacrifice. Surely, as a father, Abraham's heart would have been burdened and heavy. Most likely, he wondered why a loving God would ask him to do such a thing, but Abraham was willing to do it because he understood that God, in His infinite grace and mercy, would work it all out for good.

But could he—a proud, stubborn-as-nails man—take such a giant leap of faith and give up the most precious thing in his life? A vision of Mr. Davis that fateful night in Boston filled his thoughts, along with his wise counsel. *Give her to God, son. It's not a battle. It's not God pitted in one corner and you in the other. You'll lose every time until you're willing to surrender to His will. Only then can you possibly be a winner.*

The words were seared into his memory, imprinted on his heart. He might be a little slow on the uptake, but he eventually got it. Finally, he understood what he needed to do. But why was it so hard for him to give up? *Because it's an admission of failure.*

"In order to keep her, I have to be willing to give her up. That's what you're telling me, isn't it, Lord?" Marc lifted his head in a blind haze and focused on the sudden, dark clouds obscuring the sun. Ironic. He'd experienced a personal Damascus moment—seen the light—and yet the sun had disappeared.

The Lord knew his heart and that surrendering was one of the hardest tests for him. And he *was* being tested. "Okay, it's not a battle, but still, you win, God." His anguished cry filled the silence. Love is about sacrifice. Look what

Abraham was willing to do. Look what Christ did for him on that cross, dying a horrible, disfiguring death in order to save man from his own sin.

To save me. Marc closed his eyes. *For the promise to Abraham or to his descendants . . . that he would be heir of the world was not through the Law, but through the righteousness of . . .* "Faith." In the same way Abraham was justified by faith, he—Marc Thompson—was saved by faith in God's Son. The truth settled in his heart and wrapped itself around him, soothing his weary soul. Surrendering to God's will for Natalie, including the recovery of her memories, wasn't a failure. It was simply called . . . *faith.*

Something jarred his senses, and he turned his head, listening. Was that a voice? Maybe he was exhausted from all the thinking and possible hallucinating. Marc looked in every direction. No, it wasn't his imagination. There it was again— a distinct cry for help, but whether human or animal, he couldn't be sure.

"Is someone there?" Marc sprang to his feet. "Make a noise so I'll know where to find you!" Running to Dandelion, he unwound the rope tethering her to the tree. Cupping his hands over his mouth, he hollered, "Where are you? I'm here to help, but I need to know where you are!"

The sounds were louder this time, a plea for help. Female. Marc shuddered. "Please, God, be with me." Quickly mounting Dandelion, he guided the horse out of the clearing. He crept along at a slow pace, listening for more sounds. It wasn't long before he was rewarded with another faint cry.

"Help me! Hurry!" The fading screams held an urgency that shot deep shivers up and down his spine, quickened his pulse. Marc didn't think anything could be as bone-chilling as Natalie's scream when she fell on the stairs, or her sobs as she cried in the car here in Montana, but this was dangerously close. He stopped in his tracks for a few seconds to get his bearings, but knew he had to keep moving. God put him out here in the wilderness for a reason—several reasons, apparently.

There! The cries came from the east. So much for instinct. He turned Dandelion in the opposite direction. Galloping at full speed, he prayed he'd get there in time, and the Lord would help him know what to do. Coming out of another clearing, Marc's eyes widened in horror as he spied a woman trapped in the half-frozen water of a creek. Her face was partially submerged as she bobbed up and down in the water, flailing her arms in a desperate effort to stay afloat. Long hair was plastered to her head, and her face was deathly pale, lips nearly blue.

When her eyes moved to him, they held frozen horror yet a faint glimmer of hope. Green eyes. *Rebekah!* His heart pounding, Marc quickly dismounted. "Stay!" *Lord, please keep that horse here. I'm going to need her.* The banks running along the frozen creek offered no place to tether Dandelion. It wouldn't do either one of them any good if he ended up in that creek with Beck. They'd both be goners. He didn't want to make Natalie a widow before they had a chance to reunite. That kept him moving.

"Hang on, Beck!" How had she ended up in the creek? Tossing the loop over Dandelion's head, he fashioned a loop on the other end, thankful the rope was several feet long. He was going to need it. At least he still had some manual dexterity considering his hands were practically frozen stiff. A sense of urgency spurred him on as he unfurled the thick rope attached to the saddle as he carefully picked his way to the edge of the creek.

"Give me your hand!" Stretching out over the creek as far as possible, he extended his hand. Beck tried, but shook her head and sank a little further into the water. His foot slid on the ice on the frozen creek bank, and he muttered a few choice words under his breath. He'd ask forgiveness later. Inhaling a deep, calming breath, Marc secured his foothold as best he could as he stepped closer to the edge. He couldn't go much further. It was dangerous enough as it was, but this was where his baseball skills might come in handy.

Reach. Stretch. *Lengthen the muscles, Thompson.* Contact! He probably should have fallen in that creek, but Someone kept him steady. Losing her grip, Beck slipped back into the water. To his immense horror, Marc saw her eyes rolling to the back of her head. She was losing consciousness. "Beck, stay with me!"

Lord, please. You can't let her die. Give me strength. Help me know what to do.

He had to try another tact. Although he'd never been a pitcher, he had decent aim, and prayed his throwing arm wouldn't fail him now.

You and me, Lord. Here goes.

He quickly tossed the other end of the rope in Beck's direction. Miraculously, it landed exactly where he needed it—over her head, but with enough give for him to maneuver it under her left arm. Springing into action, every second precious, Marc pulled. He was rewarded when she slowly emerged from the water. Grunting with the effort, he grasped her hand and tugged her toward him with every ounce of strength he possessed, using long-forgotten muscles.

Beck's body temperature was so low she couldn't move, her limbs frozen. She looked up at him in a helpless stupor as he half-pulled, half-dragged her up onto the creek bank. Removing the rope, he scooped her into his arms. Beck was so cold, her long legs stiff, she wouldn't be able to get up, much less sit upright on her own. Of course, she had to be the tallest woman in the camp, at least five-foot-ten.

For a few seconds, he stared at Dandelion, trying to figure out what to do next. Beck moaned, those green eyes fading fast. He somehow had to get her to the main house. Mounting the horse, he managed to pull her upright, positioning her in front of him. He'd never be able to explain it other than it was the Lord's hand guiding him, giving him superhuman strength. Time was of the essence.

"Hold on, Beck," Marc whispered in one frozen ear as he commanded Dandelion to take them as fast as she could back to safety, back to warmth, back to the ranch and their loving friends. "Let's go home."

Chapter 33

"*N*ATALIE, A WORD, please?"

She turned away from the kitchen door, her heart rate picking up speed. "Sure, Sam." This had to be about Marc since the two had been nearly inseparable the last few days.

Leading the way to a corner of the large family room, Sam sat in the rocker and pulled it close to where she sat on the edge of the sofa. He put one hand over hers for a brief moment and squeezed. "Even if you don't remember, I'm sure you've learned I'm a pretty straightforward man. I hope you understand we're all here to help."

Tears stung her eyes. "Of course. I appreciate the sacrifice you, Lexa and all the TeamWork members made to come here and help both the Tuckers as well as Marc and me. It means more than you'll ever know."

Sam smiled. "It's not a sacrifice when love's involved. I'm sure Marc could tell you something about that." He paused when she looked at her lap, willing her hands to stay still. This man humbled her and possessed a unique ability to see straight through to her soul. Raising her head, taking a deep breath, she nodded for him to continue.

"You and I were both raised by strong Christian parents who modeled a solid marriage of faith and trust. From what he's told me, Marc didn't have that advantage. Most people don't."

"I know. I'm sure you probably also know that Marc's always been in competition with his dad."

Sam tilted his head, a puzzled expression creasing his brow. "We haven't discussed anything about his dad."

She couldn't imagine why Marc hadn't told him. "Phil Thompson. Boston Celtics? Two-time NBA champions in the 70s."

Sam's blue eyes widened. "Jumpin' Phil Thompson was Marc's dad?" He shook his head, whistling under his breath. "Marc told me he grew up in St. Louis, so I had no idea. Although," he said, running his hand through his thick hair, "he does sort of look like him, from what I remember. I think I have his autobiography, as a matter of fact. He died a few years ago, right? Cancer?"

"A decade ago, actually. His parents divorced when he was nine or ten, but his dad wasn't around much and unfortunately never took the time to get to know his kids. It's a difficult subject for Marc. When his dad left, it forced him to be the man of the family for his mom and sister, taught him to be strong and a self-made man. In many important ways, it shaped who he is as an adult." A sigh escaped. "From what I've seen since my accident, my husband works very hard for what he's earned, but sometimes I worry *he* thinks it's not enough."

Her eyes met Sam's. "He thinks he needs to impress me with a nice home and expensive things. But they're just *things*, Sam. It's not what I want."

Sam's penetrating gaze held her attention. "And what is it that *you* want?"

"For one thing, I wish Marc would understand it's okay for a guy to cry. It doesn't mean he's any less of a man. If anything," she said, twisting her fingers together, "it makes him even *more* of a man. I want him to understand life's not a competition. Especially with a dead man." Maybe it sounded harsh, but it was true.

Sam nodded. "I'm sorry he had to go through that with his dad, just like I'm sorry for your amnesia and what you two are going through now. But you and I both know God doesn't make mistakes, Natalie. In the short time I've known your husband, I've seen his heart. Marc's a good, solid, faithful man who succumbed to a sin that's trapped many, Christian or not. Men *and* women. I know how difficult this is for you, but it's in his past, and that's the key. He's open and honest with his feelings, and he's put everything on the line by bringing you here to try and reconnect."

Natalie met those blue eyes again, her resolve slipping away.

Sam leaned closer, keeping his voice low as other TeamWork volunteers came into the house. "Marc wants a second chance with you. In order to do that, he needs a clean slate. I hope you'll give him that, but there's something else I'd like you to remember. Marc's past sins are covered by the cross, by the shed blood of the Savior you and I both serve."

When she reached for his hand, Sam grasped it, squeezing tight, as they bowed their heads. As she listened to the prayer of this man—their leader in so many ways and a mentor for her husband—she couldn't imagine better role models for a strong Christian marriage than Sam and Lexa.

Finished with his prayer, Sam rose and tapped her chin. "It's my prayer you'll allow Marc to be the man he wants to be, for you *and* your child." He waited until her eyes met his. "And, from what you've told me this afternoon, I'm also sure he wants to be the kind of father *his* dad never was. You're giving him a precious gift, Natalie. I hope you can let him be the husband of your heart. Always remember, God knows what He's doing." With a smile, Sam departed.

Pulling off her boots and tucking her feet beneath her, Natalie snuggled into the corner of the sofa. Wiping a few stray tears from her cheeks, she pondered Sam's wise words. A few of the other volunteers moved quietly about the room. They were very sensitive in leaving her to her privacy, but it warmed her heart knowing that, if she needed them, they'd be there in a heartbeat.

~

An hour later, walking back to the main house from the office, Sam heard distant shouting. Shielding his eyes with one hand, he spied Beck on Dandelion,

Marc seated behind her, his arms wrapped around her waist as they appeared on the horizon. Something wasn't right. The closer they came, he saw Beck was inert, slumped over. The despair in Marc's expression was unmistakable.

His heart thundering in his chest, Sam ran as fast as he could to meet them. Dandelion barely stopped before he pulled Beck down from the horse. Soaked to the skin, her eyes were closed. Moaning, she didn't move as Sam cradled her in his arms. "What happened?" He ran with Marc keeping pace beside him.

"I don't know how, but she fell in the creek on the east side of the ranch."

"The Lord put you there, buddy. Go find Kevin. He has keys to one of the cars. Tell him to get it ready and pull it around in front of the main house. Lexa can help me get Beck out of these wet clothes and we need to get her to the hospital. Make sure to get a hot shower and into some dry clothes as soon as you can. Go. I'll take good care of her."

Glancing down at Beck as Marc ran in the other direction, Sam held her against his chest, hoping some of his body heat might transfer to her. Her limbs were stiff, unyielding. She looked so still with her lips blue, face pale and eyes red-rimmed. It scared him to death, and he murmured a quick prayer. Bursting through the door of the main house a few seconds later, Sam hollered for Lexa as he lowered her to the sofa. Beck was so cold, almost brittle to the touch. "Lexa! I need you!" Taking her hand in his, he detected a faint but steady pulse. "Lexa! Now!"

Cheeks smeared with flour, long braid swinging, Lexa flew through the door. "I'm here! Hold on to your . . ." If the situation weren't so desperate, he'd laugh. Seeing Beck on the sofa, his wife's beautiful eyes grew wide as she immediately flew to his side, falling to her knees. "Leave us for a couple of minutes. I need to peel these wet things off her."

"We don't have time. You're going to need help." Together they pried off the jeans and jacket. He rubbed and massaged Beck's feet, keeping his eyes trained on his task while Lexa did the same with Beck's hands until they both felt slight warmth. He handed Lexa a thick blanket draped over a nearby chair and laid out the wet clothes on the hearth, close to the fire.

Lexa gave him a knowing look. "Let me get the rest of her things off, and then I'll wrap her in blankets." With the back of her hand, Lexa brushed it over Beck's cheek. She stirred slightly.

"I sent Marc to get Kevin and asked that he bring the car around," Sam said. "I'm not sure about the 9-1-1 response time here, and there's a small hospital down the road about ten minutes away. We can probably get her there faster if we take her ourselves."

Lexa nodded. "Give me three minutes. I'm sure once Marc told Kevin it was Beck, he went into overdrive. That boy won't be long."

~

Marc wasn't in the dining hall that night. It wasn't like the man to skip a meal. The last time they'd been together had been so contentious, not to mention confusing, so Natalie assumed he was laying low, giving her space. One of the other men would probably take dinner to him in the cabin. Maybe she should be the one to do it?

As soon as Cassie joined them a few minutes later, she told them about Beck's rescue. Soon, all the men and women gathered around the table, listening to the tale. Natalie's eyes widened. "My Marc saved her?"

Winnie ducked her head, but couldn't hide her grin. "Yes, *your* Marc. I have to say, it's very nice to hear you call him that."

"Why should you be so surprised, Natalie?" Amy said as they all hurried back over to their cabin. Because of what happened with Beck, Sam's devotionals in the main house had been cancelled. "Look," Amy said, draping one arm around her, "I could tell you that you're being a little unreasonable . . ."

"Just spit it out." Natalie was too tired to be irritated. "Let me have it. You know you want to." After all, everyone else had been telling her the same thing all the livelong day. She caught the warning glance Winnie shot Amy's way, but it went unheeded. They sighed with relief as they reached the warmth of the cozy cabin and shed their outerwear.

Amy inhaled a deep breath. "Okay, you asked, so here goes." One hand traveled down to her hip, and she faced her dead-on. "The blessing in what happened is that if Marc hadn't been so miserable, he might not have been near that creek, and we might be mourning a close friend right now."

She stopped, and they all stared at each other before bursting into spontaneous tears. Arms around one another, they wept, holding on tight.

"Please tell me Beck's going to be okay," Natalie said, wiping her cheek. No sooner were the words out of her mouth than she felt something stir in her belly.

Winnie watched her closely. "What is it, sweetie? Is it the baby?"

"Yes!" She paused, one hand moving to her abdomen. There it was again. "I definitely felt a flutter." Winnie started telling her what she could expect, giving details and specifics. Her wealth of knowledge was amazing for a single woman who'd never experienced pregnancy or childbirth. When Cassie came back to the cabin a short time later, they were engaged in a very animated conversation, Amy and Winnie gathered around where she sat on her bed. Natalie giggled at the expression on the pretty, auburn-haired girl's face. She must think them a bunch of loons. Life with the TeamWork crew was never dull, that was for sure.

"Natalie felt the baby kick for the first time!" Winnie said, sounding like the proud Mother Hen.

Cassie's bright grin lit her entire face. "That's great, Natalie! You must be so excited."

"Thanks," Natalie said. While true, her thoughts were preoccupied with Beck's condition. "Have you heard anything more about Beck?" *Please, Lord, she has to be okay.*

"Lexa and Sam are at the hospital with her. Kevin's also keeping close watch over her. Last I heard, he was feeding her soup and planned on reading to her. He took his guitar, and provided the hospital staff allows it, I'm sure he plans on serenading her later."

Amy grinned. "I sure hope it's a love song since Kevin can't seem to find the words otherwise."

Winnie sighed. "Even if that dear boy can't find the words to tell Beck how he feels, hopefully his actions speak louder than words. He's so sweet, and it's obvious to everyone else how bad he's got it for her."

"If only Beck's brain isn't frozen," Cassie added. She frowned. "I didn't mean that to sound insensitive, considering the circumstances. From what I understand she's got some hotshot British boyfriend back in Louisiana, and that had something to do with her little tumble into the creek."

"Really? What do you mean?" Amy asked, sitting up. "Do tell."

Natalie glanced at Winnie. Her expression clued her in she might know something about it.

"Lexa said some Brit asked her to marry him, but she hasn't known him very long. Beck was trying to think things through when her foot slipped, thus the tumble into the frozen water." Cassie pulled off her hat and gloves and sat down on a chair, shaking out that luxurious mane of auburn waves. "That poor girl."

"Why on earth did she have to walk near a creek in this weather?" Amy shuddered. "I wouldn't go near one. Maybe a girl from Louisiana doesn't realize how dangerous it can be?"

"Love can do funny things to a person, and sometimes you don't always think straight," Winnie said, ignoring their stares. "Beck will be just fine, with or without the British guy. Hopefully, after what's happened, she'll finally look at Kevin and give him a chance. Of course, I don't know this other guy from Adam."

That last comment prompted a grunt from Cassie. "Funny you should say that because the other guy's name *is* Adam."

"I knew there was a guy in her life, but I didn't know his name," Winnie said.

Cassie frowned again. "I'm just thankful Marc found Beck when he did."

"I know, I know," Natalie said, raising one hand. "I've already been told how judgmental I've been about my husband, but I've also been assured that if I hadn't made him so miserable, he might not have found Beck when he did." Immediate regret squeezed inside. She sounded petty and wasn't proud of it. "I need to find Marc."

"Are you going to forgive him?" Amy lowered her eyes, a flush coloring her cheeks. "Sorry if I'm overstepping my bounds."

Natalie paused a moment, locking eyes with Winnie as she grabbed her jacket and thrust her arms into it. The look on Amy's face was expectant, mirrored by Cassie and Winnie. It was all she could do not to laugh out loud. What a bunch of matchmakers. She wasn't sure how to answer the posed question. Pulling the gloves out of her pocket, she shook her head. "All I know is, I have to find my husband."

Chapter 34

$\mathcal{N}$ATALIE KNOCKED ON the door of the men's cabin. Not hearing any sound or movement inside, she turned the knob. Although she shouldn't venture inside without an invitation, she hoped Marc might be there. Alone. Newly-fed and worn out, she figured some of the guys would surely be around. She knew Kevin was with Beck, but where could the others be? Probably tending to the horses for the night or doing some male bonding elsewhere.

"Hello? Anyone here?" She poked her head inside and darted a glance around. Typical men's cabin. She smiled at a couple of unmade beds and assorted items strewn on the floor in haphazard fashion. Probably Eliot, and no doubt Marc. Sure enough, a pair of boots beneath a bed caught her eye, and she recognized them as Marc's second pair. Feeling a pull toward the bed, Natalie sat down and picked up his flannel shirt. Burying her nose in it, she absorbed his scent, an odd but appealing combination of Irish Spring, Calvin Klein and pure masculinity. She smiled and laid it on the bed, smoothing out a wrinkle. If one of the men discovered her with her face in her husband's shirt, they'd find it amusing—and Marc would love it—but she wouldn't be able to hold up her head around the ranch.

A small stack of letters bound with a rubber band sat halfway beneath Marc's pillow. Natalie chewed her lower lip. It was an invasion of Marc's privacy, but if she didn't look, she'd always wonder. Picking up the envelopes, she randomly flipped through them. She'd know that scrawl anywhere. No return address, but they were all addressed to her at the house in Newton and dated within the last few months.

She hesitated, her hand on the top envelope. *Forgive me, Lord.* Any of the men might come back any minute, so she needed to get on with it. Pulling out a folded piece of Marc's impressive agency letterhead, her heart pounding, she darted a glance at the door before starting to read.

Dearest Natalie,

I need to tell you about something I've never talked about before. Especially because of that stupid incident with Ashley at the restaurant that ruined what should have been one of the happiest days of our lives, I need to tell you. Even if you never read this, or hear this from me, I need to write it down. Maybe it'll help.

My dad was unfaithful to Mom. Several times over. You might already have guessed as much. He was powerful, a celebrity, good looking. I know Mom thinks I look like him. That probably hurts her, too, even though she'd never hold Dad's indiscretions against me, but I witnessed firsthand what Dad's infidelity did to Mom.

As God is my witness, I vow never to hurt you like that, Natalie. I couldn't bear to see the pain of betrayal in your eyes.

Even though Mom tried to hide her hurt, I saw it. She hid behind her meetings, parties, society events, and her children. But I saw the look in her eyes the day she opened the newspaper and saw that photo of Dad with his arm around another woman, kissing her cheek. Most people looking at that photo never had a clue they weren't looking at Dad with Mom. They probably assumed it was his wife, but we knew the truth.

I think Mom suspected, but she never really knew until that moment. I was the one who found her hunched over the breakfast table, the newspaper soaked with her tears. I'll never forget it, Natalie. I was just a kid, but it changed me in a profound way. Maybe that's part of the reason why I couldn't ever bring myself to tell you about the other women I'd known before I married you.

You're so sweet and innocent, and I'm the only man you've ever known. I love that about you. Natalie, you have to know I'd take back my past behavior in a heartbeat, if only I could. But the sad truth is, I can't, but it doesn't take away what I feel in my heart for you.

He switched gears and transitioned into a prayer. *Lord, help Natalie to know in her heart that I've never looked at another woman since meeting her. That's the way it'll be until I die. I guess part of my Dad lives in me, and I got way too proud of myself when I played ball, but that's behind me now. It was stupid. My only excuse is that I didn't know You. Didn't know it was wrong.*

Okay, I knew it was wrong morally, but I didn't pay attention to anything but what I wanted and my own selfish desires. In my own mind, it wasn't the same thing as what my dad did—because I wasn't committed in a marriage relationship, but now, things are different. You know my heart, Lord, and my deepest desire is to be with Natalie.

You gave Natalie to me. I know that. She's the sweetest, greatest gift I'll ever have. She's the blessing I'll spend the rest of my life thanking You for. I want to always make her smile like a little girl with love and joy in her eyes, her voice, her heart. And now she's giving me a child. What an awesome responsibility.

Sometimes I wonder what I did to deserve her, and now another human being. Hopefully, this child will only be the first of many. A child with Natalie's gorgeous face and intelligence, and maybe some of my business sense and dogged determination. I promise I'll never let Natalie or my family down the way Dad let us down. I'll probably make a lot of mistakes—maybe some pretty big ones—but I'll never purposely tear down my family. Still, I'm human, and need Your help. Keep my eyes on the straight and narrow. Help keep my mind focused, my thoughts and eyes pure, and my sole purpose and heart's desire set on keeping myself and my family strong. May Natalie and I never lose sight of what's most precious in this life—the love we share, because You first loved us, Lord.

Natalie's cheeks were damp with tears she didn't bother wiping away as she pressed the letter to her chest. Her tears had fallen on the letter, smearing the ink just like Marc's mom's tears on that fateful newspaper photo. He'd been afraid to tell her about his dad's infidelities, but from what he'd written, he'd learned much from his dad's mistakes.

When Marc told her he'd never betray her trust, he must have been thinking of the ultimate pain his mom suffered because of his dad's betrayal. No wonder his feelings toward his dad were so bittersweet. Natalie's heart ached with newfound respect for his mom. For any woman to withstand adultery from her husband with such grace and dignity was an incredible testament of her inner courage and steadfastness. Sure, she could be flaky and temperamental sometimes, but she'd carried on and raised Marc and his sister as best she could as a single parent. They'd both turned out to be strong, independent, intelligent people, worthy of her respect, admiration, and her love.

Folding the letter, Natalie slipped it back into its envelope. There were more letters, but she didn't need to read them. Perhaps Dr. Fontaine encouraged Marc to write down his thoughts and feelings as a cathartic exercise, never intended for her eyes, but, somehow, she suspected the Lord wanted her to read this particular one. The baby fluttered. Great timing. Rising carefully from the bed, one hand on her stomach, she smiled. Unwittingly, her husband had given her the most beautiful, heartfelt birthday gift she could ever receive.

~

"Marc." She hadn't slept well, counting the hours until she could go find him again. With deep circles under her eyes, Natalie knew she couldn't look good, but seeing him sent shivers through her, and it wasn't from the cold.

I do love him, Lord.

Marc turned from talking with some of the other men gathered outside the men's cabin. Seeing her, his eyes softened, but he didn't smile.

"I need to speak with you. Alone." She didn't think the men could move so fast, but every single one of them scampered off in the direction of the dining hall without speaking. It's as if they all knew instinctually where to go as they headed out together like a silent herd of sheep. And, of course, they headed straight for the food. Well, it *was* time for breakfast, and she'd purposely planned it that way.

"Let's go inside," Marc said. Reaching around her, he opened the door of the cabin as snow fell all around them. Coming inside behind her, he closed the door hard, shutting out the cold.

Facing him, Natalie slowly removed her right glove and picked up his hand. He watched with a puzzled expression. Placing his hand on her stomach, she put hers over it, holding it steady. Marc didn't question, didn't say anything. His blue-eyed gaze swept over her—from the top of her head, to her forehead, down to her cheeks, and then to her nose before settling on her lips. It was as intimate as a kiss. Her husband loved her with his eyes, and it shot a bolt of fire straight through her. It didn't take long to feel the baby fluttering. Good girl. Marc's eyes lit with excitement.

"Is that . . . ?" She couldn't miss the catch in his throat.

"That's our baby saying hello to her daddy for the very first time. Her father the hero."

Marc shook his head, and his hand fell to his side. "I was so scared, Natalie. The Lord gave me the strength. I couldn't have done it otherwise. I'm too weak, as you know." His tone held not a trace of bitterness.

"No," she said, shaking her head, "you're not weak at all." A tear dropped onto her cheek. Another tear escaped and slid down her cheek, dropping to the floor.

"May I?" Marc asked quietly, stepping closer. "Will you let me?"

Natalie nodded while the tears continued to fall. When he bundled her in his arms, she leaned into them, feeling more at home than she had since her fall. She belonged with this man, in his arms. More importantly, it's where she wanted and needed to be. He kissed her cheek, his soft, warm lips tracing the trail of tears before repeating the same achingly sweet ritual on the other side.

"We loved each other enough to make a baby, Natalie. Now we need to love each other enough to raise our child . . . together. Please don't punish me for my past. I love you and only you, and that's all that matters. I'll be faithful to you for the rest of my natural born life. That's a promise to you and our baby. I can only pray you believe me."

The tears were flowing freely from his eyes, too, as he looked at her with all the love, and the sadness, in his heart. Her husband was *crying*, and that in itself was one of the most precious things for her heart. It was healing for both of them, and a promise for their shared future.

It was a *gift. Thank you, Lord.*

"Shhh . . ." she whispered, brushing blond bangs away from his eyes. His hair was getting longer, and curled slightly on the ends. She liked it. It made him seem younger, and somehow more vulnerable. Her hand lingered on his cheek for a moment, and he leaned into her touch. Pulling his head toward hers, she returned the favor and very slowly kissed the wet trail of her husband's tears. When he started to wipe away a tear, she removed his hand, replacing it with her lips.

"Let me. You know," she whispered, holding his face between her hands, leaning her forehead against his chin, "beneath all your bravado, Marc Thompson, you've got a very emotional heart. Thank you for not being afraid to cry, not being afraid to open your heart. That in itself is a very precious gift, you know."

It wasn't until much later Natalie remembered she hadn't told Marc she believed him. But surely he knew. Somewhere deep within his heart, he had to know.

Chapter 35

*T*HE EVENING DEVOTIONS centered on the attributes of God, and how His abundant grace flows through His own. "Every single day of my life, I'm impressed how the Lord is watching over me and providing for my needs in truly awesome ways." Slipping on his glasses and opening his Bible, Sam surveyed the volunteers gathered around the fireplace in the main house. "The Lord has blessed me by bringing people into my life who accept me unquestioningly, without pretense." He looked straight at Lexa. "His graciousness encompasses and transcends more than personal relationships and friendships. His grace comes to us in unexpected ways. In the form of a child placing her hand in yours." Sam's eyes found Marc's. "Or in the form of a job that gives you more personal fulfillment and satisfaction than you ever dreamed possible. Or when a lost soul asks questions about salvation and offers you an unbelievable opportunity to share the Savior's love."

He read a few verses of Scripture and they prayed together. "In closing," Sam told them, "when God sent His Son to die upon a cross, covering our sins, it was His ultimate act of grace. And our job is to accept that grace so freely bestowed on us. We didn't earn it, we didn't deserve it, and yet He loved us enough. We need to grow with it, learn from it, and share it." Sam smiled and removed his glasses, tucking them in his shirt pocket. "It's in our hearts every single day, and it's what we choose to do with His grace that makes our lives significant—for ourselves and others."

"You know, Natalie, I've experienced God's grace in new and unique ways since we've been here in Montana," Marc told her as they walked together a short time later. Elwood pranced around on his leash between them. It was a brisk, cold night, but the wind had eased somewhat, making it less bitter. Either that or the fact that Natalie was thawing and warming toward him, increasing his internal temperature.

"Go on. I'm listening," she said with a gentle smile.

Taking a chance, he reached his hand to her. Hesitating only a moment, still smiling, Natalie placed her hand in his. It was covered in her warm, woolen glove. "It's good to be here, out of my so-called comfort zone. I know the Lord's trying to teach me some things and, for once—and maybe because I'm physically and geographically removed from the agency—I'm listening." He laughed a little. "I'm finally open to listening."

"Kind of like removing the source of temptation?"

Curious choice of words. "I suppose that's true. When I'm at the agency, I'm the top gun. But, being here, I can see I'm no top gun." Shaking his head, Marc chuckled. "I'm a man with some decent business sense. God allowed me to build my agency into what it is today, but there's no way on earth I could have done it without His help. It's when I start thinking with my pride that He knocks me down every time."

"I know how difficult that must be for you," Natalie said quietly. "Relinquishing control." It was true. Amnesia or not, she knew him pretty well. She squeezed his hand tighter. "I'm proud of you, Marc. If you want to check your messages, I'll understand. Really, I will. You sacrificed a lot to leave the agency for two weeks and come here." She graced him with an enchanting smile. "It's true what I told Sam and Lexa at the restaurant after they picked us up at the airport. You are a man to be admired. Very much."

He desperately wanted to kiss her. Instead, he started walking again, making sure she was beside him, studying her lovely profile. Maybe it was the cold weather, maybe her pregnancy, but she was positively radiant. Stepping to the side of the women's cabin, he took both her hands in his. "Since we've been here, I've also realized something else."

Her face, so beautiful, upturned to his as her eyes roamed over his face in a slow, luxurious path. "What's that?" Her voice was quiet, curious.

"God graced me with *you*. You, Natalie, are the gift I'll forever be thankful for, and now, you're giving me a child. He could have taken you in that horrible fall, but He didn't. I realize that's a selfish attitude, but I . . ." He stared at the ground, moving his feet to keep warm before meeting her eyes again. "I'm counting on that same grace to bring you back to me, whether or not you remember everything from before. It's enough. *His* grace is sufficient."

Natalie's eyes glistened as she put her gloved hand on the side of his face, like she had in the cabin. It touched him somewhere deep inside. No other woman had ever affected him the way she did. His intent in bringing Natalie to Montana was for her to fall in love with him again, but it was also working the other way around.

"You're an incredible man."

"I have another confession." Natalie's eyes grew wide, and she started to withdraw her hand, but he caught it, holding tight. "This isn't anything you need to worry about."

"Okay, but maybe you'd better tell me quick." The beginnings of a frown creased her forehead. Now he'd worried her, and that wasn't his intention.

With one hand, he smoothed her brow. "Your fall was *my* fall from grace. In some ways, I found *my* grace because of it, sweetheart."

She was quiet a long moment, her eyes canvassing his face. "Are you saying it was a *good* thing?"

He laughed a little. "Not sure I'd go that far." Those rosebud lips parted, inviting him. He planted a soft, sweet kiss. Not wanting to tempt or tease her, he withdrew quickly. His lips grazed her temple as he whispered, "I'd say it was a *God* thing." Her skin was warm, and his sigh was deep with longing as he regained his equilibrium.

"You know what *your* problem is, Marc?"

His heart in his throat, he shook his head, not capable of words. He hoped she wasn't trying to pick a fight because he wasn't up to it tonight. The gleam in her eyes told him otherwise.

"You've put me on a pedestal, and there's no way I'll measure up to your ideal of the perfect woman. The perfect wife." Natalie shook her head. "Might as well get over it now, or I'm afraid you'll be sorely disappointed."

Marc laughed and rubbed his hand over his cheek. "You're close to perfection. Except when you're spitting mad. Even then, you're pretty cute."

"Here," she said, handing over Elwood's leash with a smile, "I think you should take our furry friend tonight."

"Thanks." Marc glanced down at the little dog. "I'm working on being an even better man for you, Natalie." Raising her gloved hand, he planted another kiss.

"Oh, I think you're pretty special just the way you are."

Not hearing the door of the cabin creak behind him as he walked away, Marc knew Natalie watched, but he didn't dare look back as a wide smile creased his lips.

Chapter 36

GLASSES IN PLACE once again, Sam opened his Bible to begin the short devotional the next evening. Listening to the passages of scripture, Marc shook his head, laughing under his breath, but he heard every word. Stealing glances across the room at Natalie, he could tell she was equally amused. When he winked, it brought that lovely flush to her cheeks. They'd been flirting with each other all day, and it was incredible.

Exhausted from another long day working the ranch, most of the crew headed back to the cabins almost immediately after the devotions. Leaving with the ladies, Natalie gave him an almost shy smile and a small wave. It started his heart pumping fast, enough to keep him warm.

Sam walked alongside him. The night was still and quiet as the snow crunched beneath their heavy boots. "Song of Solomon? Subtlety is not your strong suit." With a slight snort, Marc tossed him a sidelong glance. "I take it that message was for my benefit."

"I hate to break it to you, but the world doesn't revolve around you." Sam laughed. "Okay, I'll admit I thought you and Natalie needed to hear a biblical example of a deep, abiding love. I can tell you're both ready for it." Sam stopped, inhaling the fresh air into his lungs. "Just like the air here in Montana, it does us all good to hear about love. Speaking from experience, I can tell you the love between a man and woman is truly one of God's greatest and most awesome blessings."

"Well, I'll hand it to you. Song of Solomon is about as graphic as it gets in describing physical love within the framework of marriage." Marc crossed his arms over his chest. "All I'm saying is, congratulations."

Sam tilted his head to one side, a mischievous glint in those blue eyes. The smile lines deepened considerably. "I may regret asking this, but for what?"

Marc resisted laughing outright. It was his turn to slap Sam on the shoulder as he moved past him. "Tonight you filled our heads with thoughts of physical love and then sent us all back to our cabins. Thanks a lot. Guess I'll be going back to my own bed now . . . alone." The look he shot Sam's way was brimming with irony.

"A little tension is good for a relationship."

Marc stared into the distance. "I'll pretend you didn't just say that. Of course, it's all good and well for you, especially since you've got Lexa's twin gazelles which feed among the lilies to go home to tonight. Or however the verse goes."

Sam's laughter rang out in the stillness of the night.

"I'm not even sure what that means, but I'm sure it's all quite good. I just want you to keep in mind that others of us don't have that to look forward to . . . at least not at the moment."

"Chapter eight, verse fourteen says, 'Hurry, my beloved, and be like a gazelle or a young stag on the mountains of spices.'"

"Enough already with the gazelles." Holding up one hand, Marc shook his head. "Would I happen to be the stag in that passage?" Even though he realized he was probably taking it way out of context, he couldn't help but see the humor. After all, even the Lord has a sense of humor.

"That verse refers to separated lovers longing to be reunited and compares it to the Church longing for Christ as its Bridegroom." Sam tilted his head, surveying him. "Get the picture?"

"It's pretty clear, yes, and Natalie and I fit the whole separated lovers description. I also remember a verse in there somewhere that talks about your neck being like the tower of David, built with rows of stones. Well, old man, I think one of those stones in your tower has traveled to points north in your brain." He resumed walking, and Sam fell into step beside him.

"If I didn't know better, I'd say you're accusing me of having rocks for brains."

"Never. All I'm suggesting is that it might be better to stick with married couples when you're doing a devotional from that particular book." He shot Sam another glance loaded with meaning. "People who have someone to go home to." He paused for effect. "Get the picture?"

Sam shook his head. "I'm sorry. Sometimes I think I'm helping when it only makes it more difficult for you. My intent was for you to focus on the positive aspects of a union between a man and a woman who are blessed by God. It's something for the younger, unmarried singles to look to as the ideal in a marriage relationship, and something for married couples to reflect on and maybe gain some new insight." A slight frown creased his brow and he adjusted his Stetson. "Perhaps you're right, especially since most of my TeamWork crew isn't married. Yet."

"Natalie and I are stuck somewhere in the middle. It's like we're in some weird," Marc said, gesturing with one hand, "relationship limbo." His smile sobered as the old familiar sadness reared its pesky head.

"Marc, do you even realize how *far* you've come with Natalie since you arrived here in Montana? You two were spitting mad at each other when I picked you up at the airport. She could barely look at you, much less speak to you. Based on her body language alone, it's a miracle you've come as far as you have in such a short time. Tonight, she was practically making love to you with her eyes." Sam shook his head and snorted. "Don't even get me started on you, Moony Eyes."

"Thanks for the recap."

"Has Natalie forgiven you?"

"She hasn't said it in so many words. One minute I think she has, and the next, I'm not so sure. It's all very confusing."

"She's probably working her way through all this. In some ways, it might not be the easiest thing being within the confines of the ranch, but you can take heart in the rowdy group of cheerleaders rooting for you from the sidelines."

"What did you just say?" Marc's brows raised.

"From what Lexa told me, the other women have pretty much told your wife she needs to forgive you. And," Sam added, "that she'd best do it soon or you might start looking elsewhere. Which I assured her you'd never do."

Marc's mouth downturned. "Why would they think such a thing? I mean, I know I don't have the best track record, but I trust not everyone in the camp knows that."

Sam leaned against a fence railing and shook his head. "I think the other women have their suspicions based on what they've witnessed happening between the two of you. Remember, your wife's known Amy, Winnie and Rebekah a few years. Even though Natalie might not remember much about them, they know *her*. Know how to read her, and love her. They're rallying around her and desperately want to see you two reunited. You know how women are natural born matchmakers. They did what they could for Lexa and me in San Antonio when we were working through our own relationship issues. They're good women. None better."

Marc shoved his gloved hands as far as they'd go in the pockets of his jacket as he leaned back against the railing beside Sam. "It's comforting to know I've got a personal cheerleading contingent. A man could do worse." He allowed the beginnings of a small grin. "Let's face it. I need all the support and encouragement I can get."

"I don't think I've told you how much I admire you for telling Natalie about your past. Even though I encouraged you to do it, it still took guts some men wouldn't have. You risked a lot. It's an extreme test of strength and character to admit your past sins, especially knowing it might irretrievably break the marriage."

"Gee, thanks . . . I think. I'll never admit it out loud, but sometimes you make a lot of sense, old man." Marc was starting to lose feeling in his extremities and turned back in the direction of the men's cabin, rubbing shoulders with Sam. Walking close together trapped the body heat, making it more bearable.

"Are you meeting up with Natalie to say good night?" Sam asked.

"No, she's tired. I'm sure she's already gone back to the cabin. Everything combined—the pregnancy, the weather, the work here—she needs her rest."

"Good man. And, again, for the record, I'm sorry, buddy. I didn't mean to make you uncomfortable."

Marc gave into his grin. "Forgiven. Now, go enjoy your sweet nectar. But do me a big favor and enjoy it for me, too."

Chapter 37

$\mathcal{T}$HE NEXT DAY, they all gathered in the main house for a celebration shortly after lunch to welcome Rebekah home from the hospital. It was great to see the color in her cheeks and she seemed no worse for her experience. As they prayed together as a group, Beck thanked the Lord for putting Marc out there in the wilderness and saving her life. Her voice choked with emotion. Afterwards, the women all gathered around her as most of the men quietly departed to their various posts. Catching Natalie's eye, Marc winked and headed out the door with Eliot and Dean.

Hugging Natalie, Beck wiped away her tears. "You were the first TeamWork volunteer to ever befriend me and welcome me to the group. You showed me around the work camp and made sure I met everyone. I'll never forget your kindness to me when I was just an 18-year-kid wanting to serve Jesus with no idea what I was doing or how I could even help." She took her hands, holding them tight. "I'll pray somehow your memory will be restored, and especially your love for Marc." She smiled. "Thanks to your husband, I'll be around for a lot more TeamWork missions, Lord willing."

As Beck moved across the room to speak with Lexa, Kevin approached. "Excuse me, Natalie, can I speak with you before you leave?" Hands in his pockets, he shuffled his feet on the floor, and looked more nervous than a child ready to face the principal's wrath for a prank. She'd seen that look enough times. That thought stopped her cold. She *remembered*.

Natalie struggled to find her voice. She smiled, wanting to put the shy man at ease. "You've known me a few years now, Kevin." She shrugged, giving him a sheepish look. "At least from what I understand. You don't have to be so formal."

The tautness around his mouth visibly relaxed, and his smile reached his eyes as they strayed over Natalie's shoulder. "I'll see you later, Rebekah."

Natalie hid her grin and resisted turning to look back at Beck. That first blush of love was so sweet. Tall, dark-haired and lean but muscular, Kevin had boy-next-door, classic good looks. He and Rebekah would make a striking couple, and their personalities would complement one another.

"I'm glad she's recovering well."

Kevin nodded. "Other than an occasional numbness in her hands, she's going to be fine." His eyes met hers. "Thanks to Marc."

"Why don't we go talk in the family room." Kevin followed as she led the way. Seating herself in the rocking chair, Natalie put one hand on her belly and exhaled a long, slow breath.

"Are you feeling okay?" He moved quickly to her side, his concern for her welfare touching.

"I'm fine. Just getting used to the little butterfly kicks in my belly. They're coming with more regularity now." It seemed her body was changing every day, and it both scared and exhilarated her.

"That must be pretty awesome. Marc's talked about how excited he is to be a father." Kevin dropped onto the sofa by the chair. "He started talking one night about how he thinks the baby is a girl. How he can't wait to hold her, teach her to throw a baseball, ride a bike, take her to dinner and give her a string of pearls on her sixteenth birthday . . ."

It was surprising Marc shared that much with him, but it was good to hear. Goodness, he probably envisioned dancing with their daughter at her wedding. "He didn't happen to tell you her name, did he?"

Kevin laughed. "No, but knowing Marc, he probably has one picked out."

"No doubt."

"What do the butterfly kicks feel like?" His eyes fell to her stomach before he looked away, his cheeks coloring.

"Sort of like my stomach's growling, but it's more of a fluttering instead of a low rumble. Like I'm being tickled from the inside out." She settled back in the rocker and gave him another smile of encouragement. "But I'm sure that's not what you wanted to talk about."

"I overheard a conversation Marc had earlier today. He was talking on his phone."

Natalie's eyes widened. "If it was a private conversation . . ." She shifted, suddenly uncomfortable.

"I don't think I'm betraying any confidences by telling you. Trust me, I think you'll be glad to know."

Everyone knew Kevin was the model of discretion. She trusted him. "Okay. You've definitely got my attention now."

"Marc listened for a long time, a big frown on his face. Then he went over to the wall of the cabin and pounded it with his fist. Not real hard, but hard enough. I could tell it was someone from his agency. They must have asked him if he could go back to Boston, but he kept insisting he couldn't. Apparently, they've left him tons of voicemails since he's been here in Montana." Kevin sat up straighter, leaning close. "From what I gather, a major client of Marc's agency—some huge baseball star—is threatening to pull out of a big ad campaign and insists on speaking and meeting with him about it. I could tell by the worried look on his face how much it took out of him to say he couldn't leave, even if it meant losing that ad campaign. As a matter of fact, Marc said in no uncertain terms that he was here in Montana to reconnect with you and nothing was going to interfere with that purpose. He told them to handle it without him."

A slow smile tipped the corners of Kevin's mouth. "After he hung up, he did the strangest thing. He stomped outside the cabin, burrowed a little hole in the snow and buried his phone, all the while quoting scripture verses about patience and dealing with anger. It was pretty funny watching him digging with his hands through the snow—like Elwood burying his dog bone in the ground. Snow was flying fast and furious all over the place."

Natalie laughed. "Why do you think he did that?"

Kevin shrugged. "My guess is that if he doesn't have the phone nearby, he can't worry about what he'll miss. He's removing the source of temptation."

Natalie's eyes opened wide at that comment.

"Here's the thing. Marc made a choice. When it came down to choosing between his business and you, he picked *you*. A lot of men would really struggle with that choice." He shrugged. "I just thought you should know."

Natalie's smile came from the depths of her heart. "Thank you, Kevin. I appreciate your sharing that with me." If only he knew.

~

After supper the next evening, Marc watched Natalie as everyone gathered around the fireplace in the main house. They lounged on the sofa, in the chairs or leaned against the brick hearth as they sang together and traded fun stories and testimonials. Sitting between Winnie and Amy, she looked barely older than a teenager, fresh-faced with no makeup. Hair scooped back in a twist at the back of her head, her cheeks glowed with health from being outdoors. He breathed a prayer of thanks she no longer suffered from any morning sickness, and couldn't keep his eyes away from her. Even though he hoped she'd sit beside him, he knew it would be too much of a distraction.

Sam spoke up. "Why don't we go around the circle tonight and everyone share what the Lord's revealing to them since they've been here at Milestone Ranch."

"I'll go first," Kevin said. "God's teaching me to open my eyes to the beauty all around us in His creation." He purposely avoided looking Beck's way, but no way was he referring only to the grandeur of the Montana environment. Everyone in the room knew it. Hopefully, Beck would catch on soon enough and put the poor kid out of his misery. Since falling in the creek, she'd awakened to Kevin's special attention. From the looks of it, she wasn't exactly resistant to his charms, but no one knew if she'd made any decisions regarding her British beau back home. They were young, and had plenty of time. It was doubtful Beck would ever find a man more devoted to her than Kevin.

Marc shifted his position, catching Natalie's eye and winking. She blushed and gave into a grin. If he was really blessed, tonight might be a turning point. He startled. Why was everyone staring at him? "My turn?" Soft chuckles rippled around the group. Like Kevin avoiding Beck, he now avoided glancing Natalie's way. They'd all get the point, anyway.

"The Lord's teaching me about grace . . . and patience." They all laughed, none louder than Sam. He shot him a wry grin. Zoning out for a couple of minutes, Marc broke out of his musings with a start when he noticed the circle had moved around to Natalie. She was the last one to share.

"And what is God teaching you, Natalie?" Lexa said. If it was possible, every person gathered in the circle strained forward to hear the answer.

Natalie looked across the circle, directly at him, and smiled. "God's teaching me the power of forgiveness."

Winnie let out a delighted gasp before clamping a quick hand over her mouth and darting a wide-eyed, embarrassed glance his way. "Sorry," she mouthed. Amy was beside herself and gave him a huge grin. Marc chuckled under his breath. You'd think the TeamWork volunteers were at a tennis match, watching the volleying back and forth. It was rather comical, and Sam and Lexa's amused grins did not escape him.

After a short closing prayer, Sam rose to his feet and closed his Bible with a definitive snap. "Well, I think that about does it for tonight. Thanks everyone. Good night, sleep well. See you in the morning." Marc laughed under his breath as Sam stifled a fake yawn.

It was amazing how quickly the room cleared. Sam and Lexa excused themselves and wasted no time in retreating to their quarters at the back of the house. Within three minutes, only he and Natalie sat together in front of the fireplace.

"You sure know how to clear a room," he said, "but you're still too far away." He patted the spot on the floor next to him, giving her his best come-hither look. He didn't trust himself not to kiss the living daylights out of her. It was becoming increasingly difficult to resist. Arms resting on raised knees, he watched as she moved over, close enough, but with about two inches between them. Still too far away. She was in a receptive, playful mood. "More," he said, his voice low. Returning his smile, she moved ever-so-slightly. "More." Again, she moved another fraction of an inch. "More." She smiled but didn't budge. Leaning over, he whispered, "More. Please."

With a sexy, throaty laugh he hadn't heard in way too long, Natalie pushed his knees down to the floor. His hands fell to his sides, his blood throbbing in every pore. This night was getting more promising by the moment. "More," she murmured, scooting over onto his lap. Facing him, she cupped his face between her hands.

"The most," he whispered back. How he loved flirting with her. He repositioned her a bit. Squeezing the plastic clip securing her hair, he watched as that silky, luxurious waterfall fell about her shoulders, framing her face. "*Natalie.*" It sounded as reverent as his most heartfelt prayer. In a way, it *was* a prayer. A prayer of thanks for the gift of his wife.

She placed one hand on his shoulder and then repeated with the other, her movements slow and methodical. A secretive smile upturned those tempting lips. She leaned closer, stopping when her lips were only about an inch away. Marc memorized them, loving their fullness and softness. "*Marc.*" The sound of his name never sounded so sweet as when she breathed it against his lips. Natalie kissed him for all she was worth, and then kissed him again.

Loving every second, he wished it would never end. By the time they came up for air, it was getting really late, and his wife's chin was a bit raw from his rough stubble. "Sorry." He scratched his beard with a cockeyed smile before smoothing his thumb over her tender skin. "If I'd known the pleasure this night would bring, I would have been better prepared."

"It's my badge of honor, and definitely worth it. Besides, I kind of like it." She traced his lips in the most tantalizing way he could imagine.

"Your lips were made specifically for mine, you know. We're a perfect match." Pretty corny for an ad man, but her smile told him she appreciated the sentiment.

Releasing a sigh of extreme contentment, she slid off his lap and leaned back against him. Several minutes passed in silence as he held her close. "I can feel your heartbeat."

He laughed. "Then you can tell how fast it's beating."

"Are you nervous?"

"A little."

"Why?" She turned to look at him, those deep blue eyes searching his.

"Am I forgiven?" He watched her, his heart in his throat.

"You should know the answer to that question, especially after what I said to the entire group tonight, and especially after what we've been doing for the past hour or so."

Was that a giggle? Oh, in that moment how he wished they were back home. "I need to hear the words, Natalie."

Pressing her lips against his for another long kiss, she pulled away with a reluctant groan. "Of course, I forgive you. I just needed to work through it all in my own head. It's rather hard to rearrange my thinking sometimes when I've only thought in one direction for so long."

"I think that crazy sentence actually made sense, which must mean that I understand you pretty well, my beautiful Natalie." He shook his head and kissed the tip of her nose. "Thank you, sweetheart. Not to belabor the point, but what made you change your mind?"

She shook her head. "For one thing, you've got a whole gang of cheerleaders around here."

That made him laugh. "What else?" He kissed her cheek, nibbling a slow path down to her neck. With a deep sigh, he pulled away and tried to focus.

"It wasn't so much that I changed my mind. I think, in the back of my mind, I always knew I'd forgive you. I just had to stand back and look at it from your perspective."

"And you could do that?"

"It wasn't easy," she said, looking down for a moment, "and not to say I've worked everything out in my mind yet, but I can understand how you could have been . . . tempted, and how you could have given into those temptations, especially without the love of the Lord guiding you. That makes all the difference." She looked back up at him then, mesmerizing him. "Any woman would be crazy not to want you. As God is my witness, I'm going to do everything within my power to keep you crazy in love with me for the rest of our lives."

"I don't think that will be a problem," he said, stroking her hair. "There's only one other woman who will ever fully have my heart, you know." He chuckled. "And I'm not talking about my mother. Or my sister."

"What?" she asked, looking momentarily alarmed. "Oh." She laughed a little as her cheeks flushed a pretty pink. "I suppose we should start discussing her name soon."

"Oh, we'll have plenty of time . . . later," he said, pulling her close again. Her sigh of longing was such sweet reward. Leaving her at the door of the women's cabin a few minutes later, Marc smiled as she stood on her tiptoes and kissed him on the cheek.

Time for the full-on ammunition. He planted one of his best efforts on her. He felt dizzy, almost drunk with happiness and desire. It was quite possibly their best kiss ever, and there had been some he thought would go unequaled. But this one . . . well, this one would send them both to bed happy.

Chapter 38

"*S*AM, WE'VE GOT to have some fun."

Lexa didn't need to tell him twice. "I'll get the key."

"Not that kind of fun . . . at least not yet." She gave him a knowing smile. "We need to take the troops into town, loosen them up. With everything going on with Natalie and Marc—and with what happened with Beck—everyone's all tense. They deserve a break." She folded the dish towel and turned to face him, leaning back against the counter.

Taking his precious wife by the hand, Sam led her into the family room. Falling onto the sofa, he pulled her down with him, and she fell easily into his embrace and onto his lap. He kissed her long, passionately. "Like I told you that night Sheila went missing in San Antonio, this is exactly why I need you beside me, my love. You are definitely my voice of reason, and, as usual, you're exactly right." He kissed her again, loving how they fit perfectly, in every imaginable way. "So, tell me, what do you have in mind for the troops?" A few minutes later, after she outlined her idea, he nodded. They'd put it into action as soon as dinner was over that night. "Sounds like a plan. No time like the present. You tell the ladies, and I'll tell the men."

She smiled and slid off his lap. "Okay. And maybe later tonight, handsome cowboy . . ."

How his wife could read his mind. Scary sometimes, but also pretty wonderful. "You'd better believe it, beautiful girl." With a small salute, he headed for his coat in the other room. He couldn't wait to see the look on Marc's face when he told him their plan.

~

Three hours later, the TeamWork group, minus Kevin and Winnie who stayed behind to watch over Rebekah, piled into the SUVs stationed at the ranch as they headed into Helena to a popular country western restaurant. They squeezed into the cars so tight that Natalie was practically on Marc's lap. He didn't mind a bit, but she appeared slightly uncomfortable. It nearly drove him to distraction as he caught a whiff of her perfume as she leaned close to him as one of the other women climbed in.

If only Trevor could see me now, squished in the back of an SUV, my wife on my lap, headed to a country western joint in Helena, Montana. It felt pretty great.

After they arrived at their destination, it didn't take long to discover Sam's one weakness in life. The man had two left feet, and kept stepping on Lexa's dainty feet as they danced. She occasionally grimaced in pain, but then she'd laugh until she looked ready to drop to the floor. As the strains of a slow song began, Sam gathered Lexa into his arms.

A short time later, the TeamWork crew gathered around a large, round table, munching on snacks, laughing and chatting together. Lexa's idea to get them out of Milestone Ranch for the night was a rousing success. They'd invited the other ranch hands, but they'd begged off for various reasons.

Marc leaned close to Sam. "I'm rather surprised to see you drinking a beer, old man."

"In deference to Dirty Harry, it's about knowing your limitations. If it makes you feel any better, you can be our designated driver tonight if you're not imbibing."

"I accept that challenge, my friend." Marc laughed and raised his glass of water with lemon. What a sissy city boy he'd turned out to be. Maybe he should let out a loud belch to fully reinforce his masculine image.

"Okay, I'll confess," Sam said, chuckling under his breath, "it's non-alcoholic." He shrugged when he caught Marc's glance of feigned outrage. "I hate the taste of alcohol, or I might drink one. I only drink this stuff to boost my whole masculine cowboy image."

Marc shook his head. "You do just fine on your own in that arena without any props."

Natalie excused herself to go to the ladies room. After talking with some of the other men for a few minutes, Marc looked at his watch, wondering why she was taking so long since she wasn't one to dawdle in the ladies room. When another five minutes passed, and she still wasn't back, he decided it was time to take a little stroll. He just hoped she was okay. The fact that she was pregnant was never far from his mind these days.

As he walked toward the back of the place, he stopped short, staring in disbelief. What in the world? Natalie was in the pool room, sandwiched in-between two distinctly ungentlemanly guys. One of whom was dangerously close to putting his grubby paws on his wife. She must have sensed his presence—or his outrage—as she turned her head and saw him. Those deep blue peepers pleaded with him to get her out of there.

The bigger, burlier of the two men leaned forward, his arm trapping her means of escape as he leaned too close. She turned her head, probably to avoid the stench of his inebriated breath. The shorter man put one hand on Natalie's waist and pulled her to him in a rough manner.

A feral growl from somewhere deep in his gut escaped as Marc roared forward. He'd never been so infuriated. Stopping just short of the men—hairy apes, the both of them—something made him pause. *Try to reason with these men first. Tell them she's your wife.* Above all, he didn't want to embarrass Natalie, but he also didn't want to look like a wuss. It was bad enough he drank sissy water with lemon. He was a former professional athlete, for crying out loud. Time to prove his manhood. At least Sam Lewis had the smarts to boost his macho image by drinking fake beer. No, he'd deal with these guys another way. Still, he felt no fear—only remorse he hadn't looked for her earlier.

"Let her go. Now." The force of his command surprised Natalie, and her eyes widened. She seemed impressed, and that was enough to spur him on. He'd seen enough Clint Eastwood movies to know how to assume the tough guy persona. He was already wearing cowboy boots and a borrowed Stetson—something he might not have believed possible a year before. The thought empowered him.

"Back off, jerk. I saw her first." The second man raked a lecherous eye up and down Natalie, and she shrank away from him. Her fingers reached behind her, clutching the edge of the pool table.

"I said let her go." Fists clenched at his sides, trying to ignore the huge, immovable lump lodged in his throat, Marc paced a step forward, closer to the men. The first man threw him a threatening look and balled one huge fist against his palm. This couldn't be good. Marc's heart pounded, but he managed to nod Natalie's way to reassure her. She looked frightened now. Great.

The first guy waved a hand over his head. "Hey, boys! Looks like we've got ourselves a lover boy here." The mood of the entire room shifted as several men turned and headed in Marc's direction, one slow, menacing step at a time. From the looks of them, they'd all imbibed more than sissy water. Maybe that would be to his advantage.

Okay, Lord, you can tell me not to fight all you want, but I'm not listening.

This was about more than protecting Natalie's honor. It was about survival, pure and simple. The other men came at him fast, swinging hard as big, beefy fists met him head-on. Raising his dukes, he fought back.

~

Seeing her mode of escape, Natalie ducked and flew back into the restaurant and dance hall. Spying Sam, she called to him and ran to where he moved slowly on the dance floor with Lexa. "Sam! Reinforcements needed. Hurry!" Dashing onto the dance floor, she apologized to Lexa and grabbed Sam by the hand, pulling him behind her as she hurried back into the pool room.

Sam whistled loud enough so it could be heard over the strains of music coming from the live band at the front of the room. "TeamWork Troops, follow me!"

Marc darted a quick look in Sam's direction as he burst into the pool room, all cylinders blazing. Together they tackled the two biggest guys coming at them with full force. Dean and Eliot held back the goons' other friends who had all faded into the background, their will to fight waning when they saw her husband's more-than-capable reinforcements. Natalie gasped when the two original instigators moved toward Marc from behind, their expressions menacing. "Marc, watch out! Behind you!" Closing her eyes tight, she couldn't help but open them again. She had to watch, peeking and praying the Lord would watch over them. Should she be upset they were fighting, or grateful and proud they were fighting for her honor? Lexa came to stand right behind her, and Natalie heard her sharp intake of breath.

Sam backed the beefier, burlier of the two against the pool table. The man's eyes rolled back into his head and he collapsed, inebriated, sprawled halfway on top of the table. The vermin who'd put his grimy hands on her came after Marc. It didn't take much for him to end up next to his friend on the pool table. This one, too, was drunk and gave him a glassy-eyed stare. Natalie almost clapped, but refrained. Not that she relished seeing her husband fight. In the background, she heard the bartender holler for someone to make sure the two men got home safe. Judging by the comments she overheard, this type of thing wasn't exactly uncommon.

Pulling himself to his full height, Marc nodded at Sam. "Looks like our work here is done. And," he said, turning to make sure he made eye contact with the two men gasping on top of the pool table, "before you go bothering a lady again, you'd better first pick your fight wisely, boys."

With sudden, surprising force, one of the other men lunged forward and caught Sam unaware, shoving his fist into the TeamWork leader's jaw. Whirling around, surprised and off-kilter, Sam steadied himself. When the same man came after Marc, he retaliated by pummeling his fist into the stomach of the attacker. The man fell backward, sprawled on the ground, groaning. Shaking his fist, Marc winced and looked up at Sam.

"Like I said, a man's gotta know his limitations," Sam said. "Thanks. I owe you one for helping me out."

"You owe me nothing, or so a wise man once said. That's what I'm here for."

"Natalie," Lexa said, walking forward to claim her man as the rest of the crowd disbursed, "I think we've got ourselves Butch Cassidy and Sundance Kid here." She looked back over her shoulder. "Are those guys going to be okay?"

Sam nodded. "They'll be fine after they sleep it off. Apparently, they're not fond of city slickers invading their territory." He dabbed at the thin line of blood trickling from the corner of his mouth.

"Sam, you're hurt!" Lexa pulled his head down for a closer inspection.

"I'm fine, Lexa. Never better." He repositioned his black Stetson and draped his arm around his wife's waist.

"Are you hurt, too?" Natalie turned Marc's face toward her. The area around one eye looked a little suspicious, and might be a shiner by morning. "Does anything hurt?"

"I'll let you know in the morning. I'm not feeling a whole lot of pain right now." He gave her a wry grin, but she caught his slight grimace.

"Why don't you ladies go back into the restaurant, and we'll join you shortly?" Sam said.

"I hope they don't get into another fight," Natalie said as she and Lexa returned to their table. "Where are Amy and Cassie?" She looked around. "I should warn them how dangerous it can be to go to the ladies room."

Lexa nodded her head in the direction of a nearby table. "Look." Cassie bounced a giggling little boy on one knee and Amy did the same with a slightly older girl.

"They allow kids in here?" Natalie shook her head.

Lexa shrugged. "This is the restaurant area, and it's the only one within a ten-mile radius, so I'm sure it's pretty much the place to be. Looks to me like our two friends are giving a weary mom and dad a chance to dance while they watch their children."

Glancing at her watch and darting a glance toward the back, Natalie bit her lip. "What do you think Sam and Marc are doing back there?"

"Don't worry," Lexa said. "Knowing Sam, he'll make sure those guys are all right even if he to drive them home himself. He always has a New Testament or two in his back pocket, and I wouldn't doubt those guys might be getting a little bit of the gospel." They shared a grin.

"Sorry," Sam said as he, Marc, Dean and Eliot joined them a few minutes later. "I had no idea we'd get into a fight when we planned this outing. We thought it might be nice to get away from the ranch for a change of scenery."

"Don't apologize," Marc said. "It was quite the adventure, but before we leave, I must insist on at least one dance with my lovely wife."

Sam nodded. "We can wait a few more minutes. Have fun, kids."

"We will, but do your wife a big favor and sit this one out." They heard laughter from both Sam and Lexa as he put his arm around Natalie's waist and led her to the dance floor. Unlike his mentor with two left feet, Marc had no worries in the dancing arena. Pulling Natalie into his arms, he drew her close. The good Lord knew he needed a long, slow dance so he could hold his wife. She felt so good, and he smiled as she snuggled closer to his chest. Ah, she was worth every bit of the fight with those big bruisers. As they danced, he knew it wasn't his imagination her waist seemed a little thicker, her body softer.

In the middle of the song, Marc pulled back so he could look at her. What he saw moved him to his core. If it wasn't love staring back at him, he didn't comprehend the meaning of the word. Tilting her chin, he leaned forward, his lips only an inch from hers. He wanted to look at her, drink in her beauty, and savor the moment.

When he hesitated, Natalie leaned forward into his waiting lips, surprising him with a spontaneous, enticing kiss. "You *fought* for me."

"I hated to see that guy with his hands on you. I'd fight an army if needed."

"My hero." She tugged the Stetson a little lower on his forehead and leaned close. "By the way, I *really* like the cowboy hat." Her hands inched up his chest, moving around his neck as his hold on her tightened and they danced together until the final strains of the song. It was difficult to ease her out of his arms.

Reluctantly they parted, but the look on his wife's face warmed him all the way down to his boot-covered toes. And then some. Right then and there, Marc resolved to buy a Stetson as soon as he got back to Boston.

~

Sam sat across from Marc at the kitchen table in the main house a short while later, their wounds being nursed by their wives. Without a doubt, Sam's jaw would be his badge of honor the next morning.

"I have to say this has been one of the more exciting work camps," Sam said, running a hand over his chin. "In San Antonio, we only had Lexa falling off a house, a fire, a fight, money stolen from the safe and a kidnapping. But this one is ranking right up there. In little more than a week, we've managed to witness the birth of a calf, a near-drowning, a fistfight with a bunch of drunks in a pool hall . . . . Congratulations, buddy. We've still got almost a whole week to go."

"I promise you, I don't normally cause trouble." Marc winced as Natalie applied gentle pressure to his throbbing temple and left eye. In all his years playing baseball, he'd never had a black eye. Interesting how it took a two-week trip to Montana to accomplish that feat.

Sam chuckled. "That's Lexa's goal in life."

"Be careful, unless you want a shiner to match the one Marc's going to have tomorrow morning." Lexa steadied Sam's chin and wiped the side of his mouth, checking his cut lip.

"My wife, ladies and gentlemen. From the moment I met her, she was as stubborn and rebellious as she was beautiful. I knew I was a goner the moment I looked into those defiant eyes." Sam hauled Lexa onto his lap and planted a kiss on her cheek.

"What's this *was* business?" Lexa demanded, feigning offense.

"You know I'll always believe you're the most gorgeous woman on the face of the planet. It's simply semantics." This time, the tender kiss was fully on her expectant lips.

"Get a room, you two." Marc looked up, shooting Sam a look of apology.

"Actually, that's not a bad idea." Sam quirked a brow at Lexa.

"Just announce it to the world, why don't you?" Lexa blushed and buried her head against her husband's shoulder.

Sam rose to his feet, pulling Lexa up with him and steadying her. "Marc, since it's the end of the evening, and I think we've gotten ourselves into as much trouble as we can tonight, I'm putting you in charge."

Leaning back in his chair, he caught the keys Sam tossed in his direction. "And where do you think you're going?"

"You know as well as I do." With a possessive hand wrapped around Lexa's, Sam's piercing glance bore straight through him. "We'll be out the rest of the evening. See you tomorrow. Don't wait up."

Warmth invaded Marc's cheeks. "Of course," he said. "You two have yourselves a real good night." Pushing his fist against his mouth, he turned his head to stifle his grin.

"Care to tell me what that conversation was all about?" Natalie watched as Sam and Lexa slipped out the door, hand-in-hand.

"Natalie," Marc said, taking her hand in his, caressing it, "one of these days I'll be more than happy to tell you all about it. Trust me on that one."

Shaking her head, she smiled. "When it comes to Sam and Lexa, anything's possible."

"I'm not sure the Lord was exactly pleased by my actions tonight." He gave her a sheepish shrug.

She kissed his cheek, her lips lingering. "You were standing up for my honor, dear husband, and that's definitely pleasing to the Lord."

"I'll accept your take on it." Marc pulled her onto his lap in a move reminiscent of Sam with Lexa, pleased by how eager she was for his kiss. He liked sitting with her like this. He figured the height difference between Sam and Lexa had something to do with it, but it was pretty great, and he made a mental note to do it more often.

Wrapping her arms around him, Natalie giggled and raised her lips to meet his. As he sat at the kitchen table of the main house, kissing his wife, Marc prayed one of these days, he and Sam would need to flip a coin for that very special key.

Chapter 39

*A*FTER WORKING IN the schoolroom all morning, Natalie was thankful to get away from the ranch when Lexa drove them into town for cooking and sewing supplies. Apparently Sam brought Marc, Kevin and Dean along with him to get some more tools and feed supplies for the cattle and horses.

She observed from a distance as Marc carried a bag of feed out to an older man's truck, listening as the man's wife asked his opinion on something she planned to cook for their supper. He grabbed something off a high shelf for a young mother and smiled at everyone. Marc could pin on a nametag and get hired on-the-spot for being so friendly and helpful.

Her husband's mood had visibly improved in the last few days. Natalie smiled, knowing full well the upturn in their relationship had a lot to do with it. She couldn't help but wonder if Sam and Lexa choreographed this particular trip to the store especially for their benefit.

Natalie's smile suddenly sobered. Even though she couldn't hear the woman's words to her husband, it was plain as day what she was trying to do, what she hoped to gain as she flirted outrageously with Marc while he stood beside a rack of tools. He was trying his best to ignore her, but she was persistent. Even with a black eye, her husband was extremely appealing to members of the opposite sex, maybe even more so. It gave him that scruffy, bad boy image perhaps, and hinted at an element of danger. Some women liked that, and gravitated toward it.

Watching from several aisles over, Natalie bristled as the woman playfully tugged on Marc's arm, leaning toward him and laughing a little too hard. Typical flirtatious moves, but she wasn't exactly unattractive. Nothing new, and Marc could recognize the moves a mile away—with his eyes closed. She wasn't sure whether to laugh or give the woman a piece of her mind. What made it all the more precious was that her husband wasn't aware that she, Winnie and Amy were standing nearby, witnessing the exchange. It took everything in her not to rush forward and claim her man. Marc said something, causing the woman's eyes to widen as she looked down at his hand. For emphasis, he wiggled his ring finger in her face. Good gesture on Marc's part, but, of course, that didn't stop her. If anything, it excited her even more, and she put both hands on his arm.

"Okay, that's my cue," Natalie said between clenched teeth. "This is ridiculous. I can't stand here watching this charade anymore." With the other ladies looking on, she stalked toward the hussy with hands on her husband. "Oh, there you are, darling!" Both the woman and Marc turned in surprise. His cheeks colored, but he grinned from ear-to-ear, lighting his entire face as she reached his side. He pulled her so close she thought she might stumble over his boots. When his other hand traveled dangerously low on her backside, Natalie reached behind her to give it safe anchor while Amy, Lexa and Winnie attempted to stifle themselves. It wasn't working. With one last lingering, flirtatious glance at Marc, the woman's eyes narrowed as she tossed a withering glare her way before whirling on her heel.

"Unbelievable. Some women have absolutely no shame."

Marc pulled her closer and nuzzled her cheek. "Thanks for saving me."

"Oh, I'm certain you could have gotten yourself out of that little scene all on your own, but since I happened to be in the building, it was a whole lot more fun this way." Natalie moved one hand to her hip. "Marc, really, must you always attract female attention wherever you go? I'm going to have to fight women off for a very long time, you know. I have to say, it's exhausting being married to you." She tweaked the slight cleft in his chin. "But totally worth it."

"Let me rephrase." Keeping his arm around her waist, Marc steered her away from the others. Pulling her behind a rack of feed, he kissed her, caressing her cheeks. "Thank you for fighting for me. I love you, slugger."

"I'd fight anyone for you. I love you." She kissed him again.

Marc sighed against her lips. "Hearing you say those words again, Natalie, I could die a happy man. God's grace is so abundant." He lifted his head and laughed. "I *love* Montana!"

Pulling his head down, her lips meeting his again, Natalie showed her husband how very much she agreed with the sentiment.

~

"Lexa." Marc strode toward her, purpose in every step. Nothing was stopping his mission.

"Yes?" Lexa's mouth upturned. "You look like a man with something on his mind."

"And you're a very intelligent woman. I need you to do me a favor."

"I'm sure that can be arranged."

"I need you to assign Natalie and me to kitchen detail tonight."

Lexa laughed. "Well, that wasn't what I was expecting, but consider it done."

"Thanks. And there's one more thing."

"What's that?" Those aquamarine eyes positively sparkled.

"I need you to keep everyone else *out* of the kitchen." Not waiting for her response, Marc walked away. A few paces out, he paused and turned. Glimpsing the astonishment etched into Mrs. TeamWork's expression, he smiled and winked. He could hear Lexa's laughter all the way back to the barn.

~

As soon as he handed a dishtowel to Natalie that evening, Marc could tell something was going on. Oh, how he loved her playful moods. When their hands touched, the strong spark of static electricity startled both of them. Great thinking to ask Lexa for this particular favor. The atmosphere was charged in so many ways. "You're quite shocking tonight," he said.

She gave him a sly look, putting the towel on the counter and rolling up her sleeves, ready to plunge her hands in the dishwater. "Do you . . . like that?"

He laughed quietly. "Well, to be honest, I'd rather be shocked in more interesting ways." Raising his brows, he cocked his head to one side, air kissing her. Natalie seemed receptive, and he prayed she'd be ready for what he had in mind. She was his wife, and he'd waited a long time.

Natalie pulled a pan from the counter and submerged it in the soapy water. Turning her attention to the task at hand, she smiled. "And what ways would that be?" She ran the sponge around the outer rim of the pan, but her eyes never left his as she scrubbed it with a secretive grin.

"Woman, you're tempting me." Sidling up behind her, Marc wrapped his hands around her waist. "You smell so good." He inhaled deeply of her scent, dropping what he hoped were enticing kisses down her neck. "And you make washing dishes the hottest activity on this ranch."

"I love it when you do that." Leaning her head to the side, she allowed him much better access to her long, lovely neck. Natalie somehow managed to continue rinsing the pan, and placed it on the towel to dry.

How she could focus was beyond him. He had a one-track brain. "I know. Do you remember me doing this, too?" He ran his index finger from the top of her ear, tracing it down the back of her neck, not stopping until his finger reached the small of her back and then moved slowly and lovingly to the curve of her hip. Even through her turtleneck and sweater, Marc felt her tremble, and it pleased him.

"Yes," she whispered, leaning back against him. "Stop it. We've got work to do here. Pick up that towel and start drying." Pulling another pan from the counter, she submerged it in the dishwater, starting the same process all over again.

Marc was having none of it and continued. The dirty pots and pans could sit all night for all he cared. Rust out. What he was doing at that very moment was infinitely more important. "And do you also remember me doing this?" He moved his hands to places they hadn't been in a very long while. Much too long. He felt bold, and Natalie wasn't resistant. She leaned further back against him, her body softening and molding.

"Stop it," she repeated, her voice gentle, yielding. Even though she said one thing, the way she said it told him she wanted more, needed more. Needed *him*.

"Take your hands out of the dishwater, Natalie." Marc smiled at her quick response as she did as he asked, turning, hands raised in the air. Suds and warm water ran down her sleeves and dripped to the rug, but neither cared as she inched her hands around his neck. Her eyelashes, all dewy and damp, fluttered on her cheeks.

Finding them something beyond irresistible, Marc slowly kissed one and then the other. "I want you, Natalie," he whispered in her ear, pulling her to him. "Tonight. You are my darling wife, and I must insist." For emphasis, he kissed her long, slow and as deep as he dared. "And I pray no one walks into this kitchen right now or they're going to get themselves a real good show." All he needed was for Sam Lewis to walk in and find him groping his wife. Raising his head, he looked into her lovely eyes. "Are you ready for me?"

"Yes," she breathed. The most beautiful word he'd ever heard. Smiling, Natalie reached into the pocket of her jeans and retrieved a small metal object. Opening his hand, she placed it in his outstretched palm and curled his fingers around it. She shrugged and gave him an irresistible grin. "Lexa told me about this special key earlier today. Just in case I might want to borrow it."

Looking down at his hand, Marc smiled and pulled her close, threatening to topple them both.

~

Sam sat in the dining hall as they snuck out of the kitchen together. From the look on his face, Marc suspected Lexa already tipped him off as to his kitchen plans, and the fact that Natalie had already secured the key.

"We'll take care of Elwood tonight. You two have fun, and take as long as you need."

"Don't you worry about that, Sam. Sorry about the dishes." Shooting a grin the other man's way, Marc captured Natalie's hand in his protective grasp as he led the way to the door. Good thing he'd already asked for directions to the cabin and had the keys to the SUV tucked in his pocket. Foresight, hopeful thinking and tons of prayer paid off in the long run. Holding the door, he brushed Natalie's cheek, catching Sam's salute and smile as he followed her outside.

Marc could barely contain himself as he drove the short distance up into the nearby hill, keeping his eyes peeled for the fork in the road Sam told him was too easy to miss. By now, he had a one-track mind and nothing was stopping him. He'd waited so long to be reunited with his wife, and now that it was within reach, he could feel himself already getting worked up physically.

Down boy. You don't want to scare her.

"Marc, turn the car around." Natalie's voice was shaky.

"Hang on, love. We're almost there." He reached for her hand as he looked out the windshield, watching for that stupid fork in the road. Where was it, anyway?

"No, I mean it. Now!" Her voice was practically a wail, something he'd never heard before. Chills ran through him.

Looking over at her, and seeing the fear in her eyes, he tried to suppress the rising panic. "What is it, sweetheart? Is it the baby?"

Nodding, Natalie's eyes widened in horror. "I think I might be bleeding," she whispered. "We should go to the hospital." Her eyes were glazed, and she looked about ready to faint.

Swerving the SUV in a complete circle, he raced back down the hill to the main road. Remembering that a local hospital was about ten minutes away, he floored the accelerator, praying all the while he could get her there in time. About five minutes down the road, Marc heard the distinct sounds of a siren. Glancing in the rearview mirror, and darting a quick glance at Natalie and seeing her eyes were closed, he pressed his foot down even harder. "You can arrest me when I get there, sheriff, but I'm getting my wife to the hospital."

Please, Lord, don't take this baby from us now. Not after all we've been through together in the last few months.

The sheriff was intent on either stopping or at least slowing him down as he honked and increased his speed. Moving alongside them on the two-lane road, the lawman frowned and motioned for Marc to pull over.

Feeling like giving the ambitious deputy a select gesture of his own, Marc leaned back and motioned to Natalie, arcing his hand like the curve of a pregnant woman. By some miracle, the sheriff comprehended his meaning and, motioning for him to follow, pulled in front and escorted them the rest of the way.

Screeching to a stop in front of the small hospital a few minutes later, Marc flew to Natalie's side in seconds. Gently easing her out of the SUV, he swallowed his fear when he saw a faint spot of blood on her seat. *Please, God, no,* he silently pleaded, carrying her through the door the sheriff's deputy held open and into the ER. That blessed antiseptic smell invaded his nostrils, bringing unwelcome memories of their visit to the hospital in Boston only a few short months ago.

The nurses chatting at their station sprang into action as soon as they saw them. With his black eye and a limp woman cradled in his arms, they must make an interesting pair. They brought over a gurney and assisted him as he lowered her onto it.

"Don't worry, we'll take good care of her," one kindly older nurse assured him, patting his arm.

Desperation flooded his sensibilities. Nodding at her, Marc's eyes welled and a choke rose in his throat. Somehow, he managed to rasp, "Thank you." His hands fell to his sides and he watched as they wheeled Natalie away, taking his helpless heart with her. After answering all the perfunctory questions, feeling like he was in slow motion and in some new nightmare, Marc stumbled to a chair and collapsed into it. Lowering his head to his hands, he prayed.

Startled in the midst of lifting his thousandth petition to the Lord, he felt a gentle hand on his shoulder. Eyes wide, heart pounding, he snapped to full attention as he looked up at the young doctor.

"I'm sorry, Mr. Thompson."

"Noooo. . .!"

Chapter 40

$\mathcal{M}$ARC'S GUTTURAL GROAN was so loud and anguished, surely everyone within a five-mile radius heard it. His head dropped to his hands again, and he shook it slowly back and forth. If possible, this was as bad, if not worse, than when he thought he might lose Natalie. *Lord, this can't be happening. Not our baby. Please!*

"Mr. Thompson," the doctor said, "I only meant I'm sorry I startled you. Natalie's fine. She's *fine.*"

It took a minute for her words to sink in. He raised his head, barely breathing. "And the baby?" He rose to his feet. "Please tell me our baby's okay."

The young redhead—who looked way too young to be more than an intern—nodded. They really needed to teach kids in med school not to start off with the words, *I'm sorry,* when speaking with family members awaiting word of a loved one in the ER. Blowing out a deep sigh, relief flooded his soul, but it would take a while for his breathing to slow and his heart to stop pounding.

"The baby's heartbeat is strong. Natalie had some spotting. It's not uncommon. Make sure she rests for a few days, doesn't do any heavy lifting and doesn't overtax herself, and she'll be perfectly fine." The doctor laughed in surprise as Marc gathered her in a huge bear hug and planted a sloppy kiss on her cheek.

"Thank you," he managed. He burst into tears, sending all those sweet, maternal nurses straight to his side. God help him, he didn't care who heard him cry. His prayers were answered. He was eternally grateful and would spend the rest of his life protecting his girls.

~

As soon as they returned to the ranch, Marc pulled in front of the main house.

"Shouldn't I go back to the cabin?" Natalie's voice was subdued. Her head rested against the back of the seat, and one hand was draped across her stomach.

"I have a better idea." She nodded, but didn't comment, seemingly relieved he was taking charge. It had been an exhausting day, and she needed some peace and quiet. Marc took her hand and helped her out of the car. "Let's go find Sam and Lexa." Allowing him to assist her into the house, she leaned against him, his arm around her waist, her head on his shoulder.

"Break it up you two," Marc snapped, disgruntled as he spied Sam and Lexa cuddled together on the sofa with only the firelight illuminating the room. At least they were dressed, and weren't actively engaged in the very thing Marc hoped to be doing with his own wife at that very moment.

Stop thinking about your selfish desires and take care of your wife.

"What's up, buddy?" Sam shot Lexa a lazy grin, buttoning his shirt as he sat up straighter on the sofa. "I didn't expect the two of you to darken the doors of the ranch until at least tomorrow."

As soon as they'd entered the room, Lexa rose from the sofa to assist Natalie into the rocker by the fireplace. Retrieving a quilt, she draped it over her and placed a hand on her forehead. They talked together and Lexa looked over at her husband. "Sam." That's all it took. That one word. With the mere utterance of his name, one glance, Sam knew. Knew something had happened and now was not the time for teasing. These two had more than mental telepathy going on. It was a deep, spiritual connection, and it floored him each time he witnessed it.

"Let's go talk in the kitchen." Telling Lexa he'd put on water for tea, Sam motioned for Marc to follow. "Sit, please," he said, pouring water into a pan and putting it on the stove before pulling out the coffee pot and pouring a mugful. Placing it on the table in front of him, he reached into a cabinet to retrieve the artificial sweetener.

Marc watched as Sam poured his own coffee and sat down across the table. "How did you know I'd need coffee?"

Sam's eyes narrowed as he took a sip. "We've shared coffee a few times, you know. I pay attention." He put down his mug and leaned his chin on one hand. "Want to talk about it?"

"We didn't even make it to the cabin."

"Go on . . . when you're ready. I've got all night. Whatever you need."

"I was afraid we were going to lose the baby tonight." Marc pushed his fist against his mouth and cleared his throat, waiting until he could trust himself to speak again. "Natalie and the baby are fine, thank God."

Sam's eyes were wide. "What happened?"

"I was looking for that fork in the road when Natalie begged me to turn the car around. She was bleeding. I hightailed it onto the main road and made it to the hospital in record time. Complete with an escort from our local sheriff's department. Don't worry, I didn't get a ticket. But that reminds me, I need to clean up the car. It wasn't much, as it turns out, but it scared both of us to death since we've never been through this before. I couldn't take any chances."

Sam waved his hand. "I'll take care of it. You have more important things to do, like tend to your wife. I'm just thankful Natalie and the baby are okay. You, too." He winced and brought a quick hand to the side of his face.

"How's the jaw?"

The smile lines deepened. "About the same as your eye, I imagine."

222

"Right. Thanks again for jumping in to save my hide last night."

"That's what I'm here for. You saved mine, too. What did the doctor say?"

"She said for Natalie to rest, not lift anything heavy . . . normal procedure. If it's okay with you and Lexa, I'd like to keep Natalie here in the main house in the second bedroom for a couple of days. I know Winnie and the other women could take good care of her, but they've got Rebekah to watch over. I want to be the one to take care of my wife." He hesitated again, swallowing hard. "More than anyone else, Natalie needs her husband . . . whether she realizes it or not." The last few words were quiet, but he knew Sam heard every one.

"You're right, and I think you're exactly what the doctor ordered. I know how you feel." Something in Sam's expression alerted him there was more to it.

"Is there something *you* need to share, Sam?" Marc took a sip of coffee and waited.

The clock ticking in the quiet kitchen was the only sound for nearly a full minute. "Lexa and I lost a baby." When he looked back up, Marc glimpsed the deep emotion in those expressive eyes.

"I'm so sorry . . . I had no idea." A rush of compassion invaded his senses, and he hurt for his friend's heartache. "When?"

"Six months ago. Lexa wasn't very far along—only a month—which I guess in some small way was a blessing. But it doesn't take away the hurt, especially for Lexa. And now," Sam said, shifting in his chair, "the doctors aren't giving us a lot of hope for conceiving again." He paused, clearing his throat. "But the Lord blessed us once, and we have every hope He'll bless us again. In *His* time, not ours."

"You two are the strongest Christian couple I know." Marc met Sam's gaze, holding it steady. "Not to be flippant, but it would be a slap in God's face if you weren't able to have children. I'm sure you'll have a whole ranchful. Your kids will be the most obnoxious little Bible scholars around. Probably run around as toddlers spouting the seven rules of playpen etiquette."

Sam allowed himself a chuckle. "Thanks. I'll take that as a compliment."

They talked quietly for another few minutes as Marc fixed Natalie's mug of tea before rejoining the women in the living room. Sam spoke with Lexa for a minute, and she nodded, listening. "Natalie, honey," Lexa called, pulling on her coat, "I'm going over to the cabin to grab your suitcase."

"Let me help you." Natalie started to rise from where she was now curled on the sofa in front of the roaring fire, but Marc put a restraining hand on her. She didn't need to be going anywhere.

"You stay where you are," Lexa said, her voice firm as she tugged her hat on her head. "The other girls can help gather your things. I'll be back in a few minutes." She nodded in his direction with an encouraging smile. God bless that woman.

"I suppose you should get back to the cabin now," Natalie told him, but he could hear the disappointment in her tone. "Marc, I'm sorry . . ."

"Don't you dare apologize. Your health, and the safety of our child, is the most important thing." He looked up, but Sam had departed, leaving them to their privacy. "Listen, if it's okay with you, I'm going to stay here at the main house with you until you're feeling stronger. I'd like to be able to watch over you." His eyes held hers, and he kissed her forehead. "Please let me take care of you, Natalie."

Leaning back against the sofa, she released a heavy sigh. "You won't hear any complaints from me. It sounds wonderful." She took his hand. "Thank you."

He stroked her cheek. "Rest now. I'll get your suitcase when Lexa comes back and put it in the bedroom." Watching as she closed her eyes, Marc reached for the blanket draped over the rocking chair and gently tucked it around her. She looked so vulnerable to him in that moment, and his heart swelled. Closing his eyes, he breathed another brief prayer of thanks. *God, You are so good.* "I owe you one, Lord. Another one," he said under his breath. Not that God was keeping score, as old Mr. Davis would remind him, but he owed Him so much. And one of the very best ways to thank Him was to take care of those lives the Lord entrusted to him.

~

The next day, after lunch, they sat on the sofa again, enjoying quiet time together. Natalie's foot was on Marc's lap, and he massaged it. He didn't mind, even though foot massage wasn't one of his specialties. But she loved it, as evidenced by the look on her face.

"Thank you," she said.

"For rubbing your feet or otherwise?" He kept his voice warm, playful.

"For just being you, I suppose."

He sighed. "I still can't believe we're having a baby. And the doctor said her heartbeat's strong. She's a fighter, our daughter."

"I know." With a small smile, Natalie used her toe to prompt his fingers.

"You're demanding, Mrs. Thompson," he said with a grin, tickling the bottom of her foot.

"Do you want to paint my toenails, too?" Natalie's giggle was so infectious and great to hear. She squirmed when he tickled again, and gave him the cutest smile ever.

"If that's what you want, I suppose you could convince me."

"I love flirting with you. Remember the time . . ." She stopped, eyes wide.

"Remember what time?" He sat up straighter, but kept his hold on her foot.

"Remember the time," Natalie said, "when you . . ." Her cheeks flushed pink.

He had a pretty good idea what she was thinking. "Go on. Tell me. You've remembered something, haven't you?"

"I remember being in the bubble bath." Her eyes avoided his, and her fingers started the dance on her lap.

"Yes, you do love your bubble baths."

Those blue eyes traveled a slow path back to his. "With *you*, Marc. And you can't tell me that was before we were married because that would be a big fat lie."

"Yes, we did that." He tossed her a sheepish grin. "Normally, I'm not a bubble man." He laughed as she swatted his arm. "I know I had bubbles in places I'd rather not remember."

Natalie laughed, and it was deep and hearty, sexier than anything. "But you did it for me, you romantic fool. Come closer, please." She beckoned with one finger.

"You need to rest, sweetheart."

"Marc, release my foot, please, and come here to me." Her tone indicated she wouldn't take no for an answer, and being no fool, he obliged his wife. Scooting closer, he relished the look in her eyes. "I want to make you a promise." The intensity of her eyes mated with his soul. Resting her forehead against his, Natalie said, "As soon as I feel better . . ."

His eyes grew wide as he listened to her whispered words, and the grin that spread across his face was one of complete joy. His thumbs caressed her on top of her clothing before sneaking beneath her thick sweater.

Oh, yes. Anticipation is such a sweet feeling.

Dozing on the sofa many hours later, Marc awoke with a start. Realizing he'd fallen asleep cuddled next to her, he smiled. "Natalie?" Glancing around the room, he rubbed his tired eyes, yawning. The blanket was tucked around him now, and the fire had died long ago. Judging by the position of the sun, it was sometime in the early morning. He placed one hand on the sofa beside him. Still warm. *We must have slept here together all night.*

Trudging into the kitchen, he yawned, stretched and pulled out a pan to heat the water for Natalie's tea. She loved her tea, and he adored making it for her. It was something he'd never imagined doing, but love made him do lots of things, like share a bubble bath. He'd do anything for her. Turning on the burner, he placed the pan of water on the stove and reached into one of the upper cabinets, searching for the box he'd found the night before, some special orange blend. Natalie's favorite.

Walking past the bathroom a couple of minutes later, Marc heard running water. Standing outside the door, he called, "I've started your tea." He thought he heard a muffled reply, but couldn't distinguish her words. "What did you say?" When he heard nothing, he stepped closer. Perhaps because of their scare, he was still nervous about Natalie's physical condition and wanted confirmation she was all right.

"Everything okay, Natalie?" Taking a hesitant step inside the bathroom, he opened the door a bit wider. He should duck out and not stay a moment longer, giving her privacy, but he couldn't move, and stood rooted to the floor. Even though it was steamy, it allowed a glimpse of the outline of her through the fogged glass of the shower stall.

It wasn't the sexuality of his wife that rendered him immobilized. It was the definitive curve of a woman with child he hadn't been able to glimpse beneath the layers of clothing she always wore at the ranch. *His* child. *Their* child. Marc swayed a little, holding onto the door frame for support. She was the most beautiful creature he'd ever seen, never more so than in that moment. Natalie was oblivious to his presence as she placed a protective hand on her belly. He wasn't sure how she'd react if she spied him standing there, but somehow, he didn't think she'd mind.

Leave her to her privacy.

Quietly closing the door, Marc retreated back to the kitchen to turn off the boiling water. Standing at the stove, his head bowed, he thanked the Lord for his wife and baby. Seeing her with the curve of their child humbled and awed him beyond reason.

"Are you okay?" Wrapped in her white fleece robe, Natalie came to stand behind him a few minutes later.

Turning to face her, silent, he opened his arms. She moved into his embrace without hesitation, and he kissed the top of her head as he completely encircled her. His wife felt so warm, so wonderful.

"Does your eye hurt?" She touched the tender area with gentle fingers and leaned forward on her toes to kiss the corner of his eye. Wrapping her arms around him, Natalie rested her head on his chest.

Marc stroked her damp hair, inhaling its fresh scent. "It's fine. Not that I want to move ever again in this lifetime, but I've got the water ready for your tea."

"I love it when you play nurturer." A secretive grin flirted about her lips as she seated herself at the table. "It's time for a little talk."

"Oh?" Bringing her steaming mug of tea over to the table, he eyed her with hesitation. The look on her face indicated good things, not bad, but his heart wasn't listening.

"I think you're going to like what I have to tell you." She had no idea how seductive, how alluring, she was to him in that moment.

"Should I be sitting down for this?"

"It's probably best." She watched as he seated himself opposite her, his eyes wide.

"You're scaring me. Just tell me, whatever it is."

Reaching across the table, Natalie laced her fingers through his. Taking a deep breath, she began. "Your mother's middle name is Letitia, a name she absolutely detests. My dad keeps a stash of old newspapers in the corner of the basement, refusing to recycle or throw them out, and it drives my mom crazy. My biggest pet peeve is undeserved rudeness. Your biggest pet peeve is when you can't go to a double-header at Fenway. You keep your high school class ring in a little box in your sock drawer. I keep the tickets and programs from every play and event we ever attended together in a big box beneath the bed, marked *Courtship Keepsakes*."

She paused a moment, waiting for him to absorb her words. Marc's heart was pounding so hard he thought he might faint. This was the dream. It was even more than he'd hoped. Leaning his elbow on the table, he covered his mouth with one hand, his eyes wide. Although he couldn't speak, he nodded for her to continue.

"I had a dog, a Maltese named Max growing up, and you had a German shepherd named Shep. On our first official date, you came to my kindergarten class production of *The Frog Prince*, and then you treated the entire class to ice cream. Every single girl in my class fell in love with you and told me they wanted to marry you if I didn't." She laughed. "You were my handsome prince, and they were fighting over you."

Hearing her memories was the best thing he'd heard since she confessed her love for him—the second time around. "When did you remember all this, my love?"

"They've been coming back to me slowly over the last week or so. But I'm glad I did," she whispered, as he fell to his knees on the floor beside her, bundling her in his arms, rocking her side-to-side, and burying his face in the softness of the robe covering her shoulder.

"Did what?" he asked in-between kisses on her cheeks, her forehead, her chin, everywhere.

"*Marry* you, Mr. Thompson."

Moving the robe slightly aside, he kissed the soft warmth of her shoulder, the sweet hollow of her throat, before pulling Natalie into his arms again. If he doubted it before, he couldn't now. He'd kept the faith, but as much as anything else, the Lord—in His infinite mercy and grace—had given his wife back to him.

I was wrong, God. This is truly your grace personified.

Chapter 41

$\mathcal{S}$AM AND LEXA kept watch over both of them during the course of the next two days. Even though he offered on numerous occasions to assist Sam and the other men with chores around the ranch, Sam refused to allow him to help, telling him in no uncertain terms he was to stay with his wife. He didn't put up too much of a fight after that.

Marc read to Natalie, sang her to sleep until she covered her ears or begged him to stop, and made them a pitiful macaroni and cheese dinner. Bless her heart, she ate it and told him it was the best she'd ever tasted. Natalie could never lie convincingly, but he loved her all the more for it. They played cards, watched a couple of movies—a romantic comedy for her and an action thriller for him. Was it too much to hope that more of her submerged memories might start to resurface?

He put in a quick call to each of Natalie's doctors of her progress, including Dr. Adams. Patched straight through to the fine doctor, he sounded genuinely pleased. He also called Dr. Fontaine, but was told he was attending a conference in Switzerland. Probably sitting around smoking pipes and sharing Freudianisms.

Marc smiled, remembering Sam's rules of marriage and mentally counted off his personal scorecard, content in the knowledge he was doing the best he could to fulfill his wife's needs. That night, Natalie slept in one of the bedrooms, and he slept on the sofa in the main room, cuddled with Elwood. He barely slept, preoccupied with thoughts of his wife in the next room. It was proving difficult not to open the door separating them and crawl into the bed beside her.

After a relaxing, fun third day spent together, Natalie was regaining her strength and seemed much better. As much as he loved the private time with her—and Sam and Lexa made themselves surprisingly scarce, not to mention the rest of the TeamWork crew—he was growing stir crazy. He told Natalie he needed to help Sam and the other men around the ranch the next morning. She understood, and her eyes alone told him how much she'd enjoyed their time together.

After cuddling together on the sofa later that evening, Natalie rose to her feet. Giving him a look full of meaning, she held out one hand. "Will you come sleep with me tonight, Marc? Just sleep?" Her eyes promised more for the future. Or maybe that was his wishful thinking. A husband could hope. Digging a dog treat from his pocket, he tossed it to Elwood.

Without another word, Natalie led him into the bedroom. Watching as she lowered her robe, his heart raced uncontrollably. She wore his flannel pajama shirt with an enticing glimpse of short, silky boxer shorts underneath. He loved her long, shapely legs and drank his fill as his eyes caressed his wife. She didn't seem to mind. Dragging his eyes away, he spied the pajama pants on the bed, waiting for him. "His and hers, huh?" As she slipped under the covers, Marc undressed. Her eyes never left his as he shed layer upon layer of clothing. "Too many clothes here in Montana." Finally stepping out of his jeans, he let them drop in a heap on the floor and pushed them aside with one foot. Skip the flannel. He didn't need it to keep him warm tonight.

"Won't you get cold in only your shorts?" Natalie's eyes devoured his chest.

He savored the obvious desire in her expression. "I don't think that'll be a problem tonight." Dropping onto the bed, he curled himself around her, covering her with his warmth. "*Sleeping* will be the problem," he murmured, nuzzling the nape of her neck. "If you want to shed any more layers of clothing, that's fine by me."

"I love you, Marc."

"I love you, too, Natalie," he whispered. They were quiet for a few minutes before he became aware she moved her hands. Guiding his hand past flannel, she placed it over her heart and held it there, her hand on top of his. His eyes widened as he splayed his fingers over her soft, bare skin, glorying in the moment, feeling the steady beat of her heart, knowing it was also the heartbeat of their daughter. Even though it took everything in him, Marc left his hand where it was, not daring to start anything else. He was thankful her back was turned or he might not be able to resist the temptation. *Soon enough. Be patient.*

He held her for a long time, cherishing the soft rise and fall of her body in the rhythm of deep sleep. When Natalie turned and faced him, still asleep, he smoothed her hair away from her face. The pajama top was still parted, and he allowed his gaze to linger. *Lord, she's so beautiful. Thank you.* Raising his hand, he let it fall back to the sheets. The sight of her would keep him up longer, but it was worth it. If possible, he was more in love with his wife now than the first time around. When sleep finally threatened to overtake him, Marc leaned forward to kiss her. "Good night, sweet Natalie." Settling his hand on his daughter, he whispered another prayer for her, too.

~

"That's a goofy grin if ever I've seen one." Sam worked alongside Marc in the stables the next morning, tending to the horses. The joy in his heart must have been reflected in his eyes, based on his friend's wry, knowing grin. The man's smile lines wouldn't quit.

"Natalie remembered some things."

"Well, that's great news. Maybe it'll trigger more memories, and the floodgates will open." The hope in Sam's voice was infectious.

"Yep. That's my prayer." Marc grabbed a pitchfork to give Dandelion more hay.

"Judging from the look on your face, I'd say they were really good memories."

He laughed. "Yeah, one in particular was pretty spectacular, but don't even go there. It's not exactly the most . . . masculine . . . memory."

"Meaning you can't admit it in the presence of my overwhelming masculinity?" Sam chuckled.

"Something like that since you *can* be larger than life at times. Not to mention the way you can singlehandedly amuse yourself."

The manual labor was a great release. A slight pain radiated through his neck and traveled to his shoulders. Tomorrow, he'd rise before dawn to milk the cows again and visit the pesky hens. He didn't care. Natalie loved him again, so he could face anything. Even ornery Old Charlie.

"Sam, tell me something. Why is it that everything boils down to a certain basic subject?"

A hint of surprise registered in Sam's narrowed eyes and the corners of his mouth tugged upward. "I take it you're talking about love and marriage."

"Marriage and, shall we say, the *benefits* of marriage."

"Well, number one, we're men. Number two, we're married men. Number three . . ."

"Number three?" This one was bound to be interesting.

"Number three, you're a newlywed, you're still waiting, and you're about to go crazy from the looks of it. But then again, there's also another very important factor at work here."

"What's that?"

"We're also Christian men. Our needs and wants are fully within the scope of a God-honoring relationship with our wives. Nothing wrong with that."

Marc shook his head and chuckled. "Only you, Sam Lewis. Only you can talk about sex and the Lord in the same sentence and somehow make it sound totally spiritual. I'm sure Lexa must have to shut you up at times."

Sam handed him a bucket of oats as they moved along to the next stall together. "Oh, Lexa silences me when it's called for. In pretty creative ways."

"Sam?"

"Yes?"

"I'm not as creative as Lexa. But please, if it's possible, just be quiet. We've got a lot of work to do here." Sharing a grin, they resumed their work.

Chapter 42

*H*EARING A COMMOTION outside a few days later, Marc opened the cabin door. Sam ran into the middle of the ranch buildings, whistling and calling out to the men. Kevin, Dean and Eliot came running from the area of the barn. Grabbing his jacket and shoving his arms into it, he ran outside to join them.

"We need to head out on the range, men!" Sam shouted, cupping his hands so that his voice carried. The snow fell much heavier, blanketing the ground with a fresh layer of white powder. "The cattle have gotten out of the gates, and Cliff and the others are over at an adjoining ranch. It's up to us to round them up. More snow's headed our way, and we've got to corral the herd and get them back before the temperature drops much further. If you ride, grab a horse and let's go!"

The five men ran to the stables. It was a given Marc would ride Dandelion. Ever since that fateful afternoon when he pulled Beck from the creek, he'd faithfully brought treats to the gentle horse each evening—everything from carrots and apples to whatever else they had on hand.

Quickly saddling a black stallion named Majesty, Sam pulled himself onto the horse and tipped his Stetson as he galloped out of the stables first. Marc followed, and the other three men were right behind them as they charged onto the open range, the hooves of the horses making regular patterns in the snow.

It's beautiful out here, Lord. He pulled alongside Sam. It was a good thing he'd learned to ride when he was a kid visiting his grandparents' ranch in Colorado. Like riding a bike, it had come right back to him. They rode for ten minutes before they spied the wayward herd of cattle on the outer southern perimeter of the ranch. With renewed vigor, the men headed toward them. The snow was coming down faster, and they needed to get the job done and get the cattle and themselves back to the ranch. As they neared the herd, Marc's eyes widened. Sitting like a sheepherding watchdog was Elwood, at full attention, that tail going nonstop, as he looked every bit the taskmaster. He barked and ran back and forth, the sounds carried off by the rising wind. How on earth had he canvassed the ranch and made his way out this far?

"Thanks, Elwood." Reaching into his pocket, Marc tossed him a dog treat. A wave of affection for the mutt rushed through him. The little guy was a fighter, not afraid of anything. An unbelievably strong gust of wind sent snow swirling about them, momentarily blinding the men. It spooked some of the cattle, and a few started running. And then more. Soon, they were moving faster than Marc could have imagined. His eyes wide and his heart pounding hard in his chest, he looked over at Sam through the falling snow for the other man's direction.

Stampede! What do we do now?

Gesturing high in the air, Sam indicated he'd take the west side, Marc the opposite, and the other three men the surrounding area. Even though Sam shouted, he couldn't hear him because of the wind and the sounds of the cattle. Galloping alongside the cattle, Marc cut them off as best he could.

"Elwood, go home!" Glancing down at the ground, he felt desperately afraid for the small dog. A creature that diminutive could easily be lost and trampled by the massive beasts. Even though he loved the mutt, Natalie adored him even more. He couldn't bear the thought he might be hurt . . . or worse.

With the five men working together, they began to contain the herd in one large circle. Marc strained to glimpse Sam through the blinding snow. The wind had picked up even more, and the sun was beginning to set on the horizon, making visibility more difficult. The temperature must have dropped at least twenty degrees since they'd been out there. Cold, blowing snow burned his eyes, and he blinked hard. When he didn't spot Elwood, panic began to settle in his gut.

Suddenly, Dandelion unexpectedly bucked, spooked by one of the large creatures or maybe Elwood. Raising high on her hind legs, the horse flailed her legs mid-air, shaking her head from side-to-side, a wild look in her eyes. Struggling to hold on, Marc breathed a prayer and tried to get a grip on the bridle. When Dandelion bucked again, he couldn't hold on any longer. The world spun around him like mad.

Oh, Lord, I'm slipping . . .

~

Dandelion bucked in the air, and through the blinding snow swirling about them, Sam witnessed the terrifying sight of Marc tumbling from the saddle and disappearing from sight. "Marc!" He prayed his foot hadn't gotten tangled in the stirrups. If Dandelion dragged him, the consequences could be horrendous. Still, it might not be much better for his friend if he was on the ground with the massive beasts surging all around him. He had to get to him.

"Marc!" Sam called. "Guys, go after the cattle and round them up as best you can. I'll take care of Marc. Kevin, call Lexa on the radio and tell her to come to the southwest side of the ranch. Now!" They waved and he turned Majesty full circle and galloped over to where he'd last seen Marc and Dandelion. The herd had slowed, and the other men could round them up and head them back in the direction of the ranch without too much trouble.

Under his breath, Sam released a prayer of thankfulness for those good, selfless men. It was difficult to find dedicated men in times of hardship, and his TeamWork guys more than filled the need. Just as they'd helped him fight the fires at the houses they were building in San Antonio, they rallied to his side now to do whatever was needed to bring the situation under control.

"Marc!" Sam continued to shout his name several times, pushing his way through the remaining cattle as quickly as he could, praying all the way for the Lord's mercy. "God be with us." Dandelion stood to one side, but Marc was nowhere in sight. "Marc, where are you?" Sam shouted, cupping his hands around his mouth so his voice would carry further. His eyes canvassed the large expanse of the ranch property within range, searching for a sign or glimpse of his friend. Impatiently pushing the falling snow away from his eyes, his eyes widened in horror as he finally spied Marc's prone figure lying flat on his back about fifteen yards away. Elwood was sprawled on top of him, licking his face.

As he rushed to Marc's side, Sam breathed a sigh of relief he looked fine . . . except for the fact he wasn't moving. Sam's breath caught in his throat as he reined in Majesty and jumped to the ground. Maybe he'd been foolish to bring untrained men out on the range, but Cliff had called on him, needing their help. The Lord had a plan in all of this, but if anything happened to this man . . .

Falling to his knees, Sam pulled the small dog off Marc's chest. He leaned close and listened for signs of breathing. Not getting any response, he picked up his wrist. He detected a faint pulse, but his fingers were so cold it was difficult to tell. Internal bleeding was always a possibility in a stampede situation. After a quick assessment, he saw no outward, visible sign of a hoofprint or any sign that one of the beasts had trampled him. He had an important but split-second decision: if he performed CPR and Marc had internal bleeding, it could make it much worse, perhaps even prove fatal. On the other hand, CPR might be the only way to save his friend's life. It wasn't a choice.

Lord, I need Your guiding hand on me now.

Quickly unzipping Marc's jacket, he ripped apart his shirt. Buttons flew, landing in the blinding whiteness of the fresh snow. Pushing the shirt aside, Sam cried out as he found yet another layer of cotton. Long johns. Ripping the cotton thermal shirt right down the middle, the fabric tore under his hands, revealing an undershirt. Tearing through it, he finally reached Marc's bare chest.

Tilting his head back and pinching his nose, Sam gave him a couple of quick, resuscitating breaths. Putting the heels of both hands on Marc's chest, one on top of the other, he began to apply steady, rhythmic pressure. His mind raced, and he closed his eyes to concentrate, trying to recall all his medical emergency training. Alternating between breaths and compressions, he prayed he wouldn't break Marc's sternum in the process, but it was a small price to pay if it saved his friend's life.

Sam's prayers intermingled with his falling tears, but he couldn't stop to brush them away.

"Come on, buddy. Respond!" He put his head against Marc's chest every few seconds and listened for signs of breathing. "Come on. God, please!" Sam's guttural cry came from the deepest part of him as he kneeled on the snow, beseeching the heavenly Father to spare the life of this man.

"Marc Thompson, you did *not* come out here to reconnect with your wife only to lose your life," he said, swiping away his tears as he worked over his friend. He had to keep going. If he received no response soon, all would be lost. He wouldn't—he *couldn't*—take that chance. Sam shook his head, banishing unbidden, haunting thoughts. He wouldn't be able to bear telling Natalie her husband . . . . The mere thought of it was unthinkable and shook him to his core. He increased his efforts, watching Marc closely all the while.

Lord, I need your help. Please hear my prayer.

Chapter 43

*I*T WASN'T WORKING. Every precious second counted. Preparing him for more quick breaths, Sam tilted Marc's head back and pinched his nose, leaning forward. Relieved as he heard a soft groan, Sam continued his compressions, feverishly working the heel of his hand on Marc's chest.

Finally, Marc responded. Coughing and sputtering, his body jerked and arched in the air as he turned his head one way and then the other before gagging and sputtering some more. They were among the best sounds Sam had ever heard, and he watched for a few seconds before he gathered Marc close. Sitting with him cradled in his arms, leaning the other man back against him, Sam periodically checked his pulse while lifting prayers of thanks.

When Marc opened his eyes, Sam moved around to his side. "Hello, buddy. Welcome back."

Marc's eyes shot open, and he released a faint but audible moan. "You come any closer, Sam Lewis, and I'll deck you from here to Texas."

"Too late."

Marc groaned again. "I don't even want to know." He struggled in a vain attempt to sit up before collapsing back against Sam in exhaustion. "Guess I had the wind knocked out of me," he rasped, looking up at Sam with a wan grin. "Thanks for being here, friend."

"That's what I'm here for."

On the horizon, Sam glimpsed headlights from an approaching SUV. Knowing it was Lexa, he maintained his position. Natalie was right beside her. Crying out in alarm, both women jumped out of the vehicle and ran toward them through the snow.

~

Natalie leaned close and looked over at Sam with large, frightened eyes. "I know CPR," she said, taking Marc's wrist to check his pulse. His eyes were closed. He looked so tired, so pale. She smoothed a strand of blond hair off his face. "What happened? Is he okay?" She looked in the eyes of their TeamWork leader and appreciated the reassurance she saw reflected there.

"Natalie, trust me, he's all yours. He's going to be fine. Just had the wind knocked out of him." When Sam moved over, Natalie positioned herself so she could hold her husband. He moaned and his eyelids fluttered open. He blinked hard once, twice, three times. She nodded at Sam, and he rose to his feet and walked over to Lexa.

As Natalie hugged Marc close, she watched Sam pull Lexa into his arms and lean his head against hers. "You scared me, Mr. Thompson," she said, cupping his face between her gloved hands. His eyes closed before fluttering fully open again. He coughed a few more times, and his body shuddered with the effort. You didn't have to get yourself nearly killed in order to get my attention, you know." Squeezing her eyes tight, Natalie kissed his cold lips and nuzzled his cheek. She needed to warm him, but she also had to get him into the warmth of the car and then to the ranch.

"Excuse me," Marc said softly, "but who *are* you?" Turning his head, he coughed.

Natalie's eyes widened with terror. When the corners of Marc's mouth lifted in a slight grin, she punched him lightly on the arm. "Don't you even tease about such a thing. That's a horrible thing to say!" Nonetheless, she pressed him even closer, not bothering to wipe away her tears.

"Not that I want to complain, especially with my nose pressed against your twin gazelles, but I need to move. I've lost all feeling. Everywhere. That's not such a good thing."

Marc's entire body shuddered again. Her heart rate increased as she tightened her hold.

"I'm really cold, Natalie."

She'd been so grateful he was okay she'd not paid attention to the fact his bare chest was exposed to the elements. "I know you love my chest, but don't get any ideas," he said as she pulled the remains of his shirts together as best she could and zipped his down jacket all the way up to his neck. "Not until later, anyway."

"I can't promise that." Natalie kissed him again. Her lips warmed his, and Marc began to respond. That was a good thing. He struggled to a sitting position. "Come on. Let's get you up and into the car." Lifting his arm around her shoulders, Natalie helped him reach a standing position. Marc leaned against her as they hobbled their way through the thickening snow. When he tried to protest, saying he was too much weight on her, she tightened her hold.

As they approached the SUV, Sam hurried around to open the passenger door. "Natalie, you drive. Lexa will get Dandelion, and I'll get Majesty." Sam took over and assisted Marc inside the car. Once she was certain he was settled, Natalie tossed a glance over her shoulder. By God's abiding grace, the horses stood nearby, looking content with the relative peace and quiet after all the earlier commotion.

Elwood was another story entirely. She couldn't help but shake her head as she spied their nutty dog. He jumped around Majesty, yapping away. Thankfully, the appropriately-named stallion paid no attention to the tiny annoyance. Scooping Elwood in his arms, Sam quickly strode back over to the SUV and deposited the small dog into the backseat. Finally exhausted, Elwood collapsed on the seat, his head resting on his crossed paws.

"This little guy's had quite a night," Sam said.

"Haven't we all, buddy," Marc said, not opening his eyes. He shifted his position and blew out a deep sigh of exhaustion tempered with relief. "Take me home, please."

Sam pulled Natalie aside and lowered his voice. "We need to take him to the hospital to make sure he's okay. I'm sure Marc's fine or we wouldn't be standing here talking about it, but as a precaution, I want him checked out by a doctor and given a clean bill of health."

She nodded. "Of course. That's best."

"Come back to the ranch, and I'll drive us all to the hospital once I've secured the horses. It won't take long, and I don't think the few extra minutes are going to hurt."

Natalie swallowed hard. "I'll see you back at the ranch and we'll go from there." Sam headed toward Lexa, and as she watched, her eyes filled. Then the truth slammed her in the face—she could have lost her husband. That reality closed in and squeezed her chest so hard she thought she'd hyperventilate. "Sam!" Gasping for breath, tears streamed down her cheeks, and thick sobs came from somewhere deep inside, rolling out of her in waves. Although she needed to be strong for Marc—for both of them—it was like the floodgates opened, and she couldn't stop.

Lexa started toward her, but Sam held up one hand. "I've got her, Lexa." Through her tears, Natalie caught Lexa's gentle, compassionate smile. Without hesitation, Sam pulled her into the comforting warmth of his embrace and leaned his head against hers.

Wrapping her arms tight around her dear friend, Natalie gathered this precious man close. She raised up on her toes—not an easy feat in her heavy boots—and kissed his cheek. It was hard to know what to say. Somehow, she figured he already knew. "Thank you, Sam," she managed to whisper, "with all my heart."

"Natalie, he's okay. You're both going to be fine. I love him too, you know." His voice sounded hoarse, and he pulled her closer. "Love you both." He kissed the top of her head and held her for a couple more minutes, waiting until her body stopped shuddering and the flow of tears subsided.

"We need to get moving," she said, pulling out of his embrace. She assured Sam she was composed enough to drive, and he walked her back to the SUV.

"I heard what you said, old man," Marc called as Natalie climbed behind the wheel. "I kinda love you, too, you know."

"Yeah, I knew I should have kept my voice down, but I didn't think you'd appreciate me whispering sweet nothings in your wife's ear. Get some rest, buddy. I'll see you soon." With a small salute, Sam headed toward where Lexa waited with the horses.

Wiping away her tears, Natalie nodded at Lexa and gave her another tremulous smile. Standing nearby, holding the reins of both Majesty and

Dandelion, her mentor shed more than a few tears of her own. With a whispered prayer, Natalie climbed into the car beside Marc and took his hand in hers. As she drove them to the ranch, she told Marc that Sam insisted he go to the hospital. "Listen to him. He's a very wise man." He didn't say anything, and she prayed his masculine pride wouldn't prevent him from following Sam's instructions. He seemed exhausted and too tired to protest, even if he wanted. If so, she'd have to put her foot down.

~

True to his word, it didn't take long for Sam to secure the horses in the stables. Lexa quickly deposited Elwood in the main house and hopped in the back beside her as Sam adjusted the driver's seat and slid behind the wheel.

Walking into the emergency room a short time later, the young doctor on duty—the same as the night of Natalie's visit—moved from behind the nurse's station to greet them. "You two sure are keeping us busy these days." Her smile conveyed a combination of bemusement and concern.

"It's Marc this time." Natalie listened as the doctor instructed the nurses to take him into the ER. At least he was more coherent and able to walk unassisted.

"Natalie." Marc gestured for her to come alongside him as he walked back into the examining room. "Come with me."

"Of course." She put her hand in his.

"Don't they have any male ER doctors?" he mumbled under his breath.

"I don't think that should be a concern. She's more than capable."

With a disgruntled scowl, Marc climbed onto the table. The doctor examined him, ran a few tests and took a chest X-ray before reassuring them both he was fine.

"You were right to come here. Your friend's quick thinking might have saved your life, Mr. Thompson," the doctor said. "It also helped that you had on so many layers of protective clothing. You have some great friends, a loving wife, and I suspect a guardian angel. And," she added with a smile, "Ms. Grant told us to add hero to your list of fine qualities. Please give her my best." Telling Marc he could climb down from the table, she darted a fleeting glance at Natalie's belly. "I want you to promise me this is the last time I'll see you here in my ER. Please go home to Massachusetts and concentrate on having that gorgeous baby."

Thanking the doctor, Marc grabbed Natalie's hand again as they walked back to the waiting room. He seemed better, just tired, as he leaned against her. It was gratifying how her big, strong husband needed her, and willingly accepted her help. The frown lines etched on his forehead indicated something still bothered him as they waited for Sam to pull the SUV around to the front entrance. When she squeezed his hand, he squeezed back. "Tell me what's wrong."

In a surprise move, Marc pulled her to the side of the building, and brushed his lips over hers in a soft whisper of a kiss. "I love you so much." His voice choked. With his cheek pressed to hers, his damp eyelashes fluttered against her skin.

"I love you, too." He looked at her through eyes moist with emotion. With the fingers of one hand, she tipped his chin and rubbed her thumb against his growth of beard. It felt rough, but familiar. Wonderful. He leaned his face into the curve of her hand. "Tell me why you were so uncomfortable in there. She's a very nice doctor, and she's helped us out twice now, you know."

He shrugged. "It's nothing. You'll think I'm crazy." Seeing the car pulling into the loading area, he led her by the hand, headed toward the SUV.

"Something's bothering you. Please tell me." She resisted the pull of his hand. He paused, turning back. She glimpsed the indecision in his face. Sam could wait. This couldn't. With one hand, she brushed aside a loose section of hair that had fallen across his forehead.

"I don't want any other woman touching me again," he said. "Only you. Even if she *is* a doctor." He gave her a sheepish grin and shrugged. "I guess it's the same as you wanting a female doctor. It's not weird, just a personal preference. Never mind, I'm tired and not making any sense."

Natalie wasn't sure how to respond, but he'd never looked more vulnerable or appealing. "I never thought of it like that before, but we didn't have a choice tonight. I can't tell you how thankful I am that you're okay. Promise you won't scare me like that again."

His lips brushed hers again, achingly tender. "It wasn't intentional, I assure you. Come on," he said, "let's go. I definitely need some rest." His voice was tinged with deep exhaustion, and he yawned as Sam assisted them into the back of the SUV.

Marc's head rested against hers, his fingers laced with hers in her lap. Sam and Lexa were quiet as he drove them back to Milestone Ranch, but she saw them exchanging several loving glances. Closing her eyes, she thanked the Lord for them and their friendship, their love, and for all the TeamWork volunteers. Pressing her lips against Marc's forehead, Natalie's heart swelled as her husband's regular breathing fell like the softest whisper on her cheek, rising and falling in the rhythm of his sleep.

As they neared the ranch, a renewed stirring in her belly brought a smile to her lips. Taking Marc's hand and positioning it, she smiled as the baby moved again. She had great timing and instincts, their daughter. Without waking, Marc shifted and murmured, "So happy, Natalie."

Settling back against the seat, she closed her eyes and released a contented sigh. "Me, too."

Chapter 44

$\mathcal{S}$AM, I NEED to ask you a very important question," Marc said.

"I'm already married, thanks." Sam ushered him into the office. "Sit."

"You're not my type, anyway, and I'll stand. Here's the thing. I was wondering if you could round up a preacher for me. Have any idea where I might be able to find one—one who's ordained?" Kevin mentioned once that Sam was ordained, at least in his home state.

"And why would you need one of those?" Judging by his wide grin, Sam knew full well his intent.

"I want to marry my wife again."

Sam's laugh was heartfelt. "Are you sure she wants to marry *you* again?"

"Believe it or not, my wife wants to make the same mistake. At least I think so." Marc scratched his head.

"Asked her, have you?"

"Not exactly, no, but somehow, I don't think she'll be adverse to the idea."

"Tell you what," Sam said, "you ask Natalie, and—provided she says yes—Lexa and I will take care of all the details. Just let us know where and when to show up, and we'll be there with the proverbial bells on."

"Bells aren't necessary, but we should do it right here at the ranch. I definitely want to do it before we head home to Boston."

"Makes sense." The smile lines deepened. "Not to mention you're dying for the key to that cabin. I admire your intention to do this the right way for Natalie."

"Would you expect anything else?" Marc hesitated, his grin fading. "I'll do anything for her, and it's important. She still doesn't remember much about our wedding, so I want to give her another ceremony." He met Sam's piercing blue eyes. "I can't think of anyone better to perform the honors for us. You've become sort of special, you know. For an old guy." He ducked as Sam brought an arm around his neck and hugged him tight for a few seconds before releasing him.

"I'm honored." A frown creased Sam's brow. "I'll have to find out whether being ordained in Texas means anything in Montana."

"You know, it doesn't even matter, more the thought that counts, Sam. It's a formality, but I know Natalie will feel the same way. There's no one we'd rather marry us the second time, especially since you and Lexa couldn't be there before. It's remedying a great injustice in that regard."

Sam nodded in agreement. "Sounds about right." That infectious grin surfaced again. "About that key. I get the feeling you believe it's going to be your little love nest after the wedding ceremony, but how do you know it isn't really for a little chapel in the wilderness?"

Turning back around, Marc stared at Sam. "*Is* it a chapel? I mean, knowing you, I wouldn't doubt it. In any case, I'm pretty certain you pray either before or after you and Lexa . . ." One hand on the door, he paused to laugh. "No doubt you praise the Lord without ceasing Lexa had the good sense to marry you in spite of your obvious frailties."

"I just hope you put some chapstick on those dry lips of yours since the stampede out on the ranch. Lord knows, you needed it."

"I'm not even going to dignify that with a response."

Sam grinned. "Seriously, that little cabin is exactly what you'd expect. Tell you what. Consider that key a wedding gift from Lexa and me. Like I said, let us know the time and place, and we'll take care of the rest."

"I'll do that. By the way, you owe me a couple of shirts."

"Put it on my tab."

"Sam?"

"Yes?" Sam's eyes crinkled to match his grin, those smile lines deep.

"Thanks, friend." It sounded so inadequate.

Sam saluted. "That's what I'm here for, buddy."

How do you thank a man for helping give your life back, and helping bring you closer to the Lord in the process? The man was a miracle worker. Marc whistled all the way back to the men's cabin.

~

Standing in the doorway of his office, watching Marc walk away in the falling snow, Sam smiled. It was almost Thanksgiving, time to go home and be thankful for all that had been accomplished at the Milestone Ranch. All in all, this particular mission was a rousing success. The Tuckers had help for their ranch, one terrific young man made his move for the heart of Rebekah, his TeamWork crew spent quality time together again, and a hurting husband and wife found their way back to each other. And now, in a few short months, they'd welcome a child into God's world. Life was sweet. Sitting back down in his chair, clasping his hands together on the desk, Sam bowed his head to pray.

He thanked the Lord all over again for his many blessings, and especially for bringing a new brother to him. A brother as surely as his own two younger brothers, Will and Carson. Like all his other TeamWork men, Marc was a brother of the heart, a brother in the *faith*.

~

It didn't take Marc long to ask Natalie. He knew he should probably take more time and plan it out. The main thing at this point was that he had to ask her and do it soon. With her memories slowly starting to come back—and her love for him restored—they needed to be fully reunited. It was both a renewal and starting over all at once.

"Natalie, come walk with me." Marc held out his hand, waiting. She was absolutely radiant, with an almost ethereal glow. It humbled him to think he had anything to do with making her so happy.

Slipping her hand in his, Natalie walked beside him out into the glistening wonderland. Their boots sank into the snow, making deep footprints. As big, soft flakes continued to fall, they both looked up at the vast expanse of the Montana twilight, the stars winking at them from the heavens.

"I didn't realize you could see stars when there was snow," Natalie said, her voice full of awe. "It's so beautiful."

"*You're* beautiful." She started to say something else, but he silenced her by bringing his lips down on hers in a long, deep kiss. Pulling her as close as possible, his arms completely encircled her.

"Marry me, Natalie."

"We're already married, silly," she said. Removing her gloves, she whipped the knit cap from his head and ran her fingers through his hair. The entire time, she didn't remove her lips from his—not once.

"Marry me *again*." Reaching for her gloves, Marc helped her slip them back on again. He wanted her to have feeling in her hands, after all, and the wind was bitter. It didn't bother him. He was heated enough to keep him warm a long time, but he needed to keep her as warm as possible. "I have something for you." Reaching into the pocket of his jacket, he pulled out the small, red velvet box inscribed with the name of a famous Boston jeweler.

Natalie looked up at him in surprise. "I've never removed my wedding ring, you know."

Never in his life would he get used to how unbelievably great it felt when she adored him with her eyes like she did now. "I'm so thankful for that, my love." Opening her palm, Marc placed the box in it.

Fumbling a bit because of her gloves, Natalie opened the lid and gasped in delight when she spied the gorgeous gold locket inside. Reflected in the moonlight, a sparkling diamond in the center winked at her. "It's beautiful." She lifted it out of the box, dangling it from her hand.

"Right after we got back from our honeymoon, we went to dinner downtown and then window shopped. You saw it then." Leaning his forehead against hers, he lowered his voice. "If my calculations are correct, we conceived our daughter that same night."

"Those calculations are usually right." The smile he loved surfaced. "So, this locket is sort of an anniversary gift? A very *private* anniversary?"

"You could say that. I went back the next day and got it. I've been waiting for the right time to give it to you." He shrugged and gave her a small smile. "Feeling optimistic about this trip to Montana, I put it in my suitcase at the last minute."

She touched the locket then glanced back up at him. "This is incredibly special. I'll treasure it. Thank you."

Taking the locket from her, he turned it over. "Can you read what it says?"

She brought it closer, studying it. "Romans 8:37." Her eyes traveled back to his, but she looked puzzled.

"'But in all these things we overwhelmingly conquer through Him who loved us.' I finally reached the point where I gave you to the Lord, Natalie. The thought of losing you killed me, but He brought me to my knees at the throne of grace. It was the day I pulled Beck from the creek." He shook his head. "I've failed you in so many ways. Forgive me."

Her eyes softened. "No, Marc. You didn't fail me. If anything, you proved how much you loved me. I pushed you away. I accused you of not trusting me enough to tell me the truth, but I was the one who didn't trust the Lord enough to accept your love. Over and over, you proved your devotion to me. I pray you can forgive *me*." As she placed her palm on the side of his face, love was written in her eyes, in her expressive features. He'd remember this moment as long as he had breath in his body.

"There's nothing to forgive, sweetheart." Marc fingered the locket again and smiled. "Once our baby is born, you can put her picture in it." Whipping off his gloves, he unclasped the chain as best he could with frozen fingers and gingerly lowered it around her neck. "Gorgeous," he whispered, leaning close as he managed to finish his task, "but it'll look much better on bare skin."

Natalie laughed. "That's just like you, Marc. We talk about scripture and you get all sensual on me." Her eyes widened. "Do you realize that just slipped out, and I didn't even have to think about it?"

He chuckled. "You're either remembering or else you're getting to know me pretty well." He lifted his head to the sky. "Thank you, God!" Lowering his head, he brought his lips down on hers again. He nibbled, teased, nipped, and gloried in it all. Natalie was his. The rest of the world could simply fade away, but he was quickly losing feeling in his extremities. "I hate to say it, but we'd better head inside. We don't want them to find us with our lips frozen together."

"Wait." She tugged on his hand. "First, I have something for *you*." As he watched, eyebrows raised, Natalie reached into the pocket of her jacket. Opening his hand, she deposited a small metal object. Looking down at the shiny, gold key nestled in his palm, he laughed. The key.

Natalie shrugged. "I asked Lexa for it again this afternoon."

"I guess this means your answer is . . . yes?"

"Yes, yes, yes! A thousand times yes!"

Marc lifted her in the air like a ballerina, twirling in a slow circle. His arms held her close in the falling snow as they both raised their faces to the sky. On a whim, he dropped to the ground and made a snow angel. To his surprise, Natalie dropped down beside him, moving her arms up and down to make wings.

"Come, my gorgeous snow angel." Helping Natalie rise to her feet and steadying her, Marc laughed as she pulled away and tossed a snowball his way. Time to retaliate. Given the advantage of great aim—a remnant of his baseball-playing days—he took it easy on her. They kissed and acted like fools in love as, hand-in-hand, they made their way back to her cabin. He didn't even feel the cold anymore, and he was pretty sure she didn't, either.

~

"What's so interesting out there, Sam?" Lexa asked.

He stood beside the front window, his grin widening. Turning away, he lowered the curtain. "Just admiring these beautiful curtains made by the TeamWork ladies. Splendid job."

"Thanks, but somehow I don't think that's what you were looking at beyond the curtains." Sidling closer to him, Lexa untied the strings of her apron and draped it over a nearby chair.

Taking her hand, Sam traced a light pattern on her palm with the tips of his fingers. "In their own way, Natalie and Marc are out there enjoying their own night at the mission." Raising her hand, he kissed her open palm. "Like the night we chased a man who'd kidnapped his wife."

"In order to get to his daughter," Lexa finished, looking up at him. "A night we cemented our own relationship." She gave him the smile that melted his heart. How one woman could embody all the qualities he adored was amazing. That, and stubborn defiance, too. What more could a man ask? Sometimes it drove him crazy, but it also drove him wild with desire for his beautiful wife.

"A night we put our physical passion in check in order to wait on the Lord's timing," he said, hovering just above her lips, smiling into her eyes and loving what he saw reflected in hers.

"A night we honored Him, knowing He'd reward our faithfulness." She traced a smile line with one gentle finger.

"And how He's honored it," Sam whispered.

"And will continue to do so." Lexa pulled his head toward hers until their lips met.

As he kissed his wife, Sam tucked away the little tidbit about planning a wedding. If he told her now, it would distract her. He didn't want anything to interrupt. He'd tell her, but much later. Swooping Lexa into the cradle of his arms, he flipped the light switch and carried her through the back of the large house toward their private quarters.

"Why, handsome cowboy, I do believe you have intentions toward me tonight," Lexa mock-swooned, batting those unbelievably long eyelashes and twirling her braid.

Sam chuckled, hastening his steps. "You'd better believe it, beautiful girl."

Chapter 45

*T*HE NEXT NIGHT, Natalie walked down the flower-strewn aisle on Sam's arm. Their TeamWork friends huddled in a close circle around them as Marc stepped into place beside her, his boots sinking into the freshly-falling snow. They all wore their jeans and parkas because it was too cold for anything else, not that it mattered. It was a gorgeous, winter wonderland. He felt like bursting into a hearty rendition of "All You Need Is Love," but no one wanted that.

Kevin played his guitar and sang a duet with Cassie, his eyes falling on Rebekah time and again. God bless that lovesick boy. He needed to declare his intentions and put himself out of his misery, like Trevor, who'd sent him a message saying he planned to ask Christy for her hand in marriage on Christmas Day. Yes, life was sweet, whether back home in Massachusetts or in Montana.

Sam positioned himself in front of them and opened his Bible. The Good Book was probably never far from the man's hands. "Marriage shared by a man and woman blessed enough to have the love of Jesus Christ in their hearts is the most beautiful union of all." Stealing a quick glance at his wife, Sam shared verses of familiar scripture from First Corinthians about the patience and abiding faithfulness of love. The same verses Marc read in his hour of desperation the morning Natalie moved out of the house. It seemed like a lifetime ago, and in several important ways, it was.

"Marc and Natalie want to renew their wedding vows, secure in the knowledge the Lord brought them together not only once, but twice. As you know, their journey has not been without its difficulties, but the fact that they're standing here together in front of us tonight, pledging their love to one another, is a testament to the strength and endurance of their love. Natalie and Marc acknowledge the love they have for one another is preordained by the Lord Jesus Christ, and they look to Him to guide them through the journey of life. They'll soon be bringing their own little soul into the world, born out of their shared love and passion," Sam said, ignoring his look of warning. "But tonight, in front of God and their dear friends as witnesses, they wish to proclaim their love for one another anew." Sam nodded at him.

"Anew?" Marc whispered.

Sam leaned closer. "You're the one who's good with words. It's a word, it's appropriate, so get on with it." Those smile lines deepened, and the eyes sparkled.

Natalie's eyes caressed his face as Marc captured her hands. Promising to love this woman forever was the most honorable thing he'd ever done. "Natalie, I thought I'd never earn your love. And when I did, and then when you fell down those steps, I thought I'd lost you forever." Overcome with emotion, he paused. This was more difficult than he'd thought. "Even though your mind forgot me for a little while, your heart never did. It's always known me, just as my heart and mind know you. With the Lord's guiding hand on me, I promise to make you proud to call me your husband and the father of our children. You are my partner and my equal in every way, and I need you by my side always to help me make the hard decisions, the sweet decisions and the life-changing decisions." Raising her hand, he brushed his lips over it. "I'll love and cherish you forever."

"Marc," Natalie said, "I love you with everything I am." Her hands held his tight, but her voice never faltered. "When my mind forgot, I was lost and lonely, but your love and the Savior's love pulled me through the darkness. It would have been so easy to walk away, but you stayed by my side even when I gave you every reason to leave." Her fingers squeezed tighter, her eyes bright as they met his. "Through your faithfulness, your patience, and your unfailing love, you've shown me the way home again to your heart. And," she said, a tear sliding onto her cheek, "I can't wait to bring our child into the world. I want to introduce her to the best father a child could ever have, and the most incredible husband I could ever hope to find. The Lord is merciful, and we are so blessed."

"And now," Sam announced with great pride, "by the power invested in me by the divine Lord—and the great Lone Star State of Texas—it's my extreme honor and privilege to introduce you . . . again . . . to Marcus Alan and Natalie Dianne Thompson. Marc, you may now . . .'"

Oblivious to everyone around them as they burst into wild cheering and clapping, Marc swept Natalie in his arms, his lips finding hers, completely lost in their joy. Her cheeks were wet, and so were his, but for all the *best* reasons.

~

Pulling Lexa close as they walked together, Sam followed Marc's example. "Have I told you how much I love you today?" he whispered, nuzzling her cheek.

"Love is in the air, that's for sure," Lexa said, hooking her arm through his as they resumed walking. "Have you noticed how half the time spent here in Montana, I've either been in the kitchen or in your lap?"

Sam's laughter rang out and several turned to smile. "Are you complaining?"

"Not at all. There's only one place better." She gave him a sly smile full of meaning, and giggled as he playfully patted her. She nodded in Kevin's direction where he walked beside Rebekah. "Those two will sure be interesting to watch in the months to come."

"Without a doubt." He tossed a glance over his shoulder at Marc and Natalie. "Let's leave the newlyweds. They'll eventually come inside." Not to mention the groom's eagerness to reach the cabin. Wrapping his arm around

Lexa's waist, Sam opened the door and ushered her inside to the warmth and comfort of great friends, the tantalizing aroma of freshly-baked wedding cake . . . and maybe a pie or two.

~

"Well," Marc said a few minutes later, "I suppose we should go make an appearance. After all, this party is in our honor."

Natalie nodded. "I suppose you're right." She raised a brow and gave him a promising smile. "But only for a little while." She laughed at his broad grin. "Let's go inside."

They did the best they could for the better part of an hour, making small talk and chatting with their friends. They stole mutual glances and winks as Amy flitted about, taking posed and casual shots of them all, promising to send Marc and Natalie a special commemorative photo album. Sam toasted them, as did Kevin, Rebekah, Winnie and Amy. When Eliot and Dean turned on the music and the Texas line dances began, Marc grabbed Natalie by the hand, knowing it was their cue to escape. He loved dancing, but didn't know the Texas version. Besides, he had an entirely different kind of dancing in mind. Private, for one thing.

"Sam," he said, "seeing as how I can't stand by and watch while you pummel your wife's dainty feet, I'm taking my bride away now."

"I understand you already have the key," Sam whispered, a gleam in his eye as he looked over at where Natalie and Lexa huddled together.

"Yes, and it's all the sweeter because Natalie asked Lexa for it. *Again.* Even before I asked her to marry me again."

"God is good, my friend. Just remember those rules of marriage, and you'll be just fine."

"Thanks, Sam. I'll never forget this time in Montana with you and your TeamWork crew."

"Neither will I, my friend. Now, do yourself a huge favor, go get your bride, and . . ."

"Enough said, old man." Marc waved him away. "I can take it from here, trust me, without any instruction from my mentor, thank you very much. And one of these days," he said, "I'm going to pay someone to give you dance lessons."

"Take care, Sundance." Was that a choke in Sam's voice?

"You too, Cassidy. See you in a few days." Good grief, now *he* was getting choked up.

Sam grunted. "Like I said before, take as long as you need. Lexa and I will be at the main house if you need anything, and we'll watch over Elwood. You've got the phone number. The others are all leaving the ranch tomorrow, but we'll hang out. After all, Lexa and I have some people to feed."

"What do you mean?" Marc scratched his head, confused. His thoughts were distracted and Sam wanted to talk about feeding people. Go figure.

"Meaning we have some friends who'll need sustenance in the next few days." He leaned close. "Put it this way: whenever you hear a little bell outside the cabin, wait a few minutes—or at least make yourself decent." Those smile lines just kept getting deeper. "You'll find meals delivered daily—breakfast, lunch and dinner. Enough for snacks later on. It's part of the room service feature of that special cabin."

"I hadn't even thought of food."

Sam chuckled and slapped him on the back. "I'd worry about you if you did. Like I said, we'll provide the food. You just provide the . . ."

"I *get* your point." Marc laughed with Sam as he headed over to where Natalie still talked with Lexa. "If you'll excuse us," Marc told her with a wink, taking Natalie's hand, "my wife and I will be leaving now. Time to go to this apparently magical cabin." He planted a kiss on Lexa's cheek and whispered, "Thanks for everything. You and Sam are the best."

"I'm glad we could be here."

"Me, too." That was the understatement of the decade.

"Did Sam tell you about the bell?"

"He did. Thanks for that, too. I'll look forward to it. You two manage to think of everything, that's for sure."

"Well, Lewis and Clarke *is* a full-service operation," Lexa said.

"I'm beginning to see how true that is. None better."

"Marc." He turned to face Rebekah. Natalie nodded, releasing his hand, giving them a moment of privacy. Tears glistened in those lovely green eyes as Beck slipped her arms around him in a warm hug. "How can I ever thank you . . ."

Pulling back, he captured her eye contact. "Keep your eyes wide open to what's right in front of you. That's all I ask." Marc hoped she understood his dual meaning. Judging by her amused expression, she had a pretty good idea. "How's the numbness?"

Rebekah glanced down at her hands. "It comes and goes. It should get better in time. Small price to pay. Thank you, Marc, from the bottom of my heart. You and Natalie, and your family, will be in my prayers always. Please stay in touch."

Glancing over her shoulder, he caught Kevin's eye and winked. "Take good care of our girl, Kev." He relished the look of surprise on Beck's face, but she didn't look upset. Kevin gave him a nod and a grateful smile. That British chap didn't have a chance. These two belonged together. The Lord would see to it.

After saying their good-byes and sharing hugs and best wishes all around, Natalie shot him a curious look as they slipped out the door together. "Did Lexa say something about a bell?"

"She did. Trust me, my love, you'll find out about the significance of the bell soon enough." They stopped short when they spied the waiting SUV. It was heated up and ready to go, just like *he* was, decorated with strings of cowbells and a *Just Married* sign. No doubt the handiwork of Eliot and Kevin, or Winnie and Amy. Their packed bags waited in the backseat.

Marc chuckled when he glimpsed the beaming faces of the Teamwork crew clustered by the front window. Standing beside him, Natalie sniffled. They all waved, and he heard a few catcalls from the rowdier guys. He laughed and waved back. Pulling her close, he walked his wife to the car and assisted her as she climbed inside. "I'm very thankful you introduced me to the TeamWork crew, Natalie. They're . . . well, they're the best."

She wiped away her tears with a silent nod. As he drove them down the long driveway of Milestone Ranch, she was quiet and leaned her head back, closing her eyes. One hand moved across her stomach. She did that more and more, and he imagined it was that innate instinct women have to protect their young.

"I hope you're not too tired, but I understand if you are. It's been an emotional day," he said.

Reaching for him, Natalie's hand wrapped around his, clasping tight, making his heart smile. "That's very magnanimous of you to offer, but I need to take care of my husband."

"I like the sound of that." Marc squeezed her hand that much tighter. "We've got a few days, so I'll let you set the pace."

She looked over at him, her smile wistful. "You and Sam have really bonded in the last couple of weeks, haven't you?"

He nodded and darted a glance her way. "Don't tell the man, but he's like the brother I never had." Not only had he reconnected with his wife in Montana, but he'd made lasting, lifelong friends with all the TeamWork men, and especially Sam. Marc's eyes filled with unexpected tears. He was turning into a sap, maybe making up for all those tears he never shed in years past. Maybe being a sap every now and then wasn't such a bad thing. Raising Natalie's hand to his lips, he planted a gentle kiss and stole another glance. It was difficult to keep his eyes focused on the road. If anything happened to prevent getting to the cabin this time, he might implode.

"Do you think you'll be able to find the fork in the road?" He detected amusement in her tone.

"Natalie," he said, blowing out a deep sigh, "tonight, I'll be able to find it with my eyes closed."

"Just a tip: keep the eyes wide open." They laughed together, but his foot pressed that much harder on the accelerator, knowing it wasn't much further, praying under his breath that pesky but dutiful sheriff was on an extended coffee break.

Chapter 46

DROPPING THEIR BAGS on the doorstep of the cabin, Marc pulled out the brass key. He cocked one brow and gave Natalie a knowing grin as he turned the lock. Opening the door wide, he grabbed their bags and set them inside the door before sweeping her off her feet and into his arms. She felt so light, and he laughed at her look of pleased surprise as he carried her over the threshold.

"You didn't do that the first time." She gave him a coy grin. "My Prince."

His eyes widened. "Well, hello again, Beautiful Swan. Welcome back." He dropped a light kiss on her nose, thrilled she remembered their pet names, initiated on their honeymoon. "I'm going to be doing a lot of things in the future I never did before." Lowering her, he cupped her face and kissed that ripe mouth.

"That sounds very promising." Her eyelids fluttered as she looked up at him, as though in a trance. "Now, close that door, so we can really get this honeymoon started once and for all."

Doing as she asked, he locked the door to block out the rest of the world and insulate them in their little paradise. Bringing her to him, he focused on drinking in her loveliness. "I can't believe we finally made it here." As if their eyes were drawn to it, they both looked over at the bed at the same time. "Looks like the Lewis love elves have paid a visit," he said as they shared a grin. A path of yellow rose petals made its way from the front door to the bed and trailed across the comforter. A bottle sat chilling in a bucket on the nightstand next to a CD player.

"When did they do this?" Marc asked, surveying the cozy cabin. "We've had the key since yesterday." Walking over to the bucket, he pulled out the bottle. Sparkling grape juice.

She shrugged. "They think of everything. Knowing Sam, he probably had a second key made on one of his trips to the general mercantile. But let's not talk about that. It's time to concentrate on us. Be quiet and kiss me." Wrapping her arms around his neck, Natalie pulled his head down, raising her lips to meet his.

"You sure are demanding," Marc said, in-between kisses. Holding onto each other, they stumbled a bit as their kisses intensified, barely making it to the bed before collapsing on it.

"Wait a minute," Natalie said, gasping for air, "shouldn't we take this slower? We're acting like a couple of hormonal teenagers." He kissed her neck, and her laugh was throaty, sexy. "I don't care."

The way her eyes swept over his face—with pride and admiration—made him feel ten feet tall. "Hold that thought." Sitting up, he pulled off his boots and assisted her in doing the same. "Thank you for coming back to me, Natalie.

I hate that we had to go through all this a second time, but as weird as it might sound, it's even better in so many ways. I promise you and the Lord I'm going to spend the rest of my life making you happy."

"Oh, you do, Marc, and you've waited so long." She traced her finger along his jaw with a look of longing. "In case I haven't told you lately, I love you." Natalie wrapped her arms around him again, pulling him closer.

"I'll never tire of hearing you say that, but enough talking for now." Marc began to unwrap the wool scarf from around her neck, his eyes never leaving her face. Removing all their layers of clothing would take some time, but he'd enjoy every second. Tonight, and in the next couple of days, he was going to help Natalie remember all the ways he loved her. She was no longer hesitant, shy or scared, and she made it clear she was ready to be his wife again. *Thank you, Lord.*

With pure joy, they began the slow, loving process of rediscovering one another as they became one again. As they finally rested much later in the night, Marc smiled. Such deep-seated contentment he'd never felt before. Surely this was a glimpse of Heaven. The rest of the world could disappear. Natalie snuggled closer and traced light circles on his chest. They fell into a deep sleep, his head leaning against hers.

Waking a long while later, wrapped only in their love and a lightweight blanket, Marc pushed the blanket aside. Love swelled his heart. Feeling blessed beyond words, he leaned over and kissed her stomach, running his hand over the blossoming curve. How he loved it. "Hello, baby girl." The happy tears he shed wouldn't be the only ones he'd cry for their daughter in the years to come. But he was getting ahead of himself. His head spun at the thought of it all. Now was the time to focus on their alone time together. In a few, short months, their lives would never be the same.

"Marc, are you actually kissing my stomach?" Natalie gave him the most loving look he'd ever seen, and released the most contented sigh he'd ever heard.

Her fingers tousled his hair, and he gave her a lopsided, goofy smile. "I was just saying hello to our daughter. And wondering if your nickname should be Sleeping Beauty."

"I'll stick with the other one, thanks. You know," she said, "if this child turns out to be a boy, he might have some serious identity issues." She stretched like a lazy cat and gave him a satisfied smile, obviously relishing the look in his eyes as he skimmed the length of her.

"If it's a boy, he'll be as manly as his dad. Trust me."

Natalie welcomed him again with open arms. He was home in every possible way, and it was pure bliss.

True to his word, Sam rang a bell periodically during the next three days, leaving behind scrumptious, home-cooked feasts enough for six people. Then he'd slip away as quietly as he'd come. They fed one another as they cuddled in front of the fire, finishing every last morsel. Together they toasted Sam and Lexa and praised the Lord for bringing the entire TeamWork crew into their lives. They stocked the fridge in the cabin with the leftovers, and indulged in a few midnight snacks. "For sustenance," Marc reminded Natalie, loving the sound of her laughter.

"So," she said on the fourth day as they packed their bags, "what do we do now?" Looking down, she put a hand on her stomach. "The baby fluttered again."

"No doubt from all the exciting activity during the last few days." Marc winked as she flushed like a shy schoolgirl. Her bright eyes spoke volumes of the love she held for him. It made him feel even taller than Sam Lewis.

"We might have to come back to this cabin on one of our anniversaries, but now we go home, my love." Picking up their suitcases, he followed her to the door. "Today we go home." First, he had to move her back into the house, but it wouldn't take long. *That* he could definitely handle.

Chapter 47

"*M*ARC."

Sitting and enjoying a leisurely breakfast together in the kitchen, it was an unusually warm Sunday morning. Looking up quickly, he knew. It was time to meet their daughter. He smiled, thinking maybe the mental telepathy between Sam and Lexa was starting to rub off on them. In his eagerness, he shoved his chair back from the table and winced as it scraped the floor. Poised next to the table in a futile effort to beg a scrap of food,   Elwood barked. Marc put his plate of half-eaten pancakes on the floor. "Knock yourself out, little buddy. It's all yours. You wait here," he told Natalie. "I'll get your suitcase."

Bolting up the servant's staircase two at a time, he grabbed her bag from the corner of the bedroom. A week overdue, Natalie had grown increasingly anxious and eager to meet their child. He could handle irritable, and he'd become the expert soother and foot massager. Whatever it took. Catching a glimpse of his reflection in the mirror on the dresser, Marc grinned. "Today you become a father. Do yourself and Natalie proud. Baby, here we come." With pure joy swelling his heart, he hurried down the stairs.

Three hours later, with Natalie settled in her suite and feeling comfortable for the moment, Marc ventured down to the emergency room. He couldn't explain it, but he followed some kind of invisible pull. He figured Natalie could use a break from his pacing and nervous energy. He'd never chattered about inane things so much in his life. She'd heard a rundown of the scores of every Patriots, Celtics, and Bruins game the past season plus the prospects for the Sox in the current season. He found himself standing in front of the nurse's station in the ER.

Behind the counter was the same blonde nurse who'd been so kind to him the night of Natalie's fall. She paused, and a bright smile crossed her face when she saw him. At least she didn't frown with one of those, *Oh no, it's you again looks.* "Well, hello . . . Mr. Thompson, isn't it?"

Impressive. "Yes. Good memory."

"I take it you don't have an emergency at the hospital today."

"No. Nothing like that. My wife's upstairs in the early stages of labor."

She gave him a delighted smile. "Congratulations. That's wonderful news."

"My pacing was driving her crazy, so I thought I'd give her a much needed break. For some reason, I felt the need to come down here." Marc's smile sobered. He tilted his head, an odd sensation blanketing him. "Do you have any idea why it's like my feet just brought me here to the ER? Now?"

A surprised look crossed the nurse's face before a calm settled in her expression. "I think that feeling is called the Holy Spirit, Mr. Thompson."

"What do you mean?" Somehow, the fact this nurse was a woman of faith didn't surprise him.

She sighed. "Your friend Mr. Davis came in last night."

It would be good to see the old man again, especially on such a happy day. He'd love to make Mr. Davis smile. Marc glanced around the nearly empty ER waiting room. "Where is he?"

"He's dying."

At her words, Marc's heart slammed in his chest. "Is he . . . ?"

"Eighth floor. ICU. Tell them you're family."

He nodded and swallowed the sudden lump lodged in his throat. Tears stung his eyes. "Thanks. For everything." Punching the button in the elevator for the eighth floor, his eyes glazed, but his heart was full. Mr. Davis was ready to let go of life and be reunited with his Ruthie and their daughter. Still, Marc felt nostalgic for the dear, gentle soul who counseled him about the ways of God that long-ago night. He wished he could tell him all he'd learned in the last few months, but perhaps he already knew.

The elevator doors slid open. Two nurses talked quietly behind their station, and they looked up as he approached. "I'd like to see Mr. Davis, please," he said. One of them raised a finger and beckoned for him to follow. Coming around the corner of the hospital room, Marc paused as he spied Mr. Davis in the bed, hooked up to numerous tubes and monitors. The old man's eyes opened. In spite of the exhaustion etched in the weathered countenance, Marc glimpsed recognition in the kind eyes as he pulled a chair close to the bed.

"Mr. Thompson." Breathing labored, he outstretched a hand.

Marc captured the dry, gnarled hand. "How are you feeling?" The words sounded lame, but he didn't know what else to say or how to express what he felt. His heart swelled as he gazed on the face of well-earned wisdom, the lines gained from a life worth living.

"My chains are gone, I've been set free." The words were raspy, barely loud enough to hear.

The hand in his grew warmer as Marc held on as tight as he dared. In his off-key voice, he began to sing "Amazing Grace." Hopefully, no one would ask him to pipe down. His heart was in the right place. As he sang, the old man's eyes closed. Mr. Davis listened with a look of serenity and incredible peace. It was almost as though the hand of the Almighty caressed his cheek, whispering assurances it was all right to let go.

A few nurses gathered in the doorway. More than one wiped away tears, but they nodded for him to continue when he paused. Female voices soon joined in singing the familiar hymn. Forgetting the words of the third verse, Marc started in again with the first, and they followed his cue. Hearing a distinctly male voice, he turned and saw Dr. Adams standing behind the nurses. When he gave him a small salute, the doctor nodded and reciprocated. As they sang a few more quiet stanzas, Mr. Davis breathed his last, slipping peacefully into eternity, surrendering one final time.

"I'm not keeping score," Marc whispered, leaning over to kiss his cheek, "but God gained a great player for His team today." He rested his hand over the dear man's heart. Somewhere, that old man was smiling. God, too.

Four hours later, their dark-haired, seven-pound-ten-ounce daughter came into the world, kicking and screaming. As one soul entered the gates of heaven on that beautiful, warm April day, another came into the world, into the waiting arms of her loving parents. New life, not to replace an old one, but to claim her place in God's kingdom on earth. He'd pray for his child to one day share the strong, unwavering faith of a dear old man named . . . *Abraham.*

The miracles of God were everywhere, His favors boundless.

Holding his healthy baby girl, Marc smiled, a contented man.

Epilogue

Mother's Day — Three Weeks Later

"*H*I, SAM."

"Marc, buddy. Heard you've had some excitement in your life lately. How are things in Boston?"

"Everything's great. There's someone I want to introduce to you and Lexa." He sounded good, but weary.

"About time." Sam pushed open the kitchen door and gestured for Lexa to pick up the other extension. "Hang on a second. I'm getting Lexa on the other phone." He chuckled a few moments later. "Was that you drooling over your wife or a baby gurgling?"

"Hi, Marc." Her eyes bright, Lexa moved one hand over her heart. "Congratulations! Who's this little person you're introducing?"

"Hi, Lexa. Hold on a minute while I shift her. This," Marc said, paternal pride lacing every word, "is Grace Davis Thompson. We call her Gracie. She's three weeks old today, and she's the most gorgeous little girl you've ever seen."

Sam and Lexa both sighed. "Amazing Grace, for sure," Sam said. "I'm sure she's a beautiful child, especially if she looks more like her mom."

"Very funny."

"Is Davis a family name?"

Hesitation for a few seconds. "More like a guardian angel for my little girl."

"Marc, is everything . . . okay?" Lexa's voice was quiet, and she darted another glance his way.

"Everything's great. Gracie's perfect and healthy. Sam, you'll be happy to hear she has beautiful, dark hair like Natalie's and we think she'll keep the blue eyes. Pink cheeks, rosebud lips . . ." His voice caught in his throat, and they heard Natalie in the background. Marc lowered his voice. "I'm afraid our little princess got my temper, based on the way she's kept us up four nights straight."

"Enjoy every minute, my friend. It'll pass all too quickly, and one of these days . . ."

"One of these days you'll stop dispensing paternal wisdom and have one of your own, then we'll compare notes, Cassidy. I'm praying for the two of you." Even though he was teasing, Marc's compassion came through loud and clear.

Sam slipped his arm around Lexa as he seated himself in his favorite living room chair, pulling her onto his lap. He cocked a brow, and she nodded. Time to share the joy of their own news with their dear friends who lived too far away. "We'll be comparing notes in about seven months, Sundance."

Silence ensued for a few seconds as Marc grasped his meaning. "You and Lexa are expecting? Hallelujah!"

Sam kissed Lexa's forehead, and nestled her closer. Slipping her hand beneath his shirt, she rested it over his heart. Smiling up at him, she mouthed, "Papa Bear," her new nickname for him. How he loved it. With a smile as she kissed his cheek, Sam tightened his hold.

"We're two months along. The doctors don't know, *can't* know everything. The four of us proved that. Remember, the Lord knows more than medical science."

"Thanks for sending the book, Sam."

He smiled, kissing the top of Lexa's head. "I would have given it to you when you were here in Houston if I'd known Jumpin' Phil was your dad. I think if you'll read it, you might be pleasantly surprised."

"I already have, and so has Natalie." Sam heard the catch in his friend's throat, understood the emotion behind it. "It's given us both an entirely new and different perspective on Dad's life. On his relationship with the NBA, my mom . . . everything. I wish I'd known some of those things when I was growing up, but God's shown me it doesn't do any good to dwell on the past. I'm going to have a lot to tell Gracie, and all our kids, about their famous grandfather. I tried to get a copy, but the book's so far out-of-print, no one could find it. Only you, Sam Lewis, only you."

Sam chuckled under his breath. "Glad I could oblige. Just remember, you're every bit the champion, too, Marc, but in very different ways than your dad."

"Thanks. We love you both. Happy Mother's Day, Lexa. Talk to you again soon."

~

Marc sat in the chair in front of the window. A light breeze fluttered the eyelet curtains, and the sunshine flooding the room reflected the brightness in his heart. He closed his eyes and blew out a deep sigh. *Life doesn't get any better than this, Lord.*

"I hope that was the sigh of a happy husband." After putting Gracie down for her nap, Natalie lounged against the bed pillows. She looked tired, serene, but more beautiful than ever with the bloom of motherhood.

"You can't begin to comprehend how much I love you, sweetheart. Happy *Mother's* Day."

"I think I have a pretty good idea if what you feel in your heart is anything as strong as what I'm feeling right about now." She patted the pillow next to her with a smile.

"Oh, is that so?" A grin lifted the corners of his mouth. Closing the blinds, he dropped onto the bed beside her. "You rest. I'll listen for our boisterous daughter."

Natalie stifled a yawn. "Rest with me, Marc. Gracie will let you know when she needs something." How right she was.

"Lexa will understand that maternal instinct pretty soon herself."

His wife's smile melted him in seconds as her eyes filled. "Well, it's about time! I hope they have a boy so we can put together an arranged marriage. After all, Cassidy and Sundance need to be connected for eternity, right?"

"Oh, we already are." Draping the sheet over her, Marc curled himself around his wife, spooning her. "The best part of me is sleeping in the next room, you know. Gracie is absolutely amazing. Thank you. I can't believe what an incredible miracle she is. How can God do that?"

Natalie turned onto her back, intertwining her fingers with his. "Because He's God. We're not supposed to question. We just accept, and believe."

"Oh, I do believe, but I've got an awful lot to learn. I'll be thanking Him— and loving you and Gracie—all the rest of my days." He kissed her nose, and then her cheek, moving ever-so-slowly toward her lips. "I hope we'll be able to add another little one to our family in a couple of years."

She smiled. "Let's see how it goes with Gracie first. Kiss me."

"That's what I'm doing. I'm really trying to be sensitive to your needs here, Natalie. You need your rest."

"I repeat, kiss me. *Please.* Then we'll rest together."

"Your wish is my sweetest command." In loving obedience, Marc kissed his wife with everything in his heart, as he planned to do every single, blessed day. And there, in their home, with their baby girl sleeping in the next room, Marc followed the sage advice of his mentor and great friend, Sam Lewis. He took the time to love his wife.

Quite simply, just to *love* her.

About the Author

Second Time Around is **JoAnn Durgin's** second published novel, the follow-up to the popular *Awakening* featuring the adventures of Sam Lewis and Lexa Clarke and the lively TeamWork crew. A winner and finalist of several writing contests, JoAnn is a full-time estate administration paralegal and lives in southern Indiana with her husband and three children. She is an active member of the American Christian Fiction Writers and its Indiana chapter as well as Romance Writers of America. JoAnn's passion is writing contemporary Christian romance, and it's her desire to touch hearts with the redeeming love of Jesus Christ.

She'd love to hear from you at **www.joanndurgin.com**

Coming Soon

Twin Hearts
by
JoAnn Durgin

Joshua Grant is a man redeemed. He's worked hard to put the past behind him. A mergers and acquisitions attorney in a prestigious Baton Rouge law firm, he pours his energies into his career, hurricane relief efforts and numerous civic and charitable causes. A near-fatal event in the life of a fellow TeamWork Missions volunteer prompts him to make some apologies, starting with his friend and mentor, Sam Lewis, Domestic Missions Director for TeamWork in Houston. It's been four years since the fateful events in San Antonio when Sam threw him out of the missions camp, and he's still haunted by the bittersweet memory of his final meeting with another TeamWork volunteer. When he also seeks her forgiveness, Josh gets the shock of his life. Could turning his deepest sin into his greatest blessing be God's answer for his hurting heart?

Rebekah Grant, Josh's twin sister, is torn between two men: Adam, a dashing British aristocrat offering her a world of exotic travel, socializing with royalty, fabulous couture and the life of leisure. Then there's sweet Kevin, another TeamWork volunteer. Strong, intelligent, but incredibly shy, will the Louisiana lumber man ever take the step of faith to move their relationship to the next level? What Kevin lacks in terms of Adam's style and panache, he more than makes up for with heart-stirring kisses and soul-searching conversation. When Adam pressures Rebekah for an answer to his marriage proposal, she has a major decision to make. Juggling both suitors is wrong for so many reasons, but what's a girl to do if she wants to marry and have children in this lifetime?

When family tragedy strikes, Josh and Rebekah learn the true meaning and value of love, loyalty and what's most important in life. Leaning on the encouragement and support from Sam and Lexa Lewis and their TeamWork friends, both twins look to the Lord for His divine guidance. It's up to them to stake their claim on love before it slips beyond their reach, which means it's also time for a road trip from Louisiana to . . . the peace to be found in seeking and finding the sweetest desires of the heart.

The *Lewis Legacy Series*

by JoAnn Durgin

A God-fearing man. A God-seeking woman. For Sam Lewis and Lexa Clarke, it proves a combustible combination. You'll keep turning the pages of this sweeping romantic adventure. With great characters, plenty of humor, enough emotion to make you shed a tear or two, and an ending that'll have you cheering, *Awakening* will leave you breathless. Hold on tight.

Paperback ISBN 978-0-9912252-0-0

Newlyweds Marc and Natalie Thompson have it all, but two months after the wedding, Natalie suffers a horrible fall. Not only does she not remember their life together, but now Marc has a personal timeline to reconnect with her—seven months. You'll root for them as they fight against the odds to find their way back to one another... the second time around.

Paperback ISBN 978-0-9912252-2-4

It's been more than four years since Josh was thrown out of the TeamWork missions camp, and he's still haunted by the bittersweet memory of his final meeting with another volunteer. When he also seeks her forgiveness, he gets the shock of his life. Could turning his deepest sin into his greatest blessing be God's answer for his hurting heart?

Paperback ISBN 978-0-9912252-4-8

The *Lewis Legacy Series* is available in paperback and eBook